The Tree and Stone

The Learner Trilogy
Book 2

Andrew Monroe

For those who didn't lose hope in me finishing this book, be it friends, their very supportive parents, my family, and of course my wife, who's held my hand through all my excuses on not getting this out and still encouraged me to finish.

Chapter One

A kidnapping rarely goes well for anyone. First, there's just not an outstanding option for one human to move another. We don't have handles, and nearly every bit of us is a little squishy. This means we do not respond positively to being smashed and poked when slung over a shoulder or dragged across the ground. Acting as the one doing the kidnapping isn't as fun as it sounds, either. People are heavy, even the small ones. Plus, nobody ever likes you when you're hauling them forcibly around. If you're going in for likeability, this is not the way.

Even while he looked half-starved, Volant still felt like carrying multiple large bags of lead weights tied to an over-full-grain sack. Stealing him away from a clinic filled with other patients, Guard, and healers would be a lot easier if he was conscious and able to participate.

Groaning, I shouldered open the door leading from the room he'd spent the last few days in. I nearly dropped him with the sudden imbalance of the door giving way but recovered with stumbling, graceless steps in the moonlit hallway. Leaves rustled in a soft harmony outside, a constant in Erset.

The noise earned me a long, judgmental stare from Cassiopia, who, despite her imposing bulk of muscle, moved like a field mouse from shadow to shadow and was not helping one bit with the carrying. I found it hard to tell if she enjoyed the cloak-and-dagger plan more or my bumbling attempts at hauling Volant. Either way, a kidnapping should not be this much fun for anyone. With a mischievous smile, she leaped up and grabbed the ceiling, somehow finding handholds in the curling bark of the massive tree branch.

"This is no time for exercise," I began.

A door opened, and a pair of Guards came out, cutting me off mid-sentence. They both paused, obviously surprised to find a person equally obviously not supposed to be here. They took in my blend of dark clothes, lower face mask, and unconscious body slung across my back. Left hand, you could almost see their brains taking in the situation and deciding this was something that fell under their responsibilities.

That is until Cassiopia dropped down behind them, as soft and quiet as any zymph. Before either could let out a challenge, she smacked their heads together, knocking them out cold. Her grin hadn't changed, and I found myself wondering yet again how stable this master huntress could really be.

I winced, part in sympathy and part in pain, as I slowly stepped past the men, Volant's elbow digging into my ribs as I tried to keep him balanced. Unfortunately, I missed my footing this time, dropping onto the floor and unceremoniously dumping Volant into a sprawled heap behind me. A soft whimper was all the noise Volant made. My whole body clenched in sympathy at the sound, and I scooted back over to him.

I strained to get him up off the floor and onto my shoulder, but I wasn't strong enough.

Cassiopia finally came over, gave me another smile, and sat down on the floor with her back to him. She took one leg in her right arm and looped her other through his. Without even a grunt, she rolled forward onto her feet with Volant now strung across her back. She sat in a low squat, knees nearly touching her chest. A quick inhale, and she straightened.

The raw strength and simplicity of the movement dumbfounded me for a moment. I stopped caring about how stable her mental state was. Without her, I'd have botched this twice over already. I opened the door, gesturing her through. She just nodded politely, walking without hesitation out onto the swaying walkway on the backside of the clinic that had kept Volant since the blue robes had attacked us in the council chambers.

Shazina was waiting for us just on the other side of the rope bridge. She was sprawled out in a hand cart, looking for all the world like a spoiled kid who hadn't had her way. Which, at least on the last part, was somewhat true. Having traversed what had to be one of the most dangerous places in all of Balteris, she arrived to find Erset in the midst of civil distress, with its council killed off, half of its Guard run out, and the other half a little overly xenophobic at the moment.

All her risk-taking, hard-won survival across the causeway had been stymied by idiots. No matter how high she could jump, how fast she could run, or how hardened she was to external threats, Shazina couldn't make a single person take her plea for help as anything more than a child acting out. Despite her occasional joy at exploring Erset's maze of enormous swinging rope bridges, towering tree homes, and the myriad of cultural differences that come with living so far above the ground in a forest canopy city, Shazina was becoming more and more sullen. Her being a rather unhappy person in the first place made this genuinely miserable to be around.

We'd made a deal, though. With no one in Erset willing to listen to her, I'd told her about Volant's mother, Rook, and Halgunos and that if anyone I knew could help her, it'd be them. Of course, we couldn't get anyone to help her if we showed up, having left the captain's son trapped with the Guard after having our trial interrupted by an assassination attempt that resulted in one of the oldest and most important meeting places in Erset burning up. In return, said Guard's style of keeping order in Erset had shifted to locking away anyone they possibly could that even looked at them funny.

So, she'd agreed to play lookout and keep the hand cart ready for us to move Volant with once we'd snuck him out of the clinic.

"Are you sure taking a half-dead person away from professional healers is the best way to help your friend?" asked Shazina as we situated Volant into the cart.

The girls did the heavy lifting, both being annoyingly stronger than I was if Shazina activated her weird form of Skill. Cassiopia was so big that you had to use words like "slabs of muscle" and "ox-like" when talking about her. If I hadn't seen it with my own eyes, I'd assume she'd not be able to reach the enormous bone bow stored on what she usually wore on her back with how much muscle was in the way.

In the moonlight, Volant didn't look like an unconscious, arrow-shot, infection-fighting patient. He looked like a pale corpse. Dead and bloodless. His Wydvis tan was all but gone in the washed-out night, matching his limp and colorless hair.

"Doubt it can do him much worse than being with the healers," I replied. "Those people are just as likely to kill someone as they are to fix them back up. Never trust anyone who doesn't let you call them by their first name. They're up to something."

Cassiopia chuckled. "I agree with that, my small friend. My people from the mountains feel similar. The healers are watched just as closely as their wards. Those folk get strange ideas when no one's standing by to tell them no." She picked up the cart's handles, beginning to wheel Volant away. "You ever hear of glung fruit, Nil?"

I shivered, a hand involuntarily going to my side where the glung fruit-covered knife had cut a ragged gash in me. "Unfortunately, I know of it." The three of us navigated several bridges and curved branches until we found the lift that would lower us to the forest floor, where we'd stashed our stolen goods, including a pair of horses and a legitimately purchased wagon to transport Volant in.

"Well," she continued, "one healer tried to use it as a painkiller while operating on his patients." She shook her head. It had not gone well.

I remembered how awful I'd felt getting it out of my system with Johanna's help and cringed. "Healers," I shook my head. "I think it's more than all right that we busted him out. Probably saved his life, now that we're talking about it."

Shazina had a puzzled look on her face, so I figured they didn't have glung fruit across the causeway, but I didn't feel like explaining it to her. She'd been nearly impossible to get information out of and more than a little condescending since I'd found her. If she wanted to know more, she could ask Cassiopia.

Once we had Volant loaded into the wagon, I headed back up into the canopy to find my parents. They'd been less than supportive, and I had to borrow my mother's clinic key without her knowing to spring Volant. I stopped in front of the door of my home, staring at the faintly round wooden door I'd come in and out of so many times as a child. A pang went through me. Echoes of a lost innocence now that I'd come to understand this wasn't the safe, cozy haven I'd thought it was.

My dad, with bags under his eyes and a few days of unshaven stubble covering his face, opened the door. He had a book in one hand and was balancing a cup of tea on top of it.

I blinked in surprise, not expecting him to be awake.

"Heard you leave in the middle of the night. Couldn't go back to sleep, so..." he gestured towards the book. "Library doesn't open for a few more hours. Thought I'd wait up for you."

I headed inside, a little embarrassed. My mother came down the winding stairs from the bedroom and sat across from me at the kitchen table. I slid the key over the well-worn block of wood, unable to meet her gaze.

A small sigh and shake of the head, and she took it and dropped it into a pocket.

"We're leaving," I started.

Neither of my parents said anything. Both just looked vaguely disappointed yet unsurprisingly relieved at the same time.

"Well. Thanks, I guess. I hope you guys don't get in any trouble because of me." I stood, not wanting a drawn-out conversation.

Both shifted uncomfortably, and it was then that I realized my parents weren't in any way more adept at being adults or dealing with unusual circumstances than I was. It was my turn to be a little disappointed and a little relieved.

"Wander well," my father said. "I'm proud of you."

My mother got up and hugged me, a tight and emotional embrace. More so coming from her usually stoic self. "I'm proud of you as well. I wish we had your courage. Good luck, son. You always have a place here."

And that was it.

I left.

My emotions tangled about inside me as a jumbled mess. I'd expected an argument or condemnation, just about anything but the apparent support that my rule-following, gods-fearing family had given me.

Sunrise was beginning to filter through the treetops as I helped Cassiopia load the wagon. We didn't have much beyond Cassiopia's camping gear, Volant's rapier, and a pair of travel blankets wrapped around the unconscious Volant. A chest with some dried food acted as a seat in the back for Shazina. She lounged with a book she'd miraculously convinced my father to part with, and an angry indifference at the rest of the world painted across her face. Cassiopia cracked the reins once we'd double-checked everything we'd loaded was secure and in place. With that, we were away.

Crisp winter air smelling of earth and something ineffable greeted us as we passed out from the central forest into a more open wood with a full view of the rising sun and far away fields of Tryst. It was refreshing to be out from under the oppressive branches of Erset. We were moving forward again.

Chapter Two

I had no idea how to get in contact with Rook or Andreska. One was probably off running down pirates on the west coast of Brod near the mistlands, while the other could be just about anywhere in an airship doing whatever it was she and her crew did after helping fight off prejudiced zealots. I wrote and sent out letters to each, but it would take a long time to find them if they ever did.

So, we decided to head back to Kalaran, the most accessible place to find someone looking to be found and also the best place to hide when that's what you'd rather do. Cassiopia had never been inside the city as there was no big game to hunt in the caves of Kalaran, and the only creatures available on the mountain itself were the Night Runner's wolf mounts. It didn't matter how much you liked hunting; you did not antagonize them if you wanted to live for long. It was strange, Cassiopia having grown up so near the front gates but to never have entered. Shazina hadn't been either, but when we explained it was as close to a ruling government for the entire region of Balteris, she grudgingly agreed to the plan as well.

We took the Turtle-castle road all the way there, seeing no one else along the way. The Battle of Brod, as everyone had been referring to the start of the civil war the Equals and Xylex had attempted to instigate, looked to have shaken everyone. People all over Balteris had mostly canceled the winter celebrations. Travel was being discouraged by the Guard until they could round up the seditious Equals, and everywhere people hid behind their doors and waited for the storm to blow over.

In the letters, I explained what had happened to Volant and me after Andreska had left us and that we were heading to Kalaran to hide out and wait for them to join us. I also emphasized that I'd personally seen Shazina do some incredible things far off on the causeway and vouched that she had to be from across the sea. If that didn't get them to Kalaran, it meant Rook and Captain Andreska didn't receive the letters.

A surprise waited for us when we got to Kalaran's primary entrance, though. For the first time I'd ever seen, the gates were closed and barred. No way into the underground city with a wagon at the least. It was nightfall, and we'd been on the road for what seemed like an eternity, passing the days with sullen silence from Shazina, awkward jokes from Cassiopia, and an unwaking sleep on Volant's part.

I wanted to tear my hair out but had already shaved it down as close to the scalp as I could get it.

Instead, I knocked.

And then I knocked some more.

And finally, I furiously pounded against the ironbound gates with the back of my hatchet. As my arm grew tired, a panel slid away at eye level. Two bloodshot eyes glared out at me.

"I'm sleeping, you godspawn," an angry voice growled from beyond the gate. "Don't you know it's past curfew?"

"Curfew?" I echoed. "Kalaran doesn't have a curfew."

"We do since the Equals started blowing things up in here," the voice responded. "Gates don't open till dawn now, so you'll just have to camp out till then." With that, he slammed the panel shut, and I heard a distinct click as it locked back in place.

With the information passed back to the girls, we had no choice but to huddle together on the side of the road. We made a broth, poured some into Volant's unresponsive mouth, and then set up a small camp to spend another night out in the cold. Cassiopia was unaffected by the news. Shazina and I glowered in silence, neither of us well adapted to the chilly outdoors.

At dawn, after what might be the last cold and restless night I could bear, the gates to Kalaran creaked open. We trudged through, working warmth into limbs. An entire squad of Guard with a spear-wielding Elite at their head was standing watch just within the entrance. They didn't try to stop us. Despite possibly being exonerated of the charges against us, it was still probable I had a reward on my head. The Guard always made me nervous either way, so it was an uncomfortable walk.

At the end of the tunneled entrance, I saw splashes of light marking buildings and highlighting merchant stalls. Life was in full swing inside the cave city, and heat radiated from the cavern and warmed both my body and soul. Erset may have been where I grew up, but Kalaran was where I'd found a home at the school.

The tavern we stopped at was just around the corner from Jorcum's Higher Learning Academy, and a small part of me hoped that the letters had gotten back to Rook or Andreska, and they'd somehow be waiting for us. Broken Oar's tavern was more spacious than it seemed from the outside. The square building had two floors in a predominantly low-ceilinged part of Rootfloor. Carved stone roof artfully melded into the cave ceiling, making the building look like the mountain had birthed the place. In reality, the tavern stretched deep up into the rock, providing completely dark and fairly chilled rooms, until popping out into the residential cavern Kalaran had far above. Here you'd find Kalaran's suburban center. Homes carved into the cave walls, local shops made of thick and expensive wood, and of course, more of the school's campus as it curled its way through the mountain.

This locational perk gave the Broken Oar the honor of being one of the only buildings in Kalaran, besides the school, that you could use to access other levels of the caverns that honeycombed the mountain. It being a privilege only allowed to paying customers, a number of the wealthier residents rented out rooms just for the convenience. A common room with Kingdoms tables spread around a smoldering fireplace dominated the entryway, with a steward working behind the counter.

"Hi there," I said, trying to be cheerful. "I'm looking to get a room, but I may have some friends waiting for me. Captain Andreska or Rook happen to be here?"

A suspicious eye turned towards me, looking my travel-stained clothes up and down before settling with a less than kind gaze back on me before answering. "No. No one here by that name. How many rooms?" He looked me over again. "And you pay upfront."

Inwardly, I sighed. Luck was never my forte anyway. "One room, thanks."

Cassiopia carried Volant up to the room while I moved our meager possessions into it, and Shazina hunkered down in a corner to read. I wrote out a quick note explaining where we were and left it next to Volant in case he woke up. After a short and wonderfully warm dinner in the common room, we huddled around one of the tables while distractingly playing a three-player round despite Shazina having never even heard of the game.

Finally, she tossed her pieces on the table in frustration. "When are we going to speak to this government of yours, Nil? I'm tired of waiting. My family needs me."

With a deep breath, I tried to compose myself. "We're waiting for Andreska or Rook, as the council will respond a lot more favorably to them than to a child claiming to have crossed the causeway by herself."

She growled in frustration, crossing her. "This is ridiculous. My friends and family could be getting murdered, and all I've done is gotten further from returning home."

"It's okay, fierce one," Cassiopia said. "If we can make these people listen, we'll get Nil's friend back to his family, and then the three of us will head that way. We can train Nil to help you, and we'll try to fight these gimzers together."

"That's... not a terrible plan," Shazina said, suddenly interested. "I mean, the three of us by ourselves, yes. Terrible. But training Nil and teaching him how to become one of these Unbroken would be a good start."

"Strangely enough, I'm right here and would love to jump in on this conversation about me," I interjected. "You actually think I can become an 'Unbroken' and that it would help you with this gimzer problem back across the sea?" Beyond the first day when we'd met her, Shazina hadn't spoken of the gimzers or Unbroken. She'd been relatively quiet on all fronts once we'd gotten back to Erset and fed her. I'd nearly forgotten about this need for a council was actually to enlist several Learners to become some legendary force to fight the plague of vampiric creatures she was *almost* sure were attacking her people.

Shazina nodded. "It'd be good to have someone to practice teaching and see what kind of dangers we ran into. Supposedly, it can be rather fatal if attempted incorrectly. You seem like a perfect choice for finding out." There was almost a tinge of excitement in her voice, and I had to take a more extended look to see if there was any sarcasm lurking there.

Cassiopia laughed, a deep sound that came from her belly. "You're right again, small one! Our Nil is one of the most enthusiastic dancers at Death's Ball. He is an excellent choice for this if dying could be involved!"

I looked between the two incredulously.

These women were going to get me killed.

"Let's get started after you show me around this cave." A subtle, gleeful malice dripped off of Shazina's words, and I knew I wasn't going to enjoy this.

Outside the tavern, Kalaran was more muted than I was used to. People gave each other a wide berth and walked with fast, purpose filled strides. There was no meandering. No idle gossip-mongering. No laughter. The school, ordinarily open in the day to any visitors looking to wander its campus, was stationed with a pair of Elites that were only letting credentialed students in and out.

I found a tea shop that also served some local flare of small foods and asked Cassiopia and Shazina to save me a bite. I had somewhere I needed to go.

While on my way to the Stump, I passed by a blasted-out building. It used to be a small shop, so glass still littered the ground around where its pointless windows used to be. Pointless because it was already a tavern under a mountain, there not being much sunlight or weather around. Scorch marks peppered every flat surface as if someone had bombarded the place with balls of fire. I stopped, trying to figure out what could have caused it. I looked into a window and saw bits of stone and glass embedded into the wall itself. The place had a sharp smell, similar to manure but with ozone cutting through beneath the scent.

Further along the grooved stone road, the same that if I followed would take me back out to the port, I found what I was looking for. Time hadn't healed these wounds fully, I realized. A vice squeezed inside my chest as I tried to fight back the tears, but it was a battle I was losing. Someone had swept the ash and dust away, but the wooden stump sign's remains leaned up against our old hangout and its scorched foundation. Blackened soot covered every inch of the place. The blood and bodies had been scrubbed away as if they'd never happened.

I stepped in. Maybe not stepped in, exactly. That was a generous way to think about it considering there wasn't much more than the shadow of a threshold where a door used to be. The ceiling was gone. So were large sections of the walls. Somehow a mostly pristine table sat in one corner, turned on its side. The counter was still there, too, a blackened stone outcropping that was borrowed from Kalaran's geology and polished by hundreds of hands resting against it every day.

Enough of the wall remained that when I sank to my knees in the middle of the floor, I couldn't see out into the rest of Kalaran. Tears splashed against the floor as I remembered Bymm and his barely contained excitement at becoming engaged that night. I remembered my classmates, all full of hope and dreams, each one planning to change the world in their own way. I remembered the musician in the corner. I remembered the simplicity of a life focused on learning and making ends meet. I remembered it all, and I wept for those who never got to experience anything further. Sobs racked my body. I hadn't deserved to survive. If I was honest with myself, I deserved their fate far more than they had.

Long, painful breaths later, I reined in my sorrow. The small coal of anger I'd been stoking ever since my nights in Tryst felt hot and sharp in my gut.

I drew one of my two daggers and watched it twinkle in the odd light of a city that was it's own source of luminescence. I grasped the edge with my other hand and squeezed, letting the blade bite into my palm. Fresh, clean pain blossomed as blood dripped across the knife. I closed my hand and gathered Skill there, allowing a different kind of warmth and danger to flow into my fingers.

Pointing my index at the ground, I pushed a controlled but direct flow of Skill into the stone floor and carved a word into the floor. When finished, I uncurled my finger, letting the gathered blood splash into the six letters and fill the shallow carving.

Dark red, the word "finite" looked up at me, a reminder for anyone who ever came this way that life could and would end. Tears dropped and mixed into the word. One final touch. More Skill pushed into my hand. I drove a spear-shaped hand at the floor, gouging a deep groove, just the size for a dagger. Sliding the weapon into the tiny space was difficult with my blood slicked hand, but I managed to get it in nice and tight. I slapped the top of the pommel with a final bit of Skill, driving the blade further into the stone and wedging it in place.

I stood. A fitting token for the friends and life I lost that day. Drops of blood trailed me as I left, but my eyes were finally dry. I'd properly laid to rest my friends. It was high time I righted some wrongs.

Chapter Three

Both of the girls were still at the tea house. Cassiopia was happily munching on something covered in so much sugar that it made the dessert unrecognizable. A laughably small cup rested in her meaty palm, but she sipped at it like a high-born storybook princess. Shazina, on the other hand, had a half-eaten korbit in front of her and a sullen look. I pulled up a chair and reached for the korbit, my eyebrow raised in question.

She nodded, pushing it my way. The tea house was nearly empty, another side effect of the attacks in Kalaran, I assumed. I took the food, biting into it. Spiced bread and umami flooded my mouth, knocking me down nostalgia lane to the first days I spent in Kalaran when I'd left home against my family, and really all of Erset's, desires to become a Learner. The tears from earlier threatened to come back, but I pushed them back down.

"You all right?" I asked Shazina once I'd finished the korbit.

Hesitation, and a slight shake of the head. "I miss my sister. And my brother. And I really miss my grandma." She sniffed, fighting back the tears. "I'd know if they weren't okay, right? You feel something if the ones you love are hurt or die. So they have to be okay, right?"

Cassiopia shifted, reaching across the table to hold the much smaller girl's hand. "Of course, fierce one. They're perfectly fine. The only problem is they're probably missing you thrice over."

Nodding in agreement, I patted her shoulder. "It's okay to miss them. I bet they'll be thrilled to see you when you're back. You guys ready to explore Kalaran a bit more? We can even go by the council chambers and see if there's a play or similar."

In the heart of Kalaran's sprawling expanse of buildings was a squat, yet elegant hexagon. The de facto headquarters for all the legislation and important decision making for Tryst, Erset, Brod, Kalaran, and Wydvis. Though each was semi-autonomous, the council leaders from each city-state met here. This style of ruling mostly resulted in council members getting fat off of working people's taxes, and then congratulating each other on a job well done.

Despite my abject dislike for politicians, the building was a sight to see. Merchants had tents in clusters, selling knick-knacks, street food, and who knows what else. Kalaran's energy was in full swing here unlike the rest of the cavern. Admittedly, the Guard presence was tenfold what I'd ever seen before. Dozens of pairs walked throughout the crowd of people, alert and tense. Besides that, it finally felt like I'd found the Kalaran I'd left.

Shazina was adequately awed by the crowds and the sheer size of the sprawling architecture. "There's nothing like this back home! At most, we have some larger wooden structures. But without Skill, it takes ages for us to build or create anything of any size."

Cassiopia didn't seem to be paying attention, having headed directly to the closest street food vendor. Just like Volant would have.

It almost physically hurt waiting for him to wake up. He'd be getting along great with this strange huntress who loved food just as much as he did.

My reverie was broken by an Announcer who was hollering from the steps at the top of his lungs, barely noticeable above the hubbub.

I nudged Shazina towards him. "Let's see what he's going on about. Last time I heard from one, he was talking about a bounty on my head."

Up close, the man was young, his face acne-scarred, and his hair too well kept. "Councilman Xylex has been captured!" he yelled. "The man behind the Equal uprising, the manipulator, the fiend looking to ruin any peace in our land, has been captured! A trial will be held soon!"

When no one responded, and the crowd seemed more interested in a stray puppy that had appeared than him, the Announcer gave up. He sat on the stool, holding out small papers with Xylex's face on it and "captured" written boldly beneath the sketch.

I stepped up, taking one of the papers. "Thanks," I muttered and turned back to the girls.

"Who's that?" Cassiopia asked.

"It's him," I replied.

"Him?" Puzzled, she took the paper and examined it.

"The man who's behind the war. *God's Fury.* The group who killed my friends and employer, and the ones who were behind the whole thing. He's the one." I'd been hoping to find him myself once Andreska or Rook showed up. Instead, it looks like someone from the ragtag group of Guard that defended Brod against the Equals had brought word back about who was to blame. Honestly, I was surprised they'd listened. Supreme Dioden must have sent word before the Battle of Brod to have the Guard arrest him.

"That seems like good news! Why the glum look?" Cassiopia asked.

My mouth worked, but nothing came out at first. "It's just. I don't know. I was hoping to find Xylex myself, I guess. Though this is probably better. Hopefully, he can turn in his friends, and that particular streak of evil can be cleaned out."

With a shrug, Cassiopia handed back the flyer. Shazina had found a bookseller and was utterly uninterested in what we'd been talking about. She looked back, a small plea in her eyes. She had two books in hand, both with brightly painted covers. Cassiopia turned, and a broad smile spread across her face.

"One can never have too many books. How about you find a third, and I'll haggle with the seller?" Cassiopia said while strolling over to the vendor to begin a light-hearted discussion.

Looking back down at the flyer, I tried to figure out what this would mean. During my third read through, a vast, feel-it-in-your-chest sound exploded from the other end of the hectagon. A pair of heartbeats later, people began to scream.

I rushed towards the dust cloud, but another explosion broke through the cries of pain. The acoustics of a cave, even one as big as this, amplified the noise. It was deafening. Dust shook from the ceiling, darkening the entire area for several long moments. As it settled, I saw a woman from my nightmares, the Learner that Xylex had sent to assist the Guard in the battle against Equals. The exact same person who'd wielded Emerys' Rock to decimate hundreds of people before she'd collapsed. She also was who Captain Andreska believed to have murdered Dioden just before the fight.

She wore a long coat and held one hand inside a pocket. She didn't seem concerned by the explosion at all. More than anything, she seemed interested. With her other hand, she reached up and pulled a deep hood over her head, obscuring her face in darkness.

I stood there dumbly, not believing my eyes. She brought the hand from the pocket, a small glass sphere with thick, viscous yellow liquid suspended inside. She tossed it towards the crowd. The sphere glittered high in the air, arcing just before hitting the cavern ceiling. It shattered, glass and goo spilling across the ground.

For a moment, the last piece of optimism in me hoped she was helping. Maybe some kind of fire suppression technology. Maybe it was just litter. My brain tried to explain it away, somehow.

Then, a third explosion reverberated through me again, with the noise being so loud this close to the initial blast that all I could hear was a high pitch ringing. I staggered with the shockwave. Through more dust, I saw her walk around a corner far down the road, a light spring in her step.

I coughed, dust choking me as I turned to see what damage she'd done. There was nothing to see. Whatever alchemical concoction she'd thrown had cleared the area. Between the three successive blasts, no one was left standing. Guard members and even a pair of Elites with their long spears were swarming toward the blast site. They cordoned off the area while a few began to check for unconscious survivors.

I turned back to find Shazina and Cassiopia still at the book seller's stall, watching wide-eyed. Cassiopia had her arms around Shazina in a protective crouch, while Shazina had a similarly protective hold on her new books. She vibrated ever so slightly, and I could tell she had Skill coursing through her. I'd not seen her do much yet, but I knew she could move faster than my eyes could track, and she claimed she could bring herself to the strength of ten full-grown men for a few moments. I doubted she needed Cassiopia's protection, but it was still heart-warming.

After the shock began to wear off, people began to pack up and leave. Guard went through the crowd, encouraging this, and began to mark off the area around the council chambers. Silence had replaced the boisterous market noise, only broken up by coughs or moans. I'd had enough excitement for the day, so the three of us allowed a short Guard wearing a wrinkled uniform to shoo us out of the area.

At the Broken Oar, news of the attack was already the gossip of the common room. People huddled in corners, around tables, and even on the stairs talking in hushed, scared tones. This kind of wanton death and destruction had never happened. "Times are changing," an old man grumbled to another. "Next thing you know, we'll be back to fiefdoms and war and slavery."

We made it to the room unmolested. Once the door shut, there was blessed silence.

"Left hand of god," I sighed.

Volant was still out cold, a pale shadow on the bed. I propped his head up and poured water into his mouth, willing him to wake up. When he didn't, I gently put him back down and flopped onto the nest of travel blankets I'd laid down on the floor.

None of us spoke, and it wasn't long until sleep took us all into its deep embrace.

A problem with Kalaran is if you're used to waking up with the sun or having any external indication of time, you were hard-pressed to find that here. I woke, groggily tossing and hoping it wasn't morning already. Kalaran's bell that marked the start of the day was ringing, but my body hadn't felt the sun's rays and disagreed. That was something I hadn't missed about Kalaran.

Both Shazina and Cassiopia were up. Or at the least, Shazina was up, reading one of her new books. I couldn't see Cassiopia anywhere. She'd probably stealthed out in her unnaturally graceful way to find some delicious something or other to eat. Shazina looked up at my confused face.

Slightly annoyed, she shut the book. "You snore."

"I do not," I said reflexively.

"How would you know?" she asked while rolling her eyes. "I'm the one that had to listen to it."

For a moment, I paused. "Well, no one's ever told me I snored before."

Again, she rolled her eyes and let out a sigh. "Well, I must be wrong then. You ready to begin training?"

"I want to find the girl, the one who's behind the attacks. I don't think we'll have time for me to study." I pulled on my boots and stretched, working blood back into my limbs.

"There are no books on this side of the causeway for this. It's all about willpower, which you already are familiar with. We can work on it while you search. I'll come with." She tucked the book underneath her arm and marched towards the door, swinging it open. "Coming?"

Outside the tavern, the earthy-stone scent of Kalaran hit me more potently than usual. It must have rained on the mountain during the night. As annoying as the whole no sun thing was, the amplified pertrichor more than made up for it. I took a deep breath in, finding a center of calm in the wake of yesterday's tension. With a loud smack, I clapped my hands together, trying out Volant's meditation trick. Strangely, it felt right for once.

Streets were empty apart from the few furtive pedestrians that passed us by. Nearly every corner had a pair of Guard. It seemed to be mostly Thumpers wielding their thick cudgels, though the glint of spear tips could be seen, marking duos of Elites sprinkled about like a deadly seasoning over the smoothly carved streets. Not only was the Guard out in force, they were being far more attentive than I was accustomed to seeing these bullies act.

To start our search, I led us back to the council chambers to see if we could find anything that might help us follow the woman's trail.

There were no more merchants selling goods at the place of the attack—most of the windows dark. Just like everywhere else, the only souls to be seen were Guard and grim-faced pedestrians moving purposefully about. Shazina's size and age helped us, as I drew suspicious glares until they saw her. We must look like an older brother walking about with his little sister or something.

Still, we tried not to draw too much attention, taking a wide circuit around the hexagon, admiring the intricate carvings etched into its sides. Before we'd come all the way around to the blast site, Shazina gasp loudly.

I spun, hatchet coming up into a defensive position while Skill coursed into my hand with a buzzing tingle of energy contained in a space too small for it. "What is it?" I asked, spinning around, trying to find what had spooked her. My eyes darted everywhere an attacker could be. Rapid-fire like, I looked from rooftop to doorway to the next rooftop to an alley. Nothing.

"It's a puppy!" she squealed, rushing to a pile of rubbish that had been pushed up against the building by street workers.

I flicked my hand away, releasing the Skill in an uncontrolled spread. It struck the wall next to us and created a brief outline against the dust. The discharge was nearly ten paces tall and equally as wide. "That could be handy," I mused. Distracted by the defensive application of a widely dispersed Skill blast, I nearly forgot about the puppy. I'd never tried such a casual, wide dispersal.

"Nil!" Shazina cried out. "It's hurt!"

She'd unburied the puppy, the same one that had shown up just before the attack yesterday, and I could see even from here she was right. Its front leg had a laceration on one side, and it looked like it had been struck in the head.

Beyond the injuries, the dog was heart-meltingly adorable. It had curly brown hair with white paws. The dog whimpered softly, a miserable sound that could derail logical thinking and trigger pure emotion. Faster than I could track, Shazina had the puppy picked up and wrapped in her shirt. She was back in front of me before I'd even taken a breath.

A fire burned deep in her eyes, and a look that reminded me how this young girl had been able to do something no one else in history had been able to do painted her face in grim, stone set determination. "We're going to find that woman. And we will make her suffer," she growled the words through clenched teeth.

I took a step back, momentarily letting my survival instincts rule me. "You know, she also killed people yesterday. And lots of them when I saw her in Brod."

"That doesn't matter." Shazina softened momentarily, looking down at the shaking bundle of fur she held gently under her shirt. "She. Hurt. This. Puppy." Her words struck like the gods dictating a pronouncement to be carved in stone.

"You're right," I replied. "This puppy is way more important. Let's find a healer for it."

She nodded, the fuzzy blur of her Ukiyo dissipating back into her.

Despite the suggestion, I took us slowly by the blast site, acting like I was helping Shazina walk. Nearby, a small, half-moon of glass glinted beneath a dusting of ash. Though I'd laced my boots up well, I reached down and pretended to tie them. With a fluid motion, I stood and scooped up the shard of glass and dropped it down into a pocket. A pair from the Guard stood in our path, with one eyeing me distrustfully. But, when seeing Shazina and the puppy, his face softened immediately, almost childlike.

"Oh, hello!" he cooed to the bundle of bloody fur as he approached. "What's your puppy's name? Can I pet him?"

Shazina's eyes hardened once more, and the Guard stopped a few paces away, puzzled.

Hurriedly, I intervened before she could do or say anything that would cause us problems. "We just found him, actually, and he's hurt. Sorry, but we need to hurry and get help from a healer." I tried to move us past him, down the way I saw Xylex's massacre-happy helper disappear yesterday, but the Guard moved into our path, eyes as hard as Shazina's now.

"The puppy is hurt?" he asked. With a closer look, he saw the blood and heard the low but constant whimpering. "Left hand of god, those monsters..."

I thought he was about to blame us when he turned to his squad mate that had been watching in muted interest. "Cobb, I'm taking these to a healer, immediately. There's a hurt puppy. Cover for me."

Cobb, the bored partner with an immaculate mustache, straightened up with sudden alertness. Outrage blazed across his face, turning him from a soft-looking Guard to looking like an avenging warrior of ancient times. "A hurt puppy? Left-handed god spawns!" he sputtered. "Go! I'll cover!"

With that, the Guard turned back to us, fierce determination radiating off him. "Follow me!" And then he was sprinting away, hollering to clear the path to the few people who were still out and about.

I stood dumbly as Shazina didn't even hesitate, sprinting along right at the man's heels. Cobb looked at me like I was some halfwit. His eyes asked if I didn't realize there was an injured puppy's life at stake. With a shake of my head, I ran after the two, struggling to keep up with the pair as they ducked down alleys and leaped over obstacles like their lives were on the line.

Panting, I leaned up against the wall. My chest burned as it tried to force my lungs to catch up. Everything hurt. The Guard came out, having brought Shazina inside as I'd arrived. He stuck out his hand, somber and only slightly out of breath.

I shook it, confused.

"You're doing a good thing here. I'm honored to have helped. Name's Marle. If you even need me, I'm at your service."

"Nil," I replied. "And the same to you."

A faint look of recognition at my name came across his face, but he said nothing else. He thumped his chest in salute and walked away, as dignified as a slightly out of breath, sweat covered man can.

Within the small shop, I found Shazina anxiously watching a petite woman with strong hands feel all over the puppy. The room's back wall had a pair of barn-style doors, and I realized she must usually work on horses and similarly sized animals. Still, she seemed confident in what she was about.

A few whimpers escaped the dog, but every time the healer whispered reassuringly, scratching the dog's belly before continuing to probe around. We watched silently, unsure of what to do.

When she'd finally made her way to the small brown tail and moved it in every direction without any noise from the stray, she turned back to us, a slight smile. "He'll be all right. I just need to bandage up this cut, and then you'll need to let him rest for a few days. Preferably indoors, and most definitely with plenty of food. He's a little underfed."

Rapidly, Shazina agreed. Less sure, but with nothing to see otherwise, I nodded too.

The bandaging was quick, and I could tell this woman knew her business. "Do you only work on animals?" I asked, pointing to the table.

"For the most part, yes," she replied. "People are far less grateful and tend to complain more than animals." She tossed her head back, moving several loose black strands of hair away from her face, and hit me with a glowing smile. "Do you guys only rescue cute animals?"

With a chuckle, I shook my head. "For the most part, no. This is actually a first." She was stunning. Dark skinned, bright-eyed, and had the confidence of someone far too smart for their own good. I had to yank my gaze away before it became too inappropriate.

A slight whimper escaped the puppy as she scooped him up gently and then even more so deposited him into Shazina's hands. "Well, you certainly picked an exceptional place to start. I can't even remember the last time I saw a dog, they're pretty uncommon these days, and this one is delightfully cute."

"It was mostly Shazina. I'm just along for the ride, honestly. Nil, by the way. And this is Shazina," I said with a gesture to the oblivious child that was near tears as she rocked the puppy back and forth.

"A pleasure, Nil. Shazina. My name's Insley, and I'm glad you brought this one to see me. It was quite the treat." She motioned to the door, a warm smile on an otherwise tired face. "Please, come back sometime when the dog is doing better. I'd love to see him again. But for now, I have a client that should be here any moment."

"Thanks, Insley!" Shazina said, headed out the door.

"What do we owe you?" I asked, not having moved.

"Hush, you owe me nothing. Someone rescuing a hurt animal shouldn't be on the line for paying for it as well. This was a welcome diversion from the usual." She paused, fixing the strand that had fallen back across her face. "Just promise to come back with the dog sometime, and we'll call it even."

Offering a slight bow and grin, I replied. "Thank you. We'll do so."

We moved delicately across the remainder of Kalaran until returning to the Broken Oar. The now sleeping dog wholly enthralled Shazina. Her steps slid across the ground like a ballet dancer, the dog feeling not a bounce. The few people out paused as they saw our strange procession, small smiles lighting up their faces as they saw the dog swaddled and asleep.

Cassiopia was sitting in the room, sharpening broadheads between sips of some giant mug of spiced tea that seemed more like soup than a drink. A garrison's worth of arrows glittered in the corner already sharpened. Unlike any normal arrow, these were thick shafted, as long as a grown man's arm, and the tips could double as small knives to a regular person. Monster killers, she called them.

"Nil, you can't keep picking up strays," she said, gesturing to both Shazina and the dog. "You can barely take care of yourself, let alone them, Volant, and whatever else shows up." A goofy, lopsided smile accompanied that, and I could see she was itching to get a closer look at the puppy.

"Maybe put up the weaponry first. If anything hurts the dog further, Shazina may murder us all before you could apologize." I matched her grin, but I was half-serious.

For her part, Shazina had seemed to relax a bit now that we were inside. Ignoring Volant's unconscious form, she sat on the edge of the bed. With exaggerated care, she placed the still sleeping ball onto the bed. Volant's foot provided a headrest for the dog. Once she deemed it safe, Shazina got up and grabbed a spare shirt, and wrapped it around the creature. She made some minor adjustments and then stepped back to examine the nest. It seemed as if she found it acceptable and gestured to Cassiopia that she was allowed to approach, albeit with extreme caution and gentleness.

She did so. The giant of a woman moved forward silently until she could crouch down next to the dog. With a single finger, she gently stroked its back.

The dog didn't wake, and seemed to snuggle into the pet.

We all let out a relieved breath.

The girls had a whispered conversation on what to name the dog. They did not invite me to put in an opinion, so I headed back down to the common room, taking a seat at a table with a game of kingdoms forgotten half-way through.

A small piece, a deep onyx colored Learner, sat surrounded by a myriad of light turquoise pieces. The game variant was one I'd not played before. Maybe some homebrew rules? A double-stacked set of stones sat on the opposite side of the Learner, a configuration of pieces I'd heard of but didn't know how to play myself. It represented one of the thirteen gods, probably whichever was the player's favorite one. A god piece, earned through a stroke of luck and smart play in some game types of Kingdoms, was popular with people who wanted the winner to gain an overwhelming advantage in the endgame.

It looked like whoever had been playing had given up, recognizing the futility of playing through the rest of the game considering the lopsided forces. If I could find who'd been playing, maybe they could teach me their version of the game. It'd definitely be interesting.

I shifted around to see if anyone else was hiding somewhere in the common room when something sharp poked my leg. Gently, I slid the small shard out of my pocket. It wasn't much bigger than my thumb, and had an edge as sharp as a razor.

Glass is such a strange thing. Rigid as stone, yet you could see through it. You could also see designs in it. The world was so incredibly fascinating the closer you looked at it. Clouds, made of lighter, softer stuff than glass, could stretch further than a man could ride in a day and would block out the sun. And yet, this small piece of sharp, melted sand had contained enough power to move stone. To kill people. To strike terror in those who saw it.

Turning the shard over and over in my hands, the light caught a small shape on the inner curve. A tiny, minimalistic eye. Definitely alchemists. But, the only alchemist I'd ever met was Halgunos, and he'd not seemed the type to help create explosives. I tore a piece of paper out of the journal Volant had given me and pressed it against the glass' inner curve where the eye symbol was.

I scratched back and forth on the paper until the eye outline stood contrasted to the pencil's gray graphite. It was a start. I wrapped the shard of glass into another piece of paper and went over to the proprietor who was sitting in his own corner behind the counter, reading some small book with a picture of a Wydvis airship copied onto the front.

When he didn't notice me, I cleared my throat. It must be a good book, as he still didn't look up. I rapped on the counter and coughed again.

The man looked up with a twitch and shoved the book behind his back. "Good story?" I asked, nodding to his mostly concealed novel.

"Umm, not really," he stammered. Still caught off guard, he pushed the book further behind him.

"Well, okay then." Bemused, I turned my paper his way, the eye etching looking up to the ceiling between us. "I'm trying to find an alchemist. You happen to know where I can hire one out?"

Instead of relaxing at the new topic, the man went pale, a slight shake in his hand. "I don't know anything about the guild, and nor do I know where to find them. Good day, sir!"

Despite this being his establishment, the man came around the counter and fled. How very odd. Instead of following him, I gave up and headed upstairs to see if the girls had decided on a name or not. Before I got to the room, Cassiopia found me in the hall.

She looked flustered but the tension ebbed when she saw me. "Nil! You left at the right time. That child has no understanding of the importance of naming. The ideas she had." A scoff as she shook her head. "The less said about it, the better. Let's leave her to her new friend. I could use your eyes in this city."

Ignoring everything she said, I held out the paper. "This mean anything to you?"

She took it. A long pause, and then handed it back. "The alchemist guild. I don't like them. Why?"

I explained what we'd found along with the puppy and how the innkeeper had acted downstairs.

"Well, I may not like them, but that seems a little dramatic. My bow wouldn't have been possible without an alchemist in Brod. I just think they're creepy. Not run away in fear worthy." She huffed, her face showing she'd lumped the man in with Shazina on oddness.

"So, I was right. Alchemists are helping her with the attacks!" A smile twitched on my face.

Cassiopia looked at me in a way that said I was nearing the same judgment she'd given the other two. "Obviously. You thought there could be explosions without someone involving an alchemist? That's what they do. They make things explode or melt or whatever other unnatural things they can come up with."

"Well," I replied, "I guess you're right."

We both sat there for a moment, awkwardly waiting for the other to fill the silence.

I broke it first. "I still think if we find the local alchemist or guild or whatever, we should be able to find the woman behind the attacks."

She sighed. "I've never hunted a woman before. Let us try, sapling."

"Sapling?" I asked, mid-step to head back downstairs.

"Yes, like a young tree. Lead on." She gestured towards the stairwell.

I raised an eyebrow but shrugged. We turned towards the stairs and headed down.

Chapter Four

Out on the street, I breathed deeply. It was nice being back here and not necessarily having anyone try to kill me so far. Last time, we had to leave rather quickly, considering the death of Cralil and the burning of the Guard headquarters. And then, I knew where to go. I'd nearly forgotten about the triplets. They'd grown up in Kalaran and probably had a far less sheltered experience than I did while at the school.

I took us to the school. Jorcum's Higher Learning Academy greeted us in huge, deeply carved letters above the closed gates. They'd added more sentries since the attack on the council chambers. As soon as they saw us heading towards the entrance, two men with slung over-the-shoulder, heavy bladed scimitars intercepted us. Unlike the Guard, they had beards and wore casual clothing. They also seemed far more relaxed and far more dangerous.

"What's your business?" asked the first. Firm but polite.

"I'm a student, or was one at least," I replied. "Looking for some friends of mine that are still here."

He seemed skeptical. But, he didn't whip out the scimitar and try to behead me. "Alumn, eh. Can I see your signet then?"

I coughed. "You see, I didn't graduate. I'm looking for some triplets. Diedra, Dendra, and Joy."

Both sets of eyes hardened at hearing I hadn't graduated. But when I mentioned the triplet's names, they softened back to something closer to amusement.

"Oh, I see. Yet another suitor for the trips has come a-calling." He laughed. "Sorry boy, but for their sake, we're not letting any more of your kind in either, as harmless as you might be."

That was just downright insulting. Harmless was right up their with coward on the list of my least favorite words. Cassiopia seemed offended by it as well, as she stepped up to the man, flexing boulder-sized biceps.

"We're not suitors, boy. Begone, and let us through." She glared at the man.

To his credit, he barely flinched and didn't back down. He centered himself with a subtle shift of his feet. His amused eyes went flat.

The other sentry sensed the change and slid to the side, opening up a line of sight on us that didn't require him to go through his own man. No doubt about it, they were professionals.

"Left hand, it's not a problem," I said, arms placating Cassiopia. "If you'll pass on a message, Nil and Volant are in town. We're staying at the Broken Oar. They'll want to know."

With a tight nod, the man acknowledged this and turned back to the gate, sending a quick hand sign to the other sentry. In return, the second man relaxed and stepped back as well. Cassiopia and I backed away and followed the curve of nature-made wall.

Gray, rough-hewn stone curled like a rippling wave surrounding the school's perimeter. I traced a hand along the curving structure until we were out of sight of the sentries. Despite the smooth look of the wall from a distance, up close, and under my hand, it was a rough, pockmarked surface. The type any climber would love. And like any natural stone formation, one could always find hand and footholds if one looked close enough. It was like nature was begging for exploration. She was ever leaving interesting clues on her surfaces for those who were willing to notice the small gifts of the natural world.

I found a darkly shadowed part of the stone face with a deep groove in it that managed not to be exposed to as much public view as other sections. It was what we refer to as a chimney, one of my favorite formations to climb. I looked back and realized Cassiopia might have some trouble making it up. I'd worked this one before with Volant when we were sneaking back at night past the school's curfew, and I'd have to pull him through the narrow opening at the top. She was a lot bigger than he was.

"Spot me for a bit," I said in answer to her raised eyebrow. "I'm going to climb this, and I'd rather not fall to my death and have to be found by some random Guard."

She pursed her lips, thinking. "Yes, that would be a poor death. Not one becoming of a person who'd faced so many more interesting dangers."

"Aye, that too," I chuckled. "Just wait till I disappear and distract any Guard you see coming. After you can't see me any longer, just give it a twenty-breath count before you leave."

Cassiopia rolled her eyes. With casual grace, she leaned up against the wall just to the side of my chimney. "You're not great at playing tour guide," she huffed. "I shall await your return at the tea house we went to yesterday. But then, I expect a proper scouting expedition around this city."

No one was around, which would have been odd for this part of the day in normal circumstances. Finally, a silver lining to these attacks. I reached up, slipping my fingers into a narrow, nearly invisible groove. I pulled into it, swinging my other arm up and grasping the first asymmetrical surface I could. My feet pressed into either side of the v-shaped formation. And then I slipped, heel skidding against the stone for a pace before I fell onto my butt.

"You didn't see that," I said when Cassiopia looked my way. "Just getting the kinks worked out. It's been a while."

She gave me an encouraging pat and blessedly kept silent.

I got back to my feet and dusted off. My shoulders popped as I rolled them in circles. I jumped into the wall this time, pressing my hands and feet into the chimney's sides. Slowly, I began to ascend. Each hand carefully found its spot, a good grip here, or a stable position to press and shuffle off of. My feet did the brunt of the work, supporting my movements from a small hole I stuffed my boot tip into, and a heel kicked into the hard stone to keep me stable while I moved my hands up to the next position.

After I had to stop and catch my breath, I looked down. Vertigo threatened my focus as the ground tilted far below me. Far enough to probably kill me if I fell wrong, and at least break a lot of bones if I fell right. But not far enough for me to gather Skill and create enough drag to lighten the landing. This was how even a practiced Learner ended up dead. It was almost annoying to think about as I caught my breath and tried to ignore the tremors in my forearms. I was practically safer at a height three times this.

Fear faded as an additional hit of adrenaline coursed through me. No second-guessing. Trying to climb down would be even more dangerous. I reached up, grabbed the next hold I wanted to use. As I shifted my weight into it, the handhold broke away, costing me my balance. My right arm windmilled, but I refused to fall. I squeezed in with my other hand, pressing hard with my legs. The moment passed, and I reached up a little further, finding a better hold.

Left hand. Right hand. Left foot. Right foot. Pause, reassess, continue. I ascended further. Of course, this chimney was in one of the highest points in all of Kalaran. It couldn't be just a short one-story climb. My hands hurt, and I'd done something painful to one of my fingernails. I could feel blood dripping down it and messing up my grip. I neared the top of the climb, just below where the hole in the unforgiving wall was.

The smooth ceiling stuttered where the cave mouth met the mostly vertical wall, sticking out like a smaller ceiling. This was by far the scariest part of the whole climb. I looked up at the shelf that jutted above my head, past the chimney, and into open space. I should have just waited for the sisters to find us.

A new, unforeseen obstacle poked out above me, between the bottom of the outcropping I was climbing towards and the chimney I was currently in.

A plant of some kind, dark purple and red, protruded out from the chimney's center, pushing horizontally into the empty air. It looked like gravity had given up and let this devilish plant live in its own universe. I'd seen yucca plants before, and this almost would have qualified as one. But the shoots had curved, hook-shaped serrations running down their length, and the colors were all wrong. The projections spiraled out from the center, ending in needle-thin points. I was going to have to come out of the inner side of the chimney to get past it, and that was definitely not going to be safe.

"Gods above," I spat. This would not be fun.

With my feet set, I reached out one hand, pushing at the plant. It didn't give. The shoots were as hard as the rock wall. They were also as sharp as a blade. Tiny punctures bled from my palm where I'd pushed against the serrated hooks running its length. How did this evil little plant even get here? I cursed again. With the least sophisticated climbing technique I'd ever attempted, I pressed against the wall, arching my back and trying my best to spread my limbs out around the reach of the plant's sharp edges.

Sweat dripped into my eyes. I widened my stance even further, hoping to keep my traction just a little bit longer. I shimmied my body over the monstrous yucca, but I couldn't get my legs spread out far enough to completely clear it. What felt like knife points pierced my inner thighs. It was an easily managed pain but still noticeable. I shifted higher, and the two points of pain carved and arc down to near my knees. And just like that, I was over and tucked into the relative safety of the chimney's tightening embrace.

I took a moment to check myself, head bumping into the outcropping I had to overcome next. I found a jagged cut dribbling blood unevenly across my legs. At this rate, my body was going to be in constant overdrive healing small, self-inflicted wounds. Thank the stars I didn't cut my hand any deeper yesterday.

Slowly I climbed until I was scrunching most of my body up underneath the outcropping. My hands found first one, and then another hold, unevenly spaced on the outcropping above.

I took a breath.

I took another, slower and longer.

Then I closed my eyes and took a third and final one.

Shutting out everything, I let my feet swing out from under me over the open space and did my best not to think of the almost guaranteed death that waited below.

As my legs arced away from the wall and beneath me, I used the momentum, pulling hard against gravity before throwing my left hand up. For the briefest space, I hung in the air, anchored by only the finger tips of my right hand. I was definitely breaking the three points of contact rule Volant and I used when climbing anything.

With a primal grow, I slapped the other hand onto the lip of the shelf with wild abandon. My legs scrambled wildly until finding purchase beneath me. With a final heave, I pulled myself into a low crouch on the outcropping.

I peeked back down. The ground seemed a distant memory. Emotion burst from me, and I shook with exhaustion and a happy laugh.

There was nothing more exhilarating than facing danger and overcoming it. I felt alive like I hadn't since the moment I leaped off the cliff to help Shazina out on the causeway.

Apparently, I'd put on a fair bit of muscle since last coming through this way. It was a tight fit. I managed to squeeze myself into the small tunnel. It was more claustrophobic than I remembered. Crawling on my hands and knees, I imagined the faint trail of blood I must be leaving in my wake. If anyone ever found it, I hoped it brought them plenty of questions.

The tunnel exit was a dozen paces above and nearly as many away from the mathematics building's roof. I turned as I clambered out, my back to the structure. Feet against the wall with my knees up against my chest, I pushed out, launching myself across the space. I turned in midair, arms akimbo.

A solid thump announced my impact. I tucked into a roll as I hit, dispersing the force of landing. When I came back up to my feet, I peeked over the roof's edge to look around to make sure no one had spotted me. There was no one about. I stood and dusted myself off, happy with how it'd turned out. And then I realized I was an idiot. All this work to break in, and I didn't actually know where the girls stayed. The last place had been a hideout Volant and I'd used, and that was less than likely to be the case anymore.

Unfortunately, the campus was sprawling and maze-like in the number of places they could be, not including the fact that they might even be living off-campus like they'd been doing before their trouble with the Guard. I scratched at the stubble on my head. I hadn't thought this through at all. Without a better plan, I headed towards our old hideout. Maybe they'd left a clue or something.

Students were out and about, laughing and enjoying another day of classes. I could see all types of disciplines on display. A pair of boys holding hands while wearing dirt-covered aprons had chosen some form of herbology or gardening as Volant had. They had eyes for no one but each other and nearly ran into me, so enthralled with each other. I tried to spot any Learner's, but I couldn't get close enough to see the books being carried without seeming like a creep. The couple saw me, and the smaller boy clutched at his partner's hand and yanked him at an angle to what they'd been walking.

Confused, I looked around me, seeing if something had spooked them. And then I noticed my blood-stained pants, scratched and bloody hands, and dust-covered face. If I wasn't a dead ringer for one of the madmen in the tunnels, it was only because I looked more insane than the rumors described them. I ducked my head, hurrying to the corner of campus that I used to call home.

The people I passed all seemed so young and fresh-faced. It hadn't been that long since we'd run away. Close to a year at best. How could these people look so different? Seem so naïve? Regret bounced around in me as I strode through campus. Heavy steps carried me as I saw buildings in a new light. There was the history classroom. Would I ever get to sit in there again? Proctor Hall, an all-purpose dining room and testing area. Could I even go back to trying to learn after all this? Would the school take me back? Panic nearly set in, the potential of never going back to the school was overwhelmingly more distressing than the death-defying climb. I tried to take a few calming breaths.

Before I became too maudlin though, I found the corner that had our secret cave. It was tucked into a dark place, just high enough to be inconvenient and out of sight to the casual observer. I went up and was surprised to find a decent interpretation of a home now existing inside.

A threadbare but usable couch was in the corner. Across from it against the other wall was an actual Wydvis style hammock anchored into the stone to either side of it with sturdy iron hooks. A cooking pot hung over a smoldering fire pit that someone had painstakingly carved into the floor near the entrance. A light, sweet smell still wafted around the cave. A pile of cushions ran up along the back wall, and above them were a row of tools and cooking materials. Extra blankets stacked one on top of the other hung next to a broom. Left hand, there was even a piece of art hung on the wall above the hammock.

Then my eyes snapped to the middle of the floor, a sight that should have been my first. A man sat, perfectly still in a chair, a notebook in hand. He was snoring softly, unaware of my presence.

I froze, struggling to take in the remodel of our bachelor cave into this kitchen-forward home with some strange man dozing a few paces away from me.

The notebook slipped from his hand, thumping into the floor. I twitched, trying to back my way out of the cave.

"Who are you?" a sleepy voice asked. And then he came fully awake. "Gods above! What are you doing here? What did you do to Joy?" He half rose from his chair but slumped back into it, petrified at the sight of me.

The blood, I remembered. I looked like a storybook ghoul come to eat him more than a human who'd snuck onto the school's campus.

"Don't panic," I tried.

It didn't help. The stranger was wide-eyed now and shaking. The knot he kept his white hair up in shook as he curled up into the chair. He looked like a younger, less lean Volant now that I thought about it.

"Hey, really, I'm not here to hurt you or anything. Just looking for my friends." I slowly sat down, treating him like a scared animal. "You know Joy, I assume? And her sisters, Dendra and Diedra?"

The names calmed him. He settled his feet back on the ground and gave a nervous chuckle. "Oh, you must be one of the guys that's been trying to get a date out of them! I think you probably should have dressed better. You look a little unhygienic right now." But then he paused, remembering where I'd found him. "Wait. What are you doing here then?" His feet popped back up in the chair again, fear taking hold again.

"If you know the triplets, maybe they mentioned me. The name is Nil," I smiled, feeling the sweat streaked dust on my face crinkle against the movement.

All the fear washed away as pure relief crossed his face. He leaped from the chair. "Nil! Gods above and below, this is the best day ever! We all thought you were dead! The girls have been distraught! Is Volant all right? What are you doing here! Is there another job! I want to help!" He sputtered out, gasping to take a breath from his rapid-fire verbal explosion.

I stood and raised my hands in surrender this time, laughing. "Easy friend. Take it easy. I didn't even catch half that." I walked over, hand outstretched. "I guess you've heard of me?"

His eyes were nearly as wide as they'd been when he'd thought me some evil apparition, but in awe now. "Heard of you? You're the leafer the girls never stop talking about. Nor the school, for that matter. You and Volant are practically famous here!"

That took me back. At best, I figured the school would be remembering me in infamy, if anything, and that's only if they'd put two and two together and realized we'd stolen the horses and raided the armory.

Seeing the disbelief on my face, he continued. "Seriously. You and Volant, the cloud dancer, are all anyone talks about lately. We heard you were at the battle of Brod and have been all over having adventures."

The entire time he spoke, the thin man had been shaking my hand vigorously. Just when I thought he'd not let go until my arm fell off, he stopped and gave me an embarrassed smile. "Martino, chef extraordinaire, at your service. And, umm, Joy's boyfriend," he said sheepishly. "They set me up here so I'd have a free place to live. Hope you don't mind."

I reached down, picking up his notebook, and then handing it back to him. "A pleasure. Did you fall asleep studying?" I asked.

"Writing down my most recent recipe, actually," he replied. "But, Volant, where is he?"

I gave him the rundown on Volant's condition after being arrow shot and the smoke damage to his lungs. After a very brief synopsis on the blue robes' attack in Erset and a few more questions he wouldn't let go, he finally slowed down enough to properly have a conversation.

Volant's life being on the line sobered him up a fair bit as well. This guy was truly invested in hearing about our lives. I took in the top knot, the same way Volant wore his hair, and realized the hairstyle might be more than a coincidence.

"The girls are all in class currently, but we can go spring them out. They'd never forgive me if we didn't." Before I had a chance to respond, he was already climbing down and out of the cave. I looked back to the couch and then back to the cave entrance.

"How?" I asked, mostly to myself. I shook my head when no answer came and climbed down as well.

At the quad, I waited outside a two-story building called the mosaic as Martino went in to find the girls. All three had swapped over to studying to become Learners after meeting me. It was touching but also made me intensely uncomfortable. The building itself brought back memories of class, books, and a pang of something like regret. I ran my hands over the small, marbled squares that some builder had painstakingly embedded all over the face of the building. It would be garish if the sun were to ever shine down on this, but in the diffused light of Kalaran, it was purely artistic.

The doors slammed open, and the three practically identical girls rushed out, Joy's limp making her stand apart. "Nil!" they shouted in unison.

Despite my dirty clothes, we all hugged, and it sent a painful spike of warmth through me. My parents certainly hadn't been as excited to see me, and I couldn't remember the last time I'd had such a genuinely kind reaction to showing up somewhere.

"Where's Nil?" Diedra asked, a sidelong look at Martino before she grinned at me.

I gave them the quick story on Volant's condition as we made our way to the front gates. The mood darkened at a similar pace as if I'd announced the death of a loved one.

"He'll wake up," I promised. "Volant's strong. Stronger than anyone I know."

They bobbed their heads in agreement, and Martino grinned, fully confident in Volant's recovery despite having never met him.

Cassiopia was waiting for us, one hand holding a steaming mug of tea, and the other full with a roasted leg of some bird. "Street food here is worth the trip alone," she said as we walked up.

I introduced everyone. Cassiopia eyed my clothes with a smirk. "I thought you were just going to go climbing, Nil? It looks more like you fought off a slither."

"It feels like I did as well. The climb was a little harder than I remembered, and there was some demon plant that demanded a toll." I gestured at my legs.

Cassiopia shrugged, happy at least that I was alive and hadn't interrupted her culinary tour of Kalaran too much. With a gesture from her avian appendage, she took us back to the tavern.

We caught up on the girls' lives since we'd left Kalaran with Rook on the way back. They'd redeveloped their confidence and had moved back out of the cave and into a home in Rootfloor. Martino had begun at the school, and Joy's secret and minor crush on Volant found root in the would-be chef. At the mention of this, Cassiopia shifted over to Martino's other side, peppering him with questions on his favorite dishes, the best food spots in Kalaran, and his home in Wydvis, and demanded he make her something as soon as we arrived.

"Were you in the mistlands?" Dendra asked while Martino and Cassiopia were having a heated discussion about which kind of pepper to use in a cream-based soup.

"No, I've never made it out there." I thought for a moment. "I believe Rook was, though. You hear something?

Diedra jumped in. "Weird things were going on. Pirates and monsters. Good defeating evil, that kind of thing. We assumed you'd be involved, considering how much trouble you guys seemed to find."

"Or chase," Joy continued, "depending on the perspective."

"Nope, not us, thankfully," I chuckled. "We had enough fun on the other coast and finding Cassiopia and Shazina. Oh! I need to tell you about her." I launched into the breakdown of Shazina's Learner-like ability called Ukiyo, and the whole exchange there.

As we arrived, the proprietor was back behind his counter at the tavern, checking in or out some new patron. He watched me out of the side of his suspicious eyes, trying to find an excuse to turn us away.

Shazina was curled up on the bed with the puppy, pressing it between Volant's feet and her book. She looked up as we came in, eyes narrowing at the interruption.

"Puppy!" Diedra, Dendra, and Joy cried in unison. They rushed over to the bed, crowding around Shazina.

"Can we pet it?" one of them asked.

"You didn't tell us there was a puppy!" another accused.

"It's so cute!" a third said, simultaneous to the first two.

Shazina, for her part, was frozen and blocking the triplets with her body but not actively attacking anyone. After the initial shock wore off, she shifted, nodding to all three and allowing them to touch the bandaged dog.

"What's his name?" Dendra asked while running her fingers along its spine with delicate movements.

A smile beamed from Shazina at this. "I almost named him Obi. But I figured that's more of a girl dog's name. Instead, I went with Argo!"

Cassiopia, who'd been quietly standing with Martino, rolled her eyes in the corner. "It should have been Brutus," she muttered under her breath.

A sigh from Shazina, dramatic as any child who'd thought someone older was being stupid. Even when she wasn't actively using Ukiyo, her reflexes and senses seemed to be heightened to inhuman levels. She was smiling, though, basking in the attention of the three beautiful triplets. Watching them play with the dog, it finally clicked why the men at the front gates had assumed we were suitors. They must have them coming in droves.

Everyone's excitement calmed down after the puppy fell back asleep. Somehow it had scooted itself up from Volant's foot to inside the crook of his elbow. It wedged itself down into the blanket he had over his unresponsive body. Joy looked close to crying at this juxtaposition of cuteness. Each of the girls gave Volant a quick, soft kiss on his forehead before we went back down to the common room to all have somewhere to sit.

I pulled out the piece of glass and the etching of the alchemist's eye and showed it to them. No sign of recognition from any of the females, but Martino lit up when he had a turn to look.

"Oh! I've seen this before!" he exclaimed.

We all turned, surprise and interest splashed across our faces in varying degrees.

His face turned a shade of red at the attention, but bravely swallowed and kept going. "There was a guy I found. It was a leather shop, legitimate craftsman and all that. But, he also dealt in alchemy created products. He never said it outright, but I think he was the alchemist, and the leather was just a cover. Quite black-market stuff. He had this etched on the glass I was looking at." He bubbled with excitement, having provided something of value to the conversation.

"Honey," Joy started, looking just a little concerned. "Why were you trying to buy black-market alchemy in the first place?"

An odd look, one that was slightly hurt, crossed Martino's face. "The glass cookware I wanted, remember? I wanted some kind of hardened glass to cook in. He was too expensive, unfortunately." Crestfallen, he folded into himself.

Martino seemed a little on the emotionally sensitive side. Definitely would not have expected that from a cloudling.

Sensing his distress, Joy scooted over closer to him. As gentle as she'd been with the injured puppy, she laid a hand on his. Her smile brought him back, and he twined his fingers with hers.

Inside, a brief wave of emotion stabbed. It'd be nice to have someone care about me that way. To feel their support in such a directly physical way. Maybe one of the sisters would give me another hug, I hoped. Just a little bit of comfort would be nice. I sighed deeply, feeling the loneliness echo inside with the breath. Everyone looked over at me, and I waved it off. "It's nothing, just a sad thought." I gestured to Martino. "Can you get us back to that shop?"

Nodding excitedly, he stood. "Of course! Let's go! Do we need rope? I hear rope's important when running with Nil and Volant."

I groaned, glaring at the sisters.

"What?" Diedra started.

"It did come in handy," Dendra continued.

"And it is what Volant said you should always have with you," Joy finished, grinning.

Cassiopia chimed in, somehow having produced a bun of some kind out of her sleeveless jacket. "Rope is good," she said between bites. "Good rope makes for good plans. You never know when you need to lay a trap for a beast."

Now it was her turn for all eyes to turn on her, but unlike Martino, she was ambivalent and continued munching.

My head thumped against the built-in Kingdoms board, rattling the six-sided pieces. "You people are so annoying," I muttered.

"Speaking of annoying," Shazina interjected as everyone was laughing. "Don't think you're off the hook for Unbroken training. We need to teach you how to become an Ukiyo."

Yet again, the attention at the table shifted around, this time to Shazina. She glared as everyone looked at her, hunching in on herself.

"Ukiyo?" Dendra asked. "That's a fun word. What's it actually mean?"

Before she could respond, Diedra jumped in. "Unbroken sounds so cool. That some kind of badass title for the stupid?" She pointed at me, acting like I couldn't see.

Shazina laughed, breaking out of the moody glare she'd been holding on to. "As dumb as Nil is, he's not Unbroken. And probably won't be. It's incredibly difficult and dangerous, and requires just the right combination of grit and genius, according what what I read. We haven't had one in living memory." She sighed dramatically. "He's just practice and will more than likely die from the effort. As for Ukiyo, that's what I am. It's sort of like a Learner here, from what I've gathered. But our manipulations are internal."

It was one of the longest, most useful sentences Shazina had offered.

"Wait. Nil is probably going to die?" Joy asked.

Ignoring her, Shazina continued talking to Diedra. "Once we've worked out the issues with Nil, hopefully we can train some Learners in the Ukiyo way. Supposedly, doing so will let them discover a minor Natural Talent as well, though we'll have to find out if that's true for ourselves."

The triplets huddled together, whispering fiercely, leaving Cassiopia, Shazina, Martino, and I out of the conversation. After the hushed discussion, they turned back to Shazina.

"We'd like to learn the Ukiyo way," Joy said. The other two nodded solemnly.

In an oddly respectful nod of return, Shazina agreed. "I'd be honored to try to teach you. No promises, though. I don't know what I'm doing."

We'd struck a deal, but no matter what Shazina thought was important, finding the girl that I'd last seen Emerys' Rock with was my current priority. If we could get a hold of that massive Toron stone or root out whoever else had been involved with Xylex or was telling him what to do, Volant and I might be able to return to the school and get back to our lives. I clenched my fists. If only Volant would wake up. If he died, I don't think I'll be able to keep going. His calm, quiet determination had been the anchor keeping my ship from blowing away in the storm. And, his mother would literally kill me if he didn't pull through.

Our entire group hushed suddenly. Everyone was looking over my shoulder, though, so my momentary fear of having spoken out loud had to be untrue.

I turned around, looking back to the stairs that led to the room.

At first, I thought everyone was just looking at the puppy. And then the figure took shape and I leaped from my chair, knocking it over in a cacophony of wood on stone.

Volant leaned against the stair banister, haggard. He was pale, like the underside of a deep-sea fish you'd find washed up on the beach. His hair hung limp against his head and seemed to weigh him down.

But left hand of the gods, he was awake

"Volant!" cried Joy with excitement.

"You're alive!" Dendra added.

"And made friends with Argo!" Diedra finished.

Volant groaned, clutching the dog tighter. "So extremely creepy, I must still be dreaming." He turned, looking at me frozen in place. "Oi, Leafer," he grinned. "You find the sisters just to torment me? I know I like to sleep, but this seems cruel even for you."

I rushed over, tears of joy in my eyes as I crushed him in a bear hug. "You cloud-brained fool, Volant. You had me scared."

He awkwardly patted my shoulder with a weak hand, the other cradling the puppy protectively. "Scared you? I thought I was going to die. And then, I couldn't wake up. I tried so hard, but I just couldn't move. I heard you guys. I tasted the food. But I couldn't do anything." His voice was stricken, and not just from disuse.

Everyone else crowded around. I offered introductions, and all who could showered the puppy again with love. Despite Volant having been awake for a relatively short time, the dog seemed completely enamored with him.

I helped Volant to a chair, as he was somewhat unsteady on his feet. His eyes were haunted, but he seemed to becoming around already despite what sounded like absolute torture. He was also ravenous. Cassiopia produced another pair of the street buns, handing them both over to Volant. Now it was his turn to almost cry as he shoveled them into his mouth.

Everything felt right in the world now. The triplets gave him stories about our growing fame at the school, and Cassiopia filled him in on her adventures hunting big game. Shazina argued about naming Argo with both Volant and Cassiopia. I, on the other hand, quietly watched it all, thrilled to have my friend back.

The alchemist and Xylex and the training were all forgotten for the night. Cassiopia took Shazina to get more food. While Martino went into far, far too much detail about remodeling our old hideout into a "livable" space, the two returned with armfuls of fruit, bread, and cheese.

We talked long past the time anyone should still be awake, and the only complaint came from Volant.

"I wish Qaewin were here," he mumbled through half-lidded eyes. "That's what got me through it all, knowing that she was still out there."

Jealousy sparked in me, but I tamped it down. I couldn't blame him for thinking of her over me. We might be as close as brothers, but nothing set the heart ablaze like being young and in love.

"You should send a letter off to her in the morning. I didn't even think to try her and Slandash." I felt terrible and stupid. "I can't believe I didn't think of them. The Soft Steppers would be the easiest to reach and the most helpful."

He patted my arm, weak as he was. "Don't worry about it. We'll reach out to her in the morning."

The triplets and Martino didn't want to miss out on anything, so they brought more bedding to our already cramped room and made themselves at home. Despite the tight fit, it was nice to have so many people in one place. It was cozy and safe, a feeling that I'd been missing for quite some time.

Now that Volant has mentioned it, someone like Qaewin would be nice. I thought of Thecily and wondered where she was.

Chapter Five

I snapped awake, worried I'd only dreamed Volant's recovery. My sudden motion had caught his eye, and he turned and smiled.

He had a pencil in one hand and used the other to put down the paper he'd been holding. Be quiet, he flicked out with his free hand.

I nodded, groggily, and flicked a response. Good to have you back.

He winked, huge and exaggerated. It may have been the room's dim light, but he seemed far better this morning than he had at the table. It could also be a testament to the street buns Cassiopia had.

As quietly as possible, I shifted out from my corner and tiptoed across the bodies on the floor. I was nearly to the door when Shazina appeared by my side, not having made a noise.

The shock must have shown on my face, as a knowing look stretched across her face. My heart slowed back down, and we both headed upstairs to the access point out onto the artisan and residential district, Midcave. There was a much smaller counter in a more basic common room. In comparison to her soft as a ghost footsteps, I clomped stair by stair. It was unnerving how quickly she could so quietly move.

“Lesson one,” she began. With a wave of her hand, she gestured towards a cushion in a corner. “Stillness and meditation. We need you to practice both. You’re also going to have to work on breathing properly.”

“Meditation?” I shook my head. “I’ve done meditation. Lots of people do it here in Balteris. If that made a Ukiyo, we’d have run into them by now.”

She crossed her arms and glared. For a little girl, she could have quite the presence. “This is lesson one,” she repeated. “You’re to sit here for the entire day. You are not to speak. You are only to breathe and meditate on said breathing.”

I’d never been able to meditate for long. The best I’d done was a hundred or so heartbeats on my rock in Erset overlooking the causeway, but that was more forest bathing than anything.

I sat, closing my eyes and pocketing a coin I’d been walking across my knuckles. I breathed in, feeling the motion expand inside of me. I held it for a moment and then breathed out, matching the cadence, and holding the empty breath for another moment. Again and again, I brought air in and expelled it. What felt like an eternity passed. In reality, Shazina was probably only just now getting back to our room. This was going to be a long day.

An unending parade of thoughts interrupted my focus as time crawled by. Fears of dying. The joy of having Volant back. Questions about Xylex and why his benefactor and the leader of God’s Fury would leave him out to dry. Shazina’s role in all of this, and what life was like on the other side of the causeway. How did they kill their gods? For some reason, Captain Andreska’s friend and mentor, Berjio, popped into my head, and such a depth of regret at not staying with him in Brod to learn swordplay ate a hole through me.

More than any other interruptions, the singular scream of “what am I doing?” careened inside my skull, stealing it’s way into every moment I began to feel I was getting the hang of the meditation. It was like the wind had caught me up in its embrace, and I was stuck tumbling wherever it blew, whenever it was it chose to do so.

Hot on the heels of that, I'd inevitably find my mind turning to how would I find a place in the world after this was all settled? Could I go home? Would the school take me back? Or would I finally get out of this mess to end up on the streets, or locked up in some cell?

With each invasive thought, I tried to practice a semblance of mindfulness. Acknowledging the distraction and letting it fade away. My last sight of Thecily as I left the Skywolf invaded my headspace, and I spent a countless length of heartbeats imagining a myriad of futures with her before finally remembering my breath and letting the thoughts twist away into the ether.

Food became a distraction after an age of slow breathing. Shazina was an evil kind of cunning. I hadn't thought about how hungry you could get when sitting with nothing but breathing to distract you. In and out, I let my mind focus away from the bodily discomforts and the growling stomach. Scabs from my climb itched. My legs tingled. My back ached.

Still, I'd agreed to the Ukiyo training, and I wasn't going to give it a left handed effort on the first try.

In the middle of the afternoon, people started to pass through the room, and embarrassment became my new enemy. I squirmed, thinking of the people who'd be looking at the weird guy in the corner with the scratched-up arms taking a nap in the corner. Each set of footfalls across the floor sent twinges of unfounded shame through me. I treated these the same as I'd treated everything else and continued to follow my breath and let the feelings fade away.

By evening, I'd given in fully to the meditation. I floated in a state of mental limbo, entirely at peace with myself. It was freeing. Whether or not I could achieve the Ukiyo training or become an Unbroken, I'd need to thank Shazina for making me sit here and have this experience. It was something else entirely.

A tap on my shoulder brought me out of the meditative state. I blinked, reminding my eyes how to work.

Shazina and Volant were standing there with Argo in the latter's arms. The dog squirmed, and Volant gently scratched its ear behind the bandage. Like Volant, a little bit of rest and proper food seemed to be doing it wonders.

“You tired of lazing about yet, leafer?” Volant asked with a sly grin.

I stood, returning the grin. But then my numbed legs betrayed me, and I stumbled into the wall, feeling the anticipatory tingles of my limbs waking back up. “Oh, that’s going to be unpleasant.” Still, it felt like I’d been born again, and I just chuckled as I shook out my limbs.

Shazina rolled her eyes, offering me an arm. “Walk it off. Pain is part of the process.”

We headed out into Midcave, my legs pinpricks of pain as they still came back to life. The ceiling here was much lower, but the cave was far better lit in exchange. Man-made shafts brought light in from various corners of the smaller cavern. It was also notably more humid.

“What are we up to?” I asked, hobbling after the pair.

Volant nodded towards a squat, windowless, doorless structure across the way. Despite its austere inaccessibility, it was nearly as well patrolled by Guard as the headquarters had been. The only blemish on the cell’s impregnability was a tiny pipe that came out at an angle. I doubted if my smallest finger would fit inside it.

“I poked around today,” Volant said. “Needed to stretch my legs a bit. Found out this is where they’re keeping Xylex.” The way he said Xylex’s name was so venomous it gave me chills.

“Ah, I see.” I looked harder at the place. As handy as it would be to talk to Xylex again and find out more about who his boss was, it didn’t look like he would be receiving any kind of visitors. “Maybe we can just find the entrance to his cell? Watch it and see if any important looking men come to visit, or maybe that Learner, Patricia.”

Shazina and Volant both looked downcast. “We tried to find it, Nil,” Volant said with a sad smile. “It looks like the actual cell is in the bedrock below. The entrance is technically on Rootfloor, but it’s a lift and pulley setup with a trap door. It’s out in the open, right next to the hectagon and they are not taking security lightly after our little foray into their base. I watched all day and all night. That said, we talked to enough people and found out that this is the actual cell. The rest is just a shaft leading up to it."

Grimacing, I turned back for a second look at the singular prison.

Volant held up two fingers. "It's either cutting through the cell or somehow getting to the trapdoor, unlocking it, and then getting back out if we want a chat with him." Volant shook his head at the two impossible options.

"Aye, that seems to sum it up," I replied. Looking at Shazina, she seemed disappointed but also not overly interested in further discussion. I thought for a long moment, my day of sitting in silent contemplation giving me a sharper than usual mental edge. "I guess they'll have to move him before the trial, right? Maybe we can find him then."

Volant looked at me with a skeptical frown but kept his thoughts to himself.

On the other hand, Shazina seemed to lack his circumspection. "Now that you've seen this, can we get back to figuring out how to help my family and an entire people across the sea? The gimzers are probably killing people I know as we stare at a cell holding an already going to be punished old man." She kicked a loose stone, and it skittered like an angry insect across the cavern floor. "Volant's awake now. We can find his mother and get proper help. You said she has an airship. We can use it to take armies across the causeway."

I sighed, gesturing everyone back the way we came. "For starters, we're going to find Volant's look-alike, Martino, and go visit this alchemist. And we can't go find Volant's mother as we're waiting for her to find us. And finally, we can't take an airship across the sea. It's impossible. The causeway you crossed on foot is only slightly less so, apparently."

Nodding in agreement, Volant matched stride with me, forcing Shazina to catch up with us. "Airships run on a type of gas we harvest from the northwest. It's why Wydvis is a semi-permanent city instead of a populace of wandering nomads like Tryst. Even if we managed to transport enough fuel, which would be difficult without us floating into the void, there's the whole sea problem itself."

Shazina just rolled her eyes. "A bunch of cowards, just like I'd expect from the descendants of the ones who escaped across the strait. I don't want to hear this."

Volant and I exchanged glances, and I rolled my eyes. Kids.

Martino was with Joy in the room, snuggled up in a corner. She had a book in one hand, being almost the bibliophile that Shazina was. Martino was chewing on his pencil, notebook in hand with some recipe causing him trouble, I assumed.

They both looked up as we came in, but before they could say anything, Shazina had blurred over with inhuman speed. It was unnerving seeing her use Skill so casually. It was almost instinctual for her.

Joy flinched back in surprise but smiled as Shazina examined her book with fierce intensity. "I just started re-reading it," she explained to Shazina. "But if you need a new story, you're more than welcome to it!"

The only happiness Shazina seemed to experience in life, albeit from my extremely limited experience in knowing her, was when she had a new book. Her eyes lit up, and I was reasonably sure I saw tears forming at the corner of her eyes as Joy handed the book over to her.

"You mean, you're just going to let me have this?" Shazina asked.

"Well, of course!" Joy's laugh sounded like it would have been more age appropriate from Shazina.

I wish more people still laughed like they were young. If the world had more Joys in it, it'd be a much brighter place.

As Shazina still stared at the book in her hands, Joy laughed again, handing it over. "You silly girl, books are meant to be shared. Have you never given someone something you read and liked? That's one of life's greatest pleasures. We're meant to share stories!"

Shazina did cry then, hugging the book close to her. Soft sobs interrupted her words. "No one has ever given me a book before. I've always had to get people to buy them for me or steal them back home."

Joy's smile crashed at this, and she wrapped Shazina up in a hug, leaving Martino, who'd barely noticed the interruption. "You poor thing," she whispered. "Don't worry. I have a few more stashed away. If you promise to chat with me about it when you're finished, I'll make sure to find you another."

They hugged as Volant and I awkwardly stood there watching the suddenly intimate moment. "Umm, not to interrupt, but could we borrow Martino while you two get this book life figured out?"

Shazina ignored us, still gently crying. Joy glared over the top of the child's head, holding her tightly. "Men," she said, a hint of disgust. She softened though as Volant stepped forward, hands raised in appeasement. Argo yipped slightly, curling up with the girls and somehow seeming to agree with them.

"Don't blame Nil. He's one of those Erset folk who don't know art from arse." Volant then took Martino, still oblivious, by the elbow and led him out of the room.

Once we'd gotten him out onto the streets of Rootfloor, Martino finally looked up from the notebook, realized his surroundings, and seemed ecstatic to be included. He led us through a winding path of alleys and pathways in the general direction of Chalard Port into a mostly trade shop area of Kalaran.

Before we arrived there, an explosion went off behind us, back in the center of Rootfloor. We froze as the noise reached us.

Adrenaline spiked through me at the sound. I was torn, so close to the alchemist's shop and so far from the explosion. I turned to Volant, taking in his already labored breathing from our slow walk.

"Go," he said, pointing at the cloud of dust in the distance. "Martino and I will catch up. Find Patricia, and we won't even have to chat with this guy."

I took off at a dead sprint, bringing my will into focus and feeling the tingle as it converted to Skill. I flew down the road towards the smoke, my feet feeling like they barely touched the ground. The few people out and about were soon running by me in the opposite direction, away from the attack.

I felt a second explosion through the ground, followed by the booming sound just a block away from me. The force of the shockwave jarred me mid-step, but I kept moving forward. She had to be there, and I was going to catch her. I flinched against the ensuing wall of dust that tried to sand my exposed flesh away.

The cloud of powdered stone obscured everything. I continued forwarded hoping not to run into anything too solid. Suddenly, I was there, an eerie silence greeting my gasping lungs trying to suck in air from my run.

This attack had been far more severe. There were no injured. Only the dead. A blackened sphere ran a ten-pace wide circle around the impact site. After a moment of searching, I found the second on the cavern roof, mirroring the floor below with a large black circle from the explosion. Looking back down, I realized there were only a few victims. Still, I frantically searched the surrounding area.

She was here. Patricia was waiting for me.

Half hidden across the courtyard, she was watching me with the same neutrally inviting expression she'd had when arriving in Dioden's tent with Emerys' Rock. As soon as we locked eyes, she dipped back behind the wall.

I didn't hesitate. Dust scraped as I launched towards the alley she'd ducked into. I swung around the corner, catching a glimpse of her vaulting over a small wall at the end. I jumped, taking two steps up the wall before grabbing the lip and flipping over. Landing in a crouch, I scanned for her again.

A flash of her hair showed her turning through a gate.

I gave chase.

Every time I got close, she'd blur around a corner, never seeming to get away nor giving me any room to catch up. I was nearing the end of my stamina when I found myself in a part of Kalaran I didn't recognize. She'd begun blurring like Shazina did, disappearing faster than a human should move. My head was getting fuzzy from oxygen deprivation, and it seemed my eyesight was being affected as well.

Reflexes honed from countless days training with Volant was the only thing that saved me. A small, green shape whipped from the darkness, right for my throat. I dipped away as what looked like a pale green rope shot past. It was twice the length of a man but moved in a way that said it was alive.

The hairs on the back of my neck stood on end as I spun, instincts forcing me to turn around. Behind me, the rope had coiled itself. Except it wasn't a rope. It was a green, whip-thin snake. Narrow head, needle-point fangs exposed as it hissed. The mouth was pitch black. It struck again, lunging through the air with impossible speed.

The entirety of my body thrummed with fear. I flung myself backward, dodging out of the emerald death's way.

Snakes were worse than the borgislings. They had a similar effect on the psyche but were stealthier and just downright nasty. It slid up the wall, defying gravity.

I took a pair of breaths while it disappeared into shadow. I couldn't bring my mind to focus. I was in full flight mode. As I tried to bring Skill into my hands, the always reliable surge of power was absent. Vanished, much like my will to stay here. My hands shook. I took another set of breaths, and the panic only rose, the snake making the softest of whispers as its scales slid over stone somewhere up on or in the wall.

Reacting to the base emotion, I turned and fled, fear fueling my spent muscles and lending strength to already abused legs. It wasn't long though before the animalistic burst dissipated, leaving me gasping on the main road that led through Rootfloor.

"Godspawning left-handed, poisoned fanged, legless, evil reptiles," I spat between breaths, searching to make sure the snake hadn't slithered its way after me. At least a borgisling and its Slither rider could be seen if you were looking. Snakes just blended in with everything, stabbing out with that heart-stopping, necrotizing venom.

Plus, I'd lost Patricia. All the stillness and focus I'd found during Shazina's meditation had blown away on the metaphorical wind by running into that snake.

I thought back to the alley I'd chased Patricia into. The place she'd lured me to after she'd waited at a scene of her attack, only running when I saw her.

"Left hand of god," I cursed yet again. It'd been a trap. Somehow, she'd tricked me into that alley with the snake.

Storm clouds of dark thoughts swirled through my mind as I trudged back to the Broken Oar. She'd recognized me. She knew I'd be trying to find her. And she'd tried to kill me. Volant and one of the triplets, Dendra or Diedra, were sitting at the kingdom table.

Volant seemed better, but I could see a wave of low simmering anger rising in him. Not at me, but at himself. It had the reproachful, introspective kind of fire to it. The kind you see when you've let yourself down. His father's rapier leaned up against the chair. He'd picked up Cassiopia's street food habit, it seemed. A pair of the meat and veggie-filled buns sat on the table in front of him, the dough a soft round ball of white that still slightly steamed. He must have just arrived himself.

"Nil," he said, relief tinging his voice. "I'm sorry we couldn't come with you."

I shrugged, not trusting my voice to be steady. Even after the long walk back, I was still having aftershocks of fear-fueled tremors. I steadied my hand, petting Argo who had adopted Volant as his personal human and seemed unable to leave his lap. Still, his small tail and puppy smile said he was thrilled to see me.

"You all right?" he asked. "Guess no luck on finding Patricia? Also, you look a little pale."

One of the sisters pulled up a chair for me, and I sat, breathing deep. "Sorry I left you. I know that couldn't have been easy. But aye, I found her. Then lost her. Almost got eaten by some too-long green snake."

Volant passed me one of the buns, and I bit into it, reveling in the warm, softly steamed bun. He and Cassiopia were onto something with these. I caught them up on the chase, filling in the details as much as I could remember.

"You may have a bit of a phobia there," Dendra said with a sympathetic pat. "Snakes aren't all evil reptiles out to kill people. Generally, they're pretty useful for pest control."

I shook my head vigorously, remembering the inky depths of its mouth with the needle-sharp curved fangs. "No, you're wrong. They're pure evil."

Chuckling, Volant was starting to look like himself again. "It's okay. We all have our fears. I'm still not a big fan of heights."

"Deep water and snakes for me, it would appear," I agreed.

"I guess the alchemist is the next lead to finding this Patricia?" Dendra asked. She picked at the table nervously. None of the triplets seemed to handle being separated from the other sisters well.

As I started to agree, Shazina appeared at my elbow, book in hand as always. Too quiet footsteps, yet again.

"Lesson two," she pronounced, barely acknowledging anyone at the table as if she was talking to the air. "You must practice drawing Skill but into your mind. You'll need to build on our first lesson, find that center, and then push the Skill into it."

"What? I just got be from almost being eaten by a snake!" I glared at the child. It's not like she'd been out running around and almost died.

At this, she finally looked up at me. A vast look of disgust crossed her face as she took me in. "So? You want a break or something? I'm not here to encourage you to get even more soft. This is life. The limits you place on what you can accomplish in a day are the only limits that exist besides time. Stop whining and step up."

All three of us looked at Shazina with slight variations of stunned expressions.

She looked back.

I wanted to argue.

Yet she was right. What was stopping me? I still had breath in my lungs, and my head still worked. I was awake, had food, and was planning on spending a similar amount of energy relaxing and planning. It annoyed me, but I was being lazy.

With heavy feet, I dragged myself to the room's corner, throwing a cushion down and flopping onto it. Petulant. That's the word someone would use if Shazina were acting like I was. With an effort, I re-examined my attitude and tossed out the negativity. There was a chance here to do something no one had done in living history. It was my opportunity. Time to "step up," as Shazina said.

With the first few breaths, my remaining agitation faded into nothingness. A second wind then drove the thoughts of fatigue out of my head, and I sank deeper into the moment. I embraced the stillness, letting everything but the breathing slip away. When my mind became fully present, I started converting my will into Skill. The vibrant energy that had been scarily absent when the snake attacked began to pool in me.

First, I practiced redirecting it. Moving the current of manifested will down to my fingertips, and then back up my arm and then down the length of my body. I traced my entire body with the Skill, taking a moment to marvel at the level of control I'd developed since leaving the school. Despite the charged tingle I felt as the barely contained energy moved through me, my body stayed perfectly still and relaxed.

Then, when I had the control I felt, I tried to hold the Skill. I focused back on my breath, trying to keep the energy evenly throughout my body, unsuccessfully. The Skill began to spark, for lack of a better term, off of me like a too-hot pan being splashed with water. I willed it to stay in place but lost control of the meditative state. It was a lost cause. I flicked my hand at Volant, letting the small amount of Skill still there be released in a wide splash.

It impacted with the force of a small push, shifting him slightly in his chair. He turned, having been deep in conversation with Shazina while scratching Argo's head, and gave me a raised eyebrow.

In response, I shook my head, frustrated with myself. I closed my eyes again, rolling first one shoulder, then the second, and finally bringing them both back against the corner. Physically centered, I started my breath up. Inside, I wished I was swinging my axes instead of this. Again my will converted to Skill, and I tried to hold it like you'd do with a single hand cupping water, letting it rest within me without actually grasping it.

This time, I was able to find that perfect, present state while still maintaining the hold on the Skill. But from there, it was like running into a wall. I couldn't do anything by bringing it into my mind, whatever that meant. I tried to reabsorb it. I tried to push it onto itself, shaping it with a honed intent into itself. I tried to flex it into my biceps. I tried everything.

None of it worked.

After everyone but Shazina had long gone to bed, I shakily stood, legs having fallen asleep long ago.

"I can't do it," I said, exhaustion making it a simple, slightly sad statement.

She just shook her head, an actual laugh escaping for the briefest moment. She closed the book she'd been reading, no bookmark for this insane foreign child who just knew where she was when she'd inevitably flip it back open. "Seriously? You expected to figure it out on your first try?"

"Well," I stammered, "aye, I assumed so."

"You're an idiot," she turned, leading me upstairs. "Your people are strange. Actual results are a process. You can't just do it once and be good at it. You try over and over again until you do."

Precocious. Another word someone would use about Shazina, this time accurately. "You read too much," I countered. "Aren't you supposed to be playing with dolls or something?"

In return, her hand blurred, and a small fist slammed into the meat of my arm before just as quickly disappearing. I'd not even seen her move. But I certainly felt it.

"Okay, you win," I said, hands raised. My arm was going to have a considerable bruise now.

Chapter Six

After days of practice, I was sick of chasing the legendary Ukiyo. It was still impossible for me to do anything with Skill beyond what I could before all the meditation and mental gymnastics. At best, I at least could feel the barrier, but getting past it had proven fruitless. Even Shazina seemed to be getting discouraged. The Kalaran Council set Xylex's trial for this afternoon, and the expected bombing and escape hadn't come.

We'd scouted the boulder-like cell on Midcave, but the only change was an increased presence from the Guard. I'd have loved to get my hands on Xylex. There were so many questions I had.

Below the cell's entrance on Rootfloor, three concentric rings of Guard had formed a human wall. They'd effectively cordoned off the entire area. We couldn't even see the small hup of stone that was the cell's cap, their perimeter was so wide.

Volant and I tried to visit the alchemist's disguised leatherworking shop with Martino again. But like everywhere else in Kalaran, it was closed and tightly locked up. Xylex's trial had become a minor holiday in itself. I was beyond frustrated that I'd wasted the previous days sitting on a cushion, creating and dispersing Skill with nothing to show but a throbbing headache.

To add on to my mounting frustration, neither Rook nor Captain Andreska had shown up or responded to the letters we sent.

Noticing all of this, Volant sent the triplets and Martino on various errands and pulled Cassiopia and me aside, pretending he needed a little practice and exercise. I saw the sidelong glance he gave her and knew this was mostly for my benefit. Still, it was a welcome distraction.

While the sisters split up to find supplies for a long trip, some rope being at the top of the list, Martino went to see a wholesale food supplier, and Shazina opted for a long session with another novel and cuddles from Argo having grown tired of all of us. The three of us went by the school armed to the teeth. At the gate, the sentries still barred the way. We'd brought coin this time, knowing the school sold time on the training grounds to those who were willing to pay. Hopefully, they'd let us in, though in my sour mood, I'd been more than vocal about what I thought of our chances.

This time though, the sentries were chatting with a pair of Guard. It was Marle and Cobb. The sentries stiffened at our approach, hands twitching towards their scimitars, though only one of them touched their hilt before relaxing slightly. At the change in attitude, the Guard turned, standard-issue spears dipping in our direction ever so slightly.

Recognition flashed across Marle's face first, and he rushed over, wrapping me up in a big hug. Both Volant and Cassiopia, having been put on edge by the aggressive response, started to react less than kindly at the man's hug.

I laughed, hugging him back and giving them pause. It wasn't often men embraced in public, and it was nice to have someone showing affection instead of trying to murder me for once.

"How's that puppy?" Cobb asked, walking over and offering a warm smile in place of also hugging me.

"Argo's doing great!" I gestured to Volant. "He actually helped wake my nearly dead friend up. Miracle would have been a better name, but that kid had her own thoughts and named it without much consent from anyone else."

They both laughed, introducing themselves to Volant and Cassiopia. With everyone far more comfortable, the Gaurd finally came over, joining in.

"Did I hear that right?" the first asked, a hint of excitement. "You're the ones who saved that puppy?"

The second jumped in before I could respond. "I've got a son, who said he heard it from his friend's mom, who has tea with the healer who you guys brought it to."

"I heard it at that street vendor with the steamed buns!" the first interjected. "Says he saw it with a big woman and a little kid, a few different times."

Cassiopia blushed lightly at this. "Guilty," she said and shrugged. "Those buns are just too good to pass up."

The Guard and the school sentries competed to speak over each other in a barely understandable torrent made up of praise for the bun maker and general admiration for saving the dog and everyone's desire to see it. I stood back, bemused. Nothing like food and puppies to bring people together.

When we finally disentangled ourselves, Cobb and Marle offered to join us at the training grounds, being off for the day. The Guard, practically shoving us into the campus, wouldn't take anything but promises to bring Argo by sometime when we were free.

Still bewildered by Argo's apparent fame, I lead the group into Jorcum's Higher Learning Academy and towards the training grounds for a bit of old-fashioned sparring and target practice. The school had it all, though I couldn't for the life of me understand why they bothered.

We dragged a couple of targets around and put them as far out as possible for Volant and Cassiopia to shoot at. I pulled out my hatchet, and to the twang and thump of their bows loosing arrows that almost unerringly hit the target's bullseye, I threw at my own and much closer target. My axe followed their rhythm, embedding the hatchets as often as not.

Cobb and Marle watched me at first, impressed with the hawk-head axe I used to carve up a wooden target from seven paces. I tossed it every which way and usually followed with a knife throw or two, leaving my belt emptied of everything. Embedding all three, both Guard looked impressed. But then they looked over at the pair of archers in their corner of the yard, taking turns with Cassiopia's strange bow and even stranger arrows.

At seventy paces, half drawn, the arrows weren't even dropping midflight. The small target shivered at each thudding impact. Over a few dozen shafts peppered its surface, with only a few not within the rings at this point. Cassiopia saw them watching, and a quirk of the mouth that almost seemed friendly tugged at her as she pulled the bow to full draw. Muscles like that of some vast beast seemed to pop out of her arms and back as she strained. Even Volant took a step back, slightly taken aback by his training partner. She let the arrow fly, and it screamed with a god's vengeance as it shot through the air. The flying missile punched through the target, only stopping when the point drove into the stone wall behind it with a flash of sparks.

I clapped, slowly at first, and then faster while laughing. That was one powerful woman and an incredibly intimidating bow.

Cassiopia scowled, squinting at the target. "Left hand," she muttered, "missed the bullseye by four fingers at least. Barely even hit the target."

Our group walked over, and I gave Volant a fist bump as we neared the target. Sweat was dripping off him already, and his arms visibly shook from the strain of using the huntress' bow. She was right, though. Despite the impressive penetration, she'd only just scraped by on hitting center mass. Leaving the now partially ruined arrow in, the rest were pulled out and brought back to her specially made quiver. It had to weigh nearly as much as joy with a bag of books, and I marveled at how she traveled with so much weight.

"Still, better ratio than usual," Cassiopia grumbled as she flicked the fletching on the buried shaft. "At full pull, I'm accurate sixty to seventy percent of the time. It's really only necessary for much larger game from much further away. But still, it can be frustrating knowing that you're going to miss three or four times out of ten."

I nodded as if I had any idea what she was talking about.

The two Guards who'd been infatuated with Argo seemed to have a new idol, as from that point on, they couldn't get close enough to Cassiopia. Cobb and Marle peppered her with questions, tried and failed to draw the bow multiple times, and demanded she spar with them.

Volant and I moved to the side, letting the three of them practice with leather tipped spears. Cassiopia wasn't nearly as impressive without her bow, but her size and strength lent a certain gravitas that translated well to anything approaching violence, and in this case, hand-to-hand combat.

I drew the knife I kept at the small of my back, the long and heavy blade a comfort. In my other hand, the hawk, as I'd decided to call it. An axe meant for fighting more than for chopping wood. Volant grinned and wiped the sweat from his brow. His father's rapier flicked out with a song of steel whispering to the wind, and he sat back into a duelist's stance.

A poorly hidden wince showed he still wasn't fully recovered from the almost fatal experience involving the blue robes. He shook it off and gestured at me to start. With live edges, we moved slowly and with a fraction of the force we'd use normally. It was more like a strategy session, us pausing after a movement and reworking a defense against it. We danced, more than we fought, each of us trying to make the other just as aware of his intentions before they happened as any partner would at a ball.

Our steel-on-steel waltz dipped into something akin to the meditation practice I'd been at with Shazina. My breathing became the focus, more than our weapons. You make all the little mistakes when your mind tells your body to work in a certain way, yet your limbs don't quite translate the message correctly. I was finally finding a way to be one with myself, living in the moment fully and bypassing the communication between mind and body, merging them into one entity.

Focusing more deeply, I drew in Skill, allowing it to pool in the cupped-hand fashion I'd used while trying to understand the Ukiyo way. Instead of trying to push it anywhere in particular or do anything with it, I just kept it there, letting my breath lead me as I spun and slashed at Volant.

Too deep into the breathing, I saw his thrust coming far too late to parry. His eyes began to widen as time seemed to slow. I bent back and away, hinging my knees to drop me further out of the sharp point. It was too little too late. I willed my body to act faster. And just like that, the Skill was in my arms and legs. It was everywhere in my muscles and mind, coursing completely differently, yet with such similar familiarity. The feeling was like seeing an old friend you'd not run across in a long time.

This newfound ability did nothing to stop Volant's blade from cutting a thin line across my upper chest until it bounced off my clavicle. I fell to the ground bent in backwards in half, my shirt sliced, blood staining the material a dark red, and two fires burning in me. First, the Skill I'd somehow finally absorbed but couldn't seem to figure out what to do with. The second being the painfully bright line across my chest screaming at me that a sword had sliced it, and there was absolutely nothing to be happy about.

"All right, Nil?" Volant hovered over me, concerned.

Still laying on the ground with my legs underneath me, I breathed slow and steady despite the burning wound and sizzling spark of Skill in me. I could make this happen. I could use it. Mentally, I prodded at the Skill that felt like it'd infused itself along my skeletal structure. Part of me worried that if I didn't figure this out, I might explode from the pressure my body felt. I wiggled my fingers.

Nothing happened.

I moved my head in small circles, and still, nothing happened.

I reached up and grabbed Volant's offered hand, letting him help me up.

Still, nothing happened.

But the pressure felt more intense, and I started to grow worried. Like muscle cramps, my limbs began to twitch with the pent-up energy. I jumped, but nothing happened. I ran, sprinting across the sand-covered floor, hoping I could use the Skill before the horrible feeling I had run out of time and became a reality.

After a single lap, and out of breath, I truly started to worry. Instead of letting the panic take me, I paused and brought my breath back to its center, feeling for the Skill. I crouched down, focusing on my legs with the same meditative feeling I'd had when sparring. I pushed with my mind while simultaneously trying with my legs, thinking of how I'd used Skill to enhance my jumping abilities in the past. This time, it wasn't that I blasted will-turned-power from my feet. Instead, my entire body reacted somehow, absorbing the energy, and using it to move faster than it should.

I leaped up and practically flew towards the high ceiling. For a moment, I hung weightless in midair, giddy at having my body not torn to pieces from internal pressure. And then I dropped. Plummeting towards the ground, I reached inside again, finding the remaining Skill to be more than I thought I had gathered initially. With the lightest of thoughts, I willed it into my legs again, reinforcing them against the jarring impact as I landed.

"Umm," Marle said, first to speak. "You're bleeding, Nil."

Ignoring this, I grabbed Volant up in a hug, ruining his shirt as well! "I figured it out! I can access the Ukiyo!"

The Guard duo looked on confused, but both Volant and Cassiopia beamed. Volant returned the hug, and Cassiopia offered a goofy shoulder pat that nearly knocked me to the ground. We packed up, bandaging me, and trying to look as least guilty as possible considering the last time we had raided the armory.

By now, a crowd would be forming for Xylex's trial, and I was itching to see how it went. As we began to part ways, Volant and I cringed as Cassiopia offered for the two Guard to visit us at the Broken Oar whenever they wanted. It's not that we were actively being chased by the Guard anymore, but they also hadn't necessarily cleared us of all the charges, either.

Still, they seemed like fine people, so I offered a friendly wave as they left, with them promising to drop by soon to see Argo.

At Kalaran's council chambers, the crowd was quite a bit larger than I'd expected. A For the first time since we'd arrived back, people were out in droves. Knots of friends and acquaintances clustered around each other, catching up after what must have been weeks of limited socialization due to the attacks. Cobb and Marle had to be the only two Guard not on duty, for as many people were milling around the steps to the geometric building's main entrance turned stage, there was almost an equal number of the uniformed, truncheon wielding force of men and women looking for any sign of trouble. Black-clad Elites peppered their ranks, glinting spearpoints bristling everywhere.

I searched for the triplets and Martino and simultaneously scanned the crowd for Patricia. Surely, she was planning some kind of escape for Xylex now that he was out of the cell. I didn't see any of them yet, but at the least, the girls and Martino would be finding us if we didn't find them.

Kalaran's council and the rulers in all but name of Balteris came out, sitting in a row in heavy chairs put out for the trial. Everyone quieted as they took their places, but the silence was brief.

Rough and ready men brought out Xylex in shackles, who looked like he'd lost a healthy amount of weight. They sat him across from the council in a far less comfy looking chair. His feet twitched as the men locked the shackles to the chair, and a small bit of relief went through me, knowing he'd have a hard time getting away while chained to a heavy chair. The crowd turned ugly for a bit, yelling and throwing the occasional rotten vegetable at Xylex. It took a long time before everyone had settled enough for the trial to start.

While the incredibly tedious process of introducing the stuffy old men and women who ran the council went on, Martino slipped in next to us. He was scribbling something down in his recipe book but stopped long enough to pass on a note from the girls. The crowd's constant thrum made it hard to have a conversation without shouting, so I just nodded as he slipped away, barely looking where he went.

We're staying in. Shazina and Argo were both hungry, so we decided a picnic would be more fun than attending a crowded and unruly government function.

I passed the note to Volant, who skimmed it before shrugging and handing it over to Cassiopia. She seemed put out, probably because she was missing an outing with food more than anything. People pressed in, and it became harder to move. I was still ecstatic from being able to touch the Ukiyo that Shazina had been trying to teach me. I relaxed into the safety of numbers and listened to the mindless drone of important people reminding everyone how important they were and how even more important what they were doing was.

Xylex was rising to take his chance to speak, but without warning, his body spasmed. His eyes widened at the same time a gash opened up on his neck. The crowd quieted down, confused questions to neighbors, the only sound apart from Xylex's choked gurgle.

Patricia's a Learner. The most silent of assassins. "She's here," I hissed at Volant. "That was Skill. Xylex is as good as dead."

The same realization hit the crowd and Guard at the same time. Panicked cries crashed against shouted orders as people tried to flee, and the Guard rushed up to the council members.

A pair of glass vials arced out of the crowd towards the council, and I froze, knowing these had to be the same explosives. I drew Skill and launched a wave of it at the soaring alchemical concoctions. I hit one, making it careen into the ceiling above. It exploded, staggering me, and still possibly killing dozens. Icy terror gripped me then. The second struck home, detonating in a second shockwave that nearly brought me to my knees. The explosion sent council members sprawling. I couldn't see anything in the cloud of debris and dust, but they were almost certainly dead.

The twinkle of another vial flashed in the hazy aftermath of two explosions. Time seemed to freeze as it crossed the space toward the spot where the council and their personal Guard. I turned away from the explosion, involuntary tears in my eyes. And then I saw her, far at the back of the crowd, the only person now standing up straight. The thump and flash of the alchemical explosion rocked me, but I didn't lose her this time.

"Volant! There!" I pointed a shaky finger, trying to focus enough to draw Skill into a concentrated enough point for a killing shot.

"Left hand," he cursed, almost too soft for me to hear over my now ringing ears. "That woman? God spawning left hand, Nil."

I wasn't listening. I tried to push through the crowd, elbowing panicked people out of the way. Screams of the injured now replaced all other sounds. Both the gawking bystanders and the Guard had been hit with glass shrapnel or blasted off their feet. Volant was behind me, helping steady me as I worked my way towards her, who stood with a satisfied smile at her work.

Her smile grew wider as she turned and saw us. There was a cruel twist to it, and I grew worried. But instead of attacking us, she tossed a friendly wave towards Volant before turning and running. A flash of green at her heels made me stop dead. The snake was with her. It had been a trap, and I wasn't falling for it again.

Not that I had a choice. Fear had locked up my limbs at the sight of the green serpent racing around the corner with her.

Volant knocked into me, not having had the same reaction. We sprawled in a heap across the ground, which now had a light coating of dust. The air smelled sharp and metallic. I'd probably just killed a bunch of innocents trying to protect some questionable politicians who'd died anyway. Patricia had gotten away again. Frustrated, angry tears welled up, and I pounded the ground with my fist until blood mixed with ash and dust.

A strong hand grabbed my shoulder, and before I could protest, someone hauled me back up to my feet. Cassiopia stood there, an imposing presence in a sea of still panicking people.

"Pull it together, idiot," she said. Her eyes locked on mine.

I retook a breath, clapping my hands together once. Volant popped up, nodded in approval, and did the same. Finally, I was starting to understand that technique. At least that brought a small smile to my lips. Calmed, I took a moment to take in the damage. The council members were all dead. Xylex, too. If the Skill attack didn't do him in, the multiple blasts had. Bodies lay everywhere.

God's Fury had undoubtedly upped their body count. And one of their own? That was more surprising than anything. What had Xylex known that slated him for death instead of rescue, I wondered.

Guard were busy helping lay out the injured, and healers had swarmed the area, some from the crowd it seemed, others from nearby clinics. One, in particular, caught my eye. The woman who'd helped fix up Argo. The vet, Insley. Across the distance, our eyes met, and she nodded our way in acknowledgment.

"We should leave," I started, planning an argument against Cassiopia and Volant's far more altruistic hearts.

"Agreed," they both said in unison.

"Our friends will be worried about us, and Shazina needs to know Kalaran just lost its leadership too. You're bad luck for politicos, Nil." Cassiopia said it as a joke, but it still struck home. People seemed to be dying all around me, all the time.

"That, and we need to talk," Volant said, his voice tired. "I know your Patricia, though that's not her real name."

Chapter Seven

As predicted, the Broken Oar was a hornet's nest of activity. People crowded the common room, and rumors flew faster than a bird chasing butterflies. The sisters, along with Martino, and an Argo-holding Shazina, were all huddled in a corner. Each of them showed varying levels of concern. Even Shazina's ordinarily stoic face had a touch of wildness around the eyes.

"They're back!" Dendra or Diedra shouted upon seeing us.

The group turned, a weight simultaneously disappearing from all of them. Cassiopia left my side and went straight for Argo, producing a piece of jerky and holding it out to the puppy. The rest of us converged and exchanged details about the trial.

"You know Patricia?" I finally asked Volant once we'd caught everyone up.

"Do you remember Berjio?" he asked in response.

I nodded, a weird feeling of déjà vu. "I was just thinking about him the other day. Wish we'd have stayed and learned from him. Sword masters are hard to come by, especially such interesting ones."

Volant sighed, thinking back to it as well. "True. He was friends with my mother, if you remember. I didn't know him but by reputation, but I met his granddaughter a few times as she visited us. It's Keira, though that's not her real name. It's Keira."

"That's excellent!" I said, excited to have some kind of information finally. "If we get a hold of Berjio, he can help us find her! But why the name change from Keira?"

Volant shook his head, holding his hand up to stop me. "No, you don't get it. She's his only remaining family. He'd die before letting anything happen to her. And I assume to hide the relation to Berjio. There's not a lot of Keiras running around Balteris."

"Oh." I reevaluated. "And he's a master swordsman. The kind that's more than difficult to find these days."

He nodded.

"Well, at least he's in Brod," I chuckled nervously.

"So was she, last you saw her," he pointed out.

"Aye, good point cloudling. He could be anywhere, now."

Shazina, tired of being left out, jumped in. "What's any of that matter? You promised to help me get support for my home. The people who could do that are dead, and you touched the Ukiyo today. It's time to leave. If you just come back, you can help us become Learners again, and then I can make the Unbroken. This Keira girl is a moot point."

I sighed, turning to the child. "We still don't have a way to get back, even if we could drop our worries about this Keira."

"Well, we wait till an equinox, which will have a low tide, and use that timeframe to ride an airship below the storm," she said matter of factly.

"Oh, of course," I replied, rolling my eyes. "As easy as that."

"You promised!" she suddenly shouted, tears threatening to spill out from her eyes.

"All right, easy!" I said. "We'll figure something out. But we can't just leave my homeland to this God's Fury madness. Keira is wholesale murdering people, and we don't know why."

A hush fell over the room as someone entered. I turned and nearly bolted, seeing a figure in bright blue robes. The priests had found us again and were here to finish the job they started in Erset. They did not fail in assignments they'd taken coin for, and the priests must have uncovered our supposed deaths not having happened.

There was a staff was in one hand, and beneath a fold of his robe, I saw the glint of specially made knives that could make the staff into his strange, double-sided spear. Like a school of fish shying away from a sea monster, the crowd parted as he headed directly towards us.

My heart slowed back to normal as a grin spread across my face.

"Rook," Volant said, genuine warmth in his voice.

This was no blue-robed priest. This was one of the people we'd been hoping for, and he'd finally shown up.

"You got my letter!" I stood, hugging one of the deadliest people I'd ever had the pleasure of calling a friend.

Lean, iron-like arms returned the embrace. He released me, warmth radiating from his smiling eyes, though his mouth quirked up in amusement. Before answering, he turned and hugged Volant as well, a flash of concern as he felt Volant's frail form.

He took in everyone else but turned back to me. "Your letter?" he asked. "And Volant, what happened? You were well on your way to becoming slabs of well-earned muscle!"

We both tried to respond at once and were ignored by Rook as he took in Cassiopia properly, turning his energetic, single-minded focus on her. "My, my," he began, "your reputation precedes you, at the least. Cassiopia, huntress extraordinaire? We didn't meet, but I saw you down a rabid bear at five hundred paces. Simply amazing."

She blushed slightly. Before she could speak, Rook turned again, taking in the triplets. "And the infamous sisters! From what these boys told me, you all seemed the intelligent sort. What are you doing mixed up with them?"

They, too, seemed surprised to be known by this blue robe, but yet again, Rook turned, halting any response. He took in Martino first, turning to look at Volant and then back at Martino. A small, knowing smile twitched his lips, and then he locked on to Shazina, holding Argo.

Rooks near-constant fidgeting stilled as he took in the girl. He looked long and hard, like a predator sizing up some rather dangerous game, seeing who would run first. The moment stretched almost uncomfortably long before he finally bent down to pet the puppy, restoring his constant animation.

"The infamous puppy. It's all anyone's talked about since I landed." He straightened, looking at the small group of bewildered people.

"Oh. I'm Rook." He laughed, the quick sort of chuckle when you say something funny but know only you will find it so. "Heard Nil and Volant were in town and decided I could use some help killing someone."

To everyone's credit, no one laughed when he said it.

"So, you found us because of Argo. Not because of the letter." I said, disbelief masked by my monotone statement.

"That'd be correct," he replied. "And what an adorable puppy it is. I'm starting to see why everyone's talking about him. I've been trying to hunt down that girl who killed all the Equals. I heard Xylex was on trial today and tried to arrive as fast as I could. Unfortunately, my information network wasn't quite up to par as I've been cleaning up some of the mess in the mistlands."

"The puppy," I said. "You've got to be kidding me."

"Nil," he replied with mock severity, "I taught you better. Please pay attention, or I'll start throwing things at you again."

Without warning, Volant was suddenly laughing, great big belly laughs. He didn't stop, and soon the girls had joined in, laughing as well. Rook followed suit, adding his more resonant laugh to the mix, and then we all were laughing, mostly for laughter's sake. The tension we had built up was finally being released. It felt incredible.

It seemed Rook had been off with his not-quite-pirate crew and had been unsuccessfully monster hunting in the mistlands. Out of contact with the world, he'd missed the battle of Brod, and by the time he'd arrived there, everything had blown over. He'd gone back to the mist-lands but had started to hear rumors of Keira and her glee for violence. Not taking kindly to such rumors, he strapped on some fresh robes, something having happened to his old travel worn ones, and went back on his hunt to rid the world of evil.

Cassiopia, having taken a moment to go pick up a few dozen of the street buns, arrived with a basket full of food. We lost a solid piece of time as Rook dug in, having lived off fruit and dried meats for the better part of a fortnight. We traded stories and learned more about the triplets, Martino, and Cassiopia's past lives than in the entire time we'd spent with them, thanks to Rook's seemingly random, insightful questions. The man had a talent for made everyone around him comfortable.

After the second round of street buns, which sold out the food cart, Cassiopia finally came back around to Rook's initial introduction. "You seem like an exciting fellow," she said between bites. "Why do you want to kill anyone? And despite their odd reputations, why would these two help you?"

Rook, in response, waved his hand, moving the bun through the air in a rather vague, street magician fashion. "Some people just need killing, you know?" A chunk of the street bun fell from the central mass. With an ease belying the lightning-quick speed, he dipped the bun under the falling piece, catching it.

Cassiopia looked on, somewhat impressed, as he then tossed the whole handful of food into his mouth and swallowed it down.

"...and," he continued after picking up another bun, "these are phenomenal, by the way. These two understand this need. Volant and Nil, that is, not the buns. And they also somewhat owe me. And they also probably want the same people dead that I do." He paused, plopping another bun whole into his mouth, much to everyone's horror, but none so much as Cassiopia, who looked positively offended by the lack of appreciation. "Oh. And there's probably some form of morbid curiosity. This is kind of a thing I do. Killing bad people, that is. That's how we met if you hadn't heard. Assassin after them, me coming to kill said assassin. Volant here stealing my thunder."

As one, the triplets blinked rapidly, trying to process Rook's rapid style speech. Shazina seemed unphased, still petting Argo.

Volant blushed. "That's not fair. We wouldn't have known about the archer except for you showing up. And Nil would've died a few times over before I got to her if not for you."

I smiled apologetically at Cassiopia before turning to Rook. "I'm in. I bet Volant is too."

Another smile split Rook's face. "Excellent! Let's go there now! There's an alchemist we need to visit, yes?"

"Umm, now-now?" I asked. "Or do you mean now-let's-get-some-rest-and-make-a-plan-and-try-for-it-tomorrow now?"

Rook stood, sticking his fingers out to Argo to lick off. "What a positively adorable creature. Again, I understand all the fuss about him. And by now, I mean 'now-now' so let's get a move on Nil. Lead the way!"

Volant nudged me up, so I hopped up. It seemed this was happening. Everyone but Shazina opted to stay put, the rest not on board with an eccentric vigilante mission, understandably.

Argo yipped enthusiastically on the way to the leatherworker turned alchemist shop, so Shazina let him down. He followed behind us, finally healed up, it seemed. Despite the practically deserted city streets, people heard Argo's joyful barking and peeked out of doors and windows as we passed. A few even came out, waylaying us to say hi to the dog. If it weren't for Rook's priestly blue robes, they probably would have followed us all the way.

A light glowed from within the small shop. Late hours for a leather-worker. Rook tried the door, but it was locked. He rapped at the door softly, stepping back to join Volant and me with patient expectation.

The door creaked open, revealing a tall man, dark-skinned, with the curling scar of a terrible disease that left the few survivors with its intricate mark. The man froze in surprise. His Brod eyes, dark purple and deeply sunk, took in first Volant, then Rook, then me, and finally landing on Shazina and Argo. "Left hand," he cursed softly. "You're the ones with that puppy I've heard all about?"

"Halgunos?" Volant croaked, disbelief almost stopping him from speaking.

The friend of his mother, a man we'd all thought was a friend, grimaced almost apologetically. "They were funding my research into this," he said, gesturing to the scars that stopped just below his jaw. "No child should suffer so. And no parent should have to watch."

"But they're monsters," Volant said, a sob nearly choking him. "God's Fury killed Johanna! How could you work with them? You told us they were evil!"

At that, Halgunos flinched like he'd been slapped. I saw guilt play out across his face as heavy as any anchor. "Johanna was an accident. She saw me talking with someone she shouldn't have." Now it was Halgunos' turn to sound like he couldn't speak. Tears threatened to spill out of his eyes.

In the moment that Volant and I turned to each other, looking for some kind of reassurance that neither of us had heard what Halgunos had admitted, Rook spoke up. "Where's the girl?" he asked the alchemist.

A hand fell on my shoulder the moment I willed Skill forward, stopping me before I'd even realized what I was doing. Rook's hand squeezed painfully in the tender space between muscle and bone. I turned and growled at Rook but stopped as I saw he wasn't even looking at me. His other arm similarly held Volant. Still, Volant was straining against Rook's uncanny strength, rapier half drawn.

"She's not here." A sigh came from Halgunos. Tired. Weary. And full of regret. "I'm not sure where she's staying. I've only seen her once when she picked up the order God's Fury had me make for her."

A strangled grunt came from Volant as Rook tightened his grip, bringing him down to a knee as he fought to draw his weapon. "Don't play me for a fool, Halgunos. Where is she?"

"Xylex's place," Halgunos admitted. "Please understand, I never wanted to hurt anyone. It's just the price I had to pay to help fix the world."

Rook released us, and Volant started forward, determined to unleash a fury of emotion I mirrored.

But Halgunos wasn't willing to go without a fight. Two glass spheres appeared from his pockets. He threw them both and then slammed the door shut.

"Volant!" I roared. Rook was in motion, diving for Volant, who was in mid-stride. Time seemed to slow as the glass twinkled in the air. Instinct took over, and I flung out the Skill with both hands wide, fingers splayed. I imagined a wall launching from between my hands and pushed with my mind as hard as I could to make it reality.

Rook tackled Volant down to the ground, covering him with his body at the same time my wave of Skill crashed into the alchemical explosives. I forced my Skill to harden and stay in place, straining against my bodies limits. Shazina had blurred out of existence with Argo. I needed to figure out my Ukiyo, it'd be handy to move as fast as she did. Strange, the thoughts that pop into your head right before something terrible is going to happen.

The spheres struck my Skill-turned-shield and shattered. The resulting shock wave was like pushing Skill against the ground, and then it pushing back a hundred-fold. An unstoppable force threw me backward. My whole body felt like it would break from the sudden push back against my Skill. I maintained the impromptu wall until I skidded into the ground and my concentration was knocked clean out of me, along with my breath.

Dazed, I lay there staring at the rough-hewn cave roof. Stars, something I'd not seen since we'd arrived, twinkled high up against the shadowy ceiling. I drew a breath in, and the stars shifted, winking in and out of existence. Was I dead?

A small weight stepped on my chest. I tilted my spinning head up. Argo was there, a look of concern on his furry face. I tried to move my hand up to pet him, but it felt like it was made of pure lead. Instead, I tried to smile at the puppy. He scooted forward, nudging my nose with his, and then laid down, snuggling up for a nap. My head dropped back, and Shazina came into view.

Shazina's teeth were bared in exertion. Over one shoulder, she'd slung a slumped Volant. Over the other, Rook. She was carrying two men, easily twice her weight apiece.

Yup, I was dying and having some strange hallucination.

She grunted and nudged me with her toe. "You've got to get up, Nil. I can't carry you as well."

I groaned. Head still swimming, I tried to sit up but couldn't get my body to respond appropriately. I tried it again. Nothing.

"Breathe in. Focus. You're hurt, and you used a lot of Skill all at once. But your mind is stronger than your body. Control it." She sagged under the weight of the two bodies, but with a deep breath of her own, straightened up.

With an effort I didn't think I was capable of, I did as she said. I sucked in air, held it, and forced it out. Argo shifted at the movement but stayed put. In and out. In. Out. I drew Skill in with the third breath, opening my mind to it. I let it infuse my body. It was so much more comfortable like this. My limbs weren't my own now, and somehow that made letting the Skill flow to them become nearly effortless.

Now, instead of lead, my arms and legs were made of lightning. My head cleared, sparking with alien life. I could run all day now.

I hopped up, catching Argo as he spun off my chest. I could get used to this.

"Be careful. You'll pay for whatever strain this puts on you twice over when the Skill dissipates."

I looked at her and smiled. "Thanks for the warning. They okay?"

"No. I think Volant will be fine. He's just unconscious. Rook, though, he's got a nasty cut. We need to see a healer and quickly."

My mind spun with potential ideas. It didn't quite feel like it was me thinking, but I knew the thoughts and feelings were mine. They were too quick. And too random. It created a detached sense. Memories of people jumped through my brain like a series of still images until Argo and the animal healer froze in place. "Follow me," I said. "I know who can help us."

My feet seemed to move independently of me, responding to the thought of walking more than my actual attempt at doing so. I'd heard of phantom limb syndrome. This was something opposite of it. I wobbled down the street with energy coursing through me. Argo was back asleep in my arms, and Shazina followed along with trudging steps, still carrying both the men. I marveled at her strength but didn't slow us down to ask further questions.

With the not-phantom limb syndrome still causing a disconnect between my mind and my body, I knocked on the double-wide barn doors at the back of the clinic, facing away from the street and the front door.

The door slid open a crack. Insley, Balteris' most attractive animal healer, poked her head out. My breath caught a little, and I felt the fire I'd been keeping lit for Thecily gutter.

"Nil, I was hoping to see you and Argo again, but with maybe a little warning if it was going to be this late. I hadn't even put on..." she paused mid-sentence, seeing Shazina. "Oh. God's above. Come in!"

Shazina stumped in as Insley opened the door further. Foolishly happy considering the circumstances, I came in as well, pausing to let her pet Argo as she directed Shazina to the examination table.

With an almost gentle movement, the girl flipped first Volant and then Rook onto the table. Volant groaned but otherwise didn't respond.

"Another explosion," I explained. "They were right next to the blast."

Her brow furrowed as she examined Volant first, checking him all over. "They should be dead if they were right next to it."

She went to Rook, taking in his lacerated scalp, bleeding shoulder, and remains of his scorched Waruin braid. With an ear to his chest, she closed her eyes and listened. A moment passed, and her eyes snapped open. She grabbed his robe and ripped it open, exposing his chest. Without explaining what was happening, she hopped up onto the table and straddled Rook. She began pressing hard against his chest in a rhythmic motion.

She'd barely been at it when Rook's eyes flew open and he gasped a long, shuddering breath. He blinked rapidly and took in the room, still breathing heavily. Finally, his eyes landed on the healer. His face scrunched up in amusement. "I'm flattered, really. But you're a little young and not quite my type."

Insley rolled her eyes but hopped off, relieved. Rook shook his head, reaching up and finding his stump of a braid. "Ol' Lock is going to find that hilarious," he said with a forced sigh.

"You probably should stay seated. You were pretty close to being dead," Insley interjected as he stood up.

"Not the first time. I'll be fine, but thanks for bringing me around!" And despite having been carried all the way here, he hopped up and landed with only the slightest of wobbles. "Volant dead too?"

"No," Insley, Shazina, and I all said simultaneously.

"He's just a little concussed. Probably will come around pretty soon. It's you I'm worried about," Insley said with a hint of disapproval. When Rook continued to pace around the shop, she came to stand with me, petting Argo some more. "See? This is why I work with animals. People are dumb. And Nil?"

"Uh, yes?" I responded.

"This late-night visit comes with a price. I want food and drink and good conversation. And more time with Argo." She smiled, still playing with the puppy who was trying to lick her fingers.

"It's a date," I replied. "I mean, you've got a deal. Not that it's a date, you know."

"It's a date." She ruffled my head this time, having to reach up on the tip of her toes. "Now, I have some salts. We can wake your friend up prematurely so you guys can get him to a proper bed to rest. That fine?"

Shazina, who didn't seem to have taken well to the idea of Argo going out with me as part of some deal, gestured for her to get the salt while taking the dog from my arms.

Rook turned to me, his chest still bare, head slightly scorched, and a manic grin plastered on. The grin slipped a little as he saw me. "You're looking a little pale yourself, Nil."

The lightning had left my limbs, I realized. The tremendous amount of Skill use had sapped me. "We probably should sleep this off. Today's gone just a little too far on the excitement level for me." With that, I gracelessly slumped to the ground and passed out.

A splash of water hit my face, and Insley helped with a gentle, yet firm pat. Volant was standing with the others, looking on expectedly. "This is no place for a nap. Your friends will get you to bed," she laughed. "I'll see you soon. Don't forget. You owe me."

I let Volant help me up, and the two of us wrapped arms around each other as we stumbled back to the tavern. When I closed my eyes the second time in the seriously overcrowded room we had, I was out like a snuffed candle. This city was too small for both Patrica and Halgunos to go undetected for much longer. Dreams of explosions, Thecily, Insley, and street buns spun through my mind.

Chapter Eight

Somewhat rough hands patted my cheeks with enough force to sting. "Insley?" I asked, my mind foggy from a deep slumber.

I heard a chuckle and then a young girl's voice. "You wish, tree boy. Now be quiet. Everyone else is still sleeping." Shazina said. She followed up with a flick to my nose. "Training time."

When I rolled up off the floor, my head spun. Nausea threatened to overwhelm me, and I swayed against the near-complete mutiny my body was trying to throw. I'd been sore before from training, but this was more than overexertion. It felt like bits of muscle had been carved out throughout my whole body and replaced with acid. Bile rose, but I forced it back down. Thinking back, it felt similar to the first time I'd adequately turned will to Skill and had been scolded by the Master Learner for not properly starting with a smaller amount.

Shazina interrupted. "Outside. Now."

Painfully, I hobbled with small, cautious steps to minimize the Skill overuse, I followed her down and into the empty and darkened common room.

She pointed at the corner where I'd practiced meditation.

I groaned in response.

"None of that. You need daily practice. Yesterday could have gone a lot better if you'd known what you were doing." With that, she turned, heading back upstairs.

"Left hand," I cursed, easing myself into a seated position. She was right, and despite the warm thoughts of going back to sleep, I drew in a deep breath. I held it. One thudding heartbeat. And then a second. Out went the air, slowly. Despite my eyes being closed, I grew more alert. Guess there was no chance of falling asleep accidentally.

Hundreds of breaths followed as I focused my mind into palpable energy. Like any muscle, the will-to-Skill one ached from overuse. I pushed harder still, forcing the connection to strengthen between my mind and reality. As the little bit of power bloomed inside me, my mind wandered back to the first days at the school. Before it consumed me, I made a mental note to compare Learner lessons with the girls and then discarded the distraction to practice Shazina's training.

Time slid by in the quick yet crawling manner that comes with undivided attention and effort towards a task. As I'd just managed to kick my will from external to internal manipulations, a whole different muscle I was beginning to realize, a hand dropped on my shoulder and shocked me out of the practice.

It was the innkeeper. He stepped back cautiously. "You're starting to make the other guests uncomfortable," he said almost apologetically.

With a slight sigh, I hopped up and nodded in understanding.

Before I could go, he passed me a small cloth-wrapped bundle. "I've seen you guys eating those buns. Had to try them myself. Best food I've ever had." He paused, almost embarrassed. "Heard that black market alchemist got blown up. If that was you all, thanks."

As nonchalantly as possible, I shrugged and headed back upstairs.

Inside our little room, everyone but Volant was up. Somehow, he'd managed to stay passed out despite the constant activity around him.

Argo was playing with Cassiopia, Shazina was reading in a corner, and the sisters and Martino had shown up.

"A gift from the innkeeper," I said, dropping the bundle. Street buns were stacked on each other within, almost inciting a riot as everyone rushed over to grab one.

When everyone had a snack, Joy came over. "Shazina and I had some questions on Learner techniques. Can we take a walk?"

"Aye," I replied through a mouth full.

Rook ran into us on the way out, coming in. He'd cleaned up and pulled his remaining strands of the Waruin knot into a tight, squared-off bun. His eyes glowed with excitement, and I knew he must be itching to go by Xylex's place.

"Well, hello! Today's a good day for a spot more of violence?" Rook asked, mischief dancing across his words.

"You've got issues," I replied.

"We're going on a walk," Joy interjected. "Want to come talk about Learners with us?"

Rook bowed grandly, accepting the offer and linking arms with Joy. "Harketh!" he joked, pointing us onwards.

As we walked through the still mostly empty streets, Shazina started us off. "So, for starters, none of you become 'Learners' until you're at a school?"

"That's right," I replied, proud of our system.

"Why?" she asked.

"Because that's the most responsible choice. We don't want little kids running around with weapons, so to say."

"And what happens after you become a Learner?" she continued.

"Well, you get a job. Or teach."

"So backward," she muttered under her breath. "We're doomed."

Joy jumped in with her own question. "How'd you get past the book study into practical use? They just keep throwing books at us about visualization, control, willing the energy into existence, and whatnot. But I'm just not getting it!"

"That's always been my problem," Rook added sympathetically. "I've read most of the books on Learners, and it seems there's just a switch in some people's brain that with enough effort and focus, they suddenly flip it."

I grimaced at the description. "It's more like re-learning how to breathe." Frustrated at their uncomprehending looks and my failure to explain, I tried again. "All the books are just trying to make you shift a paradigm. You want to accomplish a task, so you focus on that task. You make yourself care about it, think about it, and follow-through. Being a Learner is figuring out how to tilt your perspective and creating a reserve of will that turns into something tangible-Skill."

Shazina nodded, liking that explanation. "That makes sense, to an extent. Our process is a little different, which may be why we lost the Learners. Ours is simply eliminating the barrier between our mind and our body. We meditate until you can create one single entity. We have to move our arm as our arm. We learn to move with our thoughts, not use our thoughts to move us."

Rook, Joy, and I all stared utterly baffled by this explanation of Ukiyo.

"Never mind," Shazina grumbled. "Nil will understand one of these days."

"Aye, I think I will," I chuckled. "I was studying and reading day in and day out, killing myself with the effort. And then I noticed the ebb and flow of that concentration. I started trying to call it up and turn it off. One day, it just kind of snapped like there had been a wall, and I'd finally found a door through it. I could open it upon reality if I just remember where it is."

Joy made some harumph-like noise in response. "And just like that, you could practically do what Naturals do?"

"No, no, no," I laughed.

Rook chuckled too, shaking his head. "This is why I went to the mountain. Jorcum's academia is slipping."

"I can't do anything of the sort like Volant. I can shape my will into something needle-sharp thin or up to a fairly large-sized table if I try really hard. The output is pretty much however I move my hands, and the Skill pushes back as much as I push out. Plus, I couldn't do much when I first broke that barrier to summoning Skill. I could knock over a plant or put a hole in a piece of paper. It's hard building up to the more impressive stuff."

Both Shazina and Joy were nodding now, grasping the concept.

"It was similar for me," Shazina added. "Admittedly, I started young, but I could only enhance my strength to the range of someone a little heavier than me. It slowly grew with practice from there."

Rook turned to Joy, still sympathetic. "It's fine if you don't ever manifest. Not everyone has enough 'muscle,' as Nil referred to it, to make a noticeable difference. With all the study in the world, you could probably break that barrier. But for me, I've tried for many, many years before realizing it was too much work when I could spend the same energy towards my actual strengths instead."

We continued in silence, everyone thinking of that.

Rook had led us to an alley across the street from Xylex's old place. The windows had new panes of glass in them now. The one we'd broken had bars on the inside, making the room more like a cell. Xylex must not have appreciated the thought of anyone else escaping through his windows.

"What are we doing here?" I hissed at Rook.

"Violence, remember?" he grinned maniacally.

"What about Joy and Shazina? They never agreed to this." I was angry. This was not a plan. This was a chaotic thrust into the jaws of fate. And fate always hit back harder.

"Shazina," Rook said, barely containing his mirth. "Would you be so kind as to escort Joy back to the tavern?"

"No!" both girls responded at the same time.

"I'm coming to help," Joy stated with an angry conviction.

"Same," Shazina growled.

He looked at them both, almost with a tinge of regret. "I truly wish you could. But do either of you think the other should come?"

"Of course not! Shazina's just a child," Joy began.

"She can't come. She's a total liability," Shazina interjected.

"And," Rook added as both girls paused and looked at each other, "Nil's the only one properly armed beside me, and I only have to worry about that cloud dancer being upset with me if he dies. Shazina, you're too important to risk. And Joy, you're far too precious." He rolled his shoulders, somehow flipping his staff around its straps and into his hand. He shrugged off his outer robe, revealing a crowded bandolier of sheathed knives. "Plus, someone's got to go warn everyone else what trouble we're getting ourselves into. So, off you two go, keep the other safe, and be sure to bring friends as quickly as you can!"

Both glared at him before turning on me.

"Rook's got a point," I said. There was no way I'd let harm come to Joy, and even if Shazina was faster and more robust than anyone I'd ever met, that didn't translate to catching a dangerous Learner.

"Go!" Rook growled. "The longer you wait, the longer we go without help."

They left. Sullen, but praise the gods, they left.

I felt for my hatchet and knife. My constant companions. A small measure of comfort came through as the leather and wood caught against my fingers. Closing my eyes briefly, I shifted my inner gaze to my toes and then moved up my body with a mental examination. Scrapes and bruises touched on my awareness as I went. Tired limbs. Nothing that couldn't be handled or ignored, though.

If Rook would have told me what we were up to, I'd have grabbed more sleep and maybe a few throwing knives. Or at the least, more people to join us.

"You go high. I'll take the front door," Rook said, gesturing to the second window, which didn't have the bars across it.

I gathered Skill, a headache starting to form with the effort.

"On my signal," he said, the joyful energy never leaving him. He drew a small throwing knife, waving it slowly in front of me. His face split into a manic smile. "Fetch!"

His hand whipped the knife out, sending it slicing through the air. Glass shattered at its impact.

"May the gods ignore you!" he wished me, shooing my still shocked self towards the now empty window.

I leaped up, pushing Skill down from my feet and helping to launch me far higher than an average person could jump. As I grabbed the windowsill, I looked down to see Rook kicking in the door. He waved up to me with reckless abandon before charging in. I pulled, bringing myself into the room receiving some minor cuts from the glass and adding to my growing list of aches and pains.

When I finished dusting myself off, I realized I wasn't the only person in the room. A thick-set man with the scarred and malformed ears of a ring fighter was standing there, waiting for me to notice him.

"Ah, is this your room?" I asked, mock surprise lacing my voice. "I must have gotten turned around."

The man's lips curled with the ghost of amusement. He shook his head and held out a meaty fist, showing Rook's dagger.

"Umm, I guess this is the right room," I said. I rolled out my wrists, flicking blood away from my hands. "Shall we?"

The ghostly amusement turned almost genuine as he raised his fists into a pugilist's fighting stance. He stepped forward, bobbing his large frame ever so slightly, trying to goad me into a rushed attack. His feet seemed to be made of ice, gliding beneath him in agile grace.

I stepped forward, closing the distance. I kept my feet underneath me, crouching slightly to center myself as I shuffled forward again, bringing myself into striking range.

He jabbed twice, forcing me to weave left and then right to avoid being brained by his sledgehammer fists.

"Not bad," he muttered, still amused.

With surprising speed, he launched a flurry of combinations at me, feinting me into opening up for his wide haymaker shot.

Fortunately, I saw it coming.

I ducked under his finishing swing, pivoting to his side while simultaneously drawing the dagger from behind my back and planting it in the huge man's knee. I pushed it deeper until the blade came out the other side.

There was a moment where we locked eyes. I expected pain or anger in his eyes. Instead, all I saw was disappointment and betrayal. Odd, that.

Then he dropped, the knee giving out on him and taking the knife with it. He hit the ground with a weighty thud, but didn't cry out. Rook's knife appeared in his hand as he rolled and curled up into a pained huddle.

He watched me as I left the room. I shut the door behind me and let out a breath. I felt dirty for some reason. The boxer's eyes had accused me of something, and it'd stuck in my brain.

Outside the room, noise from downstairs reached me. Rook seemed to have found himself a welcome party. I headed for the stairs when I heard another door creek behind me. I turned, pulling my hatchet but something hard and moving too fast crashed into my head. Stars burst, and I landed far less gracefully than the big fighter had.

My whole body seemed to be stuck in honey, unable to respond in anything but slow motion to my throbbing head's commands. I felt my arms pulled behind me and tied together with some intricately woven rope. As my eyes came back into focus, soft hands rolled me over, letting me see Keira standing there with a wicked, smug grin. Her hair was all over the place, and she had deep bags under her eyes. Playing at city bomber had taken its toll on her sleep, at least.

She leaned over, her loose hair tickling my nose while she examined where she'd hit me with the Thumper's truncheon. Mostly satisfied with her work, she nodded to herself before delivering a vicious kick to my side, adding a new shade of pain to the whole experience.

From there, she tugged me up and then poked a pair of fingers into the small of my back. The ever so slight smell of ozone that accompanied a large concentration of Skill tickled my nose. With one hand on my shoulder and the other threatening to disembowel me with Skill, she marched me down the hall until we reached stairs on the opposite side of where Rook had entered.

When I hesitated at the top step, Keira planted a boot into my back with the force of a horse's kick. Falling down a set of stairs hurts. Being shoved down a set of stairs with your arms tied behind your back is as painful and terrifying as just about anything I'd experienced. My pounding head made contact with the wall on the way down, and despite a miraculous lack of broken bones, I now had a full Soft Stepper drum circle using my brain as their instrument. This was the last time I followed one of Rook's plans.

With an effort, I stood again but the pain was too much. I threw up in the corner as Keira made her way down the stairs. My head spun with the effort. Concussion, I thought. Great.

"That was wholly unnecessary," I said through closed eyes and gritted teeth. "If you wanted to dance, all you had to do was ask."

Ignoring me beyond a slap in response, she finished dragging me to my feet and we continued walking through the massive home. We'd skipped past the first floor and were in a small cavern that must have doubled as Xylex's cellar.

I took in the room. Polished stone floor. A hundred paces across. Almost empty but for a door in one wall. Seeing it, I amended the room from cellar to hideout and escape route for Xylex, though it seemed it didn't do him any good. It was also eerily quiet.

Soft footsteps sounded from the direction we came. I turned, expecting to see Rook come to save me. Instead, I saw Berjio. Captain Andreska's former sword master. The kindly old man who'd tried to take in Volant and I back in Brod. Keira's grandfather, Volant had said.

A thin sword dangled at his waist. He looked even more tired than Keira.

"Keira," he called out with a particular weary disappointment that made my heart go out to the man. "I think it's time you left Kalaran, my dear. The fellow upstairs is making a mockery of the Thumpers you had posted. I'll hold him off, but whatever you've been up to, it's gone too far, and I can't turn a blind eye any longer."

"She's a monster," I spluttered.

"She's my granddaughter, Nil," he replied, almost apologetically.

Keira hadn't said anything. Instead, she turned, took one look at her grandfather, and then fled across to the door. She hesitated, frozen for just a moment. Her hand slashed back at us, a blade of Skill being released directly at me. She staggered from the effort and nearly dropped to a knee before stumbling her way through the door.

Interesting. I squirmed, trying to get away from whatever attack radius I was in, but my body wasn't moving fast enough. Instead, I flopped back and rolled into the wall, hoping Keira had aimed too high.

Whispering steel on leather drew my attention. Berjio took two steps towards me. He'd covered the distance surprisingly quickly. He swung his now glittering blade, and I closed my eyes against a painful death. But no feeling of a sharp bite of a sword came. I heard a strange sound like an arrow striking into a soft tree after prolonged rain. Almost inaudible.

I opened my eyes back to see Berjio's sword quivering slightly. He'd deflected the Skill, dissipating it. I'd only heard of that kind of swordsmanship in books.

"It's good to see you, my friend." Berjio's voice was worn thin but still warm. "I'm glad you're still letting that adventurous spirit guide you."

I started to respond when he dipped back towards the entrance that led upstairs. A knife spun by his head, and he deflected another with his sword. Rook was calmly entering the room, double-sided spear held loosely in one hand, the other holding an additional knife.

"Nil, I didn't bring you here to get tied up like a distressed damsel from a children's book." His arm lazily flicked out my way, the knife skidding gently at my feet.

I scrambled to it. I lost precious seconds trying to pick it up and get it angled so I could saw at my bindings.

"Master Berjio," Rook continued, bowing to the man. "My apologies, if I'd know it was you, I'd have not wasted the shot. I've been anticipating meeting you for a very long time, though I admit I'd been hoping it was something more congenial than this."

Berjio gave a half-hearted salute. "Rook, the disciple of the thirteenth god. This is indeed an unfortunate meeting place. I knew our path's would cross one day. How about we pack up, get Nil here untied, and head back to a tea house and have a chat?"

To my surprise, Rook almost seemed willing. Then he turned to me. "Was she here?"

"Aye, just left through that door at the other end a few breaths ago." I kept sawing at the rope, barely making a dent. I focused and pooled Skill, but I couldn't move my hands into a position that didn't include me doing severe damage to myself. I tried to shift to Ukiyo like I'd done the day before, but my head throbbed and wouldn't let me focus enough.

Rook shifted towards the door, but Berjio pivoted, matching him step for step, blocking the exit Keira had taken.

"I'm sorry, but she's my granddaughter," Berjio explained softly, sounding heartbreakingly sincere.

"She's killed hundreds of people!" Rook roared at him, all geniality evaporating. Snapping his spear up into a fighting stance, he took a step towards the sword master.

Berjio had gone pale, a tear rolling down his face. "It doesn't matter what she does. She's my blood, and I can't do anything but love her, despite the mistakes she's made. I hope that one day you have the same opportunity, godless."

Rook growled something and was then flowing into the fight. Sparks flew when the blades connected, though they both moved too fast for me to keep up. After a cacophony of exchanges, parries, and reposts, they broke apart.

Tears ran freely down Berjio's face now. Despite his sinewy forearms and broad, muscular shoulders, all I could see was a grandfather struggling with what was in his heart versus what he knew was right.

"I'm so sorry, this is the last thing I wanted," Rook said, all the fury having left him after the exchange. He, too, had tears cutting streaks in his face. Berjio was living art. A man who'd dedicated himself so entirely to his passion that he'd gone beyond being a mortal. Rook knew this more than anyone, as he had done the same. "Please don't make me do this. She has to be brought to justice."

Berjio shook his head slowly and attacked, moving with more powerful grace than I'd ever seen someone exhibit. Not a step wasted. Every strike and dodge of Rook's spear in perfect sync with the energy to do so. He glided around Rook, a phenomenal master in his own right, but nothing could compare to the sword master in his element.

Cut after cut, Rook gave ground to the older man, tears mixing with the small lacerations Berjio inflicted on his arms, chest, and shoulders. Both men wholly concentrated on the fight. Both men heartbroken for the necessity of it.

I was nearly through the rope when Rook let a thrust go almost unchecked. The blade scraped along his ribs. He trapped Berjio's hand with his own and tossed the shaft at Berjio. Reflexively, the man caught it, surprised.

In the same motion, Rook drew one of his spear tip shaped blades from the bandoleer and thrust, embedding it right into the elderly man's heart. An uncanny absence of sound that can only be felt after such violence enveloped the cavernous room.

The tears stopped, both men frozen inches from each other.

A soft, sad sob escaped Rook as they both sank to the knees.

"That was quite clever," Berjio said, blood flecking a cough. "I think you and I would have made great friends."

"I think we would have as well," Rook whispered, twisting and wrenching the knife.

Berjio went limp in his arms, collapsing against Rook as if they were hugging. Another cry, louder this time, escaped Rook's throat as he then embraced the old sword master. "I think so too," he said again to a man that was no longer there.

Chapter Nine

Enough slack finally came as I cut through the last strands of rope, and I stood, woozy but free. I rushed over to Rook, who was still kneeling in an embrace with Berjio, their blood and tears mixing.

"She's getting away," I said, gently resting a hand on his shaved scalp. "Don't let this death be in vain."

A final tremor ran through Rook, and then he stood. He took me in, deep sorrow in his eyes. "You're right. We need to follow." But instead of rushing off, he reached down and gently removed the sword from Berjio's grip, handing it to me. He then took the belt sheath from the corpse and buckled it on.

I stood still, confused, wanting to rush off and not understanding Rook's slowly methodical movements.

"This was a great man, Nil. His sword is not mine to give, but here we are." Rook looked me over, made a quick adjustment to the belt, and then nodded. "Let's go."

In the space of a blink, he was sprinting across the room, no hesitation in his stride. He didn't even try to open the door, instead taking a running leap and kicking it right next to the handle. The door that Keira had taken shattered on its hinges at the impact, kicking inward and slamming what remained of its wooden frame into the tunnel on the other side.

I charged after Rook, my head begging me to stop and rest with every pounding step. But I couldn't let Keira claim any more deaths.

We flew through the shaft at a dangerous speed. Rook was untouchable, twisting and turning with every surprise stone outcropping and foot-catching crack. I bounced and spun off the various obstacles, heaping more abuse onto my body. The light grew fainter and fainter until the encroaching darkness forced us to slow down enough to feel our way. It wasn't long before we found the end of the tunnel. Another solid door, but this time, barred from the outside.

Rook took several steps back and then smashed into this one as well. Wood splintered, and a bit more light came in, but the door held. He added a few kicks and it was nearly broken it down. "On three, we hit it together," he said, calm and in control.

"Aye," I agreed, still trying to catch my breath.

"One. Two," he grabbed me, holding on to my shoulder tightly, "three!"

We rushed the door, both leaning into it with our shoulders. Whatever was holding it in place gave, though I barely noticed as jolt of pain went through me, turning the world white. We fell out the other side and onto a side street of Kalaran, surprising absolutely no one as it was completely devoid of life.

To the left, a street led out of Kalaran. To the right, the city center. Rook hesitated only for a moment before grabbing me and taking me with him towards the center. We jogged, looking for any sign of the woman who'd left her grandfather to die.

He picked the correct direction. A small crowd was partially gathered around an oversized wagon. It looked to be Cassiopia's favorite street bun vendor. A portion of that crowd, specifically a short, lean man with a mustache almost as well-groomed as Cobb's, and his wife and children backing him up, was gesticulating at Keira wildly. The wife was helping none other than Shazina up, who was too preoccupied with comforting Argo to even notice the help. The dog, apparently the center of the argument, had his tail tucked between his legs and was trembling in her arms.

"You can't just go knocking people down because you're in a hurry! That dog is a symbol of our people! And you just kicked it like some rock in the street! I will hear an apology!" The man was fuming, seeming ready to wring the apology out of Keira with his bare hands if he had to.

More people came to Shazina's aid, realizing the commotion centered on the famous puppy. Joy was there too, coming to help Shazina as well.

"Shazina!" I called across the open space. "That's her! She's the one that's been blowing everything up!"

The crowd, who'd been on the brink of rioting in Argo's defense, froze. Almost as one, they turned to see Rook and me, bloody and battered. As one, they turned to Keira, whose face had frozen into a furious rage.

As the crowd exploded into movement, Keira kicked the man who'd been waylaying her and broke into a dead run away from the group. The people of Kalaran surged, crying for justice, demanding she pay for hurting Argo, and in general making so much noise that the previously quiet city seemed ready to explode from the pent-up sound.

Doors swung open, and people joined the chase as word spread. The crowd swelled as Kalaran came out of hiding to vent their pain and rage. Rook and I followed, trying to take side streets less crowded. We completely lost sight of her, and most of the crowd was yelling and screaming incoherently, because that's what mobs tend to do. If they didn't catch her, there was just as good a chance they'd string up the first questionable looking person they ran into.

I grabbed Rook and pointed to the nearest roof. He nodded and planted his back against the wall, making his hands into a stirrup. I took three steps and jumped, letting his hands catch my back foot and continue to propel me up. I made it to the roof and hung on tightly. Rook scaled my body until he, too, had a hold of the roof's lip and easily flipped himself over before dragging me the rest of the way up.

If we made it through this, my body would need a fortnight of rest and a number of feasts to recover appropriately. Once up on the roof, two things occurred at once. First, we found our quarry in the churning mass of people below. She'd made it halfway back to Xylex's place but had blended in with a mob that didn't know who they were chasing. The second was seeing Volant and Cassiopia, a long way off, but also on the roof.

They didn't seem to notice us, though it looked like Volant was helping Cassiopia pick out Keira from the crowd. She drew back her great bow, and I flinched involuntarily when she let loose, a series of screams erupting from the crowd.

Rook and I sprung from rooftop to rooftop, covering ground that would have been impossible considering the number of people flooding the streets below us. Guard were shoving themselves every which way below us as angry citizens demanded blood on Argo's behalf or in vengeance for their loved ones.

I couldn't hear myself think as I planted my hands on a raised roof after a diving leap, swinging my legs through my still planted arms and then landing in a roll across the flat and dusty roof. Rook landed beside me while Volant and Cassiopia clambered over the opposite side. All four of us winded. Using rooftops as your mode of transportation was trying in the best of times. Lugging any kind of gear, even just a sword or bow, seemed to make it into a level of strenuous best not to think of.

"She's just another building over," Volant said. "We'd just arrived at Xylex's when we heard the rioting. Climbed up to see what was going on and saw a mob chasing Keira before she pulled some tricky maneuvers and managed to dodge some guy with an awesome mustache."

"You shot her," I said, not quite a question, but close enough to one for both of them to nod.

"Well, now what do we do?" Rook asked, irritated. "If we pop down there, they'll think we're just shooting random people. This crowd is not something I'd planned for."

Volant laughed, shaking his head. "So, the student becomes the teacher, eh Rook?" He jumped the gap between roofs, turning to wave. "We just say it wasn't us. Crime 101. Never admit you're guilty." And with that, Volant was over the other side of the roof, dropping among the crowd trying to help the poor, wounded Keira.

Following his lead, I dropped down from our roof to the crowded floor and elbowed my way around the corner to the crowd. Volant's blond hair bobbed opposite me, and I pushed further in to find my friend. Guard were heading this way as well, and this was going to get a lot more complicated when they showed up.

Gritting her teeth against the arrow piercing her shoulder, Keira was surrounded by several concerned, still partially angry citizens. In their defense, they didn't know her. It's hard to be caring when you're out for blood. And, most importantly, momentum makes it hard to stand still. Keira didn't make it any easier, slashing out with a knife at anyone who came close.

Her focus seemed fractured, but I could tell she was trying to draw Skill anyway. Just in case she succeeded, I pulled in my own, sending yet more pain throughout me at the effort and causing my head to spin. Volant stepped behind me, turning a little to watch for anyone approaching from behind. Cassiopia and Rook appeared as I came, moving through the crowd with ease.

When Keira saw me, her focus sharpened. A guttural noise, somewhere between a scream and a growl, and she'd stabbed her hand out at me. Skill followed the motion, launching across the small space in a deadly line.

With both hands already primed and held together, I spread my fingers wide and drew my arms apart in a short arc. Instead of casting the Skill forward, I made a connection between my hands, feeding it back and forth. The small shield of Skill caught her attack. Unexpectedly, it deflected it some of it as well, sending the skill back at her and slicing a noticeable line through her arm and into the wall behind her. The force of it pushed me back a step, another surprise. This was going to be something I had to look into when everything settled down.

When Rook saw the exchange, he paused looking utterly astonished. For a breath, he seemed to have forgotten about his vendetta entirely. He raised an eyebrow at me.

I shrugged, not sure what I'd done.

As a group, we surrounded Keira. Volant looked like an old friend was dying before his eyes and had just told him they'd never liked his cooking. Cassiopia was stoic, alert, and somehow maintained herself enough not to pull out any food. Rook had regained the fire in his eyes.

Keira tried to stab out with the knife, her other arm now useless from the deflected Skill.

Rook caught the wrist with some underhanded grip as casually as one caught a ball tossed to them. He turned slowly until first the knife dropped out, and then a muffled cry left her gritted teeth. An audible pop announced something painful happening to her wrist as he finished the turn and let the hand drop limply in her lamp at a nauseating angle.

Bile rose in my throat, but it could have been the head injury. "Why?" I asked, directing the question at Keira but leaving it out there for Rook, too, if he wanted to answer.

She started to say something, but Rook reached down, grabbing the massive arrow and giving it a little shake. "Before you give us any lies, or run in circles, know this," he pushed the arrow again, "I will be making this as painful as possible if I think you're anything less than forthright. Understood?"

Her face was pale, white, and taut. She nodded, looking at Rook with a newfound level of fear. "Why what?" she asked.

"Why all of this," I replied, trying to ignore the feeling of cold dread Rook had put in me.

She sighed as if she wasn't on the brink of death and was talking to some village simpleton. "Xylex was a loose end, for one." She coughed, blood spilling down her lip. "Had to be removed before he could give away too many secrets. The Lady wouldn't have wanted him mentioning anything about her to the wrong people, and some of our plans have yet to bear fruit."

Rook pushed the arrow, eliciting a gasp from Keira. The crowd around us was still keeping a safe distance, but I could hear the unmistakable tone of a Guard telling people to get out of his way.

"And the bombings?" Rook demanded.

"An experiment," she wheezed. "Needed to see if we could replicate the technique. Plus, the council had to be eliminated. Can't have a queen with our sham of a republic mucking everything up."

A twist of the arrow made her eyes bulge. I looked away, unable to participate in Rook's justice, vengeance, or interrogation. Whatever you'd call it. I caught Volant's eye, who'd also turned away. Tears threatened to unleash themselves in the corner of his eyes.

"What are you not telling us?" Rook growled.

"Stones!" she cried. "Toron stones!"

Rook let go of the shaft, and Keira gasped for air for a moment. Rook's hand hovered over the custom fletching.

She regained her breath, glaring at the blue-robed man. "There's a cache of Toron stones here. I needed enough chaos to transport them out after Xylex's assassination. The one's we've been collecting. I lost Emerys' Rock at the battle. Wasn't prepared for the drain it'd have on me. In exchange for forgiveness, the rest of the stone retrievals. God's Fury isn't a forgiving bunch."

"Where are they?" I asked.

At the same time, Rook spoke up. "You lost Emerys' Rock? Where is it?"

She laughed at that, derisively. "I don't know where the rock is. Some kid probably grabbed it, doesn't know what it is. The stones are at Xylex's, obviously. Where else would I keep them? Idiots."

"Hey! You there!" a voice called out behind us. The Guard had made it through the riot to us.

In one motion, Rook ripped the arrow out of Keira. Before she could cry out at the pain, he rammed it back into her heart. "May you never find peace," Rook whispered to her as the light left her eyes.

"Left hand of god!" I cried out. "Rook, you didn't have to kill her!"

Instead of responding, he spun around, intercepting the two Guard that were now drawing truncheons. One managed to swing, and Rook stepped in, bringing his elbow and forearm up to meet the man's attack. He continued through his block with fluid motion and drove another elbow into the Guard's throat. From there, he dropped low, sweeping out with a kick to the other Guard's knee. As the man fell, Rook threw another vicious elbow, connecting with the man's head and driving him into the ground. Neither got up.

Cassiopia nodded in approval. The crowd drew back in alarm. Concern and anger turned to panic and fear. I was stunned.

Rook grabbed me, forcing me back the way we came. "Cassiopia, round everyone else up. It's time we took an exit from this place. Volant, go with her, you look like you're about to pass out, and your hair is too noticeable."

"No," Volant said with almost a sad shake, "I'm coming with you and Nil."

It seemed Rook was about to say something in argument but then shrugged. Turning to the crowd, he pointed at the now quite dead woman. "She's the one who hurt the puppy Argo and has been blowing the city up."

Someone from the crowd yelled back at that. "She hurt the dog? She deserves worse a hundred times over!" More voices joined in, creating chaos.

We slipped out as Guard came to the dazed and hurt pair that had the displeasure of arriving first. Cassiopia was already gone. She moved like a leaf on the wind when she needed to, despite her size. The three of us half stumbled, elbowed, and forced our way through the still maddened crowd who'd heard the animal abuser was just around the corner.

Chapter Ten

Xylex's old home was a surprisingly short distance away for how far it felt we'd run. The front door was ajar. A trail of blood seemed to lead away from the house. I remembered the boxer I'd cheated out of a fair fight, figuring he'd left to lick his wounds. Cautiously we stepped inside with Rook leading the way. I had the sword, but it felt wrong. It was not nearly as comforting as my axes or knives.

Eerie quiet waited inside for us, along with a pile of bodies in a small semi-circle in the main foyer. Rook's handiwork. The bodies were still warm, so little time had passed. They all looked nearly as burly as the boxer, which embarrassed me to no small amount.

We split up and began to search the labyrinthian house. Toron stones were precious, and stolen ones were probably even more important to be kept hidden than even your run-of-the-mill priceless stones. Despite this, Volant found the cache faster than it took for me to climb the stairs.

We may have given up our thieving days, mostly against our will, but a thief was precisely the kind of person you needed in a time like this. And Volant was by far the more adept of us two, despite his reluctance to embrace his gifts. He had his Talent, and then he had talent, and some days, it was hard to tell which was more impressive.

Volant was standing at the back wall, an unimaginable safe placed in the middle of the wall with an obscenely large and probably expensive painting sitting on the floor next to him. The grin on his face was huge and only a little smug.

"Getting rusty, leafer," he said as I came in. "This should have been where you first looked."

I bowed in defeat. With a gesture towards the still locked safe, I returned the grin. "How are we going to get through that?" I asked.

Rook entered then, striding across the room in a way someone only with his wealth of experience could manage. Not saying anything but offering a fist bump to Volant as he went by, Rook pulled out a pair of polished lock picks. The ever-increasingly strange man had the safe open in short order. Inside the enormous safe, only a triple sided, unusual looking key sat.

Volant and I were both surprised it wasn't a cache of stones, but Rook seemed to have been expecting it. He took the key and gestured for us to follow. We did, finding ourselves downstairs next to Berjio's body. Rook had taken the time to shift him over to the wall and lay a blanket over him.

Just to the side of his body, there was a metal plate in the wall, a keyhole just the right size for the triple edged key we'd found in the safe. Rook slid the key in. A solid click announced it landing home. One turn. And then a second. And finally, a third spin.

The entire wall shook and then slowly slid open, revealing a small room filled to the brim with glowing red crystals.

Toron stones. More hard assets than any one person had enough coin to afford.

Rook, Volant, and I all stood, slightly stunned. This wasn't just the work of a bit of thievery. This was a massive amount of effort over an incredibly long time. This many Toron stones shouldn't have even existed, according to every history class I'd ever taken.

I stepped in, picking up the stone nearest me. It was dull, no light coming from it, and a small crack showing its inability to store energy. I showed it to Volant. "God's Fury must have used it to add power to Emerys' Rock before the battle."

I started grabbing the best stones I could find, depositing them into pockets. A ring with a small, expertly carved stone inlaid like a signet made my breath catch. It was the ring Bymm had proposed with. Tears welled up in my eyes at the memory. I removed it, reverently, from the top of a stack of smaller stones.

Volant had a small length of leather I fashioned into a quick necklace with the ring tied in. I looped it over my head and felt a different kind of weight leave my shoulders. We had avenged Bymm, more or less. And we'd found his ring.

Neither of the other two were above a little wealth acquisition despite not being Learners. Pockets full, we locked the room back up. Rook slid the key away into one of the many pockets of his robes.

"My mother is never going to believe this," Volant chuckled to himself.

I nodded in agreement. "Mine neither. That said, do you know where yours is? I forgot to mention it when you woke up, but I sent her a letter ages ago to find us here, and she's not shown up."

Volant looked to Rook before turning back to me. "It's nearly impossible to get a letter to a Wydvis captain flying an airship. They essentially hold them at the main hub and hope someone stops by to pick it up. If she's running a job, it could be a fortnight or two."

That made sense. "Well, what do we do next?"

Rook looked at the two of us, almost pained. "Unfortunately, my job here is done. We'll reconnect soon, but I think it's about time I found this God's Fury leader and took care of her. I'm tired of chopping the snake's tail up."

"What about us?" I asked. "Don't you need help bringing them down?"

Rook seemed surprised. "No, of course not. I'll handle it. You two need to figure out what to do with your young foreign friend. If you can figure out a way to get across the causeway safely and back, that would be something amazing indeed."

Volant jumped in at that. "You're insane- you can't take them all by yourself!"

Rook shrugged with the confidence of a man who just single-handedly took out an entrenched house and one of the best swordsmen alive. "Go see the world, you two. Balteris hasn't been kind, and you owe that little girl some help. Make good on your promise and find me when you're back.

I flicked my fingers at Volant. I'm in. You?

He nodded to me before turning back to Rook. "Aye, we'll do that. Don't get yourself killed. I still expect to learn some more from you."

Rook and I left the house, letting Volant have a moment to pay his respects to Berjio. He may not have known him well, but the man was practically family in his mother's eyes. She would have expected it. At the least, he had to say goodbye on her behalf.

We found everyone back at the inn. The triplets Diedra, Dendra, and Joy. Martino, chef's journal in hand. Shazina and Argo, the former angry as a godspawn at being left behind, the latter just happy to be petted. Strangely enough, Cobb and Marle in their Guard uniforms sat at the table, looking incredibly uncomfortable. Finally, Insley was there, looking the most relaxed of everyone in the room. Cassiopia lounged in a corner, chewing thoughtfully on a sandwich of some kind.

I looked to Cassiopia, beyond impressed. "How'd you get everyone here so fast?"

"We were already here, minus the Guard," Insley said. "Cassiopia showed up with the two of them just a bit ago."

"Nil," Cobb interjected with a fair bit of concern. "You guys have something to do with the rioting? All of Kalaran seems to have come out, demanding blood."

I looked sidelong at Volant. "Aye, that was us," I admitted. "But not intentionally. In our defense, we ended the bombings."

Cobb's head sunk down into his hands, and he massaged his head in frustration. Marle patted him on the back.

"I hate to say it, but you guys gotta go," Marle said with a tightly neutral voice.

No one in the room seemed surprised, though the triplets shared a stiff, defiant posture that spoke more than anything they could have said.

We argued about the where and the what. Shazina was adamant that we head back to Erset so we can get her some "official" help since this trip had proven pointless on that regard.

As we all gave in to her arguments, I turned to her. "What if we swing by the school on the way out, and pick some textbooks up on becoming a Learner?"

She thought for a moment, and then smiled. A rarity, for her. "Yes, that would be great. A treasure trove of information that would help us survive. Brilliant idea, Nil!"

No one but our group was in the common room, which made the sudden thud of a door opening all the lore surprising.

A trio of heavily armed cloud dancers stood there. Traditional airship garb, rapiers, and blonde hair tied up in intricate designs. Except for the girl at the front who had the red hair and purple eyes of Brod.

Thecily was here.

My first instinct was to look at Insley, who seemed moderately alarmed but otherwise fine.

"There you are," Thecily said before gliding over to give me a more than a friendly hug.

It felt great. I'd been wishing for precisely that right up until I'd met Insley. I burned with embarrassment as she gave me a light kiss on the cheek. It was so good to see her, but part of me wanted to push her away before she cost the tenuous start to what I felt for the animal healer.

"What are you doing here?" I asked while pulling away.

A faint look of hurt crossed her face, and my heart mirrored it in kind.

Left hand, I thought. This wasn't going to go well.

She smiled, raising her hand and cocking a hip like she was posing for a portrait of an ancient queen. "We're the Sky Wolf, remember? Militarized airship for hire. Kalaran's council brought us in to stomp out some alchemical-happy bomber and get them out if we couldn't. We arrived a little late, but when I heard about a puppy and an tree-hugger-looking fellow, I knew it had to be you, so here I am!"

Rook lit up at this. "You're exactly what these people need to try to get across the causeway."

We all looked at Rook like he was crazy. You couldn't take an airship over the sea.

Thecily burst out in laughter, leaning against Volant now, who wasn't sharing in with the laugh.

She noticed. "You can't fly across the causeway. Everyone knows that," she said in a flat monotone.

"It's not that we think that you can," I replied. "It's more that Rook is partly insane, and we have to get across the causeway despite the impossibility of it."

Rook turned in a circle, taking in the group's mix of disbelief and incredulity. He smiled, gesturing towards Thecily and her two sailors. "I've thought about this before. The evidence that you can't fly there is based on only three expeditions, one of which never returned. The other two seemed to have been brought down by a sea creature, which I think you can defend against if properly prepared." He held out one of the Toron stones.

A dozen stones weighed down my pockets. If Learners could help, we at least had the resources to do so now.

"What, they're going to push the ship too fast for the sea monsters and lightning to get us?" Insley asked with eyebrow arched and dripping with sarcastic implication.

"Us?" I echoed.

"Us." She turned, a challenge in her posture like she was daring me to deny her.

"Not a bad idea," Rook replied. "But no. The lightning shouldn't be a problem. The airships are already able to handle that issue. It's the sea monsters. Some of them have quite the range. We need the ability to block them from taking the ship out of the sky. Enough Learners with enough 'oomph' and they should be able to handle it."

Everyone shifted, including Thecily, into a state of excited anticipation. You could feel the room's sudden change. The thrill of adventure grabbing their attention away from the impossibility of the task.

Rook had us, and all it had taken was a small and not well thought out plan.

Shazina, who'd been unusually quiet considering it was her homeland we were talking about, chimed in. "We use Skill, as you all call it, and that brings all the sea's attention on us."

"Razor gambit," Rook replied as if it explained everything.

I looked around, and no one else seemed to understand, except for Thecily, who was grimacing but seemed to agree.

Volant met my eyes. He didn't know either. He sighed theatrically. "And what's that, exactly, oh mysterious teacher?"

Like a kid getting a gift, Rook clapped his hands together. "I was hoping someone would ask!" He spread his hands where everyone could see the space. "It's where you have an end goal in mind, but it's time-sensitive. And the resources you use further deplete the time frame, though they also speed up the results." He took one hand and swam it to the other before punching it into the meat of his other hand like they collided. "Essentially, the Razor Gambit is an old military term referencing Learners. The more they use their Skill, the closer to burning out and dying, leaving you completely exposed. But, there's a chance you can achieve victory before that by following that strategy."

I still wasn't following. I said so.

Rook shook his head a little in disappointment. "You've got a timeline, Nil. In this case, getting across the water. You could try and not attract sea monsters by using Skill, or you can use Skill to deflect their hunting of your ship despite the cost of bringing more to you. In the long run, you'd lose with the latter strategy. But in the short run, you may scrape by in what is an otherwise losing bet."

"Left hand," multiple people said at once.

"Whatever you decide, you've still gotta get out of Kalaran," Cobb added.

Rook went over to Thecily and had a brief discussion with her and the two shipmates before turning back to the group. I saw a fat coin purse and some glowing Toron stones given to Thecily by Rook before she turned around to the rest of us.

"Well, Rook's made a financially compelling argument for us to take anyone willing to try, assuming a few Learner's come along," she grinned happily.

Everyone in the room trended towards dangerously strong thrill seeker tendencies. I shook my head, knowing I'd be joining in as well. Rook probably hadn't even needed to pay Thecily. They'd all have gone along just to be the first to try it this generation.

Shazina was the first to reply. "I'm in," she growled, almost in challenge to anyone stopping her. Argo yipped excitedly in response.

Before jumping in, I looked to Volant. Your move, his fingers flicked at me. I turned then to Insley, looking between her and Thecily. She caught me looking at her and nodded ever so slightly.

"I'm in," I replied to Thecily, who in turn beamed at me with a certain level of expectation.

"Can't let you guys have all the fun without me," Volant replied, giving a friendly wave to Thecily.

She returned the gesture happily. She and Volant had known each other for a long time. Despite a shared kiss or two, there was nothing but friendship between them.

Insley cleared her throat. "If Nil and Argo are going on this ride, I guess I'm in too. Besides, I've been getting bored fixing hoof-sore horses all day. Adventure ending most likely in death sounds like a nice change of pace."

Thecily's eyes narrowed at this, looking harder between Insley and me. But it only lasted a moment before her face softened again, and she clapped her hands together. "That's the spirit. I like to see a girl with some fire."

To my surprise, Martino raised his hand. "I think I'd like to come as well, if you guys will have me."

Dendra, Joy, and Diedra all looked over, even more surprised than I.

Cassiopia was the one to laugh, loud and long. "Well, that settles it for me! If the cook is going on your boat, so will! Good food and a chance to hunt sea monsters? I'm in!"

The triplets as one shrugged. "We're down," they said in uncanny unison.

"Plus, we get to play with Toron stones if we come, right?" Joy asked.

I nodded, happy that I'd not be the only Learner on this suicide trip, though we'd have to get the girls trained up, and quick.

Both Cobb and Marle were stony silent. Neither looked like they were ready to give up their jobs and possibly their lives just because they liked Argo. Probably the only sane people in the room, despite the slightly excessive love of dogs.

Rook clapped his hands together again with boyish enthusiasm. "That settles that, now let's get some of those delightful street buns and sneak our way out of this city."

It was less straightforward than Rook made it sound, but the sisters already had all the books we wanted to steal, and Thecily sent her two men with them to help carry the numerous tomes. Volant and I had brought practically nothing, so we went and found the street buns. Cassiopia and Shazina also didn't have much that they couldn't carry, so they stayed and chatted with Marle and Cobb and held the common room down while everyone else was getting prepped. Insley came back with an overstuffed healer's bag and a small short sword strapped to her waist. Rook took a pair of street buns and disappeared sometime between the walk back from the vendor and arriving at The Broken Oar.

"That man is mentally unhinged," Volant said when we realized he'd left. "Who just disappears on people like that?"

"Aye, he's a bit odd. I think he just likes the mystery of it all. Who knows." I replied.

A pillar of smoke rose from near the back of Kalaran, towards the port where we'd found our dead fence. Neither Volant nor I said anything, but the stream of Guard and people who rushed away from Kalaran's main entrance where Thecily had anchored her airship told us where Rook had gone and what he'd done.

It was pretty simple slipping out after that, especially with Marle and Cobb escorting us the short distance out. The only hitch was a few people stopping to pet Argo, offering advice and praise in equal measure.

We came out of the Kalaran's caves to a beautiful and too early dawn. The kind of early that only the most motivated of people experience. Or the kind of early that only rebellious teens seem to manage to stay up late enough to see. A weight was lifted from our shoulders as we stepped into the washed-out gray of an overcast sky. It was darker and colder outside than it'd been within Kalaran. Trees, rocks, and everything occupying the space between sky and ground were shades of gray only found in the morning untouched yet by the sun but still lit by an ethereal twilight.

I watched as the alien landscape slowly, almost imperceptibly, took on color and sharper contrasts as the sun inched it's hidden way up above the clouds. It was the most beautiful, peaceful experience I'd had in a long time.

Our goodbyes to Cobb and Marle were short and sweet, excepting Martino, who seemed to have some rather long request for them. The only other member who received more than a quick nod or hug was Argo, who took up more of their time and attention on the goodbye than the cumulative amount the rest of us received.

I couldn't blame them. Argo was ecstatic about being outdoors and had more energy than a puppy his size should be capable of. As he explored the trees surrounding the road into Kalaran, Cobb and Marle acted as perpetual encouragers for the dog. The rest of us were quiet. Everyone seemed to be enjoying the cold air and silent gray morning until the two Guard had their fill and headed back inside.

The airship Sky Wolf hovered above the mountain's slope just a few hundred paces away from the main entrance. We hiked up the large, boulder-strewn mountain until we came level with the ship. It was strange what a little elevation could do. We could throw rocks and hit it, but it was just far enough away from Kalaran's face for us to be unable to board without the crew tossing down a ladder for us to climb up.

Thecily whistled a few times, waking a sleeping sentry who was immediately stammering apologies. The ship lowered, kissing the hard ground. A boarding plank, complete with rope-lined handrails, was shoved out from the floating ship.

Unlike Thran's Leaf, Thecily's ship was far narrower and more loaded with uniformed, burly men and women. The whistle had woken more than the sentry, and once we'd all boarded, a dozen or so shipmates were waiting on deck for us.

Each one was armed with a short sword despite having just woken up. Behind them, axes that looked just as capable of being used in combat as for cutting rigging lined the underside of the railing every few paces.

The rest of the deck was a mess of ropes holding down the envelopes filled with secret gas that Wydvis used to keep itself, and its ships, airborne. The interwoven wood lattice to provide maximum strength and minimal weight framed the odd ship, just as you'd expect. But unlike the bow shot width of Captain Andreska's airship, this one was barely wide enough for six men standing shoulder to shoulder. It was also long. Incredibly so. It seemed to stretch back twice as far as any airship I'd seen before. This ship was less like an airship and more like a flying sword. It even had what could be described as a pommel on the back end, complete with a stern shaped like a cross guard housing what appeared to be quarters for the ship's officers.

The bridge was raised and slightly wider than the rest of the ship. It was also enclosed. As I took in more of the boat, I noticed a small ballista at the airship's bow. I'd only read about these. A gasp came from behind me, and I turned.

Cassiopia was staring at the ballista as well, and I'd only seen her with that kind of glint in her eye after we'd first met, and she'd helped us escape the octomantis. It was almost how a lover looked at their partner after a long time apart. But in her case, with a bit more feral ferocity layered in. She rushed over to it, cooing as she examined every inch of the contraption.

Thecily looked to me with an unspoken question.

"She really likes to hunt big game. I think she just found a new toy to get her some sea monsters." I coughed awkwardly as Thecily shot me a quick glare. "I'd let her use it if you get the chance. Cass has a knack for shooting at things, that's all." I smiled.

Shazina set Argo down, and the uniformed, hard-looking men and women seemed to melt as one. A wave of interest followed the sniffing dog as it explored its way in an arbitrary zigzag to the first shipman who could be seen almost trembling with anticipation.

Argo's nose bumped into the closest man, and he lost all militaristic composure. With an excited laugh, he dropped down, reaching out to Argo.

Momentarily startled, Argo hopped back, yipped, and then immediately warmed to the man. With a fierce tail wag, he jumped onto the man's boot, happy to make a new friend. The crew's remaining discipline broke, and the whole group crowded around the puppy, each being sniffed and excitedly yipped at as Argo met, greeted, and loved on each new person.

"Godspawning dog," Thecily signed with an eye roll. "I just lost my ship to an animal. Looks like the kid and puppy are now in charge."

A thought hit me, and I turned to Thecily. "Aren't you the first mate? What if the captain doesn't agree to all of this?"

A few snickers from the shipmates added to my confusion. Thecily offered me a condescending smile. "Oh leafer boy, this isn't Thran's Leaf. Volant's mommy is one of the few captains that actually does the captaining. I'm not even sure if we brought our captain along. Admittedly, he's a bit of a coward and wouldn't agree with this, but he also doesn't run the ship's day to day. That's me."

One of the men turned from Argo briefly. "He's here, Thecily. Just been below deck the whole time. Last I saw, he was drinking himself into oblivion."

"There you go," Thecily said, gesturing to the man who spoke. "Our dear captain Charn is in the cups and out of the way. If we die, we die. If we don't, he'll make some money, and maybe I'll even get my own commission."

Insley slid in next to me, close enough to brush fingertips. A little jolt went through my body at the contact, and I flushed a little as Thecily's eyes narrowed at the dark-skinned healer. "Everything on the up and up?" she asked me, not even batting an eye at Thecily's coldness.

"Aye, all good," I said, reaching out and squeezing her hand briefly. The boldness surprised me, but she seemed to take it in stride, returning the squeeze and flashing a warm smile my way.

At the same time, Thecily had turned to Volant, who was whispering something in her ear. They had a hushed conversation, going back and forth before Thecily slapped Volant on the shoulder and laughed, nodding her head while Volant looked relieved. She turned to the crew, who was still playing with the dog. "Cast off you lazy godspawns. The dog's stuck on the ship with you. It'll be there when you're off duty."

"Where to?" asked one of the now disappointed shipmates.

"Tryst," she replied with another exaggerated roll of the eyes. "We've apparently become a taxi service, and our first stop is to see if Volant's Soft Stepper girlfriend wants to join. From there, we'll be headed towards the causeway. Then, across it."

The crew, as one, froze. They all turned back to look at Thecily, who waved them on to whatever tasks require their attention to be on our way. The silence lasted only a moment longer, and then they were back to business as usual. The crew bustled around the ship, checking ropes, tying down loose crates, and generally acting busy while Thecily took us to the back of the ship.

"We don't have much in the way of extra guest quarters. So, you'll be bunking with everyone else down here." Thecily pointed to a long line of hammocks, double stacked, stretching down half the airship's length. "Of course, I have a private cabin back on the stern. Nil can show you where it is." She winked at me, and it was Insley's turn to go cold. "Speaking of, you're welcome anytime, old friend. I could always use a rematch," she paused, "for Kingdoms." She chuckled to herself, continuing with the tour of Sky Wolf.

We went through the ship, seeing a galley that was better stocked and arranged than Andreska's ship. We almost lost Martino right then and there, but we convinced him to come along and return after we'd finished the tour and been airborne for a bit. There was an armory that made up in lack of variety with quantity. The walls bristled with so many arrows that I figured if we ran into any monsters in Shazina's homeland, we'd be able to take care of them with relative ease.

Thecily's right-hand man, Toman, was at the wheel up on the deck. He nodded when the group of us came up and brightened a little at the site of Argo. Dendra seemed about to burst with questions, but her sisters reigned her in as well, using the same arguments they'd had for Martino. Toman noticed and grinned his own little self-satisfied smile.

At the ship's prow, just below the front-facing ballista, a small cargo room with a fallpack cage sat in it. Volant and I exchanged fist bumps when we saw this, but Thecily got deadly serious when we all had taken a look.

"This room is for emergencies only. And more than likely, if something happens to this ship, you won't be getting a fallpack either way. We only have enough for half of the crew. Occasionally we'll use one or two for quick trips to the ground, but otherwise, they're essentially ballast. Everyone on this ship understands that if we go down, we all go down together." She closed and locked the door behind her as we left.

The ship's nose aimed up a little, and the crew unfurled the vast sails. Soon we were skimming along above the treetops, headed for Tryst's golden smudge of plains on the horizon.

Chapter Eleven

Shazina found me as everyone was picking out hammocks. Insley and I had grabbed a pair near the starboard wall, awkwardly bumbling about the process of making it seem unintentional that we wanted to share an intimate space.

"You're overdue for practice," Shazina said, practically emotionless.

I groaned in response. "Come on. I've been beaten up, nearly killed multiple times over, and have barely rested."

Instead of responding, she handed Argo over to Insley, a pointed look at our two hammocks. "Up top, I'm going to meditate with you."

We found a spot out of the way near the ballista. With simple, efficient grace, she sat down and began to breathe in and out slowly. Clouds drifted by us, and I had to admit that there were worse places to practice meditating and potentially unlock a lost secret.

I joined her, beginning the process of centering my mind and breath. It wasn't getting easier, exactly. But the process seemed to be coming to me more quickly. In short order, I'd discarded everything about the two women I was on an airship with for the foreseeable future. I dismissed the gentle breeze tickling the stubble of my nearly shaved head. I was able to even accept and move on from the various pains that seemed to continually plague me lately.

Skill trickled in, just the smallest amount. Instead of willing it past the barrier I'd created in my head, I tried to make the Skill manifest inside my mind directly. No shuttling around like herded cattle. Just straight to the end result, the same way I did whenever I normally used my Learner abilities. It felt like I was trying to push my hand through wet dough. I started to lose the calm, patient mindset as frustration colored my failure to do what I knew was possible. The Ukiyo way slipped further from my grasp, and the further it fell away, the more that frustration took over. Finally, I punched the deck, completely breaking my concentration and letting a fist-shaped trickle of Skill dent the wood.

"That isn't productive," Shazina said, one eye open. "Start again."

"Left hand," I muttered. Again, I focused my thoughts, leading with my breath, and discarding everything else. Once I felt my center return, and I could maintain a steady heart rate, I tried again. This time, I ignored summoning the Skill and just focused on crossing that barrier into Ukiyo. Without Skill muddying the waters, it was surprisingly easy to reach it. I felt like I was looking in on my mind, seeing the currents that drove my limbs and body. While there, I let the trickle of Skill in, finding it easy to feed directly to my internal manipulations.

I flexed first my arms, feeling the Skill bolster their strength. Then a cut I didn't even realize was there split open, pain spiking up my arm. Somehow, I reflexively pushed the Skill towards it, shutting the pain down and away. My mind cleared as if nothing was there. "Shazina!" I gasped, surprised at the contrast of no pain. "I made my arm heal!"

She opened one eye, enough to give me such a skeptical look that it stopped my excitement dead in its tracks. "You can't heal yourself with Ukiyo," she said. "You can tell your body to ignore certain things though, like cold and pain, or heat and tiredness. That does not mean it is not there."

I looked down and saw the wound that had split open. She was right. I didn't feel anything, but it was still bleeding. "Well, that's interesting."

We kept at it until Cassiopia showed up with some leftovers from everyone else's lunch. In reality, she'd only brought the food because she was coming to examine the ballista. The excitement was still there, and she'd been admirably patient, having waited this long before interrupting us.

Despite the lack of any leaps in ability, I felt good. The Ukiyo was something I was beginning to be able to count on in myself.

Volant and Thecily strolled up, taking Shazina's place next to me. Despite Thecily's purple eyes and red hair making her a dead ringer for Brod heritage, she looked more like Volant's people than he did.

"Did you know actual sky pirates are back, Nil?" he asked. His whole body looked like it was vibrating with barely contained excitement. A lopsided grin also gave a window into his childhood, and you could practically see the days spent fighting with wooden swords and yelling sky pirate chants.

Thecily dampened the moment with a soft thump to the back of Volant's head. "This is nothing to be so giddy about. They're seriously bad news."

My curiosity was hooked and got the better of me. "I've only heard Volant's stories. Why are they bad?"

Thecily first looked at Volant and then at me. "You two are unbelievable. Seriously?" She huffed, actually annoyed. "They're godspawning pirates! They murder people and steal their coin and whatever else they want. They'll swoop in, turn a few people into pincushions, steal everyone's goods, and light a carriage or house or other airship on fire before disappearing off into the clouds."

Volant still grinned, though my heart sank a little. Just another piece of childhood joy being shown the ugly truth. Then everything clicked, and I nearly slapped myself for how much of an idiot I was.

"That's why this ship exists. You're not just bodyguards for hire. You're supposed to be stopping those kinds of people," I finished, gesturing at the ballista and battle-worthy airship we were riding through the sky.

"And I thought you were bad at kingdoms," Thecily returned with a small clap. "A coin for the smart boy. Yes, we scour the skies for these types. They don't appear all that often. This one though, pain in the deck. Can't find them, and they're god-spawning well supplied."

"I'm sure someone will get them," I paused, gesturing between Volant and I. "If we all come back from this in one piece, we'll even help."

Volant glared, flicking his fingers at me. Not a chance, he said.

She caught the exchange and raised her eyebrows but didn't say anything. "I guess it doesn't really matter right now. That said, get your Learners up to speed. We need to be ready for those creatures."

Grimacing, I stood up. "No rest for the beautiful," I groaned.

"Don't think that's how the line goes," Volant added cheerfully. "Nor that it applies to you, oh fearless leader."

There ended up being an actual Learner staffed on the ship, along with the triplets and I. It was a little embarrassing to be probing a graduate of the school for a demonstration, but it wasn't long before I realized just how far I'd come with so much practice compared to someone that'd gone a more traditional route.

His name was Craig, and he was nearly as embarrassed about his lack of practical application as I was trying to teach him.

First, I showed them the shield-like web of Skill I'd stumbled upon the other day. Diedra was the first to pick it up, stopping a handful of arrows tossed at her. Volant, who was watching with Shazina, cheered and clapped enthusiastically when she did it. She was proud, but the only person she looked towards for encouragement was Craig.

Joy was by far the weakest on the Skill front, not even able to pool enough Skill to make a noticeable impact on her immediate surroundings.

"It's about your willpower, short and simple," I said. "You've studied the math. You have the belief in yourself that unlocks the Skill. Now you just need to make it a reality. Work that mental muscle until you can convert it into something tangible."

She'd been glaring at her hand in frustration and slit her eyes in my direction for a brief moment. "I get the theory, Nil. It's the will that won't turn into Skill."

"Then you need to strengthen your willpower," I said. "It won't be fun. Sit in a tub of ice. Put your favorite food in front of you, and don't eat for a day or two. Exercise till you feel like you can't go on, and then keep going. Whatever it takes to make your mind stronger, you need to do."

Shazina chimed in at that. "Meditation helps on that front. That's how the Ukiyo works."

"There's your homework then," I pointed at each and one of them in turn, "Get a long meditation in before you sleep. We work on this again tomorrow."

It'd been a long day, and I was ready for bed myself. But while everyone else was filing back to the more active parts of the ship, Volant brought me up short.

"That's too nice of a sword for you not to know how to use it," Volant said, gesturing at Berjio's weapon I had belted to my waist.

I'd nearly forgotten it was there. "Come on, Volant. I'm tired. You all can't just make me train on anything and everything just because I'm awake."

He drew his sword, the rapier his mother had given him as his only possession of a father he'd never met. "Ah, that's where you're mistaken!" He swished the blade through the air. "It's time you learned to fence properly."

We spent the remaining daylight dancing back and forth, parrying slow thrusts, counterattacking even more slowly, and generally doing our absolute best to turn our muscles into pudding.

Volant corrected my arm position a hundred times over. The movements were nothing like the axe or daggers I customarily used. All the force came from the blade itself, or how you pushed with your legs. It was counter-intuitive half the time. And the movements flowed. You thrust in a certain way, and you had only a few options on what you did next.

If I'd been tired before, this was a whole different beast entirely. Even my clothes felt too heavy on me by the time Volant relented and let me head back to the bunk room.

Insley was in the hammock above mine, reading by the light of a cleverly shielded hand lamp hanging just about her space. She shifted when I trudged up, looking me up and down.

"Been busy?" she asked with a hint of hurt.

I nodded, flopping into the lower hammock and groaning softly. "Aye. Too much so," I admitted. "Everyone wanted a piece of me."

"Thecily sure seems to." Her voice was soft, but had a sharp edge to it.

I looked up, my brain telling me to step softly around this topic. "It's not what it seems. She and I, that is."

"So you two didn't and don't have a thing?" Her tone was even softer and more deadly.

"Umm, well, we did, but now we don't, I don't think," I stammered out. I nearly gave up right then and there, after such a smooth performance.

Luckily, Insley relented. "Your past is your problem. I don't even know why I agreed to this. You seemed interesting. And you needed help. And you seemed to have really seen me, unlike most of the people who just want something from me. It was refreshing."

I waited a moment, processing what she'd said. "I'm glad you came," I finally responded after the moment stretched. "I think it's a horrible idea that you came, but I'm glad you did." With more confidence than I felt, I reached up to hold her hand. She smiled and let me, and I settled back down into the swaying hammock. If she said anything else, I missed it as I was asleep almost immediately.

A few days of intense training with Shazina paired with defensive training for all five of us Learners on board and sparring with Volant and whoever else wanted to work up a sweat blurred the few days of travel it took to reach the center Tryst.

Luckily for us, the weather had been forgiving and clear, which also allowed multiple Soft Stepper tribes to converge on our low flying ship. Wydvis airships were uncommon, and the militarized ones were downright rare on the plains.

Three of Thecily's crew, and Volant who'd somehow wrangled his way into getting a fallpack, leaped off the ship to go anchor us. Once their work was done, the deck crew reeled the Sky Wolf down to hover just high enough to release boarding planks to the anchor team.

Despite their original commission to protect the council, Thecily's crew seemed to have brought along plenty of tradeable goods for just the occasion. A festive atmosphere began to take shape as the day grew on. Qaewin wasn't around, though when word spread, a familiar Soft Stepper came by. She had just seen Qaewin the day before and had a good idea where she'd be. For a few coins, she left on her zymph with a promise to return the next day with Qaewin in tow.

Volant fist-bumped me after she left, a giddy excitement making him shake like Argo when he got his paws on something particularly delicious. The poor cloud dancer looked ready to chase after the girl and ride out with her.

Before either of us got much further than a few paces, Argo skidded into Volant's boots with a furiously wagging tail. Volant bent and picked up the dog, eliciting such a chorus of admiration from the surrounding crowd of Soft Steppers you'd have thought one of the gods had dropped in among us.

People pressed in from every side, wanting to pet the dog. Someone piped up, telling a neighbor a wildly implausible story about the puppy of Kalaran, but managed to get enough details right about the riot surrounding Argo that I was modestly surprised.

"How in the godspawn," I started before a not too gentle tap on my arm had me turning around to find Shazina.

She had her head cocked to the side in a mix of impatience and a slight hint of annoyance. "Training doesn't stop because something more fun is an option. Gather your people. Meet me back up deck."

She turned to Volant, giving him a shake of the head before taking Argo back and heading on board.

"That kid is a monster," Volant whispered, admiration and awe making it a compliment.

Helplessly, I turned to my friend. "I can tell her no, right?"

He chuckled, pushing me after her. "I don't think that'd be wise. But, I'll join. I could use some kata practice."

On deck, Shazina had already gathered the other Learners. They all looked the same way I felt. Roasted meat, fresh bread, and other more exotic smells wafted over us to the background laughter of other people having fun. It was practically torture to sit on the boat and be silent and still.

Shazina took in everyone's unhappiness and narrowed her eyes. "If you're serious about becoming better, sacrifice is key." She waved a dismissive hand towards the Soft Steppers and festivities. "To intentionally strengthen your will is the goal. This is the best time to do it."

Volant had begun his kata, transfixing Shazina mid-rant. She stood, staring with uncharacteristic childlike wonder.

"We're doing that." She said it like Volant had unlocked a secret to something unimaginably life-altering.

She blurred a little, the tell-tale sign she'd summoned a lot of Skill into her Ukiyo. She fell into step next to him, pivoting and turning, matching his every honey slow arm strike and complicated triple-step foot movement. She flowed, as gracefully as if she'd been doing it the entirety of her albeit short life.

After a particular flow, she stopped, turning to us. "Why are you waiting? This is perfect! Focus on your breath, enjoy the strain on your muscles, meditate with the movement!"

Craig and I fell in next to them, slowly pivoting and stepping a move behind Volant, who'd started back over from the beginning. This Wydvis meditation kata was part intimidation dance, part combat practice, or so Volant had told me.

Sky pirating used to be the primary profession in the old days of Wydvis history. But they were still a community, just a bit more warmongering than your average one. Katas had been their supposedly secret edge.

The sisters slowly joined in but struggled to maintain their breathwork and clear mind while following the movements.

As they struggled along, Craig and I too began to lose our focus. Before any of us could quit, Shazina stopped. "Don't stop. Draw in Skill, hold it, and keep going," she barked, dropping back into the slow flow with Volant.

Despite his near-death experience, he was bouncing back well. His kata was smooth, measured, and sure. He barely hesitated when the flow demanded he use his injured shoulder, and the whole while was grinning fiercely, eyes shut as he focused entirely on the movements.

I did as Shazina said and willed the energy to life. Skill charged through me, and I let it ride, pushing it through my body to match the kata's rhythm. We drove a dagger-shaped hand in a long, arcing motion. I let Skill follow the movement, slowly sending it down my arm until it tingled at my fingertips in a dangerous, ozone-scented spark before bringing it back in and along the length of my body, following the footwork until I had a knee raised in preparation for a kick.

I took a moment, finding the barrier between my external Learner and internal Ukiyo. I pushed the Skill or maybe drew it in. It felt like both until it left my body and entered what could only be described as my mind.

A whole new sensation met each movement. It was like I'd been out of sync with my body and had suddenly found the proper ratio. I shifted my breath. Widened my feet. And danced to the wind like Volant, finally understanding the true movements of his people's pirate kata.

When Volant finished, opening his eyes as if it was the most beautiful day he'd ever experienced, the rest of us, excepting Shazina, were trembling, out of breath, and ecstatic.

"That," Dendra started.

"Was," Diedra continued.

"Incredible!" Joy finished, flushed and massaging her bad leg.

All three beamed, having found something in this kind of physical meditation that had been lacking the past few days.

Craig even seemed thrilled, despite still having trouble shaking off the fact that a dropout, has-been thief was trying to teach a full, accredited Learner how to use Skill.

"That was incredible! I've never been able to hold much Skill for longer than a breath or two. And I've never flowed as cleanly as that," he said. Smiling to himself, he sat down and began kneading his trembling limbs.

Shazina allowed us off the ship after the experience, but only with the promise we'd continue that evening. Martino took Joy to explore some culinary delight he'd found with Cassiopia, and Dendra and Diedra took Craig to see the zymphs.

Thecily was nowhere to be seen, and something about the pirate kata made me want to find her and test the sparks that seemed to still be between us.

But then Insley appeared, quiet yet confident, kind eyes and a warm smile for both Volant and I, with none of Thecily's brash, self-centered attitude.

"I was watching from the bridge. There are some crates you can climb to get on top of the roof over there. Gives you a nice comfy view of everything." She said it modestly, but I could tell she was proud of her little adventure and spying.

"You're quite the surprise, you know," I told her while gesturing towards the Soft Stepper tents that had sprung up as if from thin air all around the ship. "Volant and I spent a little time with these people, and we've got to find you some swok."

***

Twilight descended on Volant and I's sparring session. The sword was giving me an embarrassing amount of trouble to master. To add to the difficulty, I'd drunk my weight in swok and felt like I'd vomit any moment. I'd gone for quantity and quality with Insley this afternoon, and now I was dealing with the consequences.

I flicked the tip of the blade out at Volant, but he turned his wrist just slightly enough to slide his sword down the length of mine, allowing him to get in my guard and tap me on the chest with a finger.

"Sloppy," he said, stepping back. "Try this, tree hugger." He moved to my side, bringing his rapier up, and pointed at an imaginary opponent. As he lunged, he twisted his wrist in a small semi-circle outward, making the tip of the blade swing under and around.

"I don't get it," I responded honestly.

"Here, try and stop me," he said, facing back to me.

Slowly, he lunged, his point headed straight for my belly. I brought my arm in, swinging my blade across the path of his. Before it made contact, he'd already twisted his wrist as he did earlier. My defense met empty air as the tip of his sword dropped below and around my block, coming up at my heart and from the outside.

The motion was minute, but by the time I'd recovered to block again, he had the tip resting gently against my collarbone.

"See? Simple." Volant bowed, receiving applause from the growing audience who'd stayed for the evening's entertainment.

"Always showing off," a soft, gentle voice said as if whispered to the wind.

Volant spun, face splitting into a huge, ecstatic grin. He rushed over to the girl who'd spoken, wrapping her up in a massive hug and spinning her in circles before finally setting her down and planting a huge kiss despite the crowd of people.

Catcalls and whistles exploded as Qaewin kissed him back, turning a bright red despite her tanned skin and the limited lighting. She punched him in the shoulder lightly, and he pretended to stagger back, wounded.

The crowd booed, and I joined in with them. Qaewin gave in, kissing Volant once more to the wild enthusiasm of Thecily's crew. After that, everyone dispersed, heading to find entertainment with the Soft Steppers, sleep, or left-over food in the galley. Qaewin came over, hugging me warmly. After checking us over, she turned and slapped Volant. A real slap, not the gentle, loving, or playful kind.

Surprised, Volant took a step back, raising a hand to his cheek in confusion. "What was that about?"

"You scared me to death!" she hissed. "And you," she spun to point a threatening finger at me. "I had to find out through the grapevine that he almost died?"

I raised my hands in surrender, putting the pieces together. "Aye, that was an oversight," I agreed.

Volant just smiled, wrapping her up in another hug. "I'm sorry we left you. We were in the middle of that battle, and Nil and I were up next on the kill list. It was safer for you if we left. And far safer for us. Then things went a little sideways, as you know."

She relaxed, hugging him back. "I just wanted to know you knew it was a mistake. But don't think I'm letting you out of my sight again. Now, what have you been up to?"

It was then that Insley arrived, Argo trailing behind her. "The famous Soft Stepper of Volant's?" She asked, coming up to us. She had a book in one hand, and I figured she'd been reading down below until the crowd up top took their noise everywhere else on the ship.

Qaewin flashed a timid smile. "It's the other way around. He's mine, though I'm keeping the options open on my end."

We all laughed, Volant nodding along and laughing the loudest.

"There's four of us. Let's get a game of Kingdoms going while we catch you up," I suggested. "Insley, you play?"

"Oh, I've dabbled," she replied airily.

A board, awkwardly borrowed from Thecily, was set for a two-on-two match. "Nature and Nurture?" Qaewin asked.

No one objected, so we began, Insley and I falling into step with each other's moves without even discussing it. Qaewin played exceptionally well but didn't cover Volant's flank, allowing us to decimate him while her pieces were stuck on the other side of the board.

During the play, we brought her up to speed on Volant's near death and everything that happened in Kalaran, leading up to our attempt at the causeway crossing.

She paused, mid-play in a spectacular defense against Insley's nearly single-handed onslaught. "You can't be serious."

"We are, aren't we Nil?" he said with chagrin.

"That we are," I waved my hand for her to play.

Qaewin placed her piece, moving a Natural around one of Volant's dead pieces. Insley responded with a Learner of her own, finishing out a trap none of us had even seen her building. Three Learner pieces had a line of sight on Qaewin's piece if she moved out of her space.

With a surprised expression, Qaewin sat back, bringing the whole game into focus while she thought. "So, you came all this way, dragging an entire airship, a bunch of friends, and detouring them all just to bring me along on a guaranteed one-way trip to being eaten by sea monsters?"

Volant didn't take the bait, giving her a toothy smile. "That sums it up!"

She gave a theatrical sigh, looking at Insley and giving her the why-are-boys-such-idiots eye roll. Insley jabbed a thumb my way, lifting her hands in mock defeat.

"Fine," Qaewin said after the girls both had a laugh. "I'm in. You guys have had far too many scrapes without me. It's time someone kept you out of trouble."

Insley gestured to one of my pieces, and I moved it back around the board's outside corner. The game was over. It was the first time I'd ever legitimately won a game of Kingdoms. Everyone but Insley looked surprised, and she just cleared the board while Qaewin watched on in mild appreciation.

"Another round?" she asked.

I gave Insley a fist bump and nodded. "This winning is fun! I see why everyone normally likes to play against me."

We played until everyone else had fallen asleep and then stayed up talking through the night about any inconsequential thing we could, keeping our minds off the fact that our lives could very well be over before the stolen moon was full again.

I fell asleep at some point in the middle of stargazing with Insley, making up new constellations and making wishes on the occasional shooting star while lying on the deck. Volant and Qaewin were close enough to see, but far enough for us all to have some privacy. It was a perfect evening, and I drifted off, wishing it'd never end.

Chapter Twelve

Early morning sun and the bounce of heavy feet walking on woven wood woke me. Insley was nestled in my arm but was coming to life as well. One of the crew was making rounds on the boat and had been kind enough to leave us alone at the ungodly early hour. Volant and Qaewin had disappeared sometime in the night, no doubt finding somewhere more comfortable to sleep.

Helping Insley to her feet, I looked out over the side of Sky Wolf and saw life beginning to stir among the Soft Steppers. Zymphs were actively moving around, and early risers rekindled a few fires. There was no reason to stay the extra day now that we had found Qaewin.

Insley gave me a light kiss on the cheek while I was lost in thought. Before I could turn and say anything, she was already moving down the deck. Almost the moment she disappeared below, Thecily appeared, heading my way.

Thecily had dressed to impress, and she knew it. She sauntered over to me, lean arms exposed, a tight-fitting vest with a plunging neckline begging the imagination to be involved. A matching, unbelievably tight pair of pants outlined muscled legs that were a testament to a rigorous training discipline.

She'd braided her red hair in a similar fashion to the Soft Stepper style. I swallowed hard, trying to yank my eyes away. But I couldn't. If Insley would have seen me now, she'd have left the ship and headed back to Kalaran in disgust.

Embarrassment mixed with other emotions as Thecily stopped in front of me, a sultry tilt to her head.

"There you are," she said. "I had thought you'd be stopping by last night. Seems I may have some competition, though."

I fumbled for words before finally turning away from the subject entirely. "Qaewin is on board. She just needs to bring her zymph up, and we can head out whenever you're ready."

She waited a moment before responding, tapping the intricate hilt of a saber she had belted across her bare midsection, which only seemed to reinforce her chiseled physique. It looked like quite the upgrade since the floating market blade that'd broken on her. "I didn't realize she'd be bringing along one of those cats. Do they do well on airships?"

Puzzled, I gave a non-committal nod. "Maybe? I'm no expert."

"Better not scratch my ship, is all. Also, I'll see you up here tonight. I could use a little of my own sparring practice." With that, she turned back, a too casual roll of her hips that it had to be something she regularly practiced left me watching her walk away with a pang of uneasy guilt.

I paced up and down the deck, trying to focus my mind but only finding my thoughts drifting to the two women. My thoughts were interrupted by Qaewin and Volant arriving at the ramp, trailed by Slandash and a handful of zymphs.

I rushed down the ramp, intercepting the oncoming older man. He had more wrinkles, but otherwise, he was the same small man with more energy than his body seemed to know what to do with.

"Good to see you, Nil!" Slandash said after we hugged. "I hear you boys are going to try and get my daughter killed, heh?"

I paused, catching Volant's eye. He looked less than happy.

"Well, it's more that we figured Qaewin wouldn't forgive us if we left her behind," I said slowly, testing the waters.

Slandash's face turned stony, the joy at seeing me fading a fair bit. "You're right. She would've murdered you both." He paused, looking meaningfully between the three of us. "I've already argued with them all morning, so I'll save it. Just know, if she doesn't come back in one piece, the last piece of joy in my life will be gone, and my death will be on your hands as well." He looked down at his hands, a slight tremor shaking them before he regained his composure.

"Slandash," I began but was cut off with a wave of his hand.

"It's fine. I've made my peace as much as I can. You all just come back safely. I don't care about anything else." He turned, gave Qaewin a final hug. "Be safe, my daughter. I can't lose you."

As he was striding away, he turned one last time. "May the gods ignore you. Wander well!"

The zymphs seemed agitated at Slandash's exit but stayed put.

Qaewin wiped a tear from her eye before scratching her zymph, Chloe, behind the ear.

"I recognize your zymph, but these other ones?" I asked.

She paused, swallowing hard before answering. "The battle cost a lot of Soft Stepper lives. These are just some of the ones who lost riders. Mostly, they're kin to mine." She shrugged. "I'm not sure why they followed us, but they seem to want to come along."

At the top of the ramp, a comedy ensued with the felines. An uncharacteristic nervousness came over each one of them as they boarded, something in their cat instincts telling them this ship was going to be a whole different experience.

After boarding, they all hid below deck. That was almost the end of it, but when we lifted off at midday, the enormous panther like predators were practically inconsolable, hair bristling, bodies flattened out in the hold, or claws latched on to the sturdiest piece of wood available.

Thecily was in an uproar about the claw marks they were leaving all over her boat when this happened, but not even she was brave enough to try to do anything about it. Even a terrified zymph was more than a bit worrying for any person. It was a wonder they hadn't eaten all of us humans and ruled Balteris on their own.

Qaewin's zymph came crawling across the deck, arms and legs splayed like it was scaling a completely vertical cliff face. When she saw Chloe coming her way, Qaewin hurried over from the conversation we were having to console her mount. A few whispered words and a long, gentle rubdown and the cat finally relaxed enough to stand up normally.

While I worked with the Learners and Shazina, Qaewin and Volant coaxed each zymph on deck, helping them find their sky legs and overcome their fear. It took nearly a day for them to get each one taken care of, and by the time we were supposed to meet for our nightly sparring session, Volant was exhausted.

Thinking that we'd both earned some rest, we agreed to take the evening off to recover, and work on our hobbies. He'd been itching to get back to some drawings, and I wanted to pick up one of the books Insley had brought on board. Instead of reading, I ended up huddled in the hammock with Insley, just talking about reading. Despite the perfect moment, heated discussion about favorite books, and comfortably close quarters, my thoughts couldn't help but stray to Thecily and her standing invite to her cabin.

As if thinking of her made her appear, the captain of the ship found us, a pair of training swords in hand. The heavy, dulled versions Volant and I had used to grow stronger early after fleeing Kalaran the first time.

Unenthusiastically, I sparred with Thecily, mostly playing defense. It didn't take long for her to see my hear wasn't in it. With a disgusted roll of her eyes, she took the sword back, and went to find a new partner.

***

We were mid-lesson the following day when we flew directly into a storm cloud. The sisters, Craig, and I had all improved noticeably with our Skill shields. We'd not tried anything major, but we found that with the right curve of our hands and a deflective twist, we could knock projectiles away without having to worry about being strong or heavy enough to withstand the impact. Thunder rolled as lightning flashed in the distance.

It was unnerving, to say the least. Within moments of hitting the front wall of the storm, the entire world seemed to shift. Clouds shifted all around us, blotting out the sun and turning everything into a messy color-washed smudge. We couldn't see more than twenty paces in any direction, the clouds and rain were so thick.

I was about to tell everyone to head below deck and we'd practice some meditation down there when a flash of lightning illuminated the tip of a mast coming out of the clouds below us on the starboard side.

I blinked rain out of my eyes, looking up. As the phantom mast grew, it sprouted a blood-red sail rippling with storm wind. I could see an airship's envelope swinging in and out of view in the storm clouds above. Entirely confused, I watched as a full-sized airship, a dagger compared to the Sky Wolf's sword-like shape, fully materialize next to us.

A bell began to ring furiously from the bridge, an alarm if I'd ever heard one. At the sound of the bell, the dark wood of the sleek airship leaped from the clouds. Its deck was swarming with far too many people for a ship that size. Actual godspawning sky pirates. Arrows were launched and buzzed like a hundred hornets as they arced towards us.

"Deflection shields!" I shouted at the stunned Learners behind me.

The training we'd been hammering at kicked in, and each one of them, even Joy, who'd shown the most improvement despite still being woefully underprepared, threw out their hands towards the oncoming barrage. We held our hands out, fear fueling our tired wills with new energy.

Against the backdrop of the ringing bell and roaring pirates dozens of paces away, we scattered the deadly hail of arrows, saving both our lives and those of everyone on the top deck of the ship. The sky pirates aimed a second barrage at our balloon, but we batted it aside. A third wave was in the air before our impromptu counterattack had even shattered the second.

We managed to knock these away as well, though we were so worn out that we'd only deflected the more direct half. Several shafts embedded themselves along the ship's side, and two separate screams announced the arrows striking a pair of the crew, though they were nowhere near us.

Everyone, including whoever had been ringing the bell, the pirates on the smaller ship, and the crew on the deck that had seen the display of Skill took a moment to process it in dumb silence. Only the storm continued to howl its rage, uncaring of the feat we'd just performed.

Joy dropped to her knees, vomiting from the effort. Her sisters seemed about to collapse, and Craig had a faraway look that was one step away from passing out.

I cursed softly, wishing I'd carried the Toron stones with me. With just one of those in hand, we'd be still standing and ready for more.

As it was, I barely had anything but dregs left in my wheelhouse, and it looked like I'd need to save that for close-quarters fighting. The stones were down at the other end of the ship and down two flights of stairs in a locked chest.

That was time we couldn't spare.

Suddenly, the deck disappeared underneath our feet, weightlessness grabbing my stomach and making it feel like it'd shrunk two sizes as I was freefalling half a pace above the floor.

Before any of us could so much as yell, we slammed back into the ship, flattening against the springy wood as the nose dive turned into an upward sprint. Thecily must have taken the wheel and was either determined to kill her crew through violent, jarring motion, or she was trying to gain advantage and distance on the smaller ship.

I sent Craig with the sisters, the four of them stumbling in a mess of limbs and momentum. They headed across to the nearest stairwell beneath the ballista, disappearing below deck before Thecily's mad sailing threw them overboard.

We steadied long enough for the pirate ship to swing up level with us. At the same moment, Volant, Cassiopia, and a number of the crew appeared at the other end of the ship, all armed with bows and a forest's worth of arrows.

A small smile pulled at the corner of my lip as I saw Cassiopia pull back her string. She sighted and loosed. I watched the custom arrow punch through one man and skewer a second. She had another shot in the air, with the same result.

Whoever was piloting the enemy ship realized they were in grave danger from these archers and swung in, looking like they were going to ram right into Volant and the others.

The crew got off one volley, but the ship was moving too fast and high up for any of the arrows to reach its balloons high above us.

Just before impact, it pivoted, far faster than our huge ship could turn, and bumped almost lovingly into the side of our ship. Wooden planks fell across the deck's railing, locking the smaller vessel to ours with curved, hook-like contraptions at the end of the boards.

Men and women, wearing black leathers and even a bit of armor, began flooding across the ship. More pirates started roping in from the smaller ship's mast, landing all over the Sky Wolf's deck.

Simple hatchets spaced along the underside of the side railing in a sheltered alcove. Whether to cut ropes or repel invaders, I wasn't sure. But we'd definitely be using them for the latter today. I reached down, taking one in each hand. They were heavy and unbalanced, thick, sharp heads outweighing the shafts.

They'd do.

I checked my sword, making sure it was in place should I need it, and rushed toward the nearest invader, matching the storm's thundering rage with my own cry.

The pirate was focused on Volant's group, who were trying to shift over to hand-to-hand. Despite their military-style ship, they still weren't prepared for such a quick boarding party, and a number of them couldn't let go of their bows.

I dropped to a knee and spun with arms outstretched as I half slid by my target. Both hatchets bit in, the first in the back of the leg, the second in the front, both ripping away with the momentum of the spin.

I was up, only slightly dizzy, as the man collapsed behind me in a soft moan. Before me, Volant was with Cassiopia at the center of a drastically smaller number of defenders than there'd been a moment ago. The hesitation with the bows must have cost Thecily's crew.

Cassiopia was still firing arrows into the pirates, taking one down with each shot. But she had to aim carefully and wasn't making a large enough dent before Volant and her were overwhelmed. For his part, Volant was working admirably with his rapier next to the crew who'd managed to set up a perimeter.

I began to move towards them when a fresh wave of pirates jumped between the ship, these looking less like an advanced scouting party and more like the main force. They were better armed, and at their center was a huge man, tall, leanly muscled, and wearing an incredibly ostentatious hat, feather included. I skidded to a stop, taking in the new pile of people between the rest of the defending crew and me.

Two of the pirates detached themselves, drawing blades and coming my way. I tightened the grip on my two hatchets and rolled my shoulders.

I attacked first, feinting at one before whipping the heavy-headed hatchet at the other. It spun, connecting with the pirate and bringing him down with a surprised expression frozen in place as he dropped.

The second pirate paused, trying to work out the math on whether this was a good idea or not. I swung, overhand and ugly, not giving him any time to think.

He dodged.

I pivoted past him, and he delivered a kick to my kidneys while I went by. He swung his blade in a follow-up, but I caught it against the hatchet's shaft. Using the leverage to twist the weapon out of his hand, I then looped back around, smashing the backside of his head with the hammer side of the hatchet, leaving him unconscious on the deck.

I looked up in time to see two different events, one filling me with hope, the other trepidation. First, Thecily had arrived, a sizeable force with her. She, too, wore a striking hat and had her saber drawn. The rest of her fighting men and women wielded an assortment of swords, spears, and axes. They were beginning to engage the pirates, and it looked like they'd have the upper hand. Second, a woman with a pair of long daggers was preparing to leap from some rigging above Volant, her eyes trained on him with a hungry, vicious mania.

He had no idea she was there, currently battling it out with a pair of pirate swordsmen who weren't half as good as he was.

She leaped, daggers leading her charge towards my friend.

Almost unconsciously, I used the dregs of willpower left to push into the Ukiyo way, fueling my muscles with Skill. I launched the remaining hatchet at the space above Volant's head with every bit of my being. A hum, like that of an arrow, but far deeper throbbed in the wake of the hatchet. The peculiar noise made more than a few people duck.

Time seemed to stand still as the pirate fell through space towards Volant.

Just before she managed to skewer him, my throw struck, crashing into her with enough force to shatter the hatchet shaft and fling her back a pace from Volant. He turned, ducking as the resonating thrum from my throw reached him, and ducked a second time in the other direction as the woman crashed to the deck just behind him.

He looked up, finding me across a sea of pirates waving. Thanks, his fingers flashed out at me before he went back to the work of defending the ship.

While Thecily's group engaged the first party of pirates to board, making their way to Volant and Cassiopia's small resistance, I'd brought the pirate captain's attention on myself.

A few of his people shifted towards me at his command, striding across the deck menacingly. He took in the figures lying prone, either dead or unconscious, around me and clucked disapprovingly.

"That was one of my favorite girls you brought down over there," he said, his voice deep and sounding like it was made of sandstone.

"That was my friend she was trying to stab," I replied.

He unsheathed a cutlass, the blade long and sharp, the hilt studded with gemstones that flashed with every lightning strike.

I was never, ever going to leave a Toron stone off my person again. The necklace I'd made out of Bymm's ring would have saved me in this moment. I drew Berjio's rapier in response, still cursing my luck at having so much power just out of reach.

His entourage also drew their swords, and my heart sank. I wasn't much of a swordsman in the first place. Even so, this was just downright unfair.

And then a blur flew by me, a line cutting through the falling rain before bouncing off one, pirate, then two, and then the third, leaving only the captain standing. Dumbfounded, I watched as Shazina paused, staying still long enough to be unfuzzy. She nodded at me before shooting off into the crowd of invading, heavily armed, muscled, and mean-as-slithers group spreading across the ship like a plague. She cut them down like wheat until a lucky backswing of an elbow brought her to a dazed, jarring stop. Volant was near enough to grab her and drag her back behind the scrimmaging crew line, depositing her at Cassiopia's feet.

"Shall we?" I asked, flicking my blade, trying to hurriedly remember all the aspects of sword fighting I'd learned since leaving the school.

A man his size shouldn't be so nimble, but he was. His feet moved and danced. They slid and spun. He was everywhere at once, cutlass flashing from every direction, sparking off my weapon as I hastily blocked.

I tried to drop back into the Ukiyo, but I couldn't think past the immediate danger, and my willpower was virtually drained.

We broke apart for a brief moment, taking stock of the duel. I had four or five cuts around my arms and shoulders from moments I didn't even remember.

His hat's feather was slightly askew.

The pirate captain's lips twitched into the semblance of a malicious, knowing smile. He had me outclassed by quite a bit.

I lunged, stretching out like Volant had shown me, twisting my wrist ever so slightly in a small circle, making the tip of my blade flicker in a wide enough arc to go under and around the counter he was swinging through.

His eyes widened with surprise as his blade met air, and my tip drove itself into his shoulder, sinking deep.

Overjoyed, I yanked the tip out and swished it back and forth. There was no way he could continue now.

Instead of recognizing his impending defeat, the pirate grimaced, swapping hands. "I was going easy on you," he growled out between clenched teeth. "Now ya' gone and pissed me off."

He lashed out, no finesse, and no dancing footwork. Just solid, determined, brute strength. I parried, but every blow drove me a step back, bringing me further away from help and closer to the edge of the prow.

Steel sang with each swing. One. Two. Three. A fourth brought me to a knee, arm aching from the force of the attack.

He raised his arms high, ready for a killing blow. A thump. Something struck his back, making him stumble a step. A second thump followed immediately after, resulting in an arrow sprouting like a sapling from his chest.

The captain toppled over, falling face-first into the ground next to me. Two arrows sprouting from his back.

I looked up and saw both Volant and Cassiopia with bows still raised in my direction.

Thanks, I signaled back to Volant in a mirror of our exchange from what felt like only a few breaths ago.

A hair-raising series of growls echoed from the far end of the ship, and Qaewin riding her zymph, followed by half a dozen or more of the ferocious panthers, plowed into the remaining knot of pirates. As the creatures laid about with tooth and claw, the pirates' fighting spirit broke.

More pirates began to appear from the smaller ship but wearing fallpacks. They jumped over the far side of the airship, floating down into the clouds below. Apparently, the zymphs were one foe too many.

At the retreat of their companions and the slaughter of so many on our ship, the remaining pirates began to throw down their arms and surrender.

Once we'd restrained the pirate crew, I went to find Thecily.

Her face was pale, more so than her fair complexion usually was. She had a slight tremor and a wild-eyed look like a deer who'd been separated from the pack.

"You all right?" I asked

She grabbed me up in an embrace, a short shudder running through her before she let me go. I flushed, enjoying the close contact a little too much, especially given the situation.

With a steadying breath, she pulled away, regaining the steel that a lot of Wydvis women seemed to inherently be forged out of. "That was incredibly close," she said, voice quiet enough that it wouldn't carry.

She reached down, plucking an arrow off the ground, and twirled it between her fingers, letting the momentary distraction wash the wild look away. "If any of those volleys had hit us, or if they'd managed to puncture our balloon, we'd have been done for."

"Why didn't they just hit the balloon in the first place?" I asked.

"It would have destroyed the ship and only left what they could pick out of splinters." She thought for a moment. "I believe the real prize was our vessel. They didn't expect us to have such fierce resistance on board. Normally, they'd have taken us. I think Shazina singlehandedly turned the tide. If you see her before I do, pass on my thanks."

As Thecily spun away to move part of her crew over to the pirate vessel, I realized I hadn't seen any of my Learners or Insley. "Oh, gods above, let them be safe," I muttered as I stumbled towards the bunks.

Below deck, I found Craig, the sisters, Martino, Argo, and a handful of the older crew barricaded in the cramped fallpack room.

The Learners looked near collapsing. Joy was even snoring softly against Martino's shoulder, who held a kitchen knife. Insley was there, and my heart soared to see her.

"Ship is safe," I called to them, relieved to see they hadn't been injured.

Argo slipped under their makeshift barrier and came sliding into my feet with puppy enthusiasm. He jumped and yipped, ears flopping as he tried to say hello.

I reached down, scooping him up and giving him a quick hug before setting him back on to the floor. Mission accomplished, he sprinted back to the makeshift barrier as they undid their work.

With a quick stop by my locker, I grabbed the Toron stone necklace I'd made with Bymm's ring and slid it over my head.

Insley came over and was about to give me a hug before coming up short. Her eyes widened as she took in my many cuts. She didn't even say anything, just pushed me up the deck as she grabbed her healer kit.

We'd passed through the storm, and though the sky still threatened more violence on us, there was no more rain or lightning in our vicinity.

She laid me out in an unobtrusive corner on deck and began to clean and bandage the wounds. One cut needed stitches, and despite her gentle, slow pace, it was still more painful than the actual injury.

Volant came over with Qaewin, soaked even more than I was. He had a torn sleeve and the start of a black eye but otherwise seemed perfectly fine. He looked down at the cuts and shook his head, amused. "You are one lucky leafer. What made you decide to duel a captain of a pirate airship? You're lucky he didn't end you within the first few strikes."

"Locklentalis must have been watching over you," Qaewin said softly, tone agreeing with Volant. But she looked far less amused.

I grimaced at a less than gentle stab from Insley's needle. "Had a good teacher, got cocky," I said, forcing a grin past the pain.

Volant gave me a thumbs up, his relief showing through that I wasn't dead or seriously maimed.

In companionable silence and a little macabre curiosity, we all sat in silence as Insley finished her work, tightening my stitches up and putting the final knots in my bandages. The sky continued to brighten, and trees began to edge into our view of the skyline.

"Anchor's away!" A shout rang out down near the bridge.

Nothing happened for a moment, and then we came to a slow, bouncing halt. The other ship set down next to us, Toman steering the smaller craft in to sit next to us. Large, wagon-sized walkways with rope rails included were flopped across to allow easy walking between the two. Thecily herself appeared, motioning for Volant.

"I could use some help," she said to Volant. "Before we send a skeleton crew back to Wydvis with the pirate ship, we want to take stock of who they've been pilfering from."

"Sounds fun to me," Volant said, hopping up and joining her.

The rest of us stayed on board, helping clean up the whirlwind wreck up top. We'd just begun to settle back down, Cassiopia having appeared with Shazina and Argo in tow with a plate of Martino's take on a classic Wydvis bowl of sautéed veggies, sauce, and healthy chunks of bread.

***

A pale, trembling Volant arrived. In his right hand, he held a small portrait of an airship.

For a long moment, I tried to place it, while Qaewin jumped up and wrapped him in a hug, not knowing the why but seeing his distress.

I knew I recognized it from somewhere, but Volant explained, slumping down next to us while still holding on to Qaewin if his life depended on it.

"This is from my mother's ship," he gulped. "It's a commission my father had given her when she had to stay home with me. It's of her ship, the one he died on."

The news sank in like lead dropping into the river.

"The pirates got your mom's ship?" Cassiopia asked, confused. "I thought she was nearly the most battle-worthy airship captain in existence?"

Volant gave a sour chuckle at that. "She's pretty incredible but has her limits." A tear rolled down his face, followed by another. And then a third. "It seems so, though. The pirates we captured don't seem to know much. They hit a lot of different ships, and not all of them successfully. She kept this in her cabin."

It was a silence so heavy you could have screamed into it with little effect.

Cassiopia stepped over. "I'm so sorry. It's hard to lose a parent." With that, she wrapped both Qaewin and Volant in a hug.

We all joined in, Shazina grudgingly, but still she came, laying a hand on Volant with a look of impatience. The rest of us embraced, letting our support show through with our presence. Volant shook with the occasional soft sob as more tears streamed from his eyes. He wasn't the only one.

Thecily came down and joined us, offering her condolences in her stiff way. We spent the rest of the day in the hold, enjoying stories about Captain Andreska from a broken-hearted Volant, and appreciating each other in a way that's only possible when death rears its ugly head and reminds you how short life can be. Even the cold distance between Thecily and Insley thawed a little as they shared jokes and found the odd similarities between running an airship and healing hurt animals.

No one seemed inclined to find their proper hammocks, so the whole group of us slept right where we'd sat, a cozy tangle of messy humans just trying to do their best.

When Thecily's crew finished searching the pirate ship and bringing over any of the goods that would help our attempted flight over the causeway, sky pirates, wrapped in heavy chains and shackles, were shuffled over to the ship and locked up in the hold. More than the necessary skeleton crew went with the boat on its way back to Wydvis, uninterested in risking their lives for the fame of crossing across the monster filled sea.

While Thecily saw her people off on the pirate ship, I passed out Toron stones to each of the Learners. Our airship was a terrifyingly short jaunt away from the coast, and it was time we got a plan going. Near the ballista, we carefully practiced channeling energy from the Toron stones and mixing it with our Skill.

The process wasn't hard in itself, come to find out. It was not using too much energy that we had to learn. Our deflection shields were easy to throw out and maintain. Even Joy didn't break a sweat on hers, though her stone cracked immediately upon her attempt. I had her fashion it into a necklace to remind her and tossed her a second stone to continue practicing with.

We were as ready as we'd be, at least in the short amount of time that we'd had. As the others went off to enjoy the limited time they had before we made our suicidal run against nature and the gods, Shazina found me.

"Are you able to access Ukiyo as well as your Learner side of the Skill?" Her face was severe, though she was beginning to be better at showing emotions. Still, she acted more like a tired mother than the young child she was.

"No," I admitted, knowing that meant more meditation.

"Take a seat then," she said. Argo arrived, having taken to wandering a little further away from Shazina but always keeping her in sight.

With a forlorn pet to the infamous puppy, I sat and closed my eyes, drilling down on my breathing. As I pooled will, the Toron stone amplified my process.

When I reached the mental barrier that I had to slip past, it was like the door had finally been open. I immediately pushed Skill into the Ukiyo side, feeling the fibers of my muscles light up. The door was open, so I let some Skill flow back through, causing my body to layer a river of power that seemed to flow through my beings as well as sink down into the fiber of my being.

A small, sharp intake of breath from Shazina. "You did it!" She stood, pacing around me with a critical eye and slightly awed look.

"Did what?" I asked as if I didn't already know.

She rolled her eyes. "Bridged the two sides of the way. Your Learner, and my Ukiyo. I can't explain it. Something in your presence changed. Like a spark went off, and now you're balanced."

I nodded, too nervous to do anything else. We sat there, she staring at me, while I stared hard at a piece of the deck and focused on my breathing.

"Well?" Her impatience bled through like acid.

"Well, what?" I asked, actually unsure this time.

"Do something! Combine the two and see what happens!"

I thought for a moment, remembering the cliff I'd leaped from to save Shazina. I stood up, flexing my legs, feeling the connection from my toes to my fingertips.

"Not that," Shazina began, but it was too late.

With a twitch of my mind, I shoved against the deck, pushing Skill down and out. Simultaneously, I flexed my legs and jumped, urging Skill through my muscles at the same time I moved it from my feet and into the deck. Immediately, the mistake was evident.

Wood cracked beneath me as I accelerated through the air. I soared up, coming within a whispered word's distance from the balloon rigging a hundred paces above the deck below. I flailed as I hit the top of my jump's parabolic curve. Below me, the deck looked like a tiny toy ship. Beneath that, empty air.

Rope and hand met as I was momentarily motionless in the sky. My other hand swung up, grabbing onto the balloon rigging as well, stopping my descent back down to a splat-inducing end.

This high up, my head swam with vertigo, and I nearly let go. But Skill still coursed through my body and mind. I used a little, and my strength doubled, my grip vice-like on the rope. My mind cleared, too, and I was able to shake off the terror at having found myself so high up. Down on the deck, I could see people scrambling like ants all over, frantic in their inability to help me.

Guess it was time to help myself.

I let go with one hand, swinging with the momentum and latching on to more of the balloon's rigging to my right. I released my other hand, swinging it forward. With each swing, my stomach lurched a bit, and my toes tried to curl away from the emptiness below. But after an eternity, I arrived at the anchor point for the rigging, a tangled spider web of thick ropes that knotted and wove until connecting to one thickly braided piece that anchored to the ship's frame far below.

Relieved and tired, I began a slow, controlled descent down the thick rope to the crowd of people. It took far longer to climb down than the ascent. My arms were trembling by the time I reached the deck, and my head was fuzzy with the aftereffects of Ukiyo. I barely even noticed the normal fatigue from Skill use outside of that.

Fuzzy thoughts turned into something more akin to molasses as I sat on the deck. People I'm pretty sure I knew were talking to me, but I couldn't make the words sensible, and I couldn't seem to make anything reasonable come out on my end either.

Someone handed me something to eat, a flatbread stuffed with spiced meat. Mechanically, I chewed and swallowed, still sitting at the base of where I'd climbed down, struggling to make my brain work. As I finished the meal, the fog seemed to lift off, allowing names and words to flood back to me.

Volant and Shazina were there, watching expectantly. Thecily too, with a worried-looking Insley right next to her.

"Well, that was an experience," I said, my tongue thick and sluggish.

Shazina passed me a water skin. The cool, crisp liquid softened my mouth and washed away the sluggishness.

Thecily was the first to speak. "You cracked my deck, you godspawn," she said, anger mixed with relief. When I only smiled back and shrugged, she rolled her eyes. "Just, well, just be more careful next time."

I nodded, taking another long gulp of the water.

Shazina hit me in the arm, hard enough to bruise, but not really out of malice. "You are an absolute idiot. Not only did you almost die from jumping off an airborne ship, but you nearly burned your mind out with that stunt!"

Before answering, I craned my neck up, following the rope high into the sky where the balloon sat, a dizzyingly far ways away. "Aye, that was pretty dumb. But left hand, I flew."

She hit me again, followed by Insley smacking me on the other side. Volant just chuckled at my abuse. Only Argo, who'd appeared in my lap for a head scratch, seemed on my side.

"I did it though, I bridged the gap and used both at once!" A thought struck me, and I pulled out the necklace's ring. The Toron stone was okay, not a crack to be found, and it still glowed slightly. I looked back up. "I don't get it. How'd I almost burn out even though the stones not cracked?"

Shazina looked puzzled for a moment like I'd asked something childish that could be construed as a poor joke. "Because you haven't worked that muscle enough to put that kind of Skill through it." She paused, looking at me to see if I'd admit I was just pulling her leg. "It has to be the same for Learners. You have to work that muscle enough to match your will, right?"

"I guess," I said without much conviction. "But, if a Learner is to burn themselves out, it's only if the stone cracks. Otherwise, they're fine."

"Interesting," she mused. "Ukiyo may work a little differently. Because you're directly affecting your mind and how it controls the body, there's a genuine chance of burnout if you don't practice slowly and consistently. It happens all the time, honestly."

I blanched at that. "And you didn't warn me?"

She at least had the good grace to seem a little embarrassed. "I assumed you knew, being a Learner. I didn't think it was any different. Plus, Toron stones don't work for us."

Insley laced her fingers through my hands, squeezing gently despite the furrowed eyebrow and daggers she was glaring at me. "You had us seriously scared, Nil." Her voice cracked a little, and I realized that it wasn't anger she was holding back, but tears. "We couldn't help you, and if you would have slipped, or anything, we'd have been forced to watch you fall and die. That was an awful thing to do to us."

I stammered, caught off guard. "But, I didn't mean to. I was just trying to use both sides of Skill simultaneously, and I did it! Shazina, when was the last person your people knew of who did that?"

She shrugged, feigning a nonchalance that I suspected she didn't feel. "Last we heard, only the gods could do something like that."

"The gods?" I asked, momentarily forgetting about Insley's distress.

"Like, the actual gods? Locklentalis and the twelve?" Volant echoed.

She nodded, picking at a splinter. "Those are the ones. The same ones who disappeared with all knowledge of Learners across the causeway, running from the Gimzers. Long, long ago. Those gods."

Insley shook herself off, putting the emotional side she'd just shown away and bringing out the clinician. "If that's the case, why did Nil of all people just become the first to bridge that divide? No offense, of course."

I laughed, long and hard. Wiping the tears from my eyes, I gestured to Insley. "None taken, she's got a point. There's no way someone didn't accidentally figure this out before this."

Shazina rolled her eyes and spoke slowly as if she was dealing with a particularly slow child. "Only someone who's a Learner first can bridge the gap. All the knowledge on how to do that disappeared with you and your gods back before memory can even place. That, and how even to this day we're still recovering from the loss of some much progress, there's not been any way for us to discover how to become Learners. And finally, there are some rather strong theories that the ability passes through bloodlines."

She paused, taking a breath. Volant, who'd been momentarily playing with Argo, sat him back on the ground. Sensing Shazina's mood, he rushed over and hopped in her lap, planting a number of puppy kisses on her.

"As for your side of the causeway, I'd bet there's a good reason so many people fear your gods more than love and worship them. If someone comes close to discovering this bridge, they prune the troublemaker, I'd guess. Can't have too many gods running around, right?"

That caused me to pause and consider. "Good thing the gods aren't omniscient," I said. But like anytime you think a supernatural being has its eye on you, it suddenly felt like they did. The hair on the back of my neck rose up, and I had to shake off the feeling.

Despite the Toron stone having fueled the flight onto the balloon, I felt bone-weary tired. With a quick excuse, I headed back down to think.

Chapter Thirteen

Volant stood next to the hammock, hand on my shoulder and looked almost concerned.

Light streamed through the window. I felt like a sack of too ripe potatoes that'd been left in the sun. My mouth was dry. It took an unfair amount of strength to swing my legs out and plant them. "How long was I out?"

Volant let out a relieved sigh and punched me on the same shoulder. "You slept all through yesterday and half-way through today, leaf boy."

With a yawn, I stretched and felt the cuts on my arms push against the scabs they'd formed. "Finally, I'm getting on your level of lazy, cloudling," I shot back with a wink.

Volant just rolled his eyes in an excellent impersonation of Shazina. "Hope you're good to go. We're skirting the coastline down to the causeway."

That woke me up. "Already?" I frantically checked myself over, making sure I had the necklace. Despite that, I still grabbed a couple more Toron stones from the small chest near the hammock. I gulped down some water and rushed upstairs to find most of the crew watching the sea across the way. The eternity river snaked its way along the coastline below us like a crystalline trail.

Everyone but Shazina had a grim, stony presence to them. Like prisoners walking to their execution. Even Thecily, who was standing with Cassiopia at the bridge, had her lips pressed in a tight line.

Argo broke the uncanny silence with an excited bark as he saw me come up. He raced over, leaping the last few paces and landing in my outstretched arms with unabashed excitement. Idly, I wondered how many from Kalaran would have joined us just knowing this dog was along for the ride.

"You look like you've seen a ghost," Insley said, trailing Argo's mad rush with a more reserved speed.

Qaewin was a step behind her, smiling. I couldn't see a single zymph on deck. The height paired with open water so nearby must have shattered their previous confidence. It was probably for the best. The crew was still uncomfortable around the huge felines.

With an effort, I brought out a less pained expression. "I was just thinking of Argo's adoring fans back in Kalaran. And then I realized we'd be lynched if we survive this for having taken the dog on such a dangerous journey."

Insley laughed, and Qaewin joined in with her soft chuckle. Thecily saw us and came over as well, still looking slightly annoyed at me.

"So," I began, gesturing to the open water and ever-present storm clouds in the distance. "Why aren't we just cutting across straight away?"

Thecily stared like I'd lost half my senses while sleeping. Finally, she gestured around her, indicating the dozens of crew on deck. "If this goes poorly, I'd rather my crew have a second chance at making a run for it, rather than being stuck on the open sea."

"Ah," I said, feeling foolish. "That makes sense. We'll cross the sea above the causeway then?"

She nodded. With her hands clasped behind her back, she looked like a young, redheaded version of Captain Andreska. Anything coy or flirtatious about her was gone now that we were at the edge.

"Your captain really doesn't come out of his cabin?" Qaewin asked

"Never. I'd assumed he died, except our cook says he is still dropping food and drink off and getting empty plates and bottles in return." Thecily's eye twitched slightly, and I realized it must be difficult to be running a ship but not be paid or given credit for doing so.

"Pirates literally attacked us," Insley said. Her voice was measured, but there was an edge to it.

"Honestly, I thought that would bring him out." Thecily shrugged. "He must have assumed it was one of our attempts at getting him to leave the cabin. One time, we brought on a whole troop of performers just to see if he noticed."

The causeway appeared in the distance when I looked up, a thin, rocky line defying the heavy sea around it. I pointed, and Thecily turned, taking in the view.

"Nil, grab your Learners. This is about to get fun." She spun, jumping up onto the nearest rigging and getting a bit of height before barking orders.

I rushed off to find the Learners as she called for stations, rowers, and a double check on anything loose that could slide around.

The triplets were down below in the galley with Martino, playing some simplified version of Kingdoms while he watched over dinner. All three sisters had fashioned their Toron stones into bracelets around their wrists. I tossed them each an additional stone.

"Dendra, Diedra. I need you two at the middle of the ship, cover the sides and support both the front and back if need be. Get ready for some running." They nodded, standing up and rushing out without saying a word. "Joy, you're with me. Let's find Craig."

As we ran about the ship, I could hear Thecily firing off more orders from the bridge. Up top, we received an awe-inspiring view of rows and rows of wind oars spreading out beneath us. The rowers were double stacked, half below deck with their oars only visible while locked out like wings. The second set was sitting right on the top deck. Long, wing-like oars slotted straight into the ship's railing.

Insley and Qaewin both sat at an oar, paired with a crewman each. Insley smiled when she saw my confusion. "Anyone not doing anything immediately important is supposed to be rowing. I could use a little exercise," she said with a chipper tone that didn't match my dread.

I reached down and gave her hand a quick kiss, causing her to blush.

Craig was waiting for us at the front of the ship with Cassiopia and Shazina. "You and Joy are to take the back of the ship. I don't want anything lancing us from behind."

"The stern," he corrected, almost sheepishly.

I rolled my eyes. "Get to it." I tossed him his back up Toron stone as well before planting myself at the front, taking deep, steadying breaths.

"What are you going to do if we see an octomantis again?" Shazina asked.

I didn't know. "Hopefully, Cassiopia can take care of it again. Those arms of it are beyond unnatural. Even with all of us throwing up a shield, I doubt we could deflect that kind of force.

She nodded as if she'd come to the same conclusion.

"I want you up at the bridge with Thecily. You know these creatures better than anyone else on board, and maybe you can help her determine if we need to risk the storm above versus something below."

Shazina rolled her eyes but headed back to Thecily.

Shouted orders came from the bridge. As one, the oars plunged, lurching the ship forward with a burst of speed. Again and again, they swung through the air, gaining us speed and momentum. The ship turned, cutting across the final canopy of trees below and entering the open space above the sea. The causeway was growing in the distance, and I marveled at how quickly we were cutting across the water.

A shiver ran up my spine as a childhood of sea monster stories, paired with an acute fear of open water, struck home. To make matters worse, a shadow rippled beneath the choppy water, some giant creature coming up just below the surface.

The shadow shrank, disappearing just long enough for me to breathe out a sigh of relief before the water erupted as a powerful, boat-sized predator broke the surface. My breath caught in disbelief as its finned tail beat the empty air as it gnashed towards us.

It would have missed, but the long sky oars dipped down in their row, extending far below the Sky Wolf. The timing was too perfect. Right before it'd have completely missed, the sea creature's jaws crunched down, taking a chunk out of one of the oar's fan bladed ends. The motion catapulted an unlucky rower overboard, bringing us our first casualty in less than a hundred heartbeats of entering the sea's airspace.

I turned back to the bridge and saw Thecily pull back on the steering rig, bringing the airship another dozen paces higher. Our balloon disappeared above us into the ominous clouds that blanketed the sea as long as anyone could remember.

Our ship began to bump and shake, reacting to whatever nature was doing to abuse the balloon high in the clouds. After some tense moments and not a few people retching, we reached the causeway proper. Thecily brought us back down out of the perpetual storm and oriented the ship to head directly east, following the rocky path below.

It didn't take long after coming back down below the brutal storm system before shouts of alarm rang out at the far end of the ship. Bone like spikes similar to small darts skittered off the Skill bubble created by Joy and Craig. One of the crew was stumbling past the bridge, a dart embedded in his shoulder. He coughed once before falling to the ground, dead.

I leaned over the rail and looked back to see a boiling pod of oversized crab creatures with three tails each. The pod had roughly twenty of the angry amphibians, and they were pursuing the ship with a flurry of the poisoned spikes being launched from the tails like javelins.

Volant appeared at the back corner of the ship, spinning and twisting his arms, using his Talent to make a vortex of wind appear in his hands. He threw the concentrated blast of wind at the pod, scattering a volley of their tail flung spikes. He sent a second, and then a third.

The first vortex hit, spinning the crab-like creatures in a circle. The second and third sent enough confusion in their midst that they gave up the chase.

Show off, my fingers formed as he looked back my way and gave a thumbs up. He laughed, shrugging, and finding a seat in the back to recover from the exertion.

A woman appeared at my elbow, coughing politely to get my attention. I jumped, realizing I'd not been watching the side of my ship. Turning to face her, I recognized one of Thecily's crew that seemed always to be following her about.

"Thecily sent me over as support," she said with a quick salute. "I'm the resident sparker. She thought I might be able to help. The rest of the Naturals have been sent to your other Learner's as well."

That gave me pause. "Hold on, how many Naturals do you guys have?"

"Six in total, if we include your friend." She raised five fingers. "Jolen is our earther mover, Wyvie and Loc are our water warpers, and Percy is the final wind racer, like your friend."

I nodded as if that made sense. "And you are?"

"Oh! Right. Me," she said flustered. "I'm Arn."

Confused, I waved my right hand. "Arm, like a limb?"

She blushed and shook her head. "No, Arn, like a weird name that rhymes with yarn."

"Ah," I said, embarrassed now. "Got it. So, I'm glad for your help, but where were you when the pirates attacked?"

She glanced sideways, back at the bridge where Thecily was up there, steering the ship despite the rig trying to escape her grasp from all the turbulence above.

"I was down below. Honestly, not much of a fighter. In that kind of situation, I'm more like a fail-safe. Fire and airships don't belong together, so I don't do much outside of putting out fires if any appear or starting a really big one if all hope is lost."

"That, uh, oddly makes sense." I had more questions, but the sky had grown ominously much darker, and a fuzzy wall of shifting rain loomed just before us.

There were always storms over the sea, but it wasn't always storming down on the causeway itself. But sometimes, the entire stone path and surrounding sea would be shrouded in such storms that could inspire awe and fear in equal measure. It looked like one of those was on us.

Lightning flashed. I looked over to Arn, who seemed nervous as well. "You guys deal with storms all the time, right?"

Instead of answering, she craned her neck, checking down on the bridge. When she turned back, she looked slightly less nervous. "They seem fine down there, so we're in no immediate danger."

To either side of the ship, small wireframes that looked like wings extended from the sides. Lightning flashed as they expanded, striking the metal and turning it the bright white that hurts your eyes to look at. I squinted and saw the lightning trace its way down a wire that dangled far below, skimming the surface of the sea.

It was cold now, and the rain had completely soaked me through. Arn looked even more miserable, hair plastered down. She shivered involuntarily.

"What happens if one of the sea monsters grabs that wire?" I asked, hoping to distract her, but also worried that our whole ship would go down because of one small piece of metal.

She looked over the rail and pointed. With the near-constant barrage of lightning, we could see the ripples of a fast-approaching shape in the water, aiming directly at the wire. A fish, too big to be real, arced from the sea like a charging bull. It latched onto the wire, and the ship had a corresponding bounce. Almost instantly, lightning hit the metal wing and raced down to the water. When it met the fish, the whole creature lit up with charged energy before lifelessly sinking back into the water.

Now she was positively relieved. “Seen that happen with some smaller fish, wasn’t sure if there was enough punch for these bigger ones.”

Despite the storm, another pod of the lagorac, as Shazina called them, tried to bring us out of the air with their poisoned darts. Thankfully, we didn’t even need to throw up any shields, as the storm winds were too strong for the pods attack to do anything but pepper the bottom of the ship in a few places.

With the lifting of the storm, sunrise came. And a level of exhaustion none of us had been ready for. The sea was almost placid, which only made apparent the vast swath of sea that was being disturbed in our shadow. Enormous, nightmare-inducing creatures leap-frogged each other, keeping up with the ship.

With the storm over, the oars were back out and were hauling us through the sky faster than any ship this big should have been able to. Despite my lack of sleep, I still felt good. Seeing there was nothing in front of us but clear water, I made my way around the ship to check on the other Learners.

Dendra and Diedra had handled the sides of the ship with nearly no encounters. Diedra was shaken up by what she swore was a sea serpent as long as the ship and almost as wide, ghosting us through the storm. I would have laughed at the idea, but the sea was one of the greatest mysteries that existed, and we only had a few legends to tell us what lay in it. Along with that, her Natural who Thecily had stationed vouched for the story as well. The girl swore that she’d never get in the water again, despite being a water warper.

Dendra, on the other hand, was thrilled. Partly as to the lack of action, and despite her not admitting it out loud, partly due to the incredibly handsome Natural she’d ended up with. They both had the love-struck puppy eyes that screamed "in over their heads," and I was glad at least someone had a good night.

At the back, I found Craig and Joy slumped against each other. Joy was asleep, and Craig looked like it was taking almost everything he had to stay awake. I sent them both down to the bunks to rest up. The Natural was Craig's cousin, and she was only slightly better off than they were. But she wouldn't hear of sleeping. In compromise, I sent her to handle the starboard side and trade out with Dendra and her dashing Natural.

Insley and Thecily found me almost simultaneously. Both looked worn for wear. Thecily's hands shook, and I could see the red, raw remains of torn calluses and ripped blisters. Battling storm winds to keep an airship straight didn't seem to be any kinder on the body.

I took in Insley's hands, finding similarly raw abrasions. Rowing, especially for someone new to it, was far less than kind. At least she'd tried to rest through the storm, though I couldn't imagine being able to sleep through such a storm over a sea that meant guaranteed death up until Shazina had shown up.

She winced but gripped my hand back, thrilled.

Thecily's lips tightened into a line, but she regained her composure quickly. We weren't even close to being out of danger.

"I'm heading to my cabin to catch a quick nap. I'm leaving the wheel to our usual pilot, but if you see anything we can't handle, make sure they find me." With that, she turned, footsteps matching the up and down thrum of the oars pulling us beneath the storm clouds above.

A whistle sounded, and the oars all stopped moving. Thecily turned back. A thought must have occurred to her. "Shazina apparently doesn't have to sleep, if need be. I'm having her walk rounds about the ship, help gather information about the sea below. She's terrified about some octomantis."

Insley hadn't said anything but started to pull away once that whistle had sounded. "That was the oar shift whistle. I've got to go find Qaewin and help pull." She leaned over, almost like she was going to kiss me when Volant arrived, looking none the worse for wear.

"I'll come find you next break," she promised with a grin.

Volant had found all the sleep he needed while comatose. Even using his Talent throughout the night to help speed the ship while also deflecting the smaller projectiles from the unfairly endowed sea monsters, he seemed completely fine. I was almost envious of his energy.

"There you are," he said, offering a fist.

I bumped it, disappointed at the interruption but happy to see my friend looking so energized.

"I'm not recommending you get shot by an arrow or anything, but it certainly helps you appreciate life a bit more. Knowing how close I came to death makes me appreciate this little journey all the more." He was positively beaming at the dark, angry crowds above and the sea below that teemed with horrors.

I cleared my throat and pulled up the still soaked shirt. A nasty scar from the fight that'd left me half dead marred the length of my torso. "Already tried that almost dead thing myself, cloud brain."

His smile grew, clapping me on the shoulder. "Aye, that you did! So, this is fun for you too, right?"

"You're just happy to be back on an airship," I replied with my own smile.

His grin fell, and I could practically see the thought of his home, Thran's Leaf, cross his mind.

"Volant, I'm sorry," I said quickly. "I didn't mean to remind you or anything."

He shook his head, visibly hardening his resolve. "If your time comes, your time comes. I just wish I could have said goodbye to her first. Be glad you have your parents, Nil. They'll be gone before you're ready."

Chapter Fourteen

As the storms rumbled, and the occasional lightning strike arced down to the broad wire wings, we raced against sleeplessness and a murderous sea. A sea snake tried to lunge at us at one point, erupting from the water like a large black ribbon.

It climbed through the air as if it could fly. Sharp angular head with unblinking slitted eyes. The fangs were as long as my arm. I didn't even try to stop it. My legs had turned to jelly, and my body was not responding. We got lucky, as it didn't have enough height in the jump. Fangs snapped shut before falling back into the ocean. Cassiopia put two arrows in the air at the snake as it fell back to the sea, but the wind and rain completely skewed her shot.

A dark cloud of anger passed her face at this, and I thought she was going to break her bow. Just before she brought it down on her knee, she stopped and shook her head before stomping down below deck. A small jolt of speed indicated that she'd grabbed hold of two oars and was helping pull at a muscle-burning rate.

We ground our way east in this fashion, occasionally getting fitful naps between lulls in the thunderstorm, almost always to be interrupted by some new, fresh horror trying to bring down our ship. Sometimes, our watchers would sound false alarms, a person swearing they saw a tentacle reaching up through the hundred pace gap, or a dark shadow of some large creature darkening the blue, foamy water below. More often than not, they were probably right, even if nothing happened.

For just a brief afternoon, we had a respite from the lightning and sea creatures trying to eat us. Long enough for Orr, the Natural partnered with Dendra that was blossoming into something romantic, cast a fishing line over the side of the ship. It sank down below the waves and into the vast depths. Just the sight of it made me uneasy, but almost immediately, he caught one of the hundreds of small fish that seemed to teem through the water.

His second and third fish reeled in went fine, but the fourth was something larger. He and the colossal fish fought, pulling and tugging. Finally, fed up with the fight, Orr pushed his water warper Talent against the sea and gouged a small, pace wide by pace deep hole, making the fish pop out of the now empty water with ease.

At first, we all celebrated while watching Orr reel the massive fish in from far below. But as it rose up, the rest of the frothing sea seemed to calm, waves of fish scattering en masse from the point where Orr had manipulated the water. It was like a wave was expanding out from that point as if we'd dropped some stone, and it'd caused all the fish in the area to swim as hard as they could in whatever direction was opposite.

Some warning itched in the back of my head. But before I could say what it was, a dark shadow slowly formed in the depths of the now deadly calm sea. "Left hand," I swore, turning back to the celebrating group. "Tell Thecily we need to go up, NOW!"

My command was drowned out by an explosion of wood at the opposite end of the ship, towards the cabins and bridge. We lurched with the impact, and I gripped the rail tightly while peering over the side. We were a mere forty paces above the water, a dangerously low altitude. The storm above had been slowing us down so much that we'd lowered enough to completely fly beneath it, giving the rowing crew an easy time to put on speed. The gambit had caught up with us now as I saw the quivering spiked appendage of the octomantis with its serrated tip hooked into the ship.

The monstrous fisheye surfaced with its matching leviathan sized body. Tentacles writhed in the water, operating with seeming independence of the creature's focus. The eyes blinked, resulting in a hexagonal pattern of rainbows splashing across its lid before the black, beady eye locked back on to us. The second of its forward-facing arms launched out across the space, ripping through the air as it speared towards the ship.

Almost instinctually, I pushed out a torrent of Skill. My hands spread wide as I tried to catch the second claw with the deflection shield before it impacted. Immediately, the force of it threw me back, sending me catapulting across the ship's deck until I struck the back rail with enough speed to knock the breath out of me.

"That was idiotic," I mumbled to no one in particular.

The ship listed to one side, beginning to pivot as the bow was reeled back towards the octomantis down below. Something snapped, the splintering sound of wood and glass, and the ship lurched back around, flattening me to the deck with the sudden lurch in upward momentum. The oars raked against the air, and the damaged ship's bow rose up, forcing us directly into the storm clouds above. Still dazed, I watched the sea recede below us and the octomantis discover how inedible a piece of airship was.

By the time it realized its mistake, we were in the thick of the storm.

We were still climbing into the storm when what looked like a wizard from old children's books climbed up from the front of the ship's ladder to the bunks. He was old, with white hair sticking out in every direction, and a long, thick, stone-gray beard. He was tall, and he was angry, yelling something incoherent as he marched towards the bridge.

Oddly enough, he had a similar uniform as the rest of Thecily's crew, which clashed a bit with his wizard persona. His stomp turned to stumbles as the rain-slicked deck tilted and wove, something in the aerodynamics being off from the octomantis' attack. Still, he made it to the bridge, hollering incoherently in Thecily's general direction as she desperately fought to keep the airship rising into the storm.

At this point, we were far too high up for any sea monsters to reach the ship and also too high for any of us to still be on the top deck. The thought of Insley below made me turn towards the stairs, but I couldn't help myself. I made my way down the slanted deck, half-blinded by clouds. At the bridge, I could faintly hear shouting from inside, mostly from the wizard looking fellow.

I levered the door open, screaming wind trying to keep it closed. I slipped inside, finding a different kind of noise.

"We can't turn around!" Thecily shouted back as I slumped inside the doorway. Her red hair had escaped its bonds, and wet strands were whipping about in response to the jarring, shaking, and bucking airship.

"You do as I command! I'm the captain, and I want this ship turned around," screeched the man back at Thecily. His eyes were bulging, and every gnashed word was accompanied by froth and spittle.

When she shook her head, he lunged for the wheel, trying to rest it from her hands. A few of Thecily's crewmen were inside and attempted to intercept the captain but were too slow.

With a stomach-lurching drop, the wheel was yanked out of Thecily's hands by the captain's added weight and the storm's fury.

As we dropped through the sky, the ship spun, corkscrewing round and round. Spinning. Twisting. Falling.

Against anything I thought was possible, Thecily was able to bring the steering down, pointing the ship's nose back towards the sky. Still, we spun, but now up and up and up. Faster we went until the acceleration flattened me against the wall of the bridge, and my stomach tried as hard as it could to throw up everything I'd ever eaten. I squeezed my eyes shut against the spinning ship, lightning flashes, and impending death.

Finally, with a grinding creak, we came to a halt. At the same time, sunlight peeked its loving head through the large, surrounding windows. Below us, I could see the storm raging. Above, a faintly different sky than I was typically accustomed to hung, as if the colors had been washed one time too many.

I tried to suck in a breath, but it was like breathing through a too-small reed underwater. I gasped, feeling like a fish out of water. The air was too thin.

Before I could panic, I saw Thecily strapping herself into a cushioned seat on the edge of the wall. Even the captain and crew were doing so. Frantic gestures from her indicated one near me.

Confused, I sat down, still not able to breathe right. My head was spinning enough that it took far too long for me to realize what was happening. The ropes that held the balloon in place were twisted like a single braid high above us. I cinched the harness tight just as the tension in them reached the climactic moment.

A snap in the eerie quiet, and then we were spinning as if caught back in the storm, the world blurring on the outside. Something came loose from the steering, and a piece of wood shot through the front viewport in a spray of glass.

As we spun, I tried to draw Skill in and push it past the barrier to my mind, but I couldn't concentrate. Instead, the edges of my vision began to blur, darkening until only Thecily remained in the pinprick view I had. Then like a snuffed candle, I passed out.

Shouting brought me back to consciousness. My eyes snapped open and felt like they were two sizes too large for my head. My chest and shoulders ached where the straps of the harness had held me against the centrifugal force the ship had gone through. Everything tilted just enough that it seemed gravity had even been affected. I remembered the snap and looked up. Sure enough, I couldn't even see the usual rope covered gas-filled envelope contraption. At least one of the anchoring ropes must have snapped, and the ship was sagging to one corner now.

I brought my attention back to the bridge. Everyone else was still tied in, and a couple of the crew were unconscious. Thecily was coming around, but of all the people, the captain and his wild beard and hair seemed to be the most awake. His harness seemed jammed, the only thing keeping the violence at bay that his body seemed to be demanding.

"You incompetents! My cabin was half destroyed because of you lot!" he wailed, voice cracking with his anger.

Thecily's eyes locked with mine, ignoring the captain. Recognition and relief flooded across her face, and she grinned. It was a child's grin, the kind you see when they've managed to steal the cookies and gotten away with it. Her crooked smile made my already confused body flush with shared experience, and I felt the tug of two lost spirits finding kindred warmth in each other.

She popped off her harness, standing against the slanted floor, and arched her back. A whole different kind of feeling went through me, and I gulped.

I fumbled with my harness until finally untangling myself. I took a pair of dizzy, disoriented steps forward. I could breathe again, but that was all I could say with a positive light for how I felt.

As the captain continued to struggle against his harness and curse at her and the crew, Thecily went and woke each of the others up. A few gentle slaps or shakes and she had them all up and about. Finally, she came around to the captain, pulling a knife from her boot.

He froze, mid insult, and his eyes widened with fear.

She swung the knife. A clean, practiced motion, no lost economy in its movement.

I flinched, along with the wild-haired man.

When I looked back up, his harness flapped loosely, leaving him free to stand.

A momentary pause and he stood, now towering over his second in command. As the anger came back to replace the surprise, he continued his nearly incoherent tirade against everyone he could see.

"We don't have time for this, sir," Thecily finally said when all her bridge crew was accounted for. "We're over the causeway already halfway across the sea, and I have no idea how far that storm-tossed us or how much damage it did."

The look of sheer horror on the captain's face brought out a chuckle that I somehow managed to swallow and turn into an odd-sounding gulp.

Thecily dragged me out the door as he spun on me, saving my idiotic self from a tongue lashing.

Outside the mangled bridge, the ship drooped at an alarming angle. The anchoring rope attached to the stern's port side had ripped away, leaving the vessel supported loosely by the other three anchors' overstrained cabling.

The storms raged on the horizon behind us, but the waters below were clear, with the teal color of shallow water. "Godspawning left handed..." I started, pointing out past the ship.

Thecily turned, and a most un-Thecily like squeak escaped her before she regained her composure. Against the setting sun, a long, vibrant coastline stretched. It went on as far as the eye could see, jagged beaches turning to desert before finally erupting into a long, absolutely expansive mountain range.

It looked like a kid's drawing of a landscape, edge to edge on the page, uniformly tall, snow-capped peaks, and no discernible end to the mad heights blocking out the horizon.

"All clear!" a voice rang out across the ship. People began to stream from below, clogging the narrow stairs as they traipsed out onto the land.

Below us, the causeway was broad, more so than any road in Balteris. Only beginning to narrow far out where a rigid line in the water changed from the light, friendly teal to the dark, mysterious blue that signaled deep waters.

Shazina and Insley found me first, Argo trailing behind them, blissfully uncaring of the slanted deck. Volant, Qaewin, and Cassiopia stumbled over shortly after them, looking like they'd received a much more violent treatment from the ships out of control spin than the rest of us.

Nothing intelligible was said, as everyone, even Shazina, hugged and laughed and celebrated surviving the storm. We'd done the impossible and crossed through to another land. Even Qaewin's pack of zymphs came up on deck briefly to purr and weave through the closest humans who seemed the most likely to scratch their ears. The open view of the sea put them off, and they left back down into the hold as soon as the first one noticed the water was even more accessible now.

The captain's arrival cut our celebration short. A few of the crew who seemed least happy at this point about our trip flanked him. He'd regained a portion of his composure, though that only meant he looked mostly out of his mind, instead of completely.

"Arrest her!" he barked through clenched, half missing teeth.

The men moved forward, but Thecily's bridge crew intercepted them, stepping between her and the men. A few more of lower ranking members stepped in, unbending in their obedience to the ship's hierarchy though they seemed reluctant in doing so. Craig and the fellow Natural's, along with Diedra and Dendra, who had just come up, interposed themselves between the rule followers and their de-facto leader. The circle around Thecily was solid, but she looked less than happy about the situation.

"Why, exactly, are you arresting me?" she said more as a challenge than a question.

"Why?" the captain spluttered, face turning a bright shade of red. "You've nearly wrecked my ship. You nearly killed us all. My cabin is a ruin because of you!" He turned, gesturing back towards the sea and storm. "I'm taking us back to where we belong, and you'll face the Wydvis council for this. You've overstepped!"

Thecily shook her head slowly. Almost sadly. "That's not what's going to happen. Rook hired us out. We have a mission. We are going to see it through."

The captain's face hardened, changing from crazed to murderous in the space of a heartbeat. "Kill her, then."

Only the soft sound of lapping waves far below could be heard before the angry, ominous screech of steel being drawn from a scabbard announced the captain's men unsheathing their weapons.

I checked my side, finding only the Berjio's rapier. Considering how poorly I'd done with it last time, I didn't relish the idea of another sword crossing with trained cloud dancers. Still, I reach down, grasping the hilt while also summoning Skill. I pushed at it, making it cross the barrier into Ukiyo. Again, the Toron stone helped make the transition instantaneous now that I was focused.

Thecily's men, the defenders of what they saw as their true leader, whipped out blades and knives in response to the threat. Unlike the few trying to obey orders, these didn't hesitate. They leaped at their comrades in a unified rush. Only a few of the crew resisted. By the time I had my weapon free, they'd already disarmed the reluctant would-be jailers, and a sizeable expanse of empty deck surrounded the disheveled captain.

He twitched with a combination of surprise, madness, and spiteful animosity at his orders being countermanded. "This is mutiny!" he screeched, spittle flying out and his beard trembling with barely contained energy.

"Craig." Thecily pointed at the furious captain. "Please escort our esteemed, absentee captain to my cabin. He may enjoy it as his own until we return." Then, she turned to the dissenters, the ones who'd tried to follow their captain's orders. "You all have a choice to make. I respect loyalty, but honestly, to him? He doesn't even know your names." She took a step forward, pointing at each one in turn. "Second chance time, now that we've locked our façade of a captain away. You're with me. All in. Or, join him in the cabin, and we'll see what shakes out on the way back."

To their credit, they didn't look mad or vengeful. Just embarrassed to have tried to hide their cowardice under the guise of following orders. Each one saluted and apologized, offering the hilt of their swords to Thecily.

She brushed the gesture away. "Go to the captain's cabin. I want repairs started immediately, and one of you to come back to report how extensive the damage is."

After they headed down, she turned to the throng that had congregated around us. "Craig, Volant. Grab a handful of people. I want fallpacks on an advanced landing crew. We're setting the Sky Wolf down for repairs."

Volant lit up with joy, grabbing Qaewin and me while leaving the rest of the landing crew selection up to Craig. Dendra and Diedra both refused flat out, and Cassiopia probably weighed too much for a pack. We headed down into the hold with the rest of Craig's chosen landing crew.

It almost felt like home to be strapped in again. I finally was beginning to understand why Volant loved it so much. The small spike of excitement as your body caught up with the idea you were about to leap into empty air.

Volant helped me slip into the armstaps, the pack thicker than the ones we'd used on his mother's ship. The air sac attached to this one, similar to the balloon that held the airship up, was also a far slimmer profile. It didn't have nearly as much bounce to it either.

"Are these going to work?" I asked hesitantly, the excitement souring slightly as I barely felt myself lose weight from the pack.

Volant, utterly thrilled by the design, nodded vigorously. He looked as excited as Argo was when someone handed him a strip of jerky. "These are quick fall designs. We'll hit the ground noticeably harder, but as long as we aren't too geared up, you'll be fine."

Another of Thecily's crew positioned us around the ship's railing where long, strong coils of rope waited. One by one, we each were sent overboard with the end of a rope in hand. When my turn came, I leaped, letting out a whoop as I practically plummeted towards the beach below we'd slowly drifted over.

Thrill was a cheap word, but the most accurate. Similar to the pathways that Skill coursed through me when I drew it forth, a different kind of energy hummed in its place making me aware of all the ways my body clenched against the velocity of near free-fall. In short order, I thudded into the sand with a jarring impact. It didn't quite hurt, but on something harder, and with a few pieces of gear, a wrong landing would easily cause some harm. I doubted they used their fallpacks nearly as frequently as Captain Andreska's people did.

Next to where I landed, I found the large anchor spike. I picked it up in my other hand, and when Volant hit the sand and discovered his spike, we all pulled the ship up the beach towards the hard-packed earth. It was hard work, and my shoulders and legs burned from the effort, only out shadowed in pain by my lungs gasping for air.

I looked up and saw the ship had used our momentum forward to guide it to a much lower altitude, hovering at a good-sized tree's height from our heads. With a signal from Craig, we now ran in opposite directions, pulling against each other and helping the ship lower directly down. The stern touched down first, helping roll the airship parallel. Once we had it leveled out and lowered, we each drove our spikes deep into the ground.

We tied our anchors to the spikes while rope ladders were lowered from doors in the hold to allow everyone else to disembark.

Volant came over, bringing Insley and Qaewin. Both flushed from the exertion and excitement, and it was evident Volant had just added another pair of victims to the rank of fallpack-addicts. "You guys see the balloon?" he asked, pointing up to the envelope that kept us afloat this whole time.

We all looked up, a moment that Insley used to thread her fingers through mine. I looked back to her briefly, offering a warm smile.

High above us, the envelope was making a noticeable descent towards the ship. As the remaining three ropes disappeared into the hold, Volant launched into an explanation.

"Down in the cargo hold, there are wheels that we'll drop onto a gear system. It's almost always only used for repairs and the rare full contact landing. Once they get the balloon lowered far enough, a team will work on reattaching a new strand to replace the one that was damaged in the storm." He paused, gesturing to the ship's bow where a noticeable hole gaped from the octomantis attack. "It also helps keep the ship a little more stable while they work on repairs. Ground work on these airships can be incredibly dangerous."

A yip announced Argo, who came darting in a loose line towards us with barely contained excitement. Shazina strolled behind him, exhibiting her own brand of restlessness.

"Welcome to Exo," she said when the pair arrived. "We need to get Thecily to fortify the area. And someone needs to watch Argo- I'm going to go find my family."

Chapter Fifteen

While Thecily and her crew cannibalized the ship and fortified the area around the entrance to the ship with a loose wall of stakes, I tried to talk Shazina out of striking out on her own. Argo tried to play with the zymphs, who were so excited to be back on the ground they didn't even care how much the puppy seemed to resemble one of the Night Runner's wolf mounts and let him chase them around the ship.

When I couldn't convince her, despite practically begging, I made it clear I was coming along too.

"You can't come," she said in the flat, emotionless way that was so unnerving coming from someone so young. "You can't keep up, and it's dangerous."

I shrugged indifferently. "Why can't I keep up?"

She rolled her eyes with an exaggerated sigh. "I'll be running faster and longer than someone without Ukiyo..." she trailed off. "Right, you've got that covered now. Never mind. But I'm leaving now, ." She was gone, almost at a full sprint heading directly towards the desert.

"Gods below," I muttered. With a mental push that was becoming easier and easier to achieve, I opened the mental barrier to Ukiyo. "Volant!" I hollered over my shoulder as I began to chase after Shazina. I saw him look up from a conversation with Qaewin while they were helping trim too long of planks for the ship's repairs. He saw me jogging away and began to chase after me as I had chased Shazina. He caught up in no time, breathing easily as he ate up the ground in long, graceful strides.

"Odd time for exercise, eh?" he commented in between breaths.

"It's Shazina." I pointed at the small form slowly moving away from us. "Looks like we're running to her village. She made it sound like it could be pretty far." I began to tap Skill, feeling it flow easily into me. I really liked having Toron stones around.

Volant continued running for a moment before it clicked. "You're going to run all the way there?"

"Aye, that looks to be the plan. She just up and left, and I can't let her go alone. She said Ukiyo would be the only way to keep up." I pointed mid-stride, the speck of a girl getting smaller. "I think she was right. You all just don't do anything stupid until I come back. And if I don't come back, come save me."

Volant grinned, stopping mid-stride. "I don't know about that. You complain a lot. Peace and quiet would be a nice change of pace."

I waved goodbye, ignoring him. With an effort of will, I pushed the Skill across the now open barrier, flooding my muscles with alien strength. I sped up. My legs churned as I crossed over the last few rocky outcroppings and onto the hard-packed, barren desert. I pushed harder, moving up to a speed faster than I could run for even short distances, letting the Skill supplement my legs to where it felt like I was running at a comfortable, slow pace despite being able to outrun a zymph.

The speck that was Shazina began to grow larger after a while. I kept my pace steady, not wanting to burn out my Skill or legs before finding her village. The sun stretched above, moving slowly across the sky as I gained on the impossibly fast child.

Abruptly, she stopped, well into the afternoon at this point. The mountains had grown surprisingly closer, but even with Ukiyo, my legs ached, and my body felt like it'd missed a night's worth of sleep. I slowed down, padding over to the now kneeling form on the baked and cracked ground.

As I drew closer, she held up a hand, stopping me. Before her, a small shallow depression of sand surrounded an even smaller pool of water. My legs twitched forward, the thirst in me overriding the warning hand. I stopped when she waved her hand in my direction again, emphatically warning me off.

At that movement, something shot out of a small hole that was practically invisible next to the little oasis. Shazina's hand chopped out in the same motion as her body pivoted away from the attack. A small splash of blood followed the arcing blade of her hand and splattered across the ground before quickly evaporating in the heat.

Still twitching, the snake's head opened and closed mechanically as if it hoped to sink the long, curving fangs into something. The snake's body, an arm's length away, wriggled on the ground in a twisting, unintelligent denial of its headless state. The blood had an odd smell, more pronounced in the dry desert air than anything I'd smelled in the humidity of Balteris.

"You all right?" I asked, a little stunned at both the snake, which had made my knees a little weak, and at Shazina's barehanded violence in dismantling it.

Instead of answering, she dipped her hands into the water, bringing it up and drinking from it. I went to join her, bringing water to my lips in pure ecstasy. No matter what the Skill had been doing for my running, my body was still getting pummeled by the intense heat, and a drink was all I could want.

Thirst slaked for the moment; I went to look at the now unmoving snake's corpse. It was thick and not nearly as long as the one that we'd run into in Kalaran. That thought made me pause, realizing we'd not seen the creature at Xylex's house, and it could be roaming around the caverns still. This snake was also brown, with white and black bands going down its scales in a subtle pattern.

"Sand viper," Shazina commented. She left the head but picked up the now still body and tucked it into a fold of a belt that seemed more like a multilayered scarf.

I squinted against the sun. It was brighter, sharper, and hurt the eyes that much more when looking into the distance. "This place doesn't seem all that friendly," I said. "Especially for running around without supplies."

She turned back to look at me, a what-did-you-expect expression. Again, she ignored me and began to run straight towards the imposing mountain range. Clouds covered the peaks at this point, and it seemed like one of the gods had built a wall to pen us in that stretched to the heavens.

With an effort of will, I ran. The Ukiyo made me move like a predator on the hunt for prey. We ran through the desert, only stopping when Shazina saw a small oasis for us to dip our hands in to drink from, or once when she saw a trail of footprints, hundreds of them, heading perpendicular to our path. On we went until my legs lost feeling and my body stopped producing sweat. I pushed more and more Skill through me, Ukiyo driving my body even as my mind grew fuzzy and drained from the use.

Night fell, and all that we could see was desert around us. No sea at our backs, or green grass, or trees or airships. Just the brown, baked dirt with its snakes and lizards. When I was starting to worry I couldn't push any further, Shazina finally slowed down to a walk. Her breathing was just as ragged as mine.

Silently she pulled out the snake and took a bite out of it before handing the body over to me. "Are you serious?" I asked. My skin crawled with revulsion.

"Shh," she hissed back. In a low voice, she said, "they'll be out now. We need to be quiet and alert."

I took the limp snake. "Are you seriously eating this, and uncooked?" I hissed back.

She ignored me, walking on with eyes darting every which way across the desert floor before us. I followed, still holding the snake and building up the courage to take a bite. Finally, after a long battle between my ever-growing hunger pains and the gag reflex that told me it'd rebel if I tried- I took a bite.

Bile rose in my throat, and an uncontrollable gag escaped, but was able to force the chewy meat down with only a mild amount of disgust. I took another before handing the rest back to Shazina. I followed her lead as we walked across the desert for the rest of the night, realizing I'd not slept properly in some days. I was so intent on watching for snakes jumping from holes in the ground or the gimzers she was so worried about that when I took a moment to look up and see a small village of clay brick homes. I assumed I'd finally started hallucinating.

A single, old-fashioned torch flickered like a beacon in one of the huts. I expected Shazina to take off at a run again, but instead, she just continued trudging forward until we were walking between the squat buildings. The village was practically empty. No sounds, no people, not even some nocturnal animal slinking about. It was just as silent as the desert had been.

We stopped at the house with the still-burning torch. No one was within.

A single, half-strangled sob came from Shazina as she dropped to her knees. Inside, signs of violence dominated the space. Long, angry claw marks cut across the wall, some of them splashed with blood.

The run had taken its toll on us, and we were both too tired to do anything. Shazina didn't move from the floor, so I picked her up, marveling at how small and light she was. I deposited her in a bed in the room furthest from the front entrance. Grief and exhaustion had knocked her out cold, and she looked far more like the child she was while curled up on the bed.

My heart ached, a feeling becoming all too familiar as I pulled a blanket over her. Someone this young should still be having a childhood, playing in the mud, and yelling at boys for pulling her hair. Not suffering so much hardship. Or experiencing this much danger. It was cruel.

Despite everything, when a body needs rest, it is going to get it. I was asleep in front of the door as soon as my head hit the floor.

Harsh, penetrating heat and a bone-dry throat brought me out of my cramped slumber. Everything from my dehydrated lips to my blistered toes hurt. I rolled up, finding my balance after an unacceptably slow response from my body. The mix of stumbling and groans woke Shazina, who popped out of bed with enviable alertness. She took a moment to gauge where she was before her memory caught up and dropped her a second punch to the emotions.

I saw her swallow, taking a moment to blink away tears before straightening and locking the emotionless mask in place that made her seem so much older. She brushed past me, saying nothing but gesturing for me to follow. Outside, the torch still burned, flickering and letting off hazy waves of heat that could be seen in the dry air.

Behind the hut, a small well waited. Shazina cranked the handle along until deep from the darkness, a bucket arrived, brimming with water. We took turns, drinking greedily until the two of us finished the bucket off and let it slide down into the deep well again. Finally, she turned to me. A sadness was there that I'd not seen before.

"This was my home," she said, voice as flat as the ground around us. "Gimzers." With effortless grace, she leaped up to the top of the roof next to us, with no hesitation.

Not wanting to push my luck when I knew there was still a return trip to make, I climbed up behind her, windowsill to roof lip before rolling up and over onto the simple roof. I turned, taking in a full panoramic view of the area around us. Desert surrounded the homes, though faintly in the distance, I could see the beginning of rolling hills.

Hundreds and hundreds of homes dotted the landscape around us. They blended in with the landscape, nearly the same color as the ground, and no sharp edges among any of them. The population had probably been only marginally smaller than Erset. However, the build of the homes reminded me of the odd shape that was found exclusively at the bottom of the lake in Brod, the city beneath the floating harbor.

"I'm sorry we didn't make it in time," I tried, struggling to come up with something to fill the heavy silence.

She just shook her head, and I knew she was busy blaming herself, me, and everyone she'd met along the way that had slowed her return home. The warping image of heat from the torch wavered in the air just next to us, distorting the way we'd come into a roiling wave of desert.

"How long do torches like that normally stay lit?" I asked slowly, a realization forming.

Shazina stilled even further before snapping her attention to the torch. "A day, at most." Quickly, she began to scan the horizon again, doing some form of mental calculation. "If anyone were leaving from here, they'd continue east to the valley."

I looked east, seeing nothing but flat, barren ground. The mountains must be a long way away. Turning back, Shazina had disappeared. I peered over the wall to see her striding purposefully east. "Godspawning, hardheaded children," I sighed. Slowly, I climbed down, feeling every blister and ache in my overtaxed legs.

With a grunt of pain, I began jogging after her, with each step sending stabs of pain up my unsteady legs. I caught up and was about to argue when I saw she was following a single set of footsteps.

"They're fresh." She pointed at the blood dotting the ground around the print, still more red than brown.

"Could it be a gimzer?"

"No. They don't walk." She kept moving forward, speeding up a little bit. "The valley is only half a day away. Whoever left this is from my village, and where there's one survivor, there could be more."

Again, I wanted to argue. But before I could, she was off at a lope, nothing nearly as fast as yesterday, but still a brisk pace for such a small person. I pushed forward, following in her wake as we chased down her last hope. The first part of the run was pure agony, but as we went, my muscles loosened up, and we were able to put on a little speed. I tapped my Skill, and for just a moment, felt like I could bring it directly into Ukiyo without needing to cross the barrier. But, it was only for a moment before the feeling disappeared, and I had to do the mental gymnastics of shoving my will in and upon itself.

She was right. Compared to yesterday's run, it was a simple bit of effort getting to the valley village. The sun hadn't even fully risen before we hit scrubland with rolling hills forming slowly along with the vegetation.

The mountains could now be seen, but they certainly didn't seem to be getting closer as they stabbed into the sky like the walls of an impenetrable fortress. I was too busy marveling at the unending mountain peaks, Shazina called them Borin's Crown, to notice the congregation of huts scattered in the side of hills just below us.

Shazina slowed to a walk, bringing my attention to the homes around us. Apart from being half-buried in the hillsides and being spaced out a little further, there wasn't much difference in these homes than her village. People appeared at about the same time. They wielded a variety of primitive weapons. Sharpened stakes, rough wooden clubs, and an occasional knife or two.

With some Exo-known gesture, Shazina put the people at ease, and the aggression bled out of them, turning to relief. I stayed back as she exchanged a quick, hushed conversation with a tall, rail-thin woman that stepped out from a nearby home. For the rest of the village's part, they disappeared back into their huts and out of the oppressive sun.

A twitch from the shadows of one building and a boy twice Shazina's size came hurtling out at her. Before I could so much as warn her, the boy had Shazina wrapped up in a silent hug, tears flowing freely from his face. I cautiously moved closer, still at a loss for what was happening.

While I moved forward, the slender woman moved away, disappearing around a bend after a few paces. I continued, coming right up to the boy who seemed determined to hold onto Shazina despite her protestations. He said something, and she crumpled, dropping to the ground in a heap and crying. Her sobs echoed, and I knew her worst fears about the empty village had come true.

With a face nearly identical to Shazina's, only slightly older and more masculine, the boy glowered at me. His eyes brimmed with unshed tears as he held the normally emotionless girl in his arms. I waited. And I waited some more. When the shock of whatever he'd told her wore off, she turned with red-rimmed eyes and dust-covered cheeks that showed the clean lines of sadness trailing down her face.

A weak wave of the arm towards the boy that still held her in a protective embrace. "This is my brother Teo." A sniff and she wiped her nose. "My last living relative."

I flinched at that. "What happened?" I asked with such cautious hesitance. I wasn't sure the words even came out.

"A gimzer." Teo let the name drop between us like a fallen tree. Heavy, singular, and dead of feeling.

"One?" It didn't seem possible.

He glared in response. "Yes. One."

Shazina shuddered, struggling to control another wave of emotion.

"But how?" I asked.

"The first night was the worst," he said mechanically. "Fed on a few dozen before anyone knew what was happening. By the time the alarm was raised, it had already had its fill. Still killed another dozen in the process of leaving." He took a breath, using the moment to shake some emotion off. "The second and third night it came, it fed on more, and killed more. By the fourth day, we'd lost over half to its claws and another third to its hunger. Then it left."

Confused, I waited for him to continue.

With a disgusted sigh, he did. "We couldn't care for everyone. Slowly, we ran out of food. Some of the others formed a mob. Tried to give 'mercy' to those who no longer existed beyond the husks of their bodies. We fought, but they killed my mother and sister before I knew the mob's intentions. Those who could, fled. I stayed, burying the bodies and mourned. I waited and waited for Shazina to come home. Finally, I gave up and came here. I have a friend, and I wanted to warn him and didn't know what else to do."

"A single gimzer did that?"

He nodded, a dark shadow crossing his face. "They're fast. And strong. And nearly silent. I can match one if I'm using Ukiyo, but only just, and only for a short bit." Teo turned away, ashamed. "Not that I tried. When the alarm sounded, I ran. I was scared. I could have helped, but instead, I hid."

This finally knocked Shazina out of her sorrow and right into a rage. "You RAN?!" Her voice cracked like a whip, and her brother flinched as if he'd be struck by one. "You left our family unprotected? The village? You're Ukiyo makes you directly responsible for safekeeping our family," she finished, voice trailing to a shaky whisper.

Teo clenched his fists. He trembled, suppressing anger and shame. "I didn't want to die, all right? I was scared, and before I knew what I was doing, I'd left. I am so sorry. You don't understand how sorry I am. I'm the one that had to bury everyone. Had to dig a hundred graves for a hundred friends. You don't think I wish I could have done it differently?" He, too, had dropped to a whisper, and it was hard to say which of the siblings was more upset.

"A coward for a brother," Shazina said out loud, but to neither of us. "Why did I even try to bring help if this is what I'm saving?"

Crestfallen, he slumped to the ground, excitement at seeing his lost sister shifting over into a sullen shame.

It didn't seem like the time for me to be involved, so I wandered away, stretching my sore legs.

The homes were all small, mostly hidden with scrub grass rolling over the sloped roofs. The people were cautious, watching me from windows or half-cracked doors. None came out to meet or talk to me. After I realized I was hungry enough to try more snake, I began picking my way back through the maze of hills to where I'd left the two siblings to sort out their frustrations.

A near perfectly camouflaged form detached itself from the clay bricks on a house, making me stutter step in surprise.

Narrow lips twitched up into the simile of a grin at my misstep, and out of place, blue eyes twinkled with amusement. "We don't get many visitors," she said, holding out a hand.

"Nil," I replied, shaking it awkwardly. "And I can imagine. Seems a little," I paused, "desolate."

She shook her head at that, still smiling. "There's life if you know where to look. There always is and always will be. It's a lot like happiness. I'm Lonora." She looked me over once more before gesturing towards the door. "Fancy a game of Kingdoms?"

That gave me pause. "You have kingdoms over here?"

She gave a Shazina-like eye roll. "Of course, we're not barbarians." She noted my hesitation. "I've got food. And besides, I know who you arrived with here. Teo and I are..." she paused this time, looking for the right word, "close. He'll find us sooner or later."

Food was all it took, apparently. I followed her inside, my stomach rumbling. A single room carved itself into the hillside with what looked like a trap door leading to further rooms below. Loaves were stacked high on shelves in one corner, and the home had the heady, thick aroma of freshly baked bread. Lonora shut the door behind us and gestured at a threadbare rug.

I sat down and saw there was a worn kingdoms board embedded into the floor. Someone had painstakingly carved the stone with care and precision. The grooves were deep and weathered. Lonora tossed over a loaf of still-warm sourdough and a water skin. I scarfed the bread down before taking a swig. It was water, but with a bite of some kind of citrus infused with it. Perfect after the run and heat.

"Let's play," I said, riding the confidence of my last win with Insley.

She set the board, a standard, classic style with no special pieces or powers. Her playing was slow, methodical, and defensive. Positioning pieces in groups and moving them bit by bit in a march across the board. No elemental style. Nothing aggressive or built up. Just controlled, slow gain. I tried to hammer against her defense, but she had too many adjacent pieces. I tried luring her into a trap, but she ignored it. Before I knew it, Lonora had my pieces scattered around the board without any support from each other, and it was only a matter of her cleaning them up.

Back to losing like a chump. Again.

Another round, and I lost again. Still, Shazina and her brother hadn't shown up yet.

During the third game, Lonora took mercy and began to narrate. "You've been playing with too many people who focus on finesse. Sometimes, the easiest way to win is the short and simple route. Choose a move that will increase your position. Don't make sacrifices unless you need to. Simple, straightforward attacks and defense. Let your opponent make the mistakes."

Teo and Shazina arrived, both out of breath and pale.

"We saw one," Teo gasped, lacking Shazina's measured control.

Shazina, having taken a moment to bring her breathing down to a steady pace, looked between us. "The gimzer. It was crossing the desert and headed our way."

Chapter Sixteen

Our game was forgotten. Lonora shot up, a particular pressure that I was learning indicated she also could access Ukiyo. The unnatural grace that accompanied the unnatural speed confirmed it. Teo held out a hand, pausing her movement. She moved into it, relaxing into a desperate hug. It took me a moment to realize she'd instinctually reacted with Ukiyo and had to tamp it down despite her adrenaline rush.

He placed a kiss on the top of her head before looking sideways and embarrassed at Shazina.

"Friend," she commented dryly.

Teo looked guilty, but it also seemed like he'd run out of emotional rope to pull on with today. "We need to focus on this gimzer. We can't let this thing hurt this village too."

Shazina now looked embarrassed, some thought occurring to her. "I was too upset to remember the stories. Nil here is a Learner."

Some mix of fury and awe spun across both the Exo native's faces, settling down to something akin to horror. I took a step back, putting my arms up defensively. Shazina stepped forward, raising her palms in a placating gesture.

"How could you?" Teo asked, actual hurt in his voice.

A loaf of bread was tossed to Shazina and then to me before either of us could answer. My newest Kingdoms partner had transitioned past the shock and had seemed to drop back into herself. "Ignore him," Lonora said while tossing more bread his way as well. From beneath the lowest shelf of bread, she pulled out a half spear. The tip was small, more like an arrowhead attached to a quarterstaff. "We have to lead them away, the four of us should be able to take down one, and even if not, Nil here can act as a beacon for it to follow us as far from here as we can get."

I eyed the loaf of bread, and then the girl. "I'm not monster bait."

"Actually, you are." Shazina seemed almost apologetic, though less towards me and more towards the other two from Exo. "Our best choice is to get you away from where other people can be harmed. The gimzer is coming for you either way.

With a scowl, I took an sullen bite out of the fresh loaf I held. "Fine, when do we leave?"

"Now," all three said simultaneously.

Word spread through the village like wildfire. Mostly due to Teo shouting about a possible gimzer headed their way because of me being a Learner. Anyone who didn't hear him was told by neighbors in what had to be a new world record in gossip-mongering. My status as a Learner seemed to have made me even more unpopular, especially when we began to run back the way we came. Everyone seemed to understand the implication, and potential danger, of me staying in the village.

Teo and Shazina ran ahead, arguing fiercely. They did so in hushed, unintelligible whispers that left me in the dark on what the siblings were so hotly discussing. Unlike them, it required far more effort to maintain my Ukiyo well enough to keep with the speed at which we raced back over the desert towards their empty hometown.

Despite my efforts, the siblings pulled away from us, moving faster and faster. I tried to push myself, but Lonora put an arm out, slowing me back down. "They're planning something. Let them do the heavy lifting. Despite her age, Shazina's one of the smartest and strongest people I've ever heard of."

By the time we reached the clay brick homes, the two had stripped enough wood from the surrounding structures to build a solid stack that was at least as tall as man and as wide as three well fed people. It was such an impressive amount of work for just the siblings to have pulled off, the weariness of the run completely disappeared as I inspected the construction.

"Quite the fortification," I said approvingly.

Teo shook his head sadly. "This isn't defensive. This here is the trap. Come in."

Inside, Shazina stacked more wood bundles, filling the small home with strategically placed kindling. They were going to burn the whole place down, I realized. With a small amount of direction, Lonora and I helped add more wood, connecting other homes into a wood piled maze of kindling leading to the center building. The final masterstroke to the trap was all mine, and it was both the bait and the linchpin for me getting out in one piece.

I willed Skill forth, feeling the Toron stone lending me yet more energy. It'd crack soon, unfortunately. I had relied too heavily on it, and even with its size, I'd pushed too much. A problem for tomorrow. Carefully, I cut a clean hole in the roof, just large enough for a person. The use of Skill would act as a beacon, bringing the gimzer here like a fish on the line. That fish being as nasty as any of the sea monsters we'd seen, but still.

After Teo did some careful placing of the cut roof so it'd fall into place at the right time, we slapped together a makeshift bundle of heavier worked wood just above the door to the house. Evening was coming far too quickly, and with it, the gimzer. We liberally splashed precious oil inside the house, and every torch we could find was lit and delicately placed on the roof so it'd not prematurely burn down.

I sat inside. Sweat dripped from me in a steady stream. Nervousness mingling with the oppressive heat made me supremely uncomfortable as I strained to hear any approach of the gimzer.

All three of the Exo-born had lectured me on the dangers of this particular brand of nastiness. They were fast. They were strong. And they were silent. But most importantly, I had to make sure it didn't touch me. I was dead as soon as it did. To them, that was far less important than the fact that a gimzer who'd fed on a Learner was magnitudes more powerful according to legend.

It wasn't a noise or sound that told me the gimzer had arrived. A whistle had been our agreed upon signal, but it hadn't come. Instead, it felt like some external pressure. As if someone had placed my head in a bucket of water. Icy water, at that. I felt for my Skill and realized it was muted, harder to reach. Then the oppressive, cold feeling became worse, and I realized the Skill I'd drawn was fizzling away without me willing it to. "Left hand of god," I said, genuine fear blooming in the space of a breath.

Mentally I scrambled, grasping at Skill in a vain attempt to find it. Our whole plan hinged on me jumping through the roof's hidden hole, which would simultaneously bar the front door and torch the place. Panic began to set in. I breathed, forcing the fear out and clearing my mind. I stood, moving into Volant's meditation flow, trying to repurpose the burst of energy the fear was flooding my system with. While I moved, I turned my mind towards Ukiyo, hoping against hope that I could directly summon Skill on the other side of the barrier.

Nothing happened.

I went through it again, breathing more slowly, moving more slowly, all the while feeling the weight of what could only be the gimzer becoming nearly unbearable. I clapped, finishing the movement with Volant's signature focusing technique, and pushed my will into Ukiyo with iron resolve.

A spark ignited in me, Skill flooding in my mind, deep in my person. It also seemed to shield me from the gimzer's leeching effect. I pushed as much as I could into the corners of my body. Hyperawareness came to me, the slight scratch of a foot just outside the front door, a smell like dust and rotten meat.

It was here.

A whistle sounded, too little too late if I'd been relying on my Skill. The creature crashed in, four arms reaching for me. Not just one monster, I realized, already in mid-jump. Two of them. A pair. And gods above were they fast. I exploded through the hole, triggering an avalanche of clay bricks and lumber. Flames ignited through the gaps between the debris as my Ukiyo fed strength landed me just high enough on the roof's edge to avoid falling back into the hole.

An unholy pair of shrieks pierced the starry night as the home went up in flames. A thump, followed by another, rocked me from below as something impacted the clay roof with the force of a battering ram. Another hit cracked the floor beneath me, and I realized I wasn't anywhere out of trouble yet. Flames began to spread around the house, the other three having rushed in with torches and set fire to the piled wood.

I scrambled to the roof's edge and across the piled wood. Ukiyo again saved me as I wouldn't have made it across without stumbling and falling if it weren't for the incredibly heightened control I now had over my legs. A column of fire and smoke was now soaring high above the roof's edge as more wood fed the hungry, all-consuming flame.

Tongues of heat licked up at me as I jumped again, briefly passing through a burst of fire. It wasn't like when I waved my hand through a candle flame. This felt more like being bathed in a wave of tiny razors all over my exposed skin. The harsh burns washed away all other thoughts until I hit the ground. I dipped my shoulder forward, rolling in a diagonal motion to so as not to hurt my back. The movement was muscle memory at this point. I kept rolling, over and over, until all the flames that had begun in my clothes disappeared.

A blazing inferno raged as I ran from the village, finding the other three trying to escape the out of control fire as well. We made it to the edge and watched in mute awe as the flames charged from one home to another, devouring the inner timber and crumbling the dwelling from the inside out. The sky was lit with firelight as bright as any sunset evening. It wasn't until dawn that the flames died down enough that we could approach the blackened remains of their village.

Embers twinkled like dull stars in the black ashes, mirroring the night sky above that a great expanse of smoke now blocked out. None of us had expected the flames to reach beyond the maze of wood we'd encircled the home with, but what was done was done. All three of the Exo natives seemed to be more than happy to trade the empty village in exchange for knowing without a doubt that the gimzers had burned up in it.

A surreal readjusting to natural daylight came with the sunrise as the brightness of the fire disappeared. Ash was piled high around Shazina and Teo's home. The wood had burned long and hot. A bony hand, more claw-like and far too large, extended from the pile. It was charred black, but the tips of the finger still seemed sharp. Digging the monstrous corpses out of the ashes made my skin crawl, but I need to what we were. These two nightmarish corpses needed to be examined.

After we dragged the too heavy skeletons from the ashen village, I received my first introduction into what a true terror these creatures were. They were tall, much taller than anyone I'd ever met. Their skeletons had elongated limbs, ending in human-shaped hands and feet with long, talon-like claws. Their knees were double-jointed, bending in the wrong direction, more like a bird's than any human. Oversized teeth filled their mouth, all canines though Shazina pointed out that they didn't necessarily eat any flesh. Stranger still, the bones were far denser than they had any right too.

I compared my forearm to one of the creature's and found that the bone was larger and thicker than my upper arm. It'd be near impossible to break without an enormous hammer and some time. This was an apex predator, no doubt about it.

A shadow passed over us, blocking the light as we continued to examine the gimzer corpse. None of the others had seen one dead either. The shadow didn't pass, and as one, the four of us turned and looked up at the sky. The belly of an airship with a newly fixed prow floated above us. Thecily's Sky Wolf was airborne again.

Black shapes began to fall from either side of the ship. As they fell, the figures came into focus. Volant, Craig, and the rest of the landing crew were falling towards us at slightly less than dangerous speeds. Teo and Lonora were both flabbergasted at the ship and the fallpacks. They'd been intensely interested in the gimzers, but their childlike wonder at this contraption was more akin to someone discovering their lifelong dream coming true.

On the other hand, the landing crew was just as grotesquely enamored with the gimzer skeletons, marveling at the strong bones and predatory limbs. I introduced everyone as the airship lowered down its anchor ropes to hover just outside the blackened ring that used to be a village. Thecily's crew was just dropping the boarding ramps when another group of people arrived. Lonora's town had seen the pillar of smoke and had come to see what had happened, bringing every available person they could find in case the gimzer had survived our attempt to end it.

Insley and I found each other almost immediately after the ship's touchdown. We hugged, neither of us willing to let go first until Qaewin came over and interrupted us with a polite cough. The story about trapping the gimzers and burning down the village had been spreading similarly to how the flames had last night, and she wanted to hear about it firsthand. When I had finished, they all were upset that we'd done something so dumb and dangerous without having just come back to the ship instead.

Unlike our run-in with the gimzers, the ship repair had been entirely hassle-free. Thecily's people were well trained and well prepared. They'd finished the repairs and reinforced the envelope ropes that held the balloon in place with plenty of time to spare. They'd been waiting for us to come back when a crew member on night watch saw the massive fire and smoke column. They rightfully guessed we'd had a hand in it, and the crew had brought the ship up and out.

Shouts from the villagers broke through to us. Qaewin was the first to respond, rushing towards her pack of zymphs who'd been surrounded by twenty or so aggressively enthusiastic Exo natives. The massive cats were hemmed in by the onlookers. The cat's ears pulled back, and tails tucked down low. They weren't the friendliest of creatures at the best of times, but from the looks of it, they were about to turn violent on the unwitting crowd.

Qaewin pushed in, shouting at everyone to give them space. No one listened.

Volant and I shoved forward, physically moving the crowd's front row back enough to give Qaewin space to calm the animals. We finally got the crowd to open an area creating a semi-circle that allowed a visible escape route for the zymphs. This settled them down enough that a few newcomers could come close enough to pet the animals. Lonora was one of them, even more awe in her expression than when the airship had arrived.

"Why didn't you tell us you brought great cats with you? We thought they were extinct." Her tone was part wonder, part accusatory.

"I didn't know it was important," I said defensively. "Why does it matter?"

She turned, grabbing Teo and another man. They had a whispered conversation before each broke off into a run in opposite directions away from the village.

She turned back, eyes shining. "Legend has it that the great animals were what originally kept the gimzers at bay. But when the exodus happened with the gods and learners, the great animals died off as well."

"Wait, so you guys don't have zymphs, or borgislings, or lunavargs?" I asked, shocked.

She rolled her eyes. "The giant lizards being gone is the silver lining in this. But no, these are the first I've ever seen. Did you bring any of the lunavargs?"

Argo and Shazina arrived at that moment, the now much larger puppy enthusiastically greeting everyone within its field of vision. Within moments, Argo had solidified his fan base in Exo to similar enthusiasm as Kalaran had shown.

Lonora's eyes were wide with amazement. "You did!"

"Well, no," I said apologetically. "Argo's just a regular puppy."

She looked at me with an odd expression, as if I had made a bad joke. "Are you serious? This isn't a lunavarg? Look at the size of it."

"Umm, yes. Just a dog, I'm fairly certain." As I said it, a look crossed between Shazina and Lonora, and I felt like there was something I was missing. Argo did seem to have grown rather large for the short time we'd had them. I'd never really seen a dog before Argo, with them being incredibly rare, so it seemed reasonable. I'd read several books though, and he seemed to match the description. Besides, he was still as goofy as any puppy. He'd just been eating properly and putting on weight. Lots of it. An odd feeling began to niggle about the puppy.

By sunset, the runners Lonora had sent off had arrived again. Envoys from the other villages were all coming to see the zymphs and the airship. They also had news of other gimzers and wanted to build a coalition to fight back against them now that Learners, Naturals, and the great cats had returned to Exo.

Finally, some level of satisfaction broke through for Shazina. I doubted she was even close to properly having started mourning her family, but it was good to see her efforts properly appreciated and her pride in it. When the stolen moon showed its face, Insley dragged me back to the ship and forced me to get a full night's rest.

The healer knew best, as I slept through most of the following day, waking up to what sounded like a camped army outside the ship. I went up top and saw that it wasn't too far off. Thousands had arrived while I slept, giving the burned village a wide berth but surrounding the airship in every direction. Despite the loss of an entire village, the atmosphere was festive.

People were celebrating, sharing food with strangers, and giving hugs to loved ones. Village elders had the school's books in hand, reading to groups of hopefuls about lost powers in an attempt to become Learners. Zymphs prowled through the crowd, being practically worshipped by anyone they came near. Thecily's crew was busy arming the populace with steel and finishing the last touch on their repaired ship.

Far in the distance, dust clouds showed more people heading our way. The villagers elevated Teo and Lonora to a new level of famous, their Ukiyo paired with the death of the two gimzers earning them previously unheard-of status amongst their peers. Shazina though, especially with Argo, seemed to be the only other thing anyone was talking about. The girl who crossed the sea and brought back the forgotten. It'd become so overwhelming that she'd been hiding out on the ship away from her own people.

The village leader called a meeting when a runner from a neighboring village appeared, begging for us to come help eradicate a pod of gimzers that were terrorizing his people. Thecily, Volant, Qaewin, and Cassiopia were waiting for me as I headed back down to the ground. Apparently, the other village had found a den in one of the deep cracks where the gimzers had been hunting from.

There was no debate. This was what we'd come for. After having heard how they'd decimated Shazina and Teo's village, Thecily was taking it as a personal mission to stomp the creatures out. But we couldn't use the airship, as the return trip to Balteris was now a priority as well. Not a problem in itself, but there were so many volunteers from the surrounding villages that much of the ship was needing to be stripped and repurposed to provide more oars for rowing and more sleeping space for the enlarged crew.

In the end, we decided to take the zymphs, all the Learners, Naturals, and any Ukiyo volunteers from the still growing crowd. Cassiopia joined as well as Qaewin, and several crew members who refused to let Thecily go without them came along as well. We set out at a brisk but unenhanced jog almost immediately. The gimzer hunted at night, and the hope was to get there before they took another life.

A low, throaty growl came first from Qaewin's zymph and echoed from the others. Qaewin froze at the sound of it, dropping into a defensive crouch despite the empty desert around us. The rest of the group slowed down in response to the zymphs who'd all frozen, pointing just a little way to the left of the line we'd been running.

"What's the-" Thecily started before a trio of nightmares erupted from the ground a dozen paces away, moving at a blurring clip towards our group.

Chapter Seventeen

As the gimzers rushed us, our zymphs charged, bursts of speed only an oversized animal could generate. One of the gimzers, the front most one, lunged forward to meet the animals. The other two leaped clear, double-jointed knees springing them like grasshoppers high over the zymphs in an effort to get us.

Volant and I had our swords out simultaneously. We weren't as fast as Cassiopia though, who'd already sent one of her heavy arrows whistling through the air between us. With an unnatural twist, the gimzer moved midair, letting the shaft buzz harmlessly by. A second shot was already in the air, aiming for the spot the gimzer would be landing.

An ear-splitting shriek paired with a loud crack marked the second arrow's contact as it punched through the gimzer's chest, knocking it backward with its force. The third gimzer charged our group head-on, feet clawing the earth as it closed the final distance. Volant and I dove, swinging our blades with a synchronized motion that could only come from people who'd trained together as much as we had. Our swords bit deep while Thecily and her crew, a heartbeat slower, lunged forward with an armory's worth of weapons. The Ukiyo users blurred into motion as well, sending several small spears flying with deadly accuracy.

Everything was still for a moment, the gimzer hoisted in the air by the joint effort, dead before it hit the ground.

Another arrow whizzed between Volant and me. We turned as it flew by, following its path until it thudded into the second gimzer with a meaty thunk, pinning it to the hard ground. Cassiopia sent a fourth shaft flying, this one embedding itself right through the gimzer's mouth, finally finishing the creature off.

Qaewin had us wait until the zymphs came to us. The pack had taken longer to destroy the first gimzer but had done a much more thorough job of it. The large cats had spread pieces of the creature all over the immediate area they'd engaged the gimzer in. One of them had a slight limp, and another a nasty gash across its face. Otherwise, the zymphs seemed more alive and alert than I'd ever seen. They completely ignored the two we'd brought down as they rejoined us.

As a group, we slowly made our way to where the gimzers had seemingly appeared out of thin air.

Despite everything, I nearly fell into the crack that they'd jumped from. It looked like a patch of shadow, dark, and barely there. Volant grabbed my shoulder as I put a foot out over the empty expanse before my brain caught up with what my eyes were seeing. I stumbled backward, a shiver running through me at the close call. A quick torch was made and tossed down into the black. The crack was a couple of paces wide and maybe twice as many long. It was deep. Very deep. So deep, we lost sight of the torch as it fell, long before a faint, soft sound most likely indicated it'd hit bottom.

"Hidden canyons," Teo explained. "We have them all over the desert."

"A lot of the surface area up here can give way if you're not watching for it," Lonora added. "Sometime's they'll just open up, almost like a hungry mouth and swallow anything on the surface. Stories say there used to be a lake underneath the desert, but it's been drying up. We have to dig the wells deeper every year just to find water, so I believe it."

We continued, the runner urging us to haste before he lost his loved ones.

As true night began to fall, the terrain started to change. The flat desert was morphing into larger, shale like outcroppings with plinth looking pillars reaching into the sky. Boulders made out of the same orange and white rock were stacked on each other as if the gods themselves had been playing some kind of game. We stopped in front of what had appeared to be a miniature mountain from a distance, but up close became an outcropping of stones and boulders all piled in a massive, hill shaped mound. Cracks, hinting at the previously mentioned hidden canyons, dotted the area, making the footing treacherous in the pale light of the night sky.

The man who'd begged for our help pointed at the outcropping, a noticeable tremor shaking his whole body. "This is where they've started nesting. Our village is only a little way away from here, and they've already taken too many of us."

Sharp ozone, the unmistakable scent of Skill, tickled my nose.

"No!" Shazina cried out, reaching for Craig.

Confused, he turned to her. "What?"

Her warning was too late. Dark shadows boiled from the outcropping, spilling over one another until a pack of gimzers formed across the way, speeding towards us.

Zymphs surged forward as well, something about the gimzers putting them into a fierce level of aggression. I'd only seen them this furious when slithers had invaded their territory before the battle of Brod. Cassiopia and Qaewin began launching arrow after arrow across the distance. Volant moved, his hands cupping wind and shifting it like a potter shaping clay. A cyclone formed in his hands.

Thecily and her crew spread out, giving each other, and especially Volant and I, a wide berth. Cassiopia continued to shoot, but Qaewin stopped as the zymphs crashed into nightmares. The cats made a noticeable dent, but a handful of the inhuman forms were still heading our way. It was eerie how quiet the gimzers moved. Despite their speed, they didn't make a sound. I brought in Skill, shifting it to my hands, and shunting a portion through to Ukiyo with a hard, mental push. Almost immediately, a headache began to form from the effort.

With a panicked cry, startling all of us, the man who'd brought us this far ran towards the gimzers. He didn't even have a weapon. In mute horror, we watched as the first gimzer casually swung a clawed hand out. It barely touched his shoulder, and the man dropped like a stone. Panic did that sometimes. Making someone jump headlong into the danger just to make the worst come to pass.

"Single touch, and you're finished," Shazina warned the group. Teo and Lanora stood by her side, both only trembling slightly.

As the closest one neared, Volant tossed his vortex at the gimzer and charged. The blast of air knocked the towering creature over, spinning it end over end. Volant danced outside of its reach as it twisted against the cyclone he'd trapped it in. With delicate precision, he thrust once. Twice. And then a third time, the blade flicking in and out. Something like blood sprayed with each stab. He sent the vortex of wind and the creature within flying across the desert floor with a strong backhand. The effort brought him to a knee, but the creature hurtled far from us.

I jumped in front of my friend, slicing both hands out like a child pretending to fight. Each slice of the hand sent blades of Skill hurtling at the gimzers ahead of us. Chunks of dark meat ripped off at each point my attacks made contact. I pushed harder, drawing on the Toron stone until a distinct crack sounded, and a vibration shook me like that of a too-tight bowstring snapping.

Bone tired weariness flooded my body at the same time, and I knew I had summoned all the Skill I'd be able to. I pushed it through into Ukiyo, adding to the growing reserve. My muscles twitched, and my mind sharpened. And then, I danced with the nightmares of old.

Arrows flew. Swords flashed. Claws raked the air.

I lost track of time as I weaved around the creatures—fighting for my life and that of my friends.

A final gimzer, smaller and slower than the rest, was brought down by Qaewin's zymph Chloe, bringing the nightmare to an end. It looked like we'd gotten away without a loss beyond the runner.

As if thinking about him triggered something, the man's previously still body slowly stood up, his movements odd. He shambled a few steps forward. Then another few.

His movements lacked grace and coordination. He didn't seem to see us either. Faster than the eye could track, a rock slammed into the man's head. He dropped again, this time for good.

"Left hand of god! What was that about?" I turned, searching for who'd thrown the rock.

It was Shazina. A second rock was already in her hand. "He was just a shell. Remember? You're the one who asked why we didn't do the humane thing. I just saved his loved ones from making that choice."

I paused, remembering the conversation. "But, he looked fine," I tried, knowing the words wouldn't change the Ukiyo enhanced throw she'd ended the man with.

Instead of responding, she nodded her head to something behind my right shoulder. I turned and then jumped back in shock. Close enough that I should have felt his breath on my neck stood one of Thecily's crew.

His eyes were blank. No intelligence. His expression was empty, too, completely devoid of any understanding of what was around him or the violence that had just passed. He barely seemed to breathe and was almost completely still. I poked him in the chest gently. He didn't respond. I poked harder, pushing him off balance. The husk of a man fell backward, flopping against the ground.

It was then that Thecily came over, blade drawn and tears in her eyes. With one quick motion, she thrust her blade through the sailor, piercing his heart and giving him a mercifully quick and painless exit from this world.

I took another step back, almost as shocked by this as having found the dead-eyed man behind me.

She continued on to another man. Yet, another husk that used to be her crew. In and out, the sword went. Her tears were flung out with each thrust, twinkling against the night's dim light. Five of her men in total were touched and drained of their humanity by the gimzers.

We carried the bodies to the outcropping and dropped them in, an impromptu and unfitting burial.

A dark cloud hung over us after that, and no one spoke as we walked back the way we'd run, each of us wrestling with our thoughts and feelings on what had just happened.

As more and more Exo natives arrived at the impromptu gathering around Thecily's ship, a new village began to spring to life on the bones of Shazina's hometown. The triplets joined up with the gimzer hunting force, practicing almost daily with their own Toron stones. We kept a few in reserve for the ride back, but otherwise, each of us carried a pair with us, the second in case our first broke. Thecily's crew created long, heavily reinforced spears with thick cross guards similar to what you'd use when hunting boar.

Anytime a new group arrived, they'd invariably have a gimzer or two for us to go hunt down. Between the Learners, Naturals, and Thecily's impressively disciplined crew, we had exceptional success not letting the monsters drain anyone else. The zymphs provided the biggest boost to our ability to hunt the gimzers. They had an instinct in finding the creatures after having picked up the scent that first night. Despite having a group that would have even rivaled the blue robes in terms of deadliness, we mostly worked at keeping the gimzers we ran across distracted and at a spears length distance as the zymphs did the dirty work of tearing the monstrosities to shreds. They were immune to the gimzers draining touch and were easily the stronger of the two. The only thing they lacked was speed, which didn't matter if we had one of the creatures pinned with half a dozen spears.

After several successful hunts, we started training some of the villagers on how to use the spears. We repurposed nearly all of the spare wood and metal found on the Sky Wolf into additional gimzer spears. A few attacks came, most likely due to the use of Skill by the triplets or I. Exo natives were lost, but a kindred spirit began to form between them, the crew, and Qaewin's zymphs. New bonds began to appear between the big cats and some of the people.

Qaewin helped encourage it, teaching the people as much as she could about the cats and helping smooth the rough edges that formed around the new pairings. To our surprise, one of the cats had been pregnant before we left for Exo. The birth of a new litter of zymphs turned into a celebration that lasted days before we got back to the business of hunting gimzers and helping rebuild.

All the while, Shazina and I, along with the other Learners, trained until our minds or bodies gave out. Argo seemed to grow at an exponential rate, his puppy body transforming into quite a large dog that definitely seemed at least half lunavarg. He and Shazina became inseparable.

Insley worked harder than any of us. I spent as much free time as I could manage with her, and that was always in her makeshift clinic. If she wasn't training the hopeful would-be healers, she was fixing cuts and bruises of training accidents gone wrong or the myriad of injuries that seemed to crop up in what could only be called a city at this point.

During one of Volant and I's nightly sparring sessions, when I was cursing Berjio's sword and my seeming ineptness at using it properly, a villager shyly approached.

We'd taken him out on a gimzer hunt, which ended with us finding a small horde similar to the first night at the outcropping. The man had panicked at the sight of the creatures and dropped his spear. The hole in our defense almost cost him his life and that of those around him. I'd thrown up a Skill shield, similar to what we'd used crossing the causeway, and knocked the gimzer away long enough for the gap in the spear wall to be closed.

He held a small bundle wrapped in rough cloth now and seemed slightly embarrassed.

We paused.

After the first few nights, our audience had trickled down, and it was now almost always just the two of us unless someone wanted a bit of practice or Qaewin and Insley decided to join. Thecily had folded in on herself, only seeming to come alive when we were out on a hunt. She was a storm of vengeance, and I was worried she was trying to join her lost crewman in a suicidal attempt at destroying the gimzers.

The man stepped over to me, offering the bundle with a mumbled thanks. "They're a family heirloom. Supposedly from before the exodus."

I took it with half a smile on my face. The man fled as soon as the bundle was in my arms, not even waiting for me to unwrap it. Inside were a pair of matching hatchets.

Dark, sharp iron was embedded in some exotic hardwood that shined with obvious care. The blade curved in such a way that these pieces were obviously made for war. Nothing so mundane as chopping wood for these weapons. The short shafts had been carved so that they provided an impossibly comfortable grip without sacrificing any traction. I stared at them for a long time, knowing that these must have been passed down through generations of the villager's family. I didn't even know the man's name.

With relief, I sheathed the sword master's blade. I hefted the axes. They made a soothing swish as I practiced moving them through the air. By the time I was finished moving through a kata, I was grinning like a fool. Perfect balance and size. I slid them easily behind my back as if I'd done it a hundred times. It was like they'd been custom made just for me.

Chapter Eighteen

Whatever made the Exo natives Ukiyo training so effective seemed to work just as well for them becoming Learners. The elder of the villages had been studying the books we brought with us and had practically put everything else on hold. At the same time, they tried to fast track a system for finding and training people who could manipulate Skill externally as they thought of it. The village's teachers put nearly every child through a regiment of meditation, study, and physical strain in an effort to find the first batch of Learners this side of the causeway.

A large, lean-to style schoolhouse was coming together while we were out hunting the gimzers. They were generally solitary, and the use of Skill made it almost easy to find them, as the creatures would come charging in the straightest line possible at whichever Learner had manifested the Skill.

Despite the success of finding their first Learner, there was a glaring lack of interest or ability to find and train any Naturals. In Balteris, they almost always started showing signs of both the Talent and which element they were associated with at a young age. With little training, the child would generally become somewhat successful at controlling their Talent in any meaningful way, and if they pushed, possibly become a noticeably robust Natural. Not here, though. They didn't have any, nor did they seem to think it important one way or another.

Still, we continued our hunts while letting the villages come together and collectively catch their breath. It didn't take long for secondary and tertiary strike forces to form. These new groups only needed a Learner to go along as bait, and a few of the zymphs who had bonded with Exo natives. The great cats seemed even more eager than villagers to go out after the gimzers. The zymphs made the most dangerous foe on the planet a fairly even match. We'd only lost a handful of people and had taken out ten times as many gimzers.

I wove my way through the class of chattering children, their young faces alight with new found safety. Dendra had proven an invaluable resource with the kids. Laughter rang in the air, blending with the simmering excitement that coursed through my own veins. This was it —the moment we'd been working towards outside of the gimzer raids, each daily class a stepping stone to this pinnacle of success.

A young girl with a mop of untidy hair and eyes gleaming with determination stands at the center of the crowd. Her focus is unyielding as she attempts to harness Skill. I can see the childs brows furrow in concentration.

Then, a sudden shift. The smell of ozone as a ripple of energy sweeps through the throng. The girl's hands rise. The Skill responds, an incandescent dance of light that coalesces at her fingertips, a manifestation of pure potential. A cheer erupts, slicing through the atmosphere—a victorious, harmonious crescendo that marks the dawning of a new era for Exo.

Teo and Lonora had made sure I was here to witness this, to confirm what they'd been hoping for. Their child is the first Exo native to wield Skill. As the girl's success becomes palpable, the village comes alive in a way I've never seen. Dendra hugs the girl, the parents, and anyone else who comes near.

The desert heat that wraps around us does little to smother our spirits. The festivities ignite as word spreads, a spontaneous combustion of joy and unity that defies the harshness of their world. Food and drink circulate with a generosity to put any Soft Stepper feast to shame.

I stand there, amidst the revelry, my heart thundering a rhythm that matches the pulse of Exo. The joy is infectious, the pride immeasurable.

In the heart of the celebration, Teo and Lonora beam at me, their pride unmistakable. "Look," they gesture to the boy, "our first true Learner."

I smile in return, giving them both a hug. Words would never suffice for this moment.

The village, alive with a vibrancy that mirrors the desert sun, embraces this moment. Thecily's crew, alongside those villagers who'd still resented us foreigners, unite. Today, our differences are forgotten.

As I move through the crowd, I laugh—perhaps more freely than I have since our time at the school. Even in this searing, relentless desert, we carve out a space for hope, for progress. Today, Exo can finally start being more than survivors.

Not only did this mean they could begin to fight gimzers on their own, but it also meant they'd be able to try and summit the mountains and escape to the other side. I was surprised, as this was the first I'd heard of them needing skill for anything other than combat.

"Shazina," I said, seeing her and Argo go by. The dog was still as friendly and kind and energetic as ever but his size still caused me to stare. He nearly went up to her hip now, as larger than any dog I'd heard. Despite being back with her people, and brother, Shazina still seemed to keep to herself mostly.

She turned, face a mask of emotion with one eyebrow raised in question. Argo, on the other hand, hopped up and planted his paws on my chest before coming nose to nose with me- daring me not to let him lick me. I tried not to, but he did it anyway.

I laughed and pushed the dog away but kept a hand on his head to give him a scratch behind the ears. "What's with this mountain talk I've been hearing about?"

She rolled her eyes, glancing over at an elder proliferating on a raised platform down the way. "Promised land, supposedly," she said with disdain. "The mountains are too tall to climb. Gods, they're too tall even to fly over. There's no air up there. And we've tried to dig through them, but they're too deep and have too many gimzers. It's not the Learner necessarily that's supposed to get them through, but what you're becoming. The melding of Ukiyo and Learner is supposed to get them through the mountain to a land without gimzers, where the waters run clean and plentiful, and the trees all bear fruit ripe for the picking." She spat. "Children's stories. They should have more sense."

An alarm sounded from the other side of the village. Shazina and I exchanged looks. We both sprinted towards the clamor. As we came near the towering airship, running along its length, I saw Volant jumping off the railing at the far end. He pushed wind beneath him before hitting the ground and rolling with the impact. We caught up to him, and the three of us weaved through people and half-built clay brick homes.

A knot of people surrounded a smaller group who were kneeling on the ground. Insley was there, and a woman with wild eyes and the signs of heatstroke was lying on the ground before her. Volant had his sword drawn, but there were no gimzers or any other reason for an alarm to be sounded.

A boy sat in the small hut with the bell, looking sheepish, hand still on the rope. "What'd you ring the bell for?" Shazina demanded in a scathing tone, despite being half the boy's size and probably the same age.

"I saw her stumbling here. I thought she was a gimzer," he said, embarrassed.

Volant eased his sword back into the sheath. He smiled at the kid before pushing his way through to Insley. "Help me out here, Nil."

The two of us picked the woman up, Insley giving me a grateful smile in the process. We moved her back further into the village and brought her to one of the shaded wells.

Insley helped bring the woman back from the brink of heat-induced death. I recognized her as one of the hunters that had bonded with a zymph. She'd been the lynchpin for a small hunter group that went out to find gimzers. Despite the water and shade, her eyes still had a wild, panicked edge to them.

"What happened?" I asked. I tried to sound as gentle as possible, but the woman flinched anyway.

She stared wildly around. Her eyes threatened to roll back in her head, but she kept her composure just enough to stop from completely passing out. "It drained him. Corder, one of the Learners from the ship. And then, it changed. It was so fast. I only got away because I'd fallen back."

A sharp intake of breath came from one of the other Exo natives. "Not good, not good at all," a voice muttered.

I turned to Shazina, who saw the question coming before I could even ask.

"A gimzer, after draining a Learner, is supposedly a magnitude more dangerous on the scale of bad things that can happen. It's similar to an adult compared to a toddler. But it's not like we've run into one to prove that. Just legend." Despite her feigned nonchalance, she seemed as shaken as I'd ever seen her.

No further survivors showed up, including the zymph. In the middle of the wake for the lost group, zymphs everywhere came alert as one. Each had its nose pointed towards the west, ears flattened. From the village's edge, the same alarm as before sounded. This time, even more people converged at the perimeter, taking cues from the zymphs that something serious was afoot.

Hushed whispers and the occasional rocky scrape of a boot on the desert were all that could be heard. At first, I didn't see what had set the cats on edge or signaled the need for an alarm. And then I saw the flash of movement, far off on the horizon. Not having seen a gimzer in daylight, my mind tried to rationalize it as something else. Adding on that, its movements were more akin to teleportation rather than a creature made of flesh and bone.

I watched for a space of breaths, mutely horrified, as the gimzer made its way in a random series of bursts towards us. The speed was incredible. I couldn't track its movements, only seeing it briefly stop and orient before being a few paces away from the spot and appearing in the next. My skin crawled, watching the thing move. It was like a snake striking, your mind only catching up after the fact. And it just kept coming.

Volant and Qaewin, with Thecily shortly in tow returned, bristling with weapons. The gimzer had already covered a third of the distance to us. Little puffs of dust announced every time it moved. An afterimage of sorts, indicating where it had been.

The crowd ebbed and swelled as some onlookers crept away, hoping their friends and neighbors wouldn't see their cowardice. Others arrived in their place, hard expressions matching the hard steel of their spears. Clusters began to form around village heads or up and coming hunters.

With its random, scattered movements towards us, the gimzer was well over halfway when it paused for the first time. It seemed to sniff the air. Curious, I summoned Skill. The effect was immediate. Its posture snapped from a fluid, almost lazy posture into a stiff stance as it zeroed in on me. I took the Skill I'd summoned and whipped it towards the gimzer. My shot sped across the desert towards the still frozen in place creature. Just before it connected, the gimzer slapped my attack out of the air.

My blood ran cold. That shouldn't be possible.

The moment shattered, and the gimzer was heading our way. It was more than a dozen bow shots from us, but the distance seemed trivial for how quickly it ate up the ground between.

When the creature passed within what would be roughly twice that of an average human's bowshot range, the unmistakable thrum of

Cassiopia's bow went off. She loosed arrow after arrow, peppering the air with feathered shafts. Not one made contact. Within moments, it'd closed the distance, only stopping every twenty paces or so. Something about the way it moved forced the creature to stop after every burst of motion.

Volant, a few of Thecily's crew, and even fewer villagers who had bows all joined in for a volley, sending a rain of arrows down at the gimzer. It twitched and twisted, moving around and past all of the shafts. Before another volley could begin, the zymphs were pounding across the ground towards the apex monster. At this range, we could see its eyes, and they glowed a soft, shiny luminescence, unlike any other gimzer we'd seen.

Despite the number of zymphs and their beyond-human strength and speed, they were no match for the gimzer. It batted the first cat away, sending it cartwheeling to the ground. With an impossible leap, it cleared the rest of the zymphs and landed just outside of a spear's length from the front-most pocket of defenders.

They thrust anyways, fear clouding judgment. The gimzer blurred, spears cracked and shattered as it blew through the pocket of men and women, seeming to appear on the other side of them in a mist of dust and blood. It scattered the group, leaving two on the ground, and the rest flung in every direction. One of those left lying there was bleeding out with their arm torn completely free. To the credit of everyone, they not only stood their ground but went on the offensive. The fight was short and brutal. The zymphs came charging back in as spears slashed out and wind buffeted the creature from Volant. I took a swing but caught empty air as the gimzer somehow moved back and brought down a pair of Thecily's crewmen.

A lucky spear caught the creature in the center and was planted against the ground long enough for several others to anchor into the gimzer's body. Blades and spear tips and the claws of zymphs tore into the monstrosity until what was left of its body went limp, and the unnatural glow from its eyes faded to nothing.

The dust settled. So did the rest of us. A curt command from Qaewin and the zymphs backed off as well. Nineteen bodies lay sprawled around the body of the gimzer that was still held in place from spears in every direction. A dead zymph added to the sad sight. An additional group of five didn't move as the rest of us stepped back. Drained, but not deceased, at least physically. Their minds gone from this world though their bodies remained standing.

I'd been useless. All of my training, and I hadn't even tapped Ukiyo when the moment had needed it most. How many lives could I have saved? The thought haunted me.

We built pyre around the gimzer and burned its body to a crisp. A similar but more humane affair went down across the way for those who had died. Any spark of festivity that had been building around the airship and up-and-coming village had been snuffed out.

Despite the losses, the village began to grow, in part thanks to Thecily's crew helping ferry a number of workers to the edges of the mountain range and bringing back large loads of lumber for the people to shape. A wall went up around the village. Learners no longer went out solo, and everyone was on high alert to losing another.

Thecily began to make noises about the return trip, and a delicate dance of recruitment began to play out among both the village and the crew.

Volant, Insley, Qaewin, and I sat around a small table in what passed as the village's first-ever communal spot. An enterprising young woman had built the place with the help of a friend and began offering various teas for sale. Nothing nearly as nice as the floating shop in Wydvis, but it was an oasis compared to the tight confines and strict rations Thecily had moved the crew to.

An argument between father and son was happening next to us, and all four of us were eavesdropping.

"But da, how could I not go?" the son pleaded.

His father growled something before thumping the table. "And leave your brother and mother? Just to get yourself killed crossing that demonic sea?"

"I'm going," the son said after an excruciatingly long pause. "I'm sorry. But I'm going."

Before the father could say anything, the son was up and gone, rushing out the door.

Insley coughed politely, drawing the rest of our attention back to her. With a warm smile to me she then addressed all three of us. "I heard Diedra and Dendra are staying to teach at the school. And, Craig is apparently head over heels, and is staying as well."

Volant's eyes went wide, and a surprised laugh came up, causing Qaewin to chuckle at his reaction.

"Thecily is going to be seriously upset," he said. "Us wind dancers are hard to find. He's putting her in quite a bind. Plus, can we even make it back with two fewer Learners?"

Insley offered a non-committal nod in agreement on our ability to survive. "The numbers of newcomers joining in and willing to row is astounding. We might end up removing an entire generation from here. I talked with Craig, and he thinks we'll be fine."

Qaewin, in typical Soft Stepper fashion, seemed unconcerned either way.

At the ship, skilled crewmen were making fresh oars around the clock. Nearly every weapon or long-term supply or additional piece of unnecessary equipment was being offloaded from the airship and donated to the Exo village. Thecily was indeed in a mood, her arms cracking like whips as she directed her crew about their business. Her voice was hoarse from shouting orders, and I could see a vein throbbing at the side of her head.

Seeing the four of us arrive, she stormed over. "You lot better not be planning on jumping ship as well."

I raise my hands in surrender, trying to hide the grin that wanted to break free. "Not at all," I replied, "we're all coming along."

"Good. The ex-captain has opted to stay, saying 'a life here is better than a death at the sea's hands.' The cook too, but thankfully Martino and Joy are coming back and can take his place."

A village elder appeared as she was about to say something else. In his hands, he had a dark small, wooden box. He held it out to Thecily, who took it with no small amount of confusion.

"A token of our thanks," he said. "Before your departure creates any bad blood, I wanted to let you know how grateful we all are, no matter who stays and goes. We were on the brink of ruin before you and your crew arrived. We haven't been this prepared for the future since before the exodus." With that, he turned and strode off, moving well for a man his age.

Another elder arrived, offering Thecily another small token of appreciation. "We're as ready as we'll ever be, dear, so don't you worry about us now. It's time for you and yours to head home if you're still planning on it." Again, she left like the other did, leaving no room for a response.

Thecily turned to us, holding the box and a small, black-iron knife similar to the axes I had been given.

Yet before any of us could speak, a third elder who'd become the defacto leader of this village arrived, carrying an oilskin wrapped around what looked to be a large, and more than likely, ancient book.

"The knowledge of Ukiyo," he said, handing it to Thecily but bowing to each of us in turn. "Everything we know about Ukiyo, and the combination of it with the external manipulations." He bowed again, walking away just as casually as if he'd said hello to a neighbor.

Arms stuffed, Thecily had gone from confusion to a mixture of amazement and suspicion. "I think this is the politest, most generous leave-the-town I've ever received."

Chapter Nineteen

Huge ropes dropped off the side of the Sky Wolf as we finished the final checks for departure. A steady stream of Exo men and women had been filing into the ship all morning. A beautiful sunrise, the kind that only seems to come at the change of a season and lasts for far too short, started our departure day. Despite some of Thecily's crew deciding a new life on this side of the sea was better than risking death again, and a few romantic entanglements ending up with more people choosing to stay, the ship still swelled with volunteers coming on board from Exo.

At this point, the Sky Wolf looked more like a sky porcupine with the number of oars sticking out from its sides. Thecily had put her people to work, cutting additional benches, oars, and oar ports into the ship. Some complicated math that went well beyond my understanding determined how much wood they removed from the hull and cut into oars or tossed overboard. As I understood, the short version was that to maintain airworthiness, specific weight ratios had to be met so we didn't launch into the unbreathable air too high up or get dragged down to the ground by the influx of passengers.

Insley and Thecily were both admiring the ship while Volant and I finished our goodbyes with the different people we'd helped train for gimzer hunting. Since the incident with the Learner, we hadn't had anyone else lost to the gimzers, Exo or Balteran. It was a good feeling to know that we weren't abandoning them.

As I headed over to say some final goodbyes, I saw Shazina heading up the deck ramp, Argo in tow. I'd not have noticed except for the crowd waving goodbye. At first, I assumed it was for Shazina, but then I listened.

"We'll miss you, Argo!"

"Stay safe, you wonderful puppy!"

Plenty of voices called out variations on goodbye and well-wishing to the famously friendly dog.

I nudged Volant, pointing over to the group sending them off. "How does Argo do it? He has the entire village hand feeding him when he rolls by. I bet they'd have kicked us off even sooner if it wasn't for him."

Volant raised his hands out, showing he was just as much at a loss. "Pretty loveable. I'd be the same way if I hadn't had to clean poop off his paws."

"Aye," I agreed. "That said, I assumed Shazina was staying. Her brother is still here."

Volant looked trouble at that as well. "I thought the same. Maybe you should go ask her?"

Without much left to do, I headed up to do precisely that. If it weren't for Argo and his still growing form, I'd have not found her. A pile of rope in a back corner had made a shaded enclosure just big enough for Shazina to lay out under. Argo, though was bouncing around the deck, trying to get anyone and everyone to play with him.

I gave the dog a quick pet before dropping down to sit next to the rope pile. I shaded my eyes against the sun, giving her a moment to say something.

She ignored me. Typical.

"So, you're coming back with us?" I looked at her, the question as soft as I could make it.

A long, solemn pause. I could see her chewing at her lip as she thought about how to respond. Despite the time together, it was still odd seeing such a young child act so old and thoughtful.

"My brother let my family die. I can't forgive him for that." Her face was stoic, but a catch in her voice made me realize this wasn't an easy conversation for her. "My home is gone. My friends are gone. Teo has Lonora and their kid. He won't even notice if I'm here or not. It's best for both of us."

"But these are your people," I began.

"No," her voice, cracking like a whip, cut me off. "This is just where I was born. They aren't my people any more than they're your people. Besides, Balteris has so much for me to learn. And the sun doesn't beat down on you there. I failed my family. I think it's time for me to try something new."

I reached out a hand to take her shoulder before realizing halfway that she wasn't the kind to take well to comfort. I dropped it awkwardly and tried to look like I understood. "You didn't fail. We came. We brought your people hope and a brighter future. You crossed the sea twice. You're a hero to your people, Shazina. And, you've still got a whole life ahead of you to add to that."

She growled something, sounding almost exactly like Argo on the rare occasion he was woken up from a nap too suddenly. "I don't want to be a hero," she added when I said nothing.

I waited, but that was the end of it. As I stood, I turned back to look at her still huddled in the makeshift shelter from the sun. "You're still a hero to me," I said, meaning it. I left before she could respond, wanting to see what Thecily and her crew had accomplished with their renovations, my feet took me down below deck towards the belly of the ship.

Fresh cut wood has a particular smell, and that goes double for the light-weight and unique type which the Cloud Dancers used for their ships. I inhaled deeply, closing my eyes to better experience that first breath of their woodworking before it diminished.

"Nice, aye?" A voice said from behind.

Startled, I spun around. Craig, Dendra, and Diedra were in a corner, smiling. It appeared they were getting their last goodbyes in as well, and part of that involved the ship that had been Craig's home for a majority of his life.

I stepped over, embracing both the girls, thrilled at seeing them one last time. "It's an exceptional smell. Sometimes I wish I'd just kept life simple and become a carpenter. There's plenty of excitement and far more satisfaction in working some wood than being on some rich son of godspawn's payroll as a token Learner. Not that I'll ever get even that opportunity," I added dryly.

Craig shook hands with me. He seemed the most excited about staying and helping teach the people how to harness the Talent, despite the abject lack of interest the Exos seemed to have in it.

Diedra and Dendra said their goodbye in unison. Both seemed happy to stay, Craig being a large part of it, I was sure. But I think unlike the Natural, they both were staying more out of fear than anything else. To them, this was a goodbye to a friend they thought wouldn't be surviving the journey home.

I squeezed them all the more tightly, wishing I could find a way to tell them I understood their fear and appreciated having them so briefly enter my life. "Wander well, friends," I said with a heartfelt pang in my chest.

I continued through the belly of the ship, admiring the triple-stacked benches the crew had built to accommodate the influx of people who would help speed us on our way home. It looked like the inside of a sea monster's belly with its ribs bared all the way down. They'd carved out little circular holes next to every rowing platform, letting in plenty of light.

Above, even the kitchen and bunks looked retrofitted with rowing stations. Hammocks draped from the ceiling like curtains, moved out of the way until needed. Low benches dotted across the floor with the long oars already racked and ready for pulling. While we'd been hunting gimzers, Thecily's people had put in some extravagant amounts of effort to re-working their airship.

I breathed deeply again. A mix of sawdust, sweat, and whatever meal Martino was busy whipping up wafted through the room. It was time.

Back up top, I waited on the rail near Cassiopia's ballista. She'd strung a hammock and shade next to the chair and had been sleeping next to it. She wasn't around, and I was more than a little convinced that she'd been having some secret tryst with one of the Exo villagers and must have been saying her goodbyes.

The burgeoning village grew out below me. Clay brick homes almost blending into the desert. Dark soil mounds peppered the landscape, showing where laborers were excavating new wells. It was nothing so loud as Kalaran or Erset, but a liveliness could be heard if you listened closely. It was the sound of people with hope for a better tomorrow. It was beautiful.

Slow and steady steps behind me announced Insley. It was funny how differently we all seemed to walk. Volant with a quick dancer's stride. Qaewin, completely silent. But Insley seemed to always place her feet exactly where she meant to and didn't move until she was sure.

I turned, a smile on my face.

"I'm nervous, Nil," she said. She leaned up against the railing, looking out across the hot desert and towards the impossibly tall mountains. "The ride here? Not so smooth. We were incredibly lucky."

"Do you want to stay here?" I asked.

With a grimace, she shook her head. "No, it's," she began.

"Because if you want to stay," I interrupted, "I can stay with you. We can see what happens here, not risk the sea, and see what simple pleasures this desert holds."

Dark eyes widened. Insley took a measured step forward, the idea tempting her. For a moment, I thought she'd take it. But with a deep sigh, she straightened up just a little more, locking her eyes on to mine. "Fear of dying doesn't get us anywhere. We can't live if we make our choices based on being afraid." She lightly slapped my shoulder, a wicked grin flashing across her face. "More importantly, this heat is destroying my hair."

At noon, we lifted off. The ship's flat bottom dropped loose sediment and no small number of rocks in its wake as we rose into the air. Thecily was at the wheel, fiercely joyful at having the Sky Wolf airborne again, and I suspected even more so having left the captain and his small group of cowards behind.

The ship had a belly full of people ready to row, and a palpable tension began to fall as we drew nearer to the sea and its perpetual storm. A drum sounded, a new addition to keep the myriad of rowers on pace with one another. As one, they pulled against the air with the sweeping wind oars. The ship lurched, jumping forward in the air as if some giant had shoved us from behind. Another beat matched up with another gut-twisting jump. Anything not bolted in place was pushed backward by the sudden acceleration. The drum fell silent as Thecily made adjustments, and we prepared for the sprint across the deadly causeway.

Chapter Twenty

The Sky Wolf rushed towards the dark storm clouds at a breakneck speed.

Joy was on deck with me, the two of us flanking Cassiopia at the ship's bow where the giant ballista sat. We were the only Learners onboard. The Naturals, including Volant, were all manning the stern and trying to help add as much speed as they could. With how fast we were moving, the only danger should be from the front of the ship. Any sea monster that pops up as we pass will be sorely disappointed.

We bounced and shuttered at every odd air pocket. Cassiopia sat in her chair, belted in, and her huntress eyes prowled the sea before us for signs of any creatures. Joy and I had makeshift platforms that helped elevate us while also giving a little support to our backs that acted as both anchors against the speed and any Skill use, but also as something to tie ourselves to in case we fell.

It was like hitting a stone wall while simultaneously jumping off a cliff when we crossed over the line separating the sea and Exo. We dipped hard, the change in the air making us both fall and slow at the same time. Then the drumbeat grew faster as the airships nose pointed up towards the black clouds above. With each stroke we put on speed, jostling, and bumping against the fierce wind that resisted us. The crew finally established a rhythm, and soon we were skipping across air currents like a smooth rock skipping across water.

The sky itself seemed to scream all about us, and I couldn't hear Joy despite her being only a couple of arm's lengths away. Every tug on the legion of sky oars compressed me against the backrest, only matching in discomfort with the following lull in acceleration that led to a drop in altitude. Lightning flashed all around us, but the mesh wings were out and doing their job to keep it away from us. All the while, the causeway snaked below us, occasionally dotted with some nightmarish creature that disappeared beneath us before I could get a good look.

I checked my pockets as we ricocheted above the causeway. Three Toron stones left after several of them had cracked during the Gimzer hunt and leaving a majority with the Exo school. Three. It was a fortune. Yet, it was a paltry sum compared to what we initially crossed with.

Below, a massive sea snake raised its head, taking in the ship. I shivered as we flew over it despite knowing we were too high up for it to strike. Joy saw the snake as well, and her already fragile will almost crumbled then. She sagged, and if it weren't for the straps keeping us in place against the backrest, she'd have collapsed to her knees.

Still, we were moving so fast that Thecily didn't need our Skill for any kind of additional speed. The sky darkened the closer we moved towards the halfway point. I saw sections of the causeway lit by flashes of lightning that I remembered from our journey across. It'd taken days for us to make it to the coast from the halfway spot. With the wind roaring at our backs and over one hundred rowers, it seemed we'd make it before sunset.

A much slower pace was called for dinner. In intervals, a quarter of the rowers at a time moved up on deck, stretching out and letting their tired muscles relax. Martino and a small contingent of assistants rushed about serving hearty, heavy fare to the weary people. Joy unstrapped and went to join him while enjoying a meal herself.

Insley, seeing Joy's windburned face, came to the bow to find Cassiopia and me. It appeared that being a healer also meant generally not being an idiot about even simple things relating to health. She fashioned a pair of bandana-like masks for both of us, covering everything but our eyes with a soft cloth. A shake of the head, and she went and found some food as well, bringing it back over. Now that we were moving noticeably slower, there was no way I could leave the front of the ship.

Thankfully we still traveled faster than most of the sea monsters seem to be able to track. A few of the crab-like creatures took shots at us as we approached, but as I watched the small spines arc up far below, I didn't even bother tossing out any shields. The first volley thudded harmlessly into the belly of the ship. I relaxed back a little, my face no longer hurting and optimistic hope swelling warmly through me. We were going to make it.

When night fell, the storm seemed to only grow worse. Despite the near-violent jarring movements the ship repeatedly made, I could barely keep my eyes from drooping closed. I forced them open, jolting forward with the fear I'd fallen asleep. A blood-curdling keen came from the darkness below. When a flash of lightning gave me a brief, clear moment of the sea and causeway, I could see some primordial looking lizard. It was easily the size of ten men with scaly armor and angular teeth that didn't fully fit in its mouth. Despite the storm, it made an audible roar as another far too large predator bit around the lizard's midsection.

I shivered, blinking away rain and the sight of creatures best forgotten and left in the murky depths.

Even that didn't seem to be keeping my mind clear. I faded in and out of alertness, fighting to keep my eyes open. Joy slept next to me, slouched against her straps. Cassiopia, too, was asleep. I only hoped that nothing could pick us out at this speed in the night and cause any trouble for us. For all we knew, there were dozens of creatures like the octomantis in the depths that could come out at any time and bring down an airship so high in the sky.

Thunder rumbled the ship, shaking me enough to make my shoulder pop in protest. It still wouldn't have been enough, but Qaewin and

Insley appeared, soaked from the rain and looking just as tired if not more so.

"Wow, you both look terrible." I tried to make it come off as a joke, but it fell flat.

Both glared at me, and Insley looked down at the mug of steaming liquid. "Maybe we should take this elsewhere. What do you think, Qaewin?"

Qaewin looked at the cup, then back to me, then back to Insley. "He doesn't seem very appreciative. This probably could serve a better purpose with our fellow rowers."

I blinked in surprise. "You've been rowing?"

They both rolled their eyes at this, dead-on impressions of Shazina. I needed to do something about that before it caught on with everyone.

Insley passed the cup, piping hot tea with some kind of spicy undertone to it. A Martino original drink, if I had to bet.

"I've been riding zymphs since I could walk and carrying the family tents not long after. I've trained with every would-be warrior we have in Tryst." Qaewin flipped her hair back, glowering at me.

"And I," Insley added, "have been holding down animals twice your size and three times as strong to put in stitches and amputate limbs. I grew up farming rocks at the base of Kalaran."

I laughed, fending off further explanation with a wave of my hand. "I surrender, I surrender! You are both more than capable of helping pull the oars, excuse my doubt." Sipping the tea, I relished in the warmth and energy it seemed to flood my system with.

"How's Volant?" I asked. "And how are your hands?" I added as an afterthought.

Both looked down at their hands first. I couldn't make anything out in the black and stormy night light, but I knew. They'd be rubbed raw and bloody.

"Stiff, and a little sore," Insley admitted. "But, we wore some heavy gloves, so nothing there."

"Volant's fine too, though he seems tired. He asked after you, which is what brought us here." Qaewin gestured around us. "A lot less wind in the back of the ship, almost pleasant compared to up here. He wanted to come with us, but the other Naturals are all sleeping so he's holding down the currents all by himself."

I shook my head, chagrined. "Of course you wore gloves. You're not idiots like the rest of us who'd just go pull an oar without any preparation."

Both girls just shrugged, the kind that nearly every woman learns, the shrug that said boys are dumb, and we just have to love them for who they are. Insley planted a kiss on my cheek, and the two left, going back to their rowing.

I sighed deeply, my face warm from where Insley had kissed me. "I could die happy now," I muttered to the buffeting wind and flashing lightning. It felt odd to be at peace amid so much chaos. Immediately, I regretted my words. The gods loved to put you in your place, and I scanned the unreadable dark before us. If there was any single spot that you were likely to have famously ironic last words, a few hundred paces above a sea filled with too large monsters and within spitting distance of a perpetual storm was precisely where you'd be forced to eat your words.

It seemed fate was saving something up something special for me, as no horrifying sea snake was crawling over the side, and not a single octomantis had popped up to rip us from the sky. I finished my tea, finding a new sense of alertness settle in me.

We would make it across.

There was something about the sunrise while at sea, possibly combined with almost two days of no sleep, that brought tears to my eyes. Shades of orange and red mixed with flashes of yellow in majestic swirls that dappled the dangerous waters and made the world feel like one enormous painting.

. . .

Everything seemed to hit me at once. An irrational wave of emotion suckered punch me at the sight of the beautiful sun. Without really understanding why, tears began to trickle down my face as I was completely over

Cassiopia and Joy ignored my tears, staying vigilant while I watched the sky brighten in a stupefied haze. Their friendship added to the flood of emotions. Despite the danger and discomfort, I had never felt happier to be alive.

What seemed like both an eternity and a blink of the eye, the sun began to disappear behind the storm clouds again as it rose higher into the sky. Just as the light began to fade, I saw the faint brown and green shadow smudging the horizon. Erset. Home.

I turned to Joy, who'd somehow fallen asleep again in her harness. I shook my head but reached over to gently wake her up. "Go tell Thecily I can see Erset. We can be there by lunch if we row hard enough."

Joy, sleepy-eyed at first, came alive with a start. She unfastened the straps and let the rough winds push her back down the ship towards Thecily at a stumbling sprint. I turned around, relief flooding through me. We'd almost made it.

"Nil, do you see that?" Cassiopia called over to me, pointing out before the ship, just to the right of the causeway snaking its way across the sea.

A dark stain spread across a patch of sea like a shadow. Flickers of light illuminated the stain, showing a dark red hue. Red like blood.

The closer we came, the larger the mark on the sea appeared. Dead center, a carcass of some animal floated. Pieces of it drifted away as an even larger creature tore into it with gusto. Huge, saucer-like eyes floated above the surface as tentacle appendages held the body in place as it ate.

A tingle of electric fear raced down my spine and through my body—an octomantis.

As the creature gorged itself, I could see it only had one working eye. It's other was milky white and shot through with red and black where an arrow had been torn out, leaving the eye completely useless. Even from this distance, the beast was so huge that I felt like an ant in comparison. Cassiopia began cranking the seat loose from its locked in position, allowing range of motion with the ballista.

"Cassiopia, don't!" I hissed. "It might not see us. It's already eating."

Grimly, she shook her head. "We have to take a shot while we can. What if it gets us as we pass?" she asked.

"Please, no, you're just going to make it angry." I started to try and work my straps free, but in my frantic movement, I just managed to tighten them.

I could see the manic glint in her eyes. She'd gone full hunter.

She would not be denied her prize again.

With a gleam in her eye, she sighted in the ballista, aiming for the center of the bloody spot the octomantis sat in. As if in slow motion, she pulled the release. It clicked, followed by a thrum that I could almost feel more than hear. The bolt blurred, serrated metal tip flashing silver as it led the sapling sized shaft.

There was no sound when it struck. Just the slow click of the ballista cranking back to allow another bolt to be loaded. Cassiopia was all focus, moving with measured efficiency as she loaded the next bolt.

She aimed.

She fired.

I got free and staggered the last few steps forward. I watched as the second bolt arced for an eternity towards the now roiling waters as the octomantis thrashed below us.

It struck, same as the first. Now the creature knew where to look. Its colossal eye swiveled up, immediately locking on to us.

My gut sank as the ever-blowing wind, and the multitude of rowers below deck only brought us closer. Cassiopia was dutifully cranking away at the ballista for a third attempt at bringing down her prey.

The manic desire wasn't there anymore. She looked almost scared. Like she'd bet everything she had on a dice roll and lost. In a sense, she had. Our eyes locked for just a moment, and then the sharp impact of the octomantis' attack was felt. The ship lurched, and a single, faint scream could be heard against the wind.

The rowers faltered, and we slowed. I peered off the edge and saw splinters falling towards the sea. A ship's lifeblood, it's wood that kept us all stable.

The bloody waters below would have hidden any normal-sized predator. But the octomantis was just too large. Its claw-tipped, hook-shaped appendages had already snapped back into place on it's body, and it was zeroing in again.

I breathed in, and then out, willing Skill directly into my body and mind simultaneously. Despite the impending doom, a little burst of pride filled me. Then, I tried to slow down time or speed up my reflexes, whichever way it worked.

It was semi-successful. I was able to catch the tremors of motion that rippled into small shockwaves leading away from the creature in the sea as it launched its deadly mantis claws at the ship again. Beyond that, they still moved too fast. It seemed as if one moment they were locked in tight to the body, and the next, a pair of nightmare arms had erupted from below deck.

Splinters exploded everywhere as the first claw struck through the top of the bridge, while the second was only a little way off. Despite missing the bridge, it seemed to have torn through a rank of rowers as it glistened with fresh blood.

More screams and shouts added to the noise of the wind. The ship shuddered violently as the claws raked their way back through the ship, causing untold amounts of damage.

My friends could be dead. Someone I knew was almost guaranteed to be hurt. I turned away from the carnage behind me and locked onto the octomantis below. Anger and rage coursed with the Skill through my body. I pulled, tugging on the Toron stone's reserve and adding it to mine with such force that I felt one stone crack immediately.

Cassiopia loaded a bolt into the ballista, grim determination making a stone of her visage.

I pushed Skill into a condensed ball before me, molding it as I poured on more and more of my rage and fear.

A deep, chest-thumping sound announced Cassiopia firing the bolt.

I gritted my teeth, snarled, and then shoved with everything I had while trying to push against the ship with my Ukiyo to avoid being thrown off it.

To my surprise, I didn't launch off the ship. I skid and felt the entire Sky Wolf dip with the force of recoil from my Skill launching out at the Octomantis. Everything I'd had went into the sphere of condensed Skill and the stability and strength of Ukiyo. My legs gave out, and I dropped to my knees, gasping as if I'd just run from Erset to Brod in one go.

Thunderous and terrifying, the timber just behind me cracked in a shower of shards as the claws erupted up through the deck. And then just as suddenly went limp as Cassiopia whooped in celebration. It rained broken wood and dust for a long moment, silent but for the wind and creaking masts.

Cassiopia came over and helped me up, and I staggered with her to the bridge. Curled up against the wheel, Thecily waited with her arm a bloody mess. No one was rowing, and we were slowly losing speed. It didn't help that we seemed to be dragging the octomantis through the waters like a tentacle-covered anchor.

I dropped to Thecily, checking her arm, and looking for any other wounds. Cassiopia's voice boomed behind me, demanding the rowers pull as if their lives depended on it. She wasn't wrong. Their lives did depend on it. And pull they did.

A ragged gash from her elbow to her shoulder was bleeding profusely. She wasn't just closing her eyes against the pain. She was clenching them shut with every ounce of will she could, breathing hard and heavy. An uneven hole large enough to fit my head in gaped next to us. I leaned over it, peering into the belly of the ship.

"Insley! We need you on the bridge!" I hollered down the hole.

Even on an airship this size, it only took a few moments for Insley to appear, along with Shazina. Seeing the bloody arm and missing flesh, Insley sucked in a sharp breath. Hurriedly she wrapped the wound with bandages. Then wrapped it again. And then a third time.

"She's losing a lot of blood," she commented, an attempt at clinical detachment that was undermined by a slight tremble edging her words. "I can't stitch it up, we're bouncing around too much."

A large jolt, the gods adding emphasis to her point, flung us about the bridge, knocking everyone but Shazina about. The small girl seemed to hop in sync with the floor as it dipped away from under her. While we regained our footing, she'd reached down to Thecily and was walking her through the same breathing technique she'd taught me to access the Ukiyo.

"Like we practiced," she said. "Ignore the pain. Bring the breath in. Hold it. Then let it out."

Insley tried to stumble back over, but Shazina waved her away.

"She needs," Insley began but an angry motion from Shazina cut her off.

"Go help someone who needs it," Thecily is going to help herself.

In response, Thecily's breathing began to even out, and her eyes opened. She still seemed to be in immense pain, but she also seemed to be responding more coherently.

I turned to Insley and Cassiopia, shrugging helplessly. "It doesn't matter what happens to her right now if we don't get this ship home in one piece." I grabbed the wheel, feeling the ship bucking against the steering fins and sails that shaped the course the great envelope above took us. Something was wrong with the weights that ran the ship's length, making the *Sky Wolf* tilt this way and that. I couldn't make them turn left or right, only able to shift the ship's up and down.

I traded a glance with Cassiopia, who now looked almost embarrassed. "Go find me Volant. I'll need his help." She left, and I turned to Insley, who watched the attempted meditation with a fair amount of skepticism. "She's right. We need you to help others. Try and get everyone injured moved somewhere safe and do whatever you think is best. Save as many as you can."

She nodded, that spark of goodness in her taking hold as she remembered other people were just as bad off as Thecily elsewhere on the ship. She left quickly, disappearing behind the bridge to go back below deck.

We were moving more slowly now, but the horizon showed a clear outline of Erset's cliffs. We'd been knocked off the causeway and had only open sea beneath us. I couldn't do anything about it, though. The death of the octomantis and our slowed speeds made the other predators come out. A barrage of spikes from the hybrid crab and scoprion creatures began to arc down onto the deck. An unlucky Exo who'd emerged near the ballista was struck and fell to the floor, convulsing.

Behind me, Thecily's breathing had slowed. For a moment, I thought that was the end, but when I turned back, I could see her steadying, coming into complete control of her body.

"That's it, you're in charge of your body," Shazina said encouragingly.

"She can access Ukiyo?" I was both surprised and impressed. "Is this the first time?"

Shazina turned back to me, rolling her eyes in what I had decided was her default method to answering questions. "Not the time, Nil. But no, I've been working with her since we hit Exo. She's a far better student than you."

"You can stop blood loss?" I asked. Erset was growing closer, but I could feel parts of the ship shuddering disconcertingly beneath us.

A heavy, world-weary sigh came from Shazina. "If you'd pay attention, or generally care about something other than trying to get yourself killed, there's a lot of applications for Ukiyo besides being stronger and faster."

"Oh." I filed the information away as I took in the coastline before us. The trees on the other side of the eternity river began to take distinct shape, and if I wasn't mistaken, our course was headed for the largest one, still blackened from the fire Volant and I had been blamed for.

Chapter Twenty-One

Relief warred with a new level of anxiety inside me as we crossed over the eternity river, octomantis dangling below us like some obscene anchor. Volant had managed to get the ship up high enough not to crash us into the trees, but we couldn't get high enough to clear the octomantis. The drumming had stopped, and so had the rowing, and we were slowing down considerably.

The blackened tree, the same one that Volant and I had almost died in, loomed before us.

This was exactly the kind of irony the gods loved. For us to come full circle and die by crashing into it after all this. If there were ever proof needed for divine comedy, this would be it.

There weren't nearly enough fallpacks to go around in the first place. At least we'd have a chance compared to crashing at sea. As I tried to make my peace with death, a sudden lurch sent us upwards. A cheer rose below us as the octomantis corpse fell away from the ship, giving us just enough of a boost to clear the tree. A thud followed by a loud, heavy crack announced the sea monster's corpse crashing into the old council chamber tree.

Cassiopia looked like she'd be sick but didn't say anything about the crew unceremoniously dumping her prized trophy into the center of Erset.

We came to a blissfully still stop just outside the tree city where a cleared bit of earth allowed easy landing for airships visiting Erset. We slowly descended to the ground, an angry, armed group of my people below us. As the ship set down, the shouting began.

I was tired. Both physically and emotionally. There'd been no sleep for at least two days as we sprinted across the sea. Then there was the crowd. Shouting threats, being hateful, and in general making idiots of themselves, just like my hometown seemed to regularly do. I was so tired of my people being the most backward, self-absorbed sect on either side of the sea.

I pulled one of the last two Toron stones out of my hand and focused my will. I let a slow, tiny trickle of Skill leak from my hand and tossed a wide backhand out towards the crowd like I'd done when making the Skill shield.

The Skill knocked harmlessly into them with the force of a light push, but it sure shut them up. I gathered more and lazily vaulted over the railing. I let a burst of Skill slow the descent, and my Ukiyo take away the harsher effects of landing from such a height.

It had the desired effect.

The growing crowd snapped to attention, completely silent but for a few gasps.

I waited.

A burly man, slabs of muscle layered beneath a shirt that could barely contain his barrel chest, growled something and stepped forward towards me with some curse or threat on his lips.

I blurred forward, grabbing him by the front of his tunic with Ukiyo aided speed and strength. I threw him into the ground and then pressed him hard into the dirt.

"Left hand, you people shame me. You shame yourselves. You're an embarrassment to the world around us and everything good in it." I let my voice carry over and into the city hidden up in the trees just a little way away. I wasn't shouting, but I certainly could be heard.

I gestured to the ship behind me, battered, scarred with patches, and speckled with sea monster projectiles. "THIS IS HOW YOU WELCOME US HOME?" I roared, letting anger guide my voice. "This is how you treat people who need help?" I asked, letting my words carry in the wake of my anger. "This is how Erset wants to be remembered when the first people to cross the sea in living memory return? The first thing our lost cousins see in our lands, wounded and tired? Spears. Swords. Anger and hate. That's who we are as a people? You all disgust me."

I let the man up.

"But the council tree," he stammered. "You destroyed it with that horror of a creature, and now the whole city smells like rotting fish and death. Someone has to pay for that!"

I shook my head, disappointment weighing heavy on my heart. "I already helped destroy that tree once. A second time doesn't count as much in my book."

"It's you," he said, voice soft. "The Learner traitor."

Instead of answering, I pointed back towards the trees and the city within. "Go find my parents. Tell them Nil is here, and we have wounded."

The man spluttered, anger flushing his face red. "I'm no errand runner, boy," he spat.

I grabbed the man again, and this time I flung him high over the heads of the crowd. He landed with a hard crunch, and I heard him moan in pain. "You," I said, pointing at the closest person, "bring me my parents and any healers nearby. And the rest of you, either get to helping these people or get away from here."

No one moved. They all stared at me, rooted to the spot.

"NOW!" I bellowed, anger flaring up again. I'd never been so disgusted with my heritage as I was right now.

Much later, long after nearly everyone who wasn't too hurt to disembark had gotten off the ship, my parents showed up with another small crowd.

They moved cautiously as if we were wild animals that might attack. I waved Volant over, and the two of us went to greet them.

"Why are you always causing trouble, Nil?" my mom asked after we embraced.

My father looked embarrassed, and despite everything, was carrying a book as if he was planning on getting some reading in while the rest of us carried on with our disruptive behaviors.

"Good to see you, too." I pointed towards a large canopy that draped across the distance from stern to tree, making a shaded space for the injured. "Insley is over there helping already."

Luckily there were only a handful of people who were seriously injured. These were the ones close enough to the claws to be hit by wood shrapnel or given glancing blows like Thecily. Hard faced crewmen were laying out the dead on the ship's backside while others worked to bury them.

Apart from those hurt by the monster, there were also many injuries from blunt impact. There were enough concussed passengers to make me second guess ever being near the storage room in an airship during a storm.

My mother joined in with Insley, and despite the grizzly work of sewing up gashes and such, the two seemed to be hitting it off fine. That at least brought a small amount of joy.

While they worked, Cassiopia and Shazina swung by to announce they were headed into Erset to try to salvage what could be of the octomantis.

Thecily seemed almost well as she waited for her stitches in the tent but glared daggers at the two as they left. She'd learned of what drew the octomantis' ire, and whether or not it'd have noticed us if Cassiopia hadn't shot it, she was now blaming our hulking huntress for the deaths and damage.

As we ran out of ways to help, Qaewin, Volant, and I, started to head towards Erset. Qaewin's zymph had crawled up the nearest tree and was sleeping the hard, uninterruptible sleep of a recently traumatized cat.

My father caught up to me as we entered the forest, heading for the closest tree entrance. "It'd be best if you didn't, son," he said with a wince. "There's a lot of hard feelings still going around up there. Between the school, the tree, and all the other stuff, you've become more than a little infamous. It's made things hard on your mother and me, you know."

I stopped, momentarily at a loss of words. When Volant and Qaewin paused as well, I gave them a weak smile. "You guys go on, drum up some good news, and bring me back some food if you can."

They left, and I rounded on my father. "It's been hard on you two, aye?" I hissed. "You realize I've almost died, repeatedly, right? And what do you mean by hard? People calling you names? Not letting you sit under your favorite branch?"

He turned a shade lighter but carried on. "If you must know, many of your mother's friends have been less than kind to her. They've gone so far as to start excluding her from many things they did together. And my colleagues have been colder and more exclusionary as well."

I shook my head, unable to comprehend it. "You think I should cater to what backward, uneducated people think I should and shouldn't be doing?"

This time he was the one to look uncomprehending. "It's more than that. It's your mother and I's lives that are being affected by this. I'm just asking that you don't make it worse by flaunting your presence in Erset."

"Godspawning tree huggers," I growled before stalking back to the Sky Wolf.

Insley was possibly more exhausted than I was when she finally finished tending everyone that needed to. Thecily already had people working on ship repairs, recognizing the level of unwelcomeness that Erset was showing. With the construction going, we decide to avoid the ship and instead we went and laid out on the grass next to one of the large trees. Neither of us said anything. We were both too tired and too worn out. We fell asleep with a cool, seasonable breeze tickling the leaves above us, perfectly at peace next to one another.

The nap was short and sweet, with Qaewin and Volant waking us up, Argo's enthusiastic licks being the primary method to do so. I pushed away from the surprisingly heavy dog, blinking my eyes open. Insley was likewise woken up, possibly being Argo's favorite person beyond Shazina.

A sack filled with food hit me in the chest, and I fumbled to catch it. Volant chuckled, sitting down next to us, with Qaewin completing the circle.

"Your parents weren't too off base, by the by," Qaewin said in her gentle way. "There were a lot of angry people, and your name certainly came up. We even ran into the temporary council, and despite how much they loved both Volant and Argo, they had nothing but negativity about you."

Even as the food lifted my spirits, that sat like a stone in me, dark and heavy. Swallowing the mouthful of street food, I replied. "It's not that they were wrong about how people would feel, it's that they cared more about how it'd affect them than how it could hinder me."

Volant gave a knowing nod. "That's tough. I'm sorry your parents are letting you down. Again."

"I just need to accept them for who they are. It's not like they signed up to give up the entirety of their passions and pursuits just because nobody likes their son. They have their own lives to live, and I need to live mine." I took another bite and instantly felt better.

Insley was nibbling skeptically at the food. "Where did you guys get this anyway?"

Qaewin gestured vaguely at Volant. "This dolt swore he knew someplace that Nil had shown him. We wandered for more than should be reasonably expected for food before he finally asked someone. Ended up being a new councilman who'd heard of how Volant had fought against the blue robes when the council tree was burned."

Volant gave an embarrassed shrug. Somehow, he'd gained all the fame despite being half-dead throughout the ordeal, while they'd vilified me even further. Erset was becoming less and less appealing.

"So, they invited us to lunch," she continued. "After a lot of grumbling about a corrupt system, too high of taxes to cover useless positions in the system, and all the other stuff, they started to fawn over Volant. I've never seen him blush so much. 'He was so regal. Looked just like kings of old. It'd be so great just to have a single leader again,' and on and on they went until the group finally grew large enough, we were able to extract ourselves and sneak away with the food."

I laughed, long and hard. Everyone joined in, even Argo howling happily as we wiped our eyes and caught our breath.

"Volant, a king? That's amazing. We haven't had a king in what, half a dozen lifetimes?"

"More like ten," Insley added, having finally started to enjoy the food right before we all devolved into laughter.

"They're all talk," I said. "Erset hates the council system. The people have wanted a monarchy forever."

Qaewin playfully punched Volant in the shoulder before returning to petting the dog. "It's not even Volant they really want. I think it's just because Argo was around. They were all head over heels for the dog."

That was something that made sense to all of us.

A runner came panting up, some kid barely old enough to be away from his parents, and the spitting stereotype of Erset with dark hair, dark eyes, and no shoes.

"You Volant?" he asked breathlessly.

Volant looked up and nodded, curious.

"This came a while back for you, but no one knew where you'd gone. One of the new councilmen said they'd seen you earlier, and you'd arrived with the ship." He held out a letter, hands steady despite the effort.

Volant took it, and when the kid didn't leave, he fished out a coin and tossed it over to him.

With that, the kid left at a leisurely walk, and we all turned to focus on Volant.

"It's from my mother," he said. His hands trembled ever so slightly as you tried to open the letter. He scanned the note, eyes widening the further he read. He stopped for a moment as if he couldn't believe it.

"Volant, what does it say?" I asked impatiently.

He read it a second time, and then a third. Finally, Qaewin shook his shoulder a little, bringing him up for air from the note. He swallowed hard, his eyes brimming with tears though he didn't look sad.

Volant cleared his throat. "She's alive. My mom. And Thran's Leaf's crew. The pirates that attacked them had boarded the ship secretly, killing a skeleton watch crew and ransacking it before destroying the steering mechanism and getting away." He looked up, a plea in his eyes. "They're in Brod, working on repairing the ship."

I tilted my head, thinking. Out loud, I began to voice my thoughts. "It's not like we're exactly welcome here. And Thecily will need support after essentially mutinying her way into being a captain, no matter how justified it is."

Insley perked up, eyes bright with excitement. "I've never been to Brod! Are the floating harbor's gardens as beautiful as they say?"

Volant's passion for gardening flared to life as he launched into an explanation of just how beautiful the gardens were and the mastery each herbologist exhibited with every plant. He would have continued talking all day, but an unsure Qaewin interrupted.

"We just barely arrived," she said. "That letter could be old enough to be meaningless. Your mother might be anywhere. We all need sleep before we do anything ill-advised."

Insley settled down in the face of such logic. "She's right. We need to think this over before we try to convince Thecily to shift her whole crew across Balteris."

I looked over at Volant, flashing him a quick hand sign. All good, we'll go either way. "Women," I said with a pained sigh, "they're no fun. Always logical and stuff."

Insley smacked my arm while Qaewin took the opportunity to throw a small twig that bounced off my head.

"Ow! And always so quick to violence!" I cried out, covering up in defense with a chuckle.

***

With a hood pulled up over my head, I snuck into Erset in the early hours of dawn after having slept the evening away. Everything was peaceful and quiet, giving my mind plenty of room to expand into all the empty places that busy people would typically inhabit. It felt so good to be back in the trees. Curling stairs and sturdy rope bridges appeared to be a maze to the outsiders, but for me, they were the well-worn memories filtered by nostalgia's lens of times that seemed simpler.

Baking bread drifted down from somewhere in the upper levels, mixing with the woody, fresh-cut wood scent that seemed to permeate the forest around us. Mornings here were especially beautiful, with light creating mesmerizing patterns through the tree city's leaves and branches. I found my home. Or what was once my home, I realized. It'd stopped being so at some point, and I hadn't noticed it happening.

Still, I slipped in, not bothering to knock or announce myself. As was typical, my father was already up, book in hand, sipping tea and reading by the large window that let in the morning light.

He looked up and twitched, startled by the sudden visitor in his doorway.

Pulling back my hood, I waved sheepishly. "Hey, dad," I said.

His eyes darted to the window before he caught himself and relaxed. "Morning, Nil. Care for some tea?"

I sat down, a cup of tea in hand, and breathed in the sweet and spicy steam. "I just came by to say I'm sorry, and I understand now." I took a sip, burning my tongue a little.

My father shifted in his seat, uncomfortably. He'd closed the book but still held it in his hand as if it were a newborn that couldn't be left alone for too long. "No, I'm sorry. We're sorry, actually," he amended. "It's just, things have been so hard for us. Since you left. Really hard."

I checked myself before I could say anything I regretted and took a deep breath. "I know," I responded. It seemed so unfair for him even to say life had been difficult compared to what I'd had to do to keep going to school. And even more so after the night Bymm was killed. "Don't worry. I'll make it up to you guys someday. Hopefully."

We sat in silence, drinking our tea. I didn't tell him about Exo. Or the gimzers. Or Insley. We just sat. Knowing there was too much to say and no way to say it all.

The silence stretched. With a final swallow of tea, I set my cup down and gave my father a genuinely warm hug. "We'll be leaving soon. I just wanted to come and say goodbye. I understand you and mom have your lives to live and that everyone responds differently to pressure. I hope things get better for you both. I love you."

He blinked back tears and gave me another tight hug. "We love you too. I'll let your mother know you stopped by. Wander well, son."

Chapter Twenty-Two

Emotionally wrung out, I arrived back at The Sky Wolf. To my surprise, the ship was buzzing with activity, repairs being made at inhuman speeds, faster than when the damaged ship had been needed in Exo.

Shazina melted from the shadows and appeared at my side, emotionlessly watching the crew crawl about the ship like ants. "Sounds like we're going to Brod," she commented. "Volant and Qaewin floated it by Thecily and her people while you were out this morning. When Thecily heard Captain Andreska was alive and could be there..." Shazina shook her head in slight amusement. "Well, things started to happen. Fast."

"You're back," I said, making it an unasked question in response to her dump of information.

She sighed, rolling her eyes. It made me want to reach out and smack her upside the head, but I managed to hold back.

She gestured towards the front of the ship near Cassiopia's ballista. Huge fangs, and far too many of them, were being strung about the bow. Near the fangs on either side of the forward ballista, a man was embedding the octomantis' claws. Cassiopia was busy helping a dozen Exo natives skin swaths of the sea monster's hide and then nail to the ship. I'd not seen her this happy since the first time we met.

"Not mad about them making decisions without you?" she asked.

"No," I replied. "I figured it's where we would be heading. I wanted to go back to Kalaran, but I think it's fair we give the Exos a full tour."

"Oh. Forgot about that. Half of them have already disappeared into the city or the woods. A score or two are looking to sign up in Wydvis to be on a crew, and Thecily's already signed the most promising ones to her ship. All in all, not many are left that are looking for anything." Shazina seemed to have lost some of her terseness now that we were back. It was odd hearing her volunteer news like this, too.

That surprised me. I'd expected more of the people who'd come to try and set up their own community on Balteris. A small town, where they knew each other. I'd not have bet on them wildly spreading out on their own in search of new adventures and friends. "Bold," I said.

Either the extra hands or the practice at last minute repairs in Exo had the ship ready before the sun was at it's zenith. I made a circuit around the ship. It'd been raised high enough that you could sit under it without too much trouble. I touched the octomantis skin, expecting something slimy and soft. Instead, it was as smooth and hard as stone. I pushed against it with as much force as I could. It felt just as solid if not more so than the ship's wood. There was only a smidge of give in it, but I'd have as much luck cutting through it as I would the wooden hull surrounding it.

There were even strips of the octomantis skin making braces across the ship in undamaged areas. I spied Cassiopia leaning over the railing and adding some nails in. I waved and caught her eye. She was grinning like a madwoman. I grabbed the nearest rope ladder and climbed up.

"You enjoying yourself?" I asked after vaulting the rail.

She turned, towering over me and eclipsing the sun with her bulk. "Immensely!" she crowed. She pointed at more of the octomantis skin behind her. "This stuff is going to be worth its weight in gold. I've never seen anything like it. Light as a feather, tough as a rock. I donated a couple of tentacles to Erset, and they went from wanting to murder us to practically naming a tree after me."

I shook my head, laughing. "You literally drop a sea monster corpse into the middle of the city, and they love you. I merely go off to study and accidentally help burn down a tree, and not even my parents can be seen around me. There's no justice in this world."

Her broad smile weakened at that, but she patted me on the arm. "When they name the tree after me, I'll put in a good word for you."

I nodded my head east. "We're going to Brod, I hear. You joining?"

She gave a noncommittal shrug. "Don't have much choice. I need an airship to haul all of this skin. Thecily and I made a deal, she stores it, gets free use for ship repairs, and twenty percent of the proceeds if I can find a buyer. Besides, Argo is staying on board."

"You and everyone else that's met that dog," I said ruefully. "Have you noticed how big Argo is getting?"

She nodded, a serious expression on her face. "Far too big, far too quickly, if I'm any judge. Not that I've seen many dogs."

An awkward silence followed, and instead of dealing with it, I gave her a short wave and meandered off towards the bridge. Fresh sawdust covered the deck as Thecily's crew expertly replaced and fit new planking into the holes the octomantis had caused. I saw a man working with tears in his eyes and remembered that not everyone had made it. In the excitement of surviving, I'd forgotten about those who'd lost their lives on our way back. The comforting, fresh-cut wood smell soured as my mood darkened.

At the bridge, Thecily was overseeing a map. Her arm seemed perfectly fine despite the short time it'd had to heal. A new kind of energy mixed with her previous fire. A certain surety that I'd begun to associate with the few Exo's who could wield Ukiyo. It was a person who seemed completely in sync with their body. I wasn't sure how I'd missed it before, but now that I knew, it was impossible not to see the change in Thecily.

A girlish excitement entirely out of place with Thecily spread across her face when I entered. She'd cut off the sleeves of her jerkin, showing the muscled arms of someone who'd spent a lot of time waving around a sword. The floor was patched over with fresh wood from Erset woven about what I could only assume was the last of their unique lightweight planks that most airships were made almost entirely of.

"Toss me that," she said enthusiastically, gesturing to one of the black hatchets the Exo had given me.

I hesitated briefly. I'd barely used them. They'd become precious in a way I didn't realize a weapon could. She didn't hesitate. With a smooth motion, she stepped over and pulled one of the axes free from my belt, and headed over to an errant piece of wood lining the wall. She swung, sinking the blade deep before prying it out. She did it again, popping the broken wood free.

"I thought I was done for," she said in the way of explanation, gesturing to the ship. "Mutinied captain. Broken ship. Half my crew missing. A pile of foreigners, and then we dropped a sea monster into the middle of a city." She grinned. "Turns out, the only problem we haven't solved is my legal status as captain. With Volant's mother supposedly alive, and ff she vouches for me, I'm as good as cleared of any wrongdoing. We should fly together more often." Her tone took on a more predatory, sensual sound.

Before I could say anything, she slid back over to me and gracefully pushed the axe back into its loop. She was close enough I could feel her breath, and her eyes pulled at mine with an inescapable gravitas.

It was at that moment Insley cleared her throat behind us, having just walked in.

I stammered something, an attempt at an explanation, but it was too late. Tears brimmed in her eyes. "Just letting you know Joy and Martino have agreed to stay on board as well for the trip to Brod," and then marched away without a backward glance.

To her credit, Thecily had drained of her excitement and replaced it with a wince of empathy.

"Nil, sorry, I forgot myself," she tried, but I didn't even hear her.

My heart was pounding somewhere in my throat, and all I could hear was its panicked beat as I tried to convince my legs to chase after Insley. Long moments went by. Crucial moments. And then, finally, as if lightning had struck, my body and mind connected, and I sprang into action.

My feet thudded against old wood and new. I turned a corner, skidding across piles of sawdust and stumbling briefly. I couldn't find her at first, but it didn't take long. She could only feasibly call one place on the ship home—the corner in the bunks where our two hammocks waited.

When I finally found her, she wasn't crying. She was composed in a way, though her face was hard, and she was making an effort to prevent further tears. She didn't say anything, just looked at me accusingly. Pleadingly.

I sat down next to her. My heart went out to what she was feeling. Betrayed. Hurt. Rejected. She shouldn't have had to experience any of these, but I'd messed up, allowing Thecily to get so close, to make Insley think there was something between the redhead and me.

Tentatively, I reached a hand towards her. She met it, grasping mine in return. A flicker of a smile. "Look, that was really bad timing," I began.

"Nil," she said, firmly interrupting. "I'm no child, so I don't want to play games. I only want honesty." She took a deep breath. "Look. We haven't known each other for long, but I feel like there's something here. I'm scared to lose that, but if you're out just having fun, I'm not interested."

It took me a moment to process. My first thought, oddly, was how the ship felt no different sitting than flying. The second thought was I had no idea what I wanted.

"Honestly, I have no idea what I want. It feels like I've just been trying to stay ahead of this mess. Going where the wind blows me. I don't want to lose you either. There's nothing but friendship with Thecily, no matter what I'd initially felt. But I don't know what my life is going to hold. All I want is for things to go back to normal, for people to stop trying to kill the ones I care about or me. To teach a class or two, have time to read books and maybe even write one. That's about as far as I've thought about not being a child."

Her eyes twinkled at that. "Seems reasonable to me," she said in reply. "But what about Thecily and whatever was on the bridge?"

I shook my head, embarrassed. "Nothing, seriously. She was just caught up in the excitement of the day, took it a little far. Caught me off guard." I squeezed her hand. "Again, sorry." This was scarier than any of the gimzer raids. More stressful than any of the fights Volant and I had managed to get tangled up in. I'd rather fight a dozen blue robes than be talking about emotions and the future.

Insley must have sensed what I was feeling, and the turmoil seemed to be draining away from her shoulders. "Thanks, Nil. If it helps, I've never done anything but plan for the future. All of this has been rather new to me."

I stood, helping her to her feet. With a little bow, I left a light kiss on her hand. She giggled before letting my hand go. "We're going to be fine," I promised. "Unless, of course, we die. Around me, there seems a high likelihood of that."

Back on deck, night had fallen. The two of us found Volant and Qaewin, who greeted us warmly and made space on a thick, Soft-Stepper pile of blankets they'd been stargazing on. The stolen moon was shining with ethereal beauty as we joined them. Most of the crew seemed to be taking the evening's respite to explore Erset before leaving in the morning, letting us have soft, whispered conversations.

A comet crossed the sky, eliciting excited exclamations from our small group. "Make a wish," Volant said.

I didn't think I could be any happier than I was right then and there. It's a rare experience to actually be aware of just how lucky you are. To be alive and with friends, seeing something unique. It's not a happy life one should ask for, but a life filled with happy moments, or so I'd read. As Volant suggested, I made a wish. I wished for many more chances at times like this.

When we'd all taken a moment to do so, Qaewin reached around to her bag and pulled out a large bottle. Volant's eyes lit up, and I clapped slowly in admiration. It could be only one thing. Swok.

"You sneaky minx," Volant said with admiration.

Confused by our response, Insley looked to Qaewin for clarification. "It's a spiced honey flavored drink we Soft Steppers make. We don't make a lot of it, and generally, you can't get it outside of our tribe." A big wink to Insley and she hooked a thumb at Volant. "I've been saving this to celebrate our eventual rescuing of these two oafish men from their adventures."

With a grin, Insley took the proffered bottle. "To keeping the boys alive!" She took a drink, her face lighting up with delight.

Volant took the bottle next, gesturing to the ship. "To failing and flying, may we continue to do both with style."

Qaewin took her turn, raising the bottle to the moon. "To friends who can enjoy starry nights and the stolen moon with you." She took a swig, smiling softly.

I took the bottle, enjoying the chilled feel of glass and its heft. Aromas of sweet, spiced honey wafted up, mixing with the still prevalent sawdust smell all underplayed by the dense, earthy forest. I let the scents wash over me. It seemed as if I could feel autumn returning, the cool air just around the corner from us. "To a happy future, and an end to God's Fury once and for all. And to the best people in the world, who I'd surely have died a dozen times over if not for you all." I drank, savoring the swok as much as I did the first time.

Stars twinkled above us as we picked out constellations, told stories, and caught snatches of music coming from the clearing before. The music made me laugh, knowing that anyone in Erset who could hear it would be growling about the indecency of instruments and outsiders.

As we all drifted to sleep, Volant turned to me. "Oi, Leafer. We may not be where we'd planned, but we're going to get everything right one of these days. And this? This looks like we're on a good path."

"Aye," I said, nodding off. "This does feel righ, my friend."

Chapter Twenty-Three

Wind snapped against the ropes and played through my hair as we cleared the tree line and entered the open sky. My spirits rose with the ship. It was a beautiful morning.

Even with the turns at the oars being so short as to be negligible, the oversized crew made the Sky Wolf the fastest airship in Balteris by a long shot. We sped over the forest until it dwindled into rolling plains. Below, Tryst's vast expanse of grasslands looked like an unending ocean of brown and green. Despite our height advantage, we didn't see any of Qaewin's people. The plains were mind-bogglingly extensive, so no surprise that they weren't on this southern slice we were traversing.

Despite not having fully recovered from crossing the sea, Volant and I spent a fair bit sparring, even bringing in Cassiopia and Shazina. Thecily also joined in but wouldn't stop accessing Ukiyo, making us seem like slow children in comparison. I'd used the mental muscle that controlled my access to Skill and now Ukiyo so much that it physically hurt trying to access it, even with a Toron stone. It didn't take long before we sent Shazina and Thecily off to their side of the ship while Volant and I worked against each other. The hatchets the Exo gave me were put aside, along with the two heirloom-worthy rapiers. Instead, we went for full contact with some hardened wood, eliciting curses from each other as we made contact. By noon, we'd rest and go through Volant's sky pirate kata with everyone on the ship. Joy and Martino even surfaced from the kitchen, joining in and watching a few training sessions here and there. Within a few days, not a person on the ship hadn't practiced it at least once.

It was otherwise almost leisurely, something a wealthy merchant or councilman would have paid for. Arriving in Brod, the plains began to slope to a center point. From this height, I could see the crater that formed Brod's almost perfectly circular lake.

It was puzzling. My mind had trouble wrapping itself around the idea of such an enormous impact. The lake itself sat near the horizon, a small, sparkling blue gem against the grassy green slopes all around it. Small rivers ran to the lake from every direction, feeding trickles of water to the crater's center.

We began to dip down, seeing the scars of the battle still marring the landscape with large black deaths of scorched earth.

That sobered the ride a little, but as we closed in on the floating harbor city, tents dotted the edge of the lake. The trappings of a shanty town springing up around the clustered make-shift homes. In the center, eerily similar to how the set up in Exo had been, sat a crippled Thran's Leaf.

Thecily and her spotters had seen it too, and were bringing us to bear on the small settlement on the lakeshore.

A sigh of disappointment came from behind me as we turned away from our course to the city. Insley was at the tail with Shazina, and both looked highly disappointed. Argo, trailing Shazina, wagged his tail happily and trotted over to me when he saw I was looking.

Absentmindedly, I scratched his head. Something was out of place with the scene below us.

"Volant's mom seems to have lost her balloons," Shazina remarked.

"Ah, that's what it was," I said. The ropes were piled up around the vessel but weren't attached to any of the secret gas-filled envelopes that Wydvis used to make their ships fly.

As we swung around and lower, we could see the ship's envelope as a tightly rolled up bundle off to the side. A crowd was gathering at our arrival, and at least fifteen small sailing ships were beelining from the floating harbor towards the shore.

The lake's size grew more and more impressive the lower we got. Brod's cratered appearance disappeared to give way to a rocky beach, choppy water, and seemingly endless hills. If it weren't for having seen the massive crater from so high up, you'd never know there was anything odd about how the lake was formed.

Bringing the airship down seemed to take an age. Volant convinced Thecily it was of the utmost importance for Qaewin and him to take fallpacks down under the guise of finding his mother and paving the way for their arrival. Enviously, I watched as the two of them vaulted over the side, an excited whoop following Volant down.

For a moment, I thought about jumping as well. I'd used the Toron stones to soften impacts before, and I imagined it couldn't be that much more difficult from this high up. But the more rational part of me immediately shut down such a waste of energy, a potentially fatal adrenaline rush, and the possible loss of my last Toron stone besides Bymm's ring.

Below, a person ambled underneath the ship's shadow and stood there, despite numerous shouts from the crew to clear out of the landing site. The person moved oddly, reminding me of something.

Another figure hurried out from the tents and half dragged, half led the person back to the shoreline and out from under the Sky Wolf's shadow.

The anchor crew rappelled over the railing, trailing rope that looked like long, sinuous tails. The ship was as still as a flower on a windless day as they all pulled their leads taut. Then we slowly inched downwards, the horizon rising to greet us.

Qaewin and Volant were waiting. The ordinarily quiet and controlled Soft Stepper had a wildness to her, an energetic enthusiasm that came with the burst of adrenaline a fallpack gave. Her zymph bounded from the railing above after spotting her and gave a quick sniff before cavorting with a similar joy to be back on land.

Qaewin's zymph was used to the ship now but in no way liked being aboard. On the other hand, Volant's thrill-seeking bug for jumping off airships seemed to have planted itself deep in Qaewin. I could almost see the thoughts spinning in her head on how to get another chance at the fallpack.

Despite her excitement, Volant looked troubled. "There's something odd," he said. "My mother's on one of those ships heading this way, but the people here are twitchy. Something's been happening."

I looked around and saw what he meant. An airship this size would generally bring a crowd. But, this particular crowd wasn't the festive type that'd usually come running. The only people who seemed interested were Captain Andreska's crew and a series of vagabond types that seemed to follow them. All of these were well-armed and stood well away. They were hard men and women with hard eyes that watched us wearily. Beyond them, what looked like refugees stayed in tents or continued with whatever business they'd been about before the airship arrived.

I didn't recognize any of the crew. "You know any of them?"

Volant half shrugged. "A few are new. A few are freelancers. They flit from ship to ship whenever the need arises. Most of the regulars are with my mother, or so one of them told me."

It wasn't long before Captain Andreska appeared, haggard, but still with the imposing aura and chiseled-from-stone posture. "Volant, it's good to see you, son," she said as he rushed over to embrace her.

Thecily joined, along with an Exo native named Jocamo. Argo had gotten bored and followed us as well, the girls having been uninterested in joining and instead running some experiments with the octomantis remains.

Captain Andreska had a table put out in the shade of her ship, and her new first mate Finn served us tea, giving me a warm, friendly hello before sitting down. Volant still didn't seem to like the guy but managed a perfunctory nod in his direction.

"Now, this is quite a surprise," Andreska said dryly. "Last I saw you two, I'd given direct orders to stay in Erset."

Thecily, Volant, and I all shifted nervously. Despite our discomfort, Qaewin was still riding the rush of the fall pack. She snorted with the effort of containing her laugh and then ended up laughing anyway. "Wait till you hear what they've been up to," she said, unable to control herself.

As we took turns explaining, Captain Andreska's jaw dropped, closed, dropped again, and in general, she had the metaphorical rug entirely yanked out from under her feet. By the time we finished, she had sat back, taking Volant in all over again.

Then me.

Then Qaewin.

And finally, landing on Thecily.

She almost seemed like she was going to slump in the chair, something she'd not done for the entirety of the long-winded and winding story. But just as her shoulders started to sag, she used the motion instead to roll them out and sit up even straighter.

"You lot...." She paused, at a loss for words. "You lot must have Locklentalis watching over you. Blue robes? Crossing the sea? And if I'm not mistaken, that snake you talked about is a brown cliff snake. Thought to be extinct, but were some of the single most deadly creatures on Balteris for a while before enough people banded together to hunt them to the brink of non-existence."

It was my turn to chuckle. "Out of all that, the snake is what you're stuck on?"

She slid her eyes towards me, definitely a mother's look of annoyance she must have used on Volant a hundred times over. "There's a lot to take in. But moving on from that, there's something far more important that you spoke of that may have solved one of my mysteries over here."

Thecily squirmed at what seemed like a change of subject, noticeably trying to keep her mouth shut.

"Oh, yes," Captain Andreska said, as if Thecily had said something out loud. "First off, good work with those pirates. I doubt you'll even need more than a testimony from me on how they stole and crippled our ship."

A truly terrifying spasm of rage briefly flashed across Andreska's face at the mention of the pirates who'd left her ship stranded, but it disappeared just as quickly. "If I'd have found who punctured my envelope, robbed us, and left us to die, I'd have done more than take their ship. Not one of them would have lived without nightmares for the rest of their lives." She unclenched her whitening knuckles, calming down. "Still, you have my support. No matter what. You are, in every way, worthy of captaining the Sky Wolf despite your hair brained jaunt across the sea."

Thecily smiled, warm and radiant. "Thank you, Captain. That means a lot."

She nodded. "That brings me to what I meant to talk about before. When we more or less crash-landed here, the pirates having stolen our fall packs, we found several affected individuals while out scavenging near the mistlands for wood," she said, making the word affected seem like some kind of disease.

"Affected how?" I asked, thinking back to the person who'd idled beneath the ship as we came down.

Despite the dark expression that went over Finn's face, he was the one to speak up. "It's like they've gone completely dumb," he explained. "No will to live. No understanding of what's being said to them or what they're to do. They eat when given food. They sleep wherever they end up falling asleep. They're like castrated farmyard animals, just waiting to be butchered."

"Gimzers," Volant whispered, slightly horrified.

Captain Andreska looked over at her son. "Your description of the gimzers effect on their prey did make me think of parallels, but there's more."

Finn nodded and continued. "The afflicted keep disappearing. We haven't figured out the timeframe, but without exception, they each have disappeared into thin air. My twin got the disease. Or was attacked, as it seems more likely. We leashed him inside a room to make sure. Just a night ago, he was gone. The rope looked to have been ripped apart, not cut or chewed through. We haven't seen him since."

Relief momentarily salved the dread that was rising up in me. Gimzer victims didn't disappear. They were just husks for the rest of their lives. This couldn't be the work of gimzers if that were the case. Still, I had to ask. "Have you seen any creatures? Taller than man, dark gray skin? Reflective eyes?"

Both Finn and Captain Andreska flinched, and the momentary relief disappeared.

"There have been rumors, as such," Captain Andreska said in a reserved tone. "We've not been able to confirm them, but supposedly the mist-lands have some monster of the night with glowing eyes. Everything is gray out in the mists, though."

Unsettled, I exchanged glances with Volant and Thecily. They'd seen how beat down the Exo's had been. They'd also experienced up close just how dangerous a gimzer could be. But disappearing victims? That couldn't be them. Plus, we were home. We were in Balteris. Gimzers didn't exist here and couldn't have crossed the straight.

With a wave of her hand, Captain Andreska tabled the subject. "Just stay alert, and see if these affected exhibit similar characteristics to your gimzer victims. There's slightly larger fish to fry."

If gimzers had somehow crossed over to Balteris or been hiding in Brod, this would be a larger fish than whatever she thought was more important. "If you say so," I said with obvious worry.

"God's Fury is on the move again. More specifically, they've come out of the shadows and have risen into quite a bit of power. Kassandra has taken over the Kalaran government. She's essentially legitimized the Equal movement as a political, misaligned, and oppressed group looking for equality for all. Factions have been springing up at an alarming rate from the sound of it."

"Aye, that does sound bad," I agreed.

Qaewin growled something soft and incoherent before clearing her throat. "Those left-handed lizard faces. Do you know where my father's been?"

"Yes," Andreska said simply. "He's gone into politics of a sort, trying to actively oppose the Equals with a coalition of people. He's not made it out this far."

Uncomfortable after sitting so long, I unconsciously adjusted Berjio's sword at my waist. The movement froze me, an awful realization that I'd left out Rook's duel with Berjio and the sword. I'd nearly pushed the memory out of my head.

"Andreska, I mean, Captain," I stammered. "I forgot something."

Bemused, she gestured back towards the Sky Wolf. "If it's so important, please go fetch it."

"No, I replied. "Not on the ship." I unbuckled the rapier, laying it across the table.

Her eyes fell on the sword, and before I even said anything, her carefully composed appearance began to crumble. A war of emotions flickered where amusement had been before. "How did you come by that sword, Nil?"

I swallowed, pushing it a little across the table. "You haven't seen Rook, have you?"

"No, though I did hear he passed through these parts just before we arrived. Still have yet to have the pleasure of your," Andreska paused as if the word was hard to say, "teacher."

Again, I swallowed. "Rook ran into Berjio after they'd chained me up. The two fought. Rook won." I tried to add more, to talk about how Berjio had seemed to intentionally lose after he thought his granddaughter was safe. How Rook seemed to hate himself for it. The Toron stones we found. But none of it came out.

It was like looking at a marble statue. Her face was chiseled, stony, and unmoving. After the initial wave of understanding passed, she became unreadable. Only the twin sets of tears welling up in the corners of her eyes gave away that she was still alive.

Abruptly she stood, tears flashing as they caught the light. "Excuse me. I need a moment to process this." She then clasped her hands behind her back and strode off and out of sight. A heavy sob echoed from beyond the curve of the ship.

I turned to Finn. "How many of these affected have you found?"

He looked up for a moment, doing some quick math. "I'd say around fifty or so. It seems just about every day, we find one or two out in the mistlands. Most are homesteader types from what we've seen. Loners who live out in the wild away from civilization, surviving on the land and their wits." He seemed wistful for a moment before waving the statement away. "It's hard to tell because there hasn't been anyone keeping track, and they end up disappearing anyways."

Goosebumps broke out on my arm. That was a lot of people for such a light amount of caring to be going on.

Chapter Twenty-Four

It was a long time before Andreska came back. The rapier was still where she'd left it. She picked it up, eyeing the lines with a professional intensity. She unsheathed it, checked it over once more, and then slammed it back home with practiced precision. "Rook and I will be having words when I find him. But I think it's right for you to have the sword. Far better a weapon than those gaudy axes you carry around."

I bowed, taking the sword from her. "Thank you," I managed, embarrassed with the solemnity.

As I straightened, a man in a flamboyant checkered jacket, and an insanely large hat that reminded me of the little boat thief that Volant and I had escaped from Brod with the last time strode up, followed by two bodyguards. The man's clean-shaven face was pale and soft.

"Captain Andreska, I hope I'm not interrupting anything important."

Before she could respond, he gestured to one of the guards, who strode over to her while clutching a bulging purse of coins. He carefully placed it on the table.

"I understand you and your crew are currently out of work. I'd like to hire you to join us in fighting off these usurpers and their unsavory ilk." He pointed at the bag. "A gesture of goodwill, from the Council of Brod."

"Excuse me, but I feel I must have missed something." Andreska was nonplussed.

He looked at all of us in turn and then gestured towards the Sky Wolf. "Haven't you heard? The Equals have taken over Kalaran. They've also begun torching Tryst's plains. Civil war has broken out."

This time Finn stepped in. "Can we get back to you with an answer? We'll need to discuss a bit in private. Is there somewhere in Brod we can find you at?"

Slightly deflated, the man stepped back. "Ah, of course. But please, don't wait too long, this is urgent. The name's Lopool. Councilman Lopool, that is. I'll more than likely be at the chambers behind the gardens but just ask around. Everyone knows me."

When Captain Andreska merely stared, the man gestured to his guards again, and the group disappeared just as quickly as they'd appeared. We watched them fade away among the tents until a small sail ship detached itself from the beach and headed back to Brod.

Massaging her temples, Captain Andreska turned to us. "You lot came from Erset, did you hear anything about this? See fires? Anything?"

Mutely, Volant, Qaewin, and I shook our heads. Thecily though, made a wavering gesture with her hand. "One of the watchmen saw smoke while we were crossing Tryst. But we skirted down near the southern cliffs to catch the stronger air currents."

"Left handing Equals," Andreska sighed. It was a deep and weary sigh, the kind only both a mother and the stand-in mother of a ship could manage. It made me feel like I'd disappointed someone and had to make up for it. Then she slammed her fist into the table. "Guess they've hired us. Captain Thecily, I'm going to need a ride to Wydvis. We're going to finish this if we have to sacrifice every airship our home has."

Thecily saluted, something I'd not actually seen her do before.

Finn picked up the bag of coin and tossed it to her.

"Finn!" Thecily barked, all captain. "Get that ship emptied! Anything unnecessary is to be pulled out and stored. We'll attach to the Sky Wolf and get towed back to civilization." She turned to Qaewin, Volant, and me. "No offense Qaewin, I think you're a testament to your father's will and such a woman for any father to be proud of. But you two," she said, stabbing a pair of fingers at Volant and me. "You two should be tied up, tossed into a closet on my ship, and left there until all of this is over. You're irresponsible. You're bad influences upon each other, and those around you, and have an unbelievable ability to attract the gods attention and bring trouble upon your heads." Her arms spread out, encompassing the tents and broken airship and sloping hills. "Unfortunately, I must leave you here. Again."

Volant bristled, half rising out of his chair before his mother raised a placating hand. Funnily enough, Qaewin was nodding her head along with Captain Andreska, obviously agreeing with what she said.

"This is not abandonment this time. I need that mischief-magnet here in Brod."

Volant paused mid-motion and sat back down heavily, lacking his usual grace. "What?"

"You and Nil will find this source of the afflicted. You will find where they have been disappearing. If possible, you will fix this problem with that stubborn, bullheaded luck you two seem incapable of losing." She turned back to Qaewin. "Also, if possible, I'd like to request you and your family's support in general, and in this issue in particular. Please, pass on my regards to Slandash if you see him before I do."

As the crew prepared for the airships' departures, reports began to come in. Riders on horse thundered into the camp with general proclamations. They seemed to be hired out by the Equals as three of the four riders were spouting nonsense about the bombings in Kalaran being the work of Naturals in the deployment of councils from each region trying to cover up the people's voice.

Kassandra was praised for pulling back the curtain on these activities and was putting up her personal wealth to hire "freedom fighters" to join the Equal movement.

Unfortunately, some of the Exo natives who'd come along liked the sound of quick coin and began disappearing while Thecily and Andreska prepared their ships. Shazina watched with mute disappointment as clusters of her people struck out in the direction the riders indicated.

News began to spread on where the war's loyalties were appearing. Wydvis was neutral, which was received by the crew with similarly neutral care. Wydvis was more a community of aggressively independent people with similar living situations and passions. As a whole, they didn't go in for politics.

Erset, of course, would end up siding with Equals but hadn't officially done so. They were probably just finding out now. Tryst and its various tribes split their allegiances. Having already shed blood against the Equals, Soft Steppers had their plains preemptively burned, though the story went that the same wild Naturals who'd blown up portions of Kalaran were to blame. The Slithers were with Kalaran, for the same reason the Soft Steppers weren't, and the Night Runners ignored the rest of us as they never strayed down from their mountain peaks.

Worst of all, news of the same crazed Naturals attacking the school made it to us. My blood began to boil when I heard this, and I grabbed the man talking roughly by the collar before spinning him around to face me.

"What's this about Jorcum's?" I asked, trying to keep my voice level.

Voice dripping with sarcasm, the dirty man turned to look down at me. "Better watch ya' self, boy. Some jealous Naturals tried to bring the school down. But it sounds like they bit off more than they could chew. Equals won't let that kind o'thing fly when they're in charge."

Part of me was glad to hear they hadn't destroyed the school, but part of me was annoyed at having run into yet another Equal sympathizer.

That annoyance showed, and the man scowled, pushing me in the hallmark move of starting a brawl. He had two friends, as dirty as he was, and both looked bigger and meaner. "Ah, so you're one of the sympathizers, huh? That's somethin' I can fix."

I hadn't said anything, but I also guessed having grabbed the man might not have been the wisest move. He seemed to be taking it personally and, having decided I wasn't one of "them," was going to take full advantage and let loose some steam.

He swung big and wide, another embarrassingly predictable start to a brawl. His meaty fist arced through the air.

Disdain permeating every bit of the motion, I leaned back, letting his fist pass by harmlessly. The man had overextended. He stumbled when his overcommitted punch met empty air, and his friends laughed.

Red in the face, he snarled and whipped out a long, wicked-looking knife. Seeing this and taking in the weapons I had, his friends stepped forward, brandishing their own blades. This had turned from a beat down to something far more deadly in the space of a chuckle.

The knife bit out wildly, the man trying to cut me to ribbons before I had a chance to draw my axe. Instead of doing so, I stepped forward, weaving around his wild attack. The knife hissed by the exact spot where the glung fruit coated blade had cut me so long ago. Unfortunately for him, I'd been practicing since then.

I snaked my arm up and around, immobilizing the elbow and taking away his momentum. His hand wavered uselessly behind me. A breath passed as I locked eyes with his two friends, who'd paused mid-stride. And then I pivoted, swinging the man up and across my hip against the angle of his arm. He struck the ground. Hard.

Something gave as he hit the ground, and a muffled cry came out of the man before he passed out.

Still, I didn't reach for the axes or draw Berjio's sword. I gestured to the two men. When they didn't move, I gave an encouraging smile. "Come on. You wanted to dance, let's dance you Laker inbreds."

They waded forward, only a little staggered by the ease of me handling their friend.

Again, I moved forward to meet them, feinting a jab first before dropping low and around the second. Not giving them time to change tactics, I landed a series of knuckle-first punches into the second's kidneys, eliciting a howl of surprise and pain.

He lashed out with the knife backward, swinging for where my face should have been. Instead, I'd already begun to move again, crossing underneath his swing and snapping a kick out. I landed the kick right at the knee, and the man went sprawling.

The third man's eyes had gone wide at the edges. His pride seemed to urge him on, and he jumped forward anyways, stabbing frantically with a knife that looked more like a toothpick in his large hands.

I raised one hand. Summoning and converting Skill before I'd even pointed my fingers. I didn't even touch the Toron stone's source, and the effort had happened in the blink of an eye.

Terrified, the man froze. "You're a Learner?" he asked, despair nearly choking the words off at the end. He tried to take a step forward, but I waved the pointed fingers at him. He didn't understand just how big a hole I could put through him.

"I am. Name's Nil," I answered. "How about we say this is over, you help get your friends to some healer, and maybe take my advice to heart-the Equals are using people like you to enslave all of us. There's nothing good that comes from them succeeding."

Hastily the man nodded. I left, drawing the Skill in and through me, converting it to Ukiyo instead. The world seemed to sharpen in every way, and though nothing changed outside, it almost felt like the sharpness of my senses helped the world slow down just hair, or at least my understanding of it.

Chapter Twenty-Five

As night began to fall, Qaewin, her zymph, Shazina, Cassiopia, Volant, and Insley gathered around a small campfire with me. Everyone understood what we had to do while the airships were headed back to Wydvis. Now that they were gone, the lakeshore seemed desolate. Cassiopia had scheduled us passage on a small boat to get across the lake and upriver.

The only real plan we'd come up with was to run around the mistlands until we found something. There wasn't much to the area, a few hills and cliffs, maybe a valley here and there, and plenty of caves on the shoreside. The problem was visibility. You could see twenty paces or so around you at any given time. It was easy to get lost and near impossible to find anything out there.

A ship, mostly looking like a dark shadow in the fading light, eased up just a way out from the shore. "We don't have all night," a voice shouted across the water to us. The ship looked oddly familiar, at least as a silhouette. A tiny man stood near the wheel, a magnificent hat obscuring his face entirely from view.

We waded through the shallow water towards the ship. A shiver ran up my spine, remembering the warning I'd received about not disturbing the lake. I wasn't the only one uncomfortable with the experience, and everyone seemed to find a store of energy to climb aboard quickly, the zymph the fastest of us all. A pair of deckhands helped pole the ship away from the shallower water and into the lake's deeper, choppier waves.

"Gods, you lot are brave! Don't you know there are monsters in these waters?" The small form hopped down, bypassing the ladder entirely. Even with the hat, he was barely taller than Shazina.

"Tervlik?" Volant half shouted, half asked with childish excitement.

The kid pulled off the wide hide, bringing his face out of shadow. Not only was he barely a hair or two taller than Shazina, but also of similar age.

An enthusiastic growl came from Tervlik, who lost all semblance of the severe but diminutive boat captain as he rushed over and hugged Volant. He turned, seeing my surprise, and hugged me as well. "I just knew I'd run into you two again."

We traded stories as his much older crew spun us around and began crossing the lake. The nocturnal lake creatures kept us company with occasional too close and too loud splash. Occasionally something large either bumped into the ship, or the ship bumped into it. A jolt of fear went through us every time, but despite all this, the Tervlik's crew seemed unconcerned as we made our way.

"After you guys dealt with those pirates, thanks for that by the by, I had my family's old ship reconstructed from memory, with a few tweaks here and there," Tervlik said, gesturing around us. He seemed able to talk all night and planned on doing so.

Mid conversation, we passed the floating harbor and the multitude of lights on rocking ships and bobbing homes that made up the Brod's upper portion. Like a smooth mountain, the chimneys that acted like four gargantuan straws giving airflow to the below rose out of the center of Brod's floating harbor. From down here, they seemed like only a god's plaything, nothing that people could have made.

"My family wasn't poor by any means," he continued, "so when everything was said and done, I found myself with a house I didn't need and a pile of coin. Turned the house into a tavern, let a family friend run it, and used the rest of the money to get a ship. I pay the crew from the inn's profit if work is slow, but overall, we've had a pretty good time of things."

We were all impressed. Volant and I had barely managed to survive our world turning upside down, and only Insley had any experience with genuinely making money.

Tervlik and his crew took us up one of the small rivers, and as the stolen moon reached its zenith, we hit the first roiling mist of the mistlands and were swallowed up. The mood on the boat took a somber tone after that, and our chatter died down into wary alertness.

We'd not been too long riding up the river into the mistlands mist when one of the crew softly called out to Tervlik that the depth was closing in on the boat. The boy issued a few commands, and the boat slowed to a stop before dropping a short anchor.

"Alas, our journey comes to an end," Tervlik said with a bow. Though his voice hadn't even dropped yet, he bent regally at the waist and kissed first Qaewin, then Insley, and finally Shazina's hands. "It was a pleasure, my ladies." He turned to Cassiopia, unsure if such gallantry was proper or not with a woman of her size and obvious muscle.

She saved him from any decision making by sticking her hand out for a hearty shake.

With a companionable nod to Volant and me, he smiled. "Still have those rocks of mine?"

Volant smiled back and shrugged. "Pretty sure I've got it somewhere on my mother's airship."

I gestured in response at Volant. "Same here, I hope."

Tervlik tried to look wounded, but he could only hold the pose for a moment before cackling happily. "Still, I am at your service, rock, or no rock. But, if you ever need my help, be sure to send it my way. I still owe you both at least another favor."

With that said, his crew hustled us off the ship and into the cold river. Qaewin and her zymph had a crisis of conscience and I was sure they'd try to mutiny before going back in. The water wasn't deep, and we were able to wade to shore. From there, Tervlik's boat was only a ghostly outline as it turned and began to head back downstream. We'd packed light, planning to work our way back towards the lake through the night and see if we came across any gimzers or anything of that sort.

First, we warmed ourselves by running towards the coastline's edge, following the river as it snaked its way towards the western ocean. With such low visibility, the mass of water snuck up on us. I heard it long before actually stepping onto the beach. It was eerie, with the mist sucking up both sound and light. Almost like a dream.

And just like a dream, a colossal shadow began to take shape in the distance before us, just off the edge of the beach.

"What in the godspawn is that?" asked Insley through labored breaths.

None of us had an answer.

It looked like some mythical castle out of legend, squared edges, turrets, the whole package. The mist made it hard to see details beyond the rough shape, so we began to edge closer. Closer up, the fog gave way to a rocky growth of granite and stone that supported the foundation of what seemed to be a large beach fort.

It wasn't quite a castle, but close enough to be striking and also downright intimidating. The tide was low, so we crept along the sandy edge. On the other side of the fort, a smaller shadow tilted in the mists. We had a hushed argument on whether or not to try to explore the fort more thoroughly or not, with Volant and I wanting to head straight up the side of the rockface and the girls arguing that we needed to see what else was out here before doing anything rash.

There being four of them to the two of us, we made our way to the distant shadow on the beach while keeping a weather eye on the fort behind us.

Just out of bowshot range, a ship began to materialize much as the fortress had. One we recognized immediately. Rook's ship, the Aye, was beached on the sand and leaning haphazardly to one side. It seemed to be a night for old friends and coincidences. Thinking of the rogue blue robe, a bounce came to my step, and I began to jog towards the ship.

Only reflexes honed by hundreds of sparring sessions saved me. The mist-muffled twang of a bowstring came from the ship. I ducked, letting my momentum turn the movement into a full-on lateral roll before coming up, axe in hand and Skill surging through me. The arrow impacted just where I'd been in a spray of wet sand.

Another arrow sang out, parting the mist a few paces out from me. I stepped to the side, batting it away with the swing of an axe. I whipped my other hand forward, sending a blanket of Skill surging out. An otherworldly keen sounded from the fort behind us, making the hair on my neck bristle. The mists briefly parted before us, but Skill was a poor conductor for moving so much air as to increase visibility.

Volant saw what I had meant to do, and in a swinging, twirling dance sent a wave of wind blasting across the length of the beach towards the Aye. A surprised group of sailors with bows blinked across the distance to us.

I waved and then gave them a rude gesture as the mists closed again.

No further arrows came, so we cautiously made our way over to the pirate-turned-anti-pirate ship. A rope snaked down from the railing as we reached its base. "Hurry," a voice hissed from up above.

Taking them at their word on the need for haste, the group of us took turns quickly scaling the rope with help from the men above, with Chloe using her feline agility to bound up the side of the ship. When a zymph gets on a boat quickly, it's wise to follow its lead.

Something, a feeling perhaps-- the kind all prey feel when a predator has them in their sights, sounded the alarm in the back of my brain.

Everyone else was up above. I spun, searching the mists towards the fort that still loomed like a dark hill in the distance. I heard the rope thump into the sand behind me. And then there were eyes shining in the mist, closely followed by an elongated body. It wasn't quite a gimzer, less sleek, less naturally organic looking. Still, it had the eyes. And the claws. And the speed.

I shoved my will straight into Ukiyo, lighting up my senses and muscles and even thinking more quickly for it. I thrummed with the pent-up energy. The not-gimzer surged, clearing a dozen paces easily. I dropped to my knees and bent backward nearly double, touching the back of my head almost all the way down. The nightmare crunched into the side of the ship, barely missing my folded body.

With a simultaneous turn, I sliced through the air but found the ground before me empty. The thing had hit the ship and stuck, looking for all the world like a terrible four-legged spider clinging to the wall.

Growling, I let the missed swing pivot me and brought the other axe around for a spinning backswing. My aim was short yet again. With a third spin, I let the backhand become the start of a throw, sending the axe head a single full rotation before it struck into the back of the creature.

It let out the same, spine-tingling keen I'd heard before. I stabbed out, but the creature blurred, leaping off the side and landing behind me. If it weren't for Ukiyo, it'd have won then and there, but I could move faster than the laws of nature should have allowed. I dipped under the swing that I knew was coming. Air parted like cut silk above me, the claws ripping the space where I'd been. I slashed out with the black metal axe and severed the not-gimzer's leg.

A backhand from the creature sent me flying through the air. At first, it was an odd feeling, being almost weightless before the pain lit up like fireworks. I skidded in the sand, breathless and stunned.

The creature staggered and fell, but despite the axe still buried in its back and missing a leg, it crawled forward in a creepy, three-legged skitter that ate up the distance. I flung my remaining axe but missed, the creature dancing back and sideways. It was close enough to human to be downright disturbing.

It's remaining leg and arms coiled beneath it. Unnatural eyes met mine. The limbs snapped to extension, springing it forward with claws extended and a mouth wide with a soundless scream. I flinched back, fear overwhelming me.

Then Volant was crashing down into it, glittering steel blade driving point first into the creature's skull as he landed on its back, crushing it to the ground. Even in the muffling mists, the sharp snap of a blade breaking cracked through the air like a whip.

Volant rolled with the impact, coming off the creature and holding his father's sword hilt. When the not-gimzer laid perfectly still, he looked down at the sword hilt. A moment of despair tinged his features, but he shoved it aside. I finished standing with his help, and we cautiously approached the creature.

It's back was crushed, and the head impaled deep into the sand by the broken blade. It was a gimzer, more or less. At the least, it had all the gimzer features and a bit more bulk to it. On the less side, it was shorter and seemed less evolved than the ones in Balteris.

"This isn't good," Volant said.

"Aye, that it isn't," I agreed. "One might even say this would constitute as a bad situation."

Another keen sounded, followed by a second, neither from the fort. The noise jolted both of us, and we hurried back to the ship, retrieving my axes on the way, and finally climbing up to join the others in the approximate safety of height and numbers.

The fight had lasted just long enough for everyone else to have barely begun to realize what was happening before Volant had landed on the thing. Rook's right hand, Jacob, had a cutlass drawn almost immediately. Everyone else still was processing what had happened.

"There do, in fact, seem to be gimzers in Balteris," I cheerily announced. "We're all probably going to die."

Insley slapped my arm but smiled nonetheless. Shazina just shook her head, and Qaewin looked worried, and her zymph's agitated twitches mirrored her.

Jacob clapped me on the back. "Good to see you two again," he said with a tired but genuine smile. "I must admit, I surely must, that I did not expect to find you two out here." His gray hair was tied back, and he seemed to have aged a dozen years since we'd last seen him.

"The same here, actually," I said. "Now, where's Rook, and why are you in this godspawning place?" I looked around, seeing just a few men. "And where's the rest of the crew?"

With a gesture to one of the men to keep watch, Jacob led us to a small space in the hold where they'd made a meeting place of sorts. We all sat, tired from the run.

"So here's the thing," Jacob began. "We came lookin' for those creatures, and we found them. Unfortunately, they're not the only bad stuff out there. While we were out chasing them, a bunch of toughs came and grabbed Rook and dragged him off to that fort. Killed some of the crew, too. We lost a few more trying to get through the gates. Can't leave, either, and not just out of loyalty. We're stuck, and those creatures seem to be growing more numerous."

The update took him less time than it'd taken us to even get comfortable around the table.

"Left hand," Qaewin muttered under her breath. "What kept you out?"

"There are men with bows and spears. Maybe ten or so. We're just a bunch of washed-up pirates. Rook is a whole other story, worth a dozen of us. But without him, we're pretty run of the mill on storming forts and such.

Our group exchanged glances. Small nods came from everyone, Volant giving me a wink when everyone had given their assent. "It'll be nice for him to be on the receiving end of some help for once," I said. At the same time, I unbuckled Berjio's sword. I passed it over to Volant, who hadn't stopped fidgeting with his father's hilt. "And you," I added, "are going to need a new sword for this."

Words failed him, but the appreciation shone through the way he reverently took up the sword. It felt good to not be carrying it. Whatever Captain Andreska thought, the sword wasn't for me, that much I was beginning to be sure of.

We bent our heads together and began to plan, eschewing sleep for quick action and a chance to get out of the mistlands as quickly as possible.

Some invisible bird, a crow or raven maybe, cawed out from the impenetrable mists as the ship went up in flames. Shazina and Argo stayed with Rook's crew, ostensibly because they couldn't imagine a little kid going with us, but mostly to keep them safe.

We watched the group of them flee from the ship, large torches made from decking. The blaze was downright bright in the pre-dawn mists. The mass of light streamed from the ship, moving deliberately out and around towards the fort's front gates.

Our squad of gimzer hunters-turned-jailbreakers watched from the shadows between the fort and the ship. We'd gotten as close to the structure as we felt comfortable before ducking down to wait for the blaze. It was a sad sight, seeing the Aye burn so. Our time with Rook on it had been short but memorable, and I almost missed the simplicity of sailing along the coastline with them.

Men appeared at the top of the fort, vague shadows that were hopefully watching either the burning ship or the trail of torches headed towards their front gate.

I moved, rushing towards the rock outcropping the fort was built on. The others followed, none of us trying to be exactly stealthy. Cassiopia had her bow out and an arrow knocked as she scanned the dark wall above us. Insley stayed with her, a look of worry on her face.

Qaewin, Volant, and I began to climb. The rock was cold and slick, but the handholds were plentiful. Qaewin's zymph made it to the base of the fort before us but hesitated at climbing the wall. The rest of us climbed the boulders as quickly as we could, making it to the base of the fort well before Jacob and his team had come within bowshot of ramparts above. I checked the rope around my waist, finding the heavily braided sailor's rope dry and comfortably thick. Its weight would have made someone else's climb a lot harder, but I was beginning to have the suspicion that Ukiyo use trended towards something more permanent in my body.

I focused my will, bringing Skill and Ukiyo both to life. I nodded to Volant, who began to gather the air and mist into a tightly packed shape before him. Qaewin patted me on the back before stepping a few paces away.

Shoving against the ground with unnaturally enhanced legs, I jumped. Three things happened at once.

First, I exploded into the air, flying up towards the edge of the fort's parapet with extreme velocity similarly to when we'd been on Thecily's airship.

Second, the Toron stone in my pocket cracked, leaving a vortex of emptiness in me. A burst of exhaustion slammed into me like a hammer.

Third, a keen wailed out from the fortress, a soul-rending sound far too close for comfort. The sound shook me enough that I nearly missed the ledge and plummeted back down to Volant and Qaewin.

The ledge was wet, but the stone was roughly hewn and had thousand ridges. If not for that, my tired hands would have slipped completely. Instead, I hung, briefly too exhausted to pull myself up and over the ledge. I gritted my teeth, digging down further until I found that warm piece of anger. That resentment towards the way the world was compared to the way I wanted it to be. An arrow sliced from below as I pulled up, embedding itself in a man a few paces away from where I flopped over the ledge.

Wasting no time, I tied the rope off and tossed the loose end over the wall. An intense burst of wind came from below, and mist pooled around where I crouched with a denseness that only a Natural could achieve.

Qaewin and Volant made their way over without any further mishaps. Another arrow hissed through the darkness and mist, striking someone with a meaty thud. Bowstrings began to twang from across the courtyard as whoever these thugs were began to fire upon Jacob's group. The noise was uncannily muffled, making my hair stand on end. Death shouldn't be so soft.

Volant and Qaewin followed as I sprinted down the ramparts towards the nearest man who was drawing a bead on the group. He loosed, then heard my footsteps, turning suspiciously around. He got a halfway shouted alarm out before I slammed into him with both axe blades in a vicious overhand swing.

Qaewin and Volant flowed around me, taking out another two men as they spun at the shout.

Dislodging my axes, I caught up to them, then passed, moving further along the rampart's walkway as arrows rained down in our direction.

Fortunately, we didn't carry any torches, whereas the men guarding the castle did. Their flames revealed their positions while simultaneously blinding their night vision and limiting the range they could see at.

Shooting at a line of torches down on the beach was one thing. Shooting at three, hard to see shadows moving far too fast was a whole other problem.

It was almost too easy. Volant, Qaewin, and I all moved as if we'd practiced this kind of thing together for years. None of the fort thugs fought cohesively, coming in at as in ones or twos, swinging wildly. At least one man was shot by one of his own, and two more ended up running into each other and making things that much easier. I was beginning to guess they must have been washed up or washed-out Guard.

Unfortunately, it didn't last. One man who seemed to have run away touched down in the courtyard. Half a dozen reinforced metal cages dominated the area. Rook was in one, I realized. Two gimzers were in another pair. I tried to summon enough will to take a shot, but the pain was too much. "Qaewin!" I shouted, pointing at the man running across the courtyard towards the cages. "Shoot him!"

She took a step back, short bow at the ready. She was already drawing back, tracing the line of my finger before she saw the man.

She loosed. Then again in rapid succession. The first two arrows missed by mere fingertips. Her third arrow struck the man in the calf, but he'd already thrown the bolt home for the first cage. The psuedo-gimzer erupted from it, streaking towards the wall we were on.

The man opened the second cage as the fourth arrow finally brought him down, too late. The other followed the first's lead, moving straight for the wall below us. The world seemed to hold its breath for a moment.

I peered over the edge. Just as I did, a dark and sinewy hand latched on to the ledge next to my foot. I jumped back in shock as the nightmare creature raked its way up from the sheer stone wall below. A second set of hands appeared as I took another step back.

Neither creature hesitated. Neither did I.

As they lunged forward, I jumped, aiming for a small stone roof just below our wall. I felt the psuedo-gimzers cut the air beneath me as I flew over them before the lurch of freefall took any focus I had and brought it to bear. I hit the roof and rolled before springing up and jumping again to the courtyard below. Two thumps behind me announced the monsters following my lead.

Dashing towards Rook's cage, I tossed one axe through the thin bars to the waiting man. With the other, I took a two-handed grip and swung as hard as I could at the bolted shut chain. The impact vibrated up my arm and nearly knocked the small axe out of my hands. Miraculously, the weapon didn't break. The chain, on the other hand, did.

The door swung into me, shoved with such force from Rook it knocked me down. The gimzer behind me thudded into the iron bars as I sprawled out across the ground below it, Rook having saved me yet again.

Then the fight really began. Rook and I whirled between and around the creatures, barely keeping them at bay but moving so well together that we were almost dancing.

An eternity passed with us barely surviving before Volant and Qaewin appeared.

Daggers from Qaewin filled the air, biting up and down the first gimzer's flank. The second had an arm chopped off by Volant, the momentary distraction and imbalance giving me an opening to swing my axe through its neck. Rook seemed to have the same opportunity and smashed my other axe down into the gimzer's face, leaving it embedded deep into the thing as it fell over.

I couldn't hear anything but our heavy panting. As we caught our breath, a knock came from the gate. It came again, more insistent. I straightened up and checked myself over as a third round of pounding came, even more, aggressive than before.

"Impatient fellow, isn't he?" Volant said dryly before going over to the gate and pulling back the bar that locked it.

Jacob came rushing in as the gate swung open, torch held in one hand, cutlass in the other.

"Oi, Jacob," Rook said with a silly wave of my axe. "Don't carry on like that, acting as if the less savory inhabitants of this fort would have let you in to fight them. Have some dignity, man. Put that sword away."

Sheepishly, the first mate began to do so, when a ferocious scream came from the shadowy gatehouse. The battle cry was attached to a short, slightly stocky man who was running with a spear stretched out towards Jacob.

Halfway to sheathing the cutlass, he flung the torch at the charging man. He slid past the spear with a surprisingly agile parry and lunge as the man flinched back from the torch. As if posing for a portrait, the two men stood briefly locked in the moment, one with a surprising amount of steel buried up to the hilt in him, the other still shocked that he hadn't had a spear put through his heart.

A grunt, and Jacob broke away, retrieving his sword as the man collapsed. He looked over at Rook but said nothing.

Rook cleared his throat awkwardly. "Ah, yes. Dignity. Easy come, easy go, eh?"

After a cursory search, there only seemed to be one entrance into the rest of the fort. The gatehouse the man had charged out of was the only place there seemed to be a door or any other kind of structure beyond the walls around us. Cassiopia arrived last, huffing after running her way around the sandy beach and up the road to the front gate. She took a position on the wall, bringing Insley, Argo, and a slinking Chloe along and settled in. Volant tickled the lock open, and our entire group moved down the stairs en-masse.

It was bright inside, torches decorating the spiraling stairs. A single heavy wood door, unlocked this time, waited for us at the bottom. Still, Rook kicked it hard, sending it crashing open. Or half-open. The door struck a man and sent him sprawling.

Cries of alarm echoed within as we rushed into the torchlit cave-like sub-level. Another half dozen armed and rough-looking men waited. A tall, light-skinned man with blue runic tattoos covering his hands and exposed arms stood behind them. An alchemist.

"Left hand," I muttered.

We had them outnumbered, not to mention outclassed, considering Rook was armed and ready for some payback. Still, the men attacked, charging in with the reckless overconfidence that mean men who've survived a few fights seem to have. They went down as smoothly as one would wheat at harvest. Qaewin and Rook took two in the blink of an eye, the iron smell of blood filling the enclosed space almost immediately. Volant and I took down another, and Rook's small yet angry crew mobbed the final one.

Despite the short space in time, the alchemist had been busy. As the last man fell, I looked up to see him holding two glass bottles in one hand, their contents a viscous, metallic black and blue. In the other, he had a much larger bottle, faintly red and bubbling. The alchemist's grin was wide with too-white teeth. An unhinged glint of joy electrified his face. The eyes were bloodshot, and didn't seem to actually see us. Despite the far-away look, I knew he knew who was at fault for disrupting his plans.

"You'll not take me alive," he crowed happily, "and neither will any of you leave here alive."

"Jacob, you lot need to run. Now," Rook said under his breath.

To their credit, only a hardened look passed over their faces before they turned and charged back up the stairs from where we'd entered.

The alchemist, surprised, paused with his arm cocked back. "Such cowards," he said, disappointed. Then he pulled back, taking aim.

We all moved as one, it seemed. Rook and I sent axes flying, while Qaewin hurled a pair of knives, spinning them through the air. Everything seemed to blur. Then Rook's throw took the man's right arm, and Qaewin's blades hit the left. My axe missed. Volant twitched at our movements, but recovered, embarrassed.

Rook shoved both Qaewin and Volant towards our retreating friends, indecipherable yelling who's meaning was clear. Run.

I turned to see a spiraling cloud of green fire and blue smoke erupting around the mad alchemist. I bolted up the stairs behind the other three, taking the steps two at a time.

Heat chased us up exit as we scrambled onto the courtyard.

Back up top, the dawn sun shone faintly more like a smudged idea of the sun than what we were used to. The mist here never let up. As the wind changed directions, and the rich, burned timber smell of The Aye wafted across to replace the acrid smell of the alchemist's fire.

Rook turned, catching the different scent. He turned back, eyes narrowing as he took us all in. "Did you burn my boat?"

Feet shuffled. Eyes found anything but the man with the Waruin braid and robes that could have passed as blue, once upon a time.

Finally, the first mate stepped forward. "Well, you see," he began and launched into a quick, thorough explanation of the crew's losses, the damage to the ship, and the need for a distraction.

It took a long while before the gatehouse stopped emitting the noxious smoke and burning green light, and even longer still until the heat dissipated. When Rook declared it safe enough, we made our cautious way back down into the now blackened sub-level.

It was warm, and faintly smelled of cooked fish for some reason, my axes were otherwise unharmed. Qaewin's knives, on the other hand, were twisted, burned, and useless now. Another door stood in the back, and we found a barracks, followed by what looked like a pair of cells in the final room.

They were empty, but made my skin crawl none-the-less. Something evil had been done here.

Chapter Twenty-Six

It was midday before we'd hiked back into Brod and out of the mists. Once there, Rook called a stop and gathered us all around. He had a small scroll, more like a page out of a book that someone had rolled up, though the paper's quality was thick.

"Now that it's a bit lighter outside, I think it's time to talk about things that go bump in the night." Rook unfurled the paper, weighing it down with rocks on the corners.

As the river burbled happily off in the distance, I stepped closer. The paper was written in clear, concise handwriting, with exceptionally detailed drawings. Multiple diagrams showed steps to take, and only its archaic grammar made anything confusing. It was a guide on creating gimzers, dating back to before the exodus to Balteris.

"I found this while Nil was fondling his axes after the fire," Rook explained. "It seemed better to get into proper daylight before speaking of that place again."

When no one objected, Rook rolled the parchment back up and slipped it into a small, blackened tube that then disappeared into his threadbare robes as if by magic.

Despite the calmness of his tone, I knew Rook at this point. We'd spent far too much time together on the road and his ship. This man was masking his rage just beneath the surface with a calm, lecturing tone.

He smiled, brittle and sharp. "That man down there has unleashed a weapon as that manuscript refers to these gimzers on our land. He also made his own little tweaks, resulting in a less than perfect creature, similar to what Shazina and her people have faced. Instead of cunning and longevity, these versions are shorter-lived but wilder, and their victims, if not killed, eventually become a gimzer as well." He took a deep breath. When that wasn't enough, he picked up one of the stones and squeezed it. "That monster wearing the skin of a human is who created two of these gimzers. We killed both originals. However, that doesn't matter. He let them loose for hunting every night for a fortnight. There are dozens upon dozens of people who were turned into nightmares from before the time of gods."

Up until this moment, our moods had been lifting as the sun kissed us hello as we walked. I'd been having a fun debate with Insley on whether or not dessert was the best food group, and we'd laughed back and forth as each made their arguments. Volant and Qaewin had been quiet, listening to the exchange but just smiling, holding hands as they walked. Cassiopia, unaffected by the dark or mists, whistled tunelessly as we went. Even Shazina had seemed almost not emotionless for a bit there, playing fetch with Argo while keeping a sharp watch on Qaewin's zymph, who in turn seemed morbidly curious about Argo's ability to chase any thrown object and bring it back.

Now though, I looked around and saw dark, sour, and unhappy looks across everyone's face.

A deep sigh came from Rook as he finally dropped the rock. "This is the final atrocity from those God's Fury folks that I can allow. Plus, I hold them personally responsible for the destruction of my boat. Which, I was quite fond of."

"What can we do to help, then?" I asked.

Rook offered the sharp, humorless smile. "Be your usual, charmingly destructive and annoying circle of friends."

Brod's floating harbor and the subterranean Below, or Brod Proper, if one was pedantic, seemed to be sleepily waiting for us to come back. Fishing boats dotted the lake, bobbing like a hundred discarded children's toys. It was quiet and calm. Tervlik and his ship were waiting just at the edge of the river's mouth.

We hopped aboard and headed into the floating harbor.

Rook ran off for a moment, disappearing into the bobbing mass that made up the thousands of homes and shops and everything in between that the Lakers on the surface needed to live out their lives. Unsure what else to do, the rest of us waited with Tervlik and his small crew.

It wasn't a long wait.

Oddly enough, with a large bundle in his arms and covered in soil and flowers, Rook returned. His mood had only darkened in the brief wait. He dumped the rag down, spilling out a small horde of coin and weapons. He pushed the weapons into the arms of his men and tied up the coin, slinging it over his shoulder. Tervlik's eyes had gone as wide as saucers at the sight of the wealth but stayed quiet as Rook finished his task.

A moment passed as he considered Volant and me and the merry little band we'd gathered. Finally, he shook his head against whatever he'd been thinking. "Good luck with being all charming and destructive," he said and gestured towards the floating harbor. To Tervlik, he handed the coin he'd just tied back up. "We need a boat and a crew. You seem up to the task."

Tervlik took the bag. With a little jig of excitement, he swept off his marvelous hat and bowed low to Rook. "We're ready to get you anywhere the waters go."

Rook returned the bow, looking at us all expectantly. When no one had moved, he rubbed at his mostly shaved temples and gestured again to the bobbing dock. "This is your stop. You lot need to hold the harbor down and protect these people from gimzers." He reached past me and down to Argo. "You take care of these blundering fools now, all right, Argo?" Rook cooed, scratching the dog behind the ears, and made a few faces at the dog. Standing up, he seemed determined but softer after his brief interaction with the dog. "I'll be back, just need to go call in some favors and hunt down some information. There's boarding for you all at Sunken Stone. It's right next to the gardens.

With nothing left to do but get off, we disembarked from the ship and watched Tervlik and Rook fade across the lake's expanse until they disappeared from our view.

While everyone else settled in, Volant and I went to the gardens. Despite the sunshine, the tendrils of autumn's brisk air had finally come to Brod. The cooler weather meant fewer people about, but as we strolled through the gardens and Volant was enthusing over the variety of rare plants, I heard a muffled tumult.

Promising to come back for a closer inspection of the plants, I managed to drag him towards the growing susurrus. It was hard to walk, so we made our way slowly. The ever-shifting ground was like being on a small boat, but less predictable. The harbor's movements were small, almost imperceptible, but it was just enough that I kept catching my heel on the wood planking or shifting my weight the wrong way at the wrong time.

Just beyond the gardens was a small market square, the same as you'd find around the corner in a Kalaran or an Ersetian neighborhood. One of the traveling town criers was there, having just finished passing on the information. Unlike me, he seemed perfectly at ease on the decking and had disappeared before we were within earshot of any parting words he might have had.

"What's everyone so excited about?" I asked a tall, reed-thin Laker with a stained apron on.

"There's some kind of auction happening in a few days," she replied.

"And why's that have so many of you very fine and interesting people of Brod talking about it?" Volant interjected.

She rolled her eyes, but Volant had his easy smile, and it was hard for most people not to want to chat with him. “There’s a Toron stone going up for sale. Supposedly it’s pretty big, but for the price, you could set yourself up for life and never worry about coin again.”

That made Volant and I pause. Long enough so that the Laker took the opportunity to move away from us and blend further into the crowd.

“Do you think?” Volant half asked, half mused.

“Aye, I do,” I replied. Emerys’ Rock. The left-handed Toron stone that had started this whole thing. Keira had lost it supposedly, but apparently, it’d shown back up after all this time. Or at least someone was pretending to have found it.

We pushed around and through the crowd, trying to find out more info. All that we got was there was going to be an auction on a boat out in the harbor. But that wasn’t what had the rest of the crowd riled up.

“Those godspawned, dirty, good for nothing equals didn’t do enough damage last time? Now they’re coming to Brod?”

Yet again, we stopped in our tracks. I held out a hand to Volant and flicked a couple of fingers. Listen. Wait.

The man was talking loudly to a younger woman, his daughter, maybe. Or an apprentice, possibly. “What if they’re right and can make things better?” She asked, unconcerned by the reddening face of the man.

“Better?” he practically shouted. “They won’t make things better! Those people are just out for power. They don’t care about what happens to Naturals or Learners, and especially about those who don’t have Talent or Skill. It’s just a political movement.”

The girl looked like she disagreed and was about to say so. Before she could, the man raised a sausage-shaped finger. “Marissa, not here. Not now. Get your tools packed up. We’re taking the first ship off the harbor. Sounds like the Equals are only days away, and the Guard can’t save us this time.”

Her eyes hardened, but she nodded. “Fine.”

We moved further through the crowd and realized that the crier had only been a sideshow for this group. Talk of disappearing relatives on the shore, Equals coming to enforce rule on Brod, and a general level of panic pervaded the milling crowd. It was contagious, and by the time we slipped away back to the garden, I felt a little shaken myself.

Chapter Twenty-Seven

Everywhere we went, people were talking about Emerys' Rock, though none knew that name or the growing disappearances of Toron stones. The auction for the "special" Toron stone would be happening in a few days, from what we heard. A colossal luxury ship was coming down the eternity river on its maiden voyage. From all accounts, it sounded like someone took a small mansion and stapled it to a barge.

Strangely enough, it seemed the more we heard about the Equal incursion and the ship coming, the seller of the stone was looking to play both sides off each other. No one knew about the stone's unique properties, but the auction seemed to be specifically waiting to start so the Equals and everyone else who didn't like them would have a chance at buying an ace for an impending civil war.

"Volant," I finally said, finishing a korbit we'd found near a busy corner to eavesdrop from. "We're going to need more rope."

His face split into a wide, knowing grin. "You always need rope when doing heisty things," he said.

Back at the tavern Rook had put us up at, the girls seemed to have heard additional rumors right in the common room.

"We're stealing Emerys' Rock," I announced. Volant chuckled, but the girls all looked around furtively, checking to see that I hadn't been overheard. "Don't worry," I said, plopping down at the table and stealing one of the roasted almonds that Insley had. "No one knows it by that name. And besides, they're going to be expecting someone to steal it anyway."

Volant dropped a truly magnificent coil of rope on the ground and sat as well. Rope was all the rage in Brod what with all the boats and tied-together docks.

The room smelled old with a hint of lake. Despite the cozy confines, the group around the table seemed excited. Theft was far more fun then fighting ancient and nearly unkillable monsters.

We huddled together more closely. Only the zymph was missing, being far too large for anything as pedestrian as a common room. Argo had already won over the whole tavern judging from the pile of scraps and bones he was chewing on in the corner.

"Let's get started," I said.

"Cassiopia," Volant began, pointing at her, his voice a conspiratorial whisper. "We have only a day or two before this ship arrives. You and your bow will be manning a getaway boat. You'll need to find one, preferably something covered and with minimal crew. We just have to get back to the harbor. You able to take care of all that?"

Two thumbs up from the huge woman. "What about the Equals?"

Volant nodded. "Good question. Sounds like if we get Emerys' Rock, we don't need to sweat anything. But if it's not really on the ship, or whatever, we'll be running a secondary campaign leading up to the heist. We're going to go work on finding anyone and everyone we can to prepare defenses. Attacking the floating harbor is going to be difficult, even if they manage to find some ships."

I gestured towards the moving floor. "Besides, there's always the Below. That's a fortress in its own right."

"Or a death trap," Qaewin added.

We all looked at her.

"The below can be flooded," she said uncomfortably. "Everyone knows that."

Volant laughed but grabbed her hand. "That's just a myth," he said gently.

She squeezed his hand back but looked him hard in the eye. "No, it's not. Trust me. My father said that it's definitely floodable."

We all took a moment to think about that. The tavern keeper dropped off some additional Laker food that Cassiopia had ordered, and we all dug into the pile of oddly spiced potatoes and fish that seemed to be a staple here.

I gestured to Insley, moving the conversation forward. "We were hoping you'd spearhead the preparation movement. We're also going to need a way to convincingly fake an illness, and also a way to cause a lot of people to get sick quickly if possible."

Her eyebrows went up at this, but it seemed like the start of an idea was forming, and she gave a half shrug of agreement.

"Shazina," I said, making it almost a question. "You up for playing to your age, looking like some innocent kid tagging along when the auction happens?"

She nodded, though a tightness in the gesture made it seem like she didn't want to.

Volant pointed at Qaewin and himself. "We're going on as buyers, we'll have Shazina with us when we go, but once we're on board, she'll start scouting the ship for the stone."

I nodded. "I'll come along as well, posing as a manservant. I'll go 'find' Shazina and see if I can find the stone as well. Once one of us finds it,

Volant will make a distraction. We'll meet at the back of the ship, get down to the boat with Cassiopia, and escape back to the harbor."

"Easy," Qaewin commented dryly.

"Aye, it should be," I said with a smile.

Insley looked unconvinced. "What if it doesn't work that way? What if the stone is kept somewhere you can't get to, or what if this whole thing is a trap, or they have too many guards?"

That gave me pause for a moment, and it seemed to do so for everyone else. Finally, I shrugged. "It'll work. We're good at this kind of thing."

"Once we're off," Volant continued, "we can try to light a couple of fires to keep them occupied."

I put my fist out, meeting Volant's. "Everyone knows their parts?" Another four fists stacked on top of ours. "Let's get it done!"

Energized from the planning session, I strolled outside with Insley to help her start gathering support. Old planks creaked between freshly replaced planks as the unending harbor bobbed below us. A thought occurred, and I steered us towards the giant air stacks that dominated the center harbor. They were so big as to be out of mind as you made your way around the floating harbor in general, but the real Brod lay below the lake, down on the floor. I wanted to pay my respects at Berjio's house.

We went through the guardhouse at the top without much more than a cursory nod before getting our stamps and heading down.

The stairs wound below us in a vertigo-inducing height. It was humid and had the strange mix of scents that came from a cave with a log burning fire inside and the mossy smell of somewhere inundated with water. Sunlight bounced around from the shafts at odd angles, but for the most part, the center of Brod's below shone, and the only shadows there stretched out from the city's edges to the dome's walls.

News had come ahead of us of Berjio's death. Neighbors and disciples had turned his home into a memorial, flowers lay in heaps around his door's entrance, and poems were tacked up all over the small wooden structure. Candles in the hundreds surrounded the boat-shaped home, spilling wax across the beach sand floor in puddles.

The memorial itself was surprising. But even more so was the crowd of people, eerily silent, kneeling, sitting, or praying in their own little ways. A score or so of men and women, black being the predominant color of dress, surrounded the home with their sorrow.

Briefly, I assumed that they must have just received the news and his death was a fresh source of pain for them. But, there were candle stubs that would have taken days to burn down, and a few of the flowers had dried and wilted into dead things themselves.

Insley stayed back as I found a scrap of paper and then a piece of leftover charcoal. I wanted to write something moving. Something thoughtful and powerful. But my mind was blank. Instead, I wrote something simple.

I watched you die, friend. And I couldn't do anything to stop it. Thank you for having sheltered me. And thank you for the lesson you taught me at the end.

If I end up half as loving of a man like you, I'll count myself lucky.

The short note still brought tears to my eyes and a lump in my throat. I tried to clear it but only made myself shift closer to losing control. While tacking up the note to Berjio, a hand fell on my shoulder.

A man, kind eyes darkened by sorrow and a face framed by a heavy beard, was next to me. I was still confused when the man summarily embraced me. I went rigid as he hugged me. It wasn't like many people in my life had been giving me many hugs, and I'd especially not had any from strangers.

He pulled away, gave me a gentle squeeze of the shoulder, and then turned to the note I'd put up. It was his turn to stiffen as he read it, and his hand squeezed at my shoulder as I tried to back away.

"You saw Berjio die?" he asked in a hoarse, not-quite-whisper.

Heads that had been bent down or looking away snapped up all around us, locking in on the man and me.

I stuttered, grasping for words before finally deflating. "Yes, I saw him die," I said, knowing I'd deserve whatever violence this group was about to take out on me. But no blow landed. Instead, the man brought me into another embrace, weeping openly now.

"You are most welcome here, friend," he said through the tears. "Please, when you're ready, we'd like to hear how it happened, if you can."

The score of people pushed in around us. A hand slipped into mine, and I looked down to find Insley looking even more surprised than I was holding tightly to me. Slowly, I began to tell the story, explaining about his estranged granddaughter and how she'd mislead him, the bombings, and in the end, how he'd let Rook kill him.

They listened.

When it was all said, fresh tears were in all of our eyes. They were also filled with a sense of purpose. Knowing it versus using that were two different things. I was so caught up in the telling of Berjio's end to make sense of much else.

Unlike me, Insley seemed ready for this. She stood up, gesturing to the crowd around us. "There's a better way to honor the sword master's memory," she said. "We're building a resistance group. We need fighters. Brave men and women who will stand up for what Berjio would have stood up for. We need to fight the Equals. Here, and then in Kalaran."

Her words echoed as Berjio's more committed mourners, close friends, distant relatives, and not a few students mulled what she asked for.

As she was about to say something else, the bearded man who'd first embraced me stood next to her. "She's right," he said with simple, unshakeable authority. "Berjio didn't dedicate his life to learning and teaching the sword so people could go about dueling and feeling good about how dangerous they were. He did it to fight against injustice, to protect those you love, and to be the strength of a person who can't be strong for themselves."

Heads nodded all-around at this, and I caught the distinct feeling of a quote. It must have been something Berjio said often.

"We're with you," the man said. "What would you have us do?"

Relief visibly washed over Insley. "First, I need help growing our numbers. We only have a few days before the Equals will be here, and we need a lot more support."

He waited expectantly.

"That's it for now. But next, we'll actually have to fight. This isn't some convoluted plan. We're staying at Sunken Stone up top on the floating harbor. We'll be using that as the headquarters. Send your people there when you find them."

The man nodded, part in understanding and part as a dismissal to us.

He had work to do.

Berjio's mourners had the pent-up kind of energy that only seems to come when death has knocked on the door of someone you loved. They went off enthusiastically, knocking on neighbor's doors, accosting people walking through the winding spaces between homes and shops, and refusing to take no for an answer from anyone.

We watched in awe as Brod's previously sullen and quiet Below began to echo with defiance. With men and women finding their courage. With parents vowing to find their lost children and wreak havoc on those who'd caused said loss, and children promising the same in a sad parallel. The gimzers had taken enough people that everyone seemed to have felt the sting of the Equals machinations in one fashion or another. The time for revenge was nearing.

The volume rose like water in a sinking ship. Insley's eyes grew wide as the story spread before us in a visible wave. The people had taken us at our word that Rook wasn't the real cause of Berjio's death, but I worried what would happen if Rook did return and found his role in such a beloved man's death so widely known.

Our detour having accomplished more than I'd ever imagined, we quietly left the Below and headed up the winding stairs to the floating harbor.

"As above, so below," Insley muttered as we stepped out onto the small platform that perched above the crowded harbor.

Voices of a hundred people merged into a low, oppressive buzz that rippled out across the water. I could see Volant, Qaewin, and Argo on a low balcony from Sunken Stone in the middle of the crowd. People were shouting, not at them, but with them. One of the only discernible phrases I could pick out was "for Argo!" which would send the dog into a brief spasm of howls before he settled back down.

"Looks like our friends didn't want you to carry the whole weight of saving everyone," I said.

She nodded dumbly. "And I thought we did so well down there."

"Hey, we didn't do anything. You did incredible, though," I said. "Besides, they cheated." I pointed at Argo and his goofy, canine grin. "That dog can get one of the mad cave dwellers in Kalaran to offer up his last morsel of food and die of starvation."

Chapter Twenty-Eight

All around, the shadows reached out. A humidity you could swim through lay heavy on us as we examined the large lever bound and locked with chain. The man showing it to us had a bland, bored expression that matched both his personality and clothes.

I crouched down to get closer underneath the curving slope of the dome. It was unnerving, seeing the man-made handiwork that kept an entire lake at bay above me. The lever was old but well made. It gave me chills.

I looked over to the builder. "This would flood all of Brod?"

"If you unchained it and pulled it down," he said, making a gesture, "then yar, it'd flood the city up just right."

I waddled my way out from the curve until I could stand back up. The lever was as long as I was tall. With a bewildered shake of my head, I followed the man out of the damp, untraveled section of Brod and back towards the brightly lit Below.

Volant was waiting for me near Berjio's old place. A smithy had spawned back before his death partly due to the proximity to the famous sword master's home and the visitors it brought. But also partly out of a need for a blacksmith so close to the home. With Berjio dead, the woman running the smithy had transitioned into mass production of weapons.

Volant had been helping, hoping the menial labor would take his mind off the burglary we were hoping to accomplish.

Flashing a hand signal when our eyes met, I said, Let's go.

He said something to the blacksmith, and she nodded in response. He waved farewell and came and joined me. Together, we headed up to the harbor.

A majestic, more-art-than-boat floating mansion was anchored a few hundred paces out from the harbor. The ship caused both of us to pause and take in the sight as we came out of the stairwell that led down into the Below.

Volant rolled out his shoulders and grinned. "Nil, this is going to be fun."

I chuckled. "Aye, but it'll be dangerous, too."

The rest of the crew found us, minus Insley and the animals. Argo was just as happy following her around as Shazina, and Qaewin sent her zymph to protect them both.

The rest of us wore finer than usual clothes, but only Volant wore a visible weapon. Cassiopia had her bow and arrows hidden under a bundle along with my axes. I'd placed a pair of knives up my sleeves, but still felt naked. The absence of my Toron stones I'd grown so used to drawing on made me even more anxious. Bymm's ring still hung around my neck, but the stone was so small to provide almost no comfort on that front.

With a large fishing pole, Cassiopia rowed out beyond what would be reasonably considered bow shot range for any normal human. The rest of us boarded the ferry-style boat that was waiting for all who went to the auction.

People were everywhere on the ferry. Merchants with their air of snobbery that screamed Equal supporters huddled in groups of two or three while strong, tough-looking men and women half encircled them, facing out. We were some of the last to board, and before we could begin to get a feel for the crowd, we'd already pulled up to the ostentatious new ship.

Shazina was up first, with Qaewin and Volant moving right behind her, climbing the ornate wooden staircase that uniformed men lowered down to receive us. I brought up the rear, absorbing every detail and planning on how I'd escape attention and search the ship. I crested the stairs, and ahead of me, an ox of a man favoring one leg was grinning down at me as if I'd just gifted him his own seat on the council.

I took in the leather braced knee, the back-alley brawler scarred knuckles, and saw all my plans crashing around me.

Quick and subtle, I flicked fingers at Volant, who'd just turned back to see what'd stopped me at the stares. Keep going, I signed.

"My, my, my," the big man said, gliding rather smoothly forward despite the still healing knee. "I'd been hoping to run into you again."

I reached for the hidden knives, but the man held up a hand in warning. His smile twisted towards something sharper, but otherwise, he still seemed to be welcoming a friend on board.

"This is between you and me, son. I'm thinking you'd rather keep it that way?" His eyes flicked over to my friends and came back to me, and then tracked around to the half dozen thugs that a fine set of clothes couldn't quite disguise their previous affiliation as thumpers from the Guard.

I weighed it out for a breath.

He was right.

I spread my arms, a greeting and surrender. "My friend, I certainly hadn't expected to see you. Shall we?" I stepped forward, and the burly brawler's smile turned warm again while his eyes twinkled with malice.

Following behind the man, I flicked the message again at Volant. In turn, he nodded and turned to whisper something at Qaewin before leading her and Shazina along with the crowd.

We stepped into a storage room that was larger than most boats I'd been on. Light streamed in from large windows, making the floor practically shine.

"You bounced back quick," I commented as the man shrugged out of the stiff coat he'd been wearing.

He grunted. "That little kneecapping you did to me was one of the single most unpleasant experiences I've had. But, here you are. And here I am. You moved well. I'd like to see how this goes."

I reached into my sleeves and pulled out the two knives, and sank into a fighting crouch.

Bemused, the man shook his head. "None of your tricks this time. As I said, I want a fair, straight match. I assume you're here for that god spawning stone? Toss the knives, and I'll tell you where it is. If you win, you'll be free to take it. If you lose, maybe your friends will still manage."

Disbelief wrote itself across my face. "Why would I take that deal? I'll cut you to ribbons and find it for myself."

"Ah, yes, fair point." He acknowledged. He rolled his neck around, loud pops accompanying the motion. "Thing is, that too-large Toron stone ain't here. And, I can yell real loud. I've got a couple former Elites hiding out on the payroll, and they could cause all kinds of mischief for your friends."

"Left hand," I cursed and tossed the knives towards the wall. I brought my hands up, palms open in a modified brawler's stance.

A genuinely pleased grin flashed across the man's face before he danced forward, scarred fists at the ready. He moved unfairly well for having taken a knife in the knee. There were plenty of top tier performers who'd have been jealous of his grace.

Knives or not, I wasn't going to fight fair. There was too much at stake. I pushed directly into Ukiyo, strengthening my muscles and sharpening my reflexes.

"Where's the stone?" I demanded as we closed in on each other in the center of the room.

Two left jabs blurred out at me, and even with my enhanced speed, I barely had time to get an elbow up to take the blows on my arm.

A hook followed, and I rolled under it, letting my hand curl into a fist as I dropped a hit into the man's ribs before coming back up.

He didn't even seem to notice the blow.

A quick shuffle and he was just short of striking range. "Fairs fair," he said. "That Toron stone is in Kalaran. Locked in that place they kept that prick Xylex in."

Lightning-fast he danced forward, sending a blur of strikes and feints in a dizzying combination.

I dodged one or two, keeping my hands up and receiving several painful strikes to my arms and far too many hits to the body to be healthy. One rib, in particular, felt like it'd cracked under his massive fist.

I staggered back, gasping from the onslaught.

He didn't press the attack. Instead, he watched as I caught my breath and shook out my arms.

Even with tapping into Ukiyo, he was better than me by a long shot. Time to play even dirtier.

Will turned to raw energy coursed through me as I focused harder, pushing deeper into me. I layered the Ukiyo with Skill, letting both sides of the power course through me. I flashed forward, and time almost slowed as I charged the man. I brought my open palm back and pushed Skill there.

The brawler's face took on a surprised expression as he tried to bring his hands up but was too slow. A Ukiyo enhanced palm smashed into his face while a wide swath of Skill followed the motion through and sent the man flying.

I skidded backward from the expulsion of Skill, using what remaining willpower I had to ground myself. The floor cracked, and the ship rocked as I anchored myself against flying backward.

I'd put too much into it. The brawler crashed through one of the windows on the opposite side of the room, knocking crates aside and leaving a gaping hole out to the crowd of potential buyers.

An alarm bell began ringing furiously at the opposite end of the ship. I could just make out a figure pumping his arm furiously to make the racket before forms of heavily armed thugs flooded the storage room from that end.

Weariness washed over me from the exertion, and I made one of my better decisions and ran out the back door I'd come through and dove headfirst off the ship and into it the chilly lake water.

Arrows struck the water all around me as I surfaced. What seemed an impossibly far distance away, I could see Cassiopia and her little fishing boat bobbing on the waves.

Something large and scaly brushed my feet as I fought against the choppy water. An arrow buzzed within inches of my ear at almost the same time, and my adrenaline spiked hard enough to push me to start swimming.

Pulling at the water felt like a wasted effort, but I didn't know what else to do. Slowly, the large ship grew smaller behind me while Cassiopia's grew in size.

A disturbance in the water brought my head around, and I saw the spined back and chainmail scales of a nightmare curling back down into the murky water.

Panic struck, and I swam harder.

A monster much like some we'd seen below us while flying over the causeway surfaced again, slicing causally through the water while keeping pace with me. Its mouth was filled with snake looking fangs, hundreds upon hundreds in rows. Its unblinking eyes focused in on me, and I froze, barely staying afloat.

I tried to bring my will into focus, but I was too cold and too scared. Like a rabbit paralyzed by the screech of an eagle, I floated dumbly before the sea-turned-lake monster.

The serpentine head rose slowly out of the water. In the back of my head, I noticed that whoever had been shooting at me on the ship had stopped. At least there was that.

Then the fang-filled mouth opened wider. Much wider. It lunged, and I clenched but refused to close my eyes as it took me.

Despite the lapping waves and muscle paralyzing fear, I picked out the double thump-thrum of Cassiopia firing two arrows in rapid succession. My mind caught onto this fact as the arrows ripped through the back of the creature's skull and out the eyes that had been locked onto me.

With huge, spasming lurches and gut-wrenching twists, the monster thrashed in the water, nearly ending me then and there.

Hurriedly, I back paddled from the churning foam and waves, but the creature was large, and the death throes too wild.

Like a smith's anvil, its tail crashed down onto me, shoving me deep into the water.

While dazed, a different fish with rough sandpaper scales bumped into me, sending me swirling through the lake water like a top. I got my bearings, and a mouthful of water, and surfaced, spluttering and gasping. Then my mind clocked the size of the fish that bumped me, and I grew even colder. A fin, the kind that anyone who grew up near large and deep waters learned to watch out for and fear, sliced by, a dark shadow as long as a boat attached to it.

In an eruption of water, the shark exploded with such speed that it was briefly airborne before it crashed into the writhing serpent, and both disappeared beneath the surface with only a faint red stain on the water indicating either had been there at all.

I turned in the water and found Cassiopia and her boat just a few paces from me. The huge woman had a long rope spinning in her hand. She let go, sending it flying to me.

I grabbed a hold and let the strong woman reel me in.

When I flopped over the side, she pointed out back towards the ship.

First, I noticed the luxury ship had small fires dotted around it and was ever so faintly burning.

Second, and even more interestingly, it seemed that Cassiopia hadn't been the cause of it. Faint echoes of what sounded like angry shouting crossed towards us.

With both of us pulling at the oar, we sliced through the water and came upon the auction ship in short order. Steel rang out, matched by screams and cries of pain. It seemed like the Equals had decided to try to take Emerys' Rock for themselves.

"Our plan might have been a little flawed," I admitted.

Cassiopia shrugged in what seemed to be a caring way and reached back for a lantern she had burning despite the sun high in the sky. Her hands worked efficiently, turning an ordinary pair of arrows into fire tipped shafts. She took careful aim and sent the first through an open window, and the second arcing unbelievably high into the sky before it screamed its fiery way back down and struck the roof of the room I'd fought the brawler in.

A few returning arrows whizzed back at us, but Cassiopia hauled up a shield-shaped piece of floor that deflected most of their shots and caught the few that had hit straight on. After a moment, we peeked over the wood to see the archers had been distracted by something else. Calmly, the huntress plucked the arrows from the shield, wrapped them in rags, set them on fire, and then sent the shafts back onto the boat with just the strength of her arm.

Finally, the shape of Volant and Qaewin came flying off the back of the ship before crashing into the water after a brief free fall. The lake shark still being at the front of my mind, I quickly tossed the rope over to where they'd disappeared. They came up together, and both grabbed on. Shazina appeared next, standing at the back of the ship. She sprung off the vessel with a Ukiyo enhanced leap and landed in the water, an arm's length away. Her head barely went under before she popped back out and flipped over the rail like some kind of acrobat.

"Couldn't find the stone," she said simply.

I frowned and filled them in as we rowed back to the harbor, explaining the brawler and where the Emerys' Rock supposedly was. No one was thrilled to hear it.

We ditched the fishing boat and hurried our way deep into the floating harbor's maze of structures. It looked like the fires had been put out on the ship, which I'd have felt better about, except at the edge of the river, I could just make out a small flotilla at the edge of the lake heading towards Brod. I reached out, bringing Volant to a halt. The others turned to see what had stopped us. We all stared as the tide of ships became more visible, taking shape and solidifying into individual vessels overladen with people. Each one of them flew a red and white flag with a large black circle dominating the center.

The Equals were no longer on the way. They'd arrived.

With its fires put out, the auction vessel gamely tried to put distance between itself and the oncoming navy, but it was too slow. It was like watching a colony of fire ants descend on a larger, slower ant. They surrounded and engulfed the ship, and we could almost see the last twitches of resistance before everything stilled again. The Equals tossed some bodies over the side, and then the ship was entirely blocked from view by Equal vessels.

That same flag furled out from the tallest mast. At least Emerys' Rock was about as far as it could be. But that also meant we had a losing fight on our hands.

Everyone on the Floating Harbor seemed to erupt into motion at the same time. Watchers blew alarm whistles, and the scant remaining Guard swarmed from homes and up out of the Below. A few Elites began gesturing with their spears, sending their squads to various ships with more militaristic leanings. The harbor itself bobbed about violently as boat homes pushed off and fled the city.

Insley appeared, flanked by Argo and Chloe on a roof just behind us. Volant and I boosted Qaewin up, and then the rest of us climbed on top. The harbor was in a panic.

Insley said something to Volant, who nodded, and then spun his arms twice and then shoved outward. Wind blasted away from him in a buffeting expulsion that was all the more impressive during this previously windless day. The gale caught everyone off guard and brought their attention to us.

Argo howled, long and loud in response. It was the kind of howl that echoed through our ancient history, the kind that kept children up late at night telling ghost stories and campfires burning well through the dawn by our ancestors. I did a double-take, really taking in the puppy who'd managed to grow far too large, far too fast.

Before I could voice anything on that subject, the dog saw me staring and trotted over to rub his head against my leg until I pet him.

Silence rang out as Insley stepped to the ledge. "We knew this was coming!" she began, voice ringing out across the harbor. "Stand by what you believe. The lake belongs to Brod, not some rabble of idealists wanting to destroy our civilization."

The panic subsided, and a throng began to grow around the building we stood on. The fear slowly was replaced with anger. I could see the crowd's mind shift from fear for their lives to the realization that they could do something about it. Whatever Insley had been up to, she'd planted the seeds well.

Noise from hundreds if not thousands of people began to stir again as the message spread like wildfire.

"Brod!" Insley continued. "You were once the center of our military prowess. You brought us the strongest men and women to protect us from those who wanted to harm others. You trained warriors to lead them. You are the foundation of the Guard, and you have beaten these people back before. This time, they're here on boats, on your lake. How. Dare. They." Insley finished, venomous.

A roar came back to her at that, and the wild mob turned into a determined force in the blink of an eye. Weapons appeared. Friends were found, and anyone without a boat found those who had one. Faster than it'd taken us to climb the roof, Brod's citizens had launched a fleet of their fishing boats and river barges and every ship they seemed to have in a scattered wave at the encroaching Equal flotilla.

Sinking weights of dread dropped through my stomach. Seeing these people empty out into the lake made me realize the Equals weren't making the same mistake as last time. They'd given no time to prepare, and they'd brought a horde. The ships were more prominent and more numerous than the Lakers. There wasn't any chance of winning with the defenders.

Everyone else saw it too.

"Hey, looks like they could use some help," I said, trying to inject some levity into my tone.

Shazina looked at me like I'd lost my mind. "You'll die if you go out there."

Feigning confusion, I turned to Volant. "What is this death she speaks of?"

"Death? Oh ho," he chuckled in as grandiose a manner as he could. "You don't recognize our walking companion? The one who gives the endless sleep? The restful and silent night? Our friend?"

I grinned wickedly. "Aye, now that you mention it, I do remember something like that!" I turned back to Shazina, who was far less amused than we were. "We're here. They need help. And so far, we've managed to scrape by. It's the path we ought to walk."

She shook her head. "We can just leave, take a boat back in the other direction, go back to Erset, or Kalaran and get that stone."

Sadly, I shook my head. "We won't stop you from doing that. Left hand, it's probably a good idea for you to do so. But I'm going, and I know Volant is too."

Argo barked excitedly. Qaewin nodded too, and Cassiopia shrugged her agreement.

Insley, on the other hand, looked worried. And she had every reason to be so. She was a healer, not a fighter.

"Shazina, how about you take Insley and Argo, and you guys help coordinate the rest of the city in an evacuation? I don't think this will end well for Brod." As I pointed back the way we'd come, I noticed something even more chilling. Grayish shapes began to appear in the water, moving inhumanely fast. Gimzers.

Qaewin, tracking my gaze, cursed loud and long. "God spawning alchemists," she growled. Hearing such fierceness at such a higher volume from her was almost as surprising as the arrival of the abominations and their too-specific timing.

Screams, terrified and then violently cut off, changed our course almost immediately. I took one look back at the ship-on-ship battle happening in the lake and saw a losing fight. But gimzers were here, and we had to do something about it.

I vaulted down. Soft thumps followed me. I didn't turn to make sure. A black axe in each hand, I charged down the mostly empty harbor towards where the screams came from. In no time, we'd found the source, three gimzers still soaking wet, a drained woman slumped on the ground across from them.

I didn't even break stride, leaping into them despite my weariness. Axes flashed, and I brought two down. One of Cassiopia's arrows thumped into the third. I began to smile, but it faltered and broke as I looked back and up. Hundreds of the gimzers were climbing up the air stacks like some demented insects crawling up a tree.

"Someone's using Skill, and lots of it," I said while pointing.

Cassiopia began to steadily shoot arrow after arrow, each one knocking one of the creatures down from the side of the towering masonry. But there were too many.

Qaewin's zymph growled, the feline noise far deeper and louder than anything a dog or wolf could make. It left us moving at a speed that only a large predator seems capable of starting at.

Volant let loose his strange sky pirate battle cry and followed the huge cat towards the air stacks.

Chapter Twenty-Nine

Without warning, thunder and lightning began to rage. I was halfway up the stairs that led into the air stacks and ultimately down into the Below. Looking back, I saw fire, wind, water, and wood moving in spirals of destruction across the boats. Naturals pushing their Talent too hard, with too many in this close of proximity, seemed to be whipping up a storm on the lake.

Waves out on the lake grew larger, beginning to rival those of the sea that surrounded Balteris. The battle of ships had turned into a scattered, uncoordinated maelstrom of wood and sails trying to stay afloat and not be crushed beneath water or larger vessels. Dozens of the boats had already beached themselves onto the harbor's docks, having been unable to control the suddenly wild wind and waters. An ugly situation was getting uglier.

I brought my attention back to the task at hand and saw the door above us burst open, and a fleeing mass of people began to pour out of the Below. We were at a chokepoint, and like a cork in a bottle, our little group was about to be stampeded by the same people we were trying to help. Without any other options, we turned and sped back down the stairs ahead of the fleeing Lakers.

People streamed by. I bounced from foot to foot, anxious to get back at the gimzers when I heard the violent clash of battle from much too close. Exasperated, I turned to Volant.

"This is getting frustrating," I said.

He nodded. "We can't get down below with all these people, and they're about to run into a meat grinder of Equals from the sounds of it. Guess we go back to the original fight?"

"And leave a pile of gimzers behind us?" Qaewin interjected. "Not good."

I thought for a moment. "We need a place to defend from. And we need to flood the Below."

A silence fell. I'd told them that flooding the below would be a one-way trip for whoever did it.

Volant began to speak, but I cut him off. "I'm doing it. I'm the one who knows where it's at. You lot get to the inn. Try and get it walled off, and if I can somehow get out after I bring it down, I'll find you there.

We split up. The rest of them heading towards the inn and trying to gather as many people as they could on the way. I watched them go for a moment. Insley was going to be livid when she found out. On the positive side, I'd probably not have to worry about that if I died.

The crowd was beginning to thin some, so I started elbowing my way through, shoving against the tide of people. It felt like running a gauntlet. I was bruised and battered, adding to my already exhausted state. When I finally pushed my way past the packed door, I saw my worst fears happening down on the Below's floor. I jumped, smacking into the support pole, and slid down the rest of the way.

A small band of old men with old spears were shakily guarding the foot of the stairs when I landed. As one, they impaled a gimzer that careened out from behind the building. Eight spear tips plunged into the alchemist's creation. A second gimzer came out from the other side of the building and hurtled into them, biting deeply into one man's arm and flinging him aside like a rag doll.

I sent an axe spinning, watching it embed deeply into the creature's skull. This bought the men enough time to stab down again with their spears, taking the creature out of the fight.

"I'm flooding the Below," I yelled over my shoulder as I landed, taking back my axe and sprinting toward the corner the builder had shown me.

Confused yells followed me, but I'd already moved up on top of the closest roof. I leapfrogged from one wooden beam to another, skipping above the gimzers below and summoning the dregs of Skill into my weary body. Whatever Learner had been using enough Skill to bring all these monstrosities running had either stopped or had been taken down by them as my scant use brought the horde of nightmares locking in on me.

I ran faster, leaping over gaps like a squirrel on the run for its life. I stoppered my Skill, pushing it deep within me while I moved further across the Below. Gasping for air, I dropped onto the sand like ground with a roll. I used the roll's momentum to get up and saw the gimzers had stopped following me.

A new source of Skill was emanating from across the empty expanse of sand that was the edge of the Below where the curve of stone was too much for many to be claustrophobic. I saw what almost seemed to be a dome of energy pulsating from an ancient man, back bent with too many years of life.

I faltered, wanting to go to his help. I couldn't make out much beyond the shape of him as the gimzers were charging between us. Then it clicked in my head he was offering himself up to the monsters to allow whoever it was he loved so dearly the time to escape. And coincidentally, me to make them pay.

I found the small stone hut with the lever chained to the wall. I smashed my axes over and over again into the chain until a link finally snapped and gave way.

My mind was numb with weariness. I stared dumbly at the freed lever, remembering how afraid of drowning I'd been as a child. Sometimes life was unfair, and the only choice you had was to embrace that unfairness.

With both hands, I grasped the lever. I took a calming breath, which did nothing to stop the trembling in my arms.

I braced to throw my weight into a downward yank, but in the heartbeat before I did, a glint of gears caught my eye. With a quick inspection, I realized a small bolt was all that held a lake back, and the lever was the mechanism to remove said bolt. I carefully tested the lever's strength.

I'd far overestimated what was needed, as barely pressing a single hand on it began to move it easily. With the gentle push, I watched as the lever's action slowly slide the bolt out, one gear ratchet at a time. I let go, and the lever stayed in place, held by the geared teeth and friction.

Hope blossomed in me. Any chance of not drowning was something worth taking. I brought the lever almost all the way to the floor, leaving a finger width's worth of bolt left in the wall. A strong sneeze might dislodge it and bring the whole lake in.

Holding my breath, I stepped back, one gingerly placed toe at a time, as if I was dancing in the spring on an iced over river on a sunny day. The noise of the panicked evacuation fell into background buzzing as I focused on moving away from the open door and barely-inserted pin. I gauged the distance to the shaft of light coming down from the air stack with a quick look behind me. It was far.

I looked back to the lever. It, too, was far. Or at least as far as I'd be able to throw with any accuracy. My body clenched against the thought of drowning. I thought of Volant and breathed in slowly, before ever so softly clapping my hands together once with an involuntary flinch. The tension bled out of me, and I found my resolve.

Everything I had went into the axe throw. Not necessarily the force of the toss. Or at least not only, though there was plenty of effort put there. More importantly was the direction, just underneath the door frame, with the slightest curve to the throw to increase the axe's probable contact surface area. It was intentionally wild, with the most heart-stopping wish for accuracy shoved into it as I released.

The spinning black blade and handle disappeared into the shadowed door.

Without a moment's hesitation, I pushed off in the opposite direction. Raw will bloomed into Skill, my fear feeding the squashed down bits of Skill I'd kept in reserve.

A horrendous roar of rushing water nearly drowned out the muffled sound of stone scraping stone.

I couldn't help it. I looked back and saw the side of the dome had collapsed.

Black waves of water were erupting from the hole and moving faster than I seemed to be able to run.

I let out a strangled cry as I pushed harder towards the shaft of light and ripped off the necklace with Bymm's ring. A group of gimzers were running towards me in a creepy, almost-human gait.

"Left hand," I spat. It didn't change anything. I yanked everything from the Toron stone set in the ring. My whole body thrummed with energy. There was a crack as the stone failed, but that barely registered as I threw the last pieces of my focus and the borrowed strength from the Toron stone into a final attempt.

Paces away, the Gimzers began to jump. With a burst of will, I showed them how to do it properly. I shoved Skill into the ground below me while simultaneously pushing into a leap as hard as possible with Ukiyo. The resulting movement nearly gave me whiplash as I blasted through the air high above the gimzers. A wave of water crashed into them below me. There wasn't time to see what happened next as the air stack's inner wall was waiting to meet me. I hit it with enough speed to knock the breath out of me. My fingers scrambled for purchase on the roughhewn stone.

A moment to catch my breath lingered like an eternity before I mustered enough nerve to look down. Despite the water raging below, I was still high enough up that falling back down would break a bone at the least, assuming I didn't land on a building or gimzer.

Slowly, I climbed. Not too far above me, the inner stairs of the air stack spiraled up. I reached the railing and flopped over, panting from exertion and the aftershocks of adrenaline. Water rose beneath me, and homes began to bob as the Below's floor disappeared under roiling lake water.

"Huh," I mused, "guess they really do float." A deeper part of my mind reminded me that it probably wasn't a good sign I was talking out loud.

I pushed myself up and began to climb the narrow stairs. There was nothing left for me to give but sheer stubbornness and grit. My friends were out there fighting, or dying, or somewhere in between. Nearly at the top, I felt the structure shake and move, as if one of the gods had punched the ground. Dust and small pieces of stone shook around me.

Not wanting to wait and see what would happen if I became stuck in this shaft, I pushed my burning legs into action and covered the remaining flight of stairs with only some mild cursing.

With a heave, I crested the lip of the air stack, no longer even able to form coherent thoughts. My vision swam as I flopped down onto the ridge of the massive chimney-like structure. I looked over, and as my breath began to come more steadily.

A battle worthy of songs and stories raged around and on the Floating Harbor. Ships rode the lake waves and rammed into each other. The inn where we'd stayed was surrounded by hundreds of fallen Equals and hundreds more of murderous fanatics willing to kill for their cause.

Torches were being lit and thrown at the inn. Fishing boats armed with Brod's last-minute militia were sinking beneath the crushing numbers of the Equals ships. Small pockets of the Guard stood against the tide of fanatics, but they'd be overwhelmed soon.

Even from this high up, I could see an arrow strike Qaewin in the arm. I couldn't hear anything, but I saw Volant and felt the rage that washed over him. A gale turned into storm winds and finally condensed into a raging tornado. He flung it forward, cutting a line through the attacking equals and completely stopping the assault for a brief, awed moment.

Another rumble shook the stack, nearly rolling me off the side. It wasn't just me that felt it either. I saw confusion spread through everyone below.

Then another rumble, louder than the first. The air stack vibrated and shook. With an alarming and unbelievable slowness of too-large objects, my perch began to sink down into the lake.

Too weary to do anything else, I looked out across the lake, past the raging waves and carnage. On the horizon, I saw ships. Not the small fishing boats of Brod, nor the chaos of would-be warships the Equals brought. These were like the Aye, not just river floating vessels, but the kind that traveled up and down the coast and out to deeper waters from the south sea, to the west, and up to the north. These were pirate ships, which were one and the same as merchant ships depending on the season. They were the bravest of crews who were willing to traverse the open waters that were traversable and through the deep rivers that carved their way through Balteris.

And at the front of those ships was a much smaller one, something akin to a large fishing boat. It was Tervlik and Rook, returning with reinforcements.

Chapter Thirty

Chapter Thirty-One

With a final shudder, the Below collapsed. The structure I was on didn't topple over. It merely sank. It was like riding a cart down an ever so slightly slanted hill. Smashed together homes and debris filled the entire air stack's opening far below. As I descended, the flotsam rose to meet me.

On the outside of the collapsing chimney, it was chaos. The Floating Harbor used the stacks as anchor points. Now those anchor points were being dragged down into the lake and taking the harbor with it.

And despite the literal ground disappearing out from under them, the fighting raged on.

I tried to draw in strength to stand but only managed to get onto one knee. I searched for any energy left in me, any will to turn to Skill. I couldn't find it. When I tried despite the lack of reserves, a pain stabbed into me as if my blood had turned into fire. Everything went dark as I blacked out.

When I came to, the stacks had sunk to within fifteen or so paces from the roiling lake. I could see hundreds upon hundreds of people treading water, swimming for a too-distant shore, or just hanging on to the city's debris. Lower I sank. Without the stamina to get up and swim to safety, I rolled over the edge and dropped a few feet down onto the pile of compacted homes. It hurt, but at this point, what didn't.

Despite being amid what seemed the start of a civil war, on a lake that had at least one shark and who knows what else, I laid back and watched the rest of the air stacks sink beneath the surface. Interestingly enough, the engineers must have measured them almost precisely to the depth of the lake. The great stone chimneys came to a stop just beneath the lake's surface.

With a groan, I rolled over and stuck out my foot. I could almost reach the lip of the air stack's crown. I took a deep breath and pushed off, letting the water take most of my weight. And then I was standing, lake waves pushed me about, but between them, the water only came up to my chest as long as I kept my footing on the lip of the sunken chimney.

Rook and Tervlik's fleet had arrived, and they were spreading through the chaos and pulling Equals and Brod's citizens aboard with impartial abandon. At this point, only the most fervent of the fanatics seemed willing to suicidally attack the rescuing ships. Most everyone was just happy to be out of the cold and exceptionally dangerous water.

I paddle-walked my way across the lip until I found the inn, half-submerged. I almost gave up then and there, but a voice called out from behind me.

"Need a lift?" a huge, muscle-slabbed and hairy man with no shirt asked. Beside him was a wolf, easily larger than the biggest zymph I'd seen.

"You're a Night Runner," I stupidly replied.

Something caught his eye behind me. I turned to see a pair of gimzers climbing out of the depths. One seemed to have lost its arm and part of its torso to a lake predator. A whistle sounded behind me, and then a black shadow passed over my head. The creath hit a piece of roofing before using it to spring at the gimzers. A sickening crunch sounded as it crushed the first.

The other gimzer attacked the wolf with the speed and ferocity that I'd come to associate with the monstrosities, but as soon as it struck, the wolf merely rolled its shoulders and flung the monster away. Another lightning-fast bite and the second gimzer was down.

"If you're done taking a bath, Nil, we'd all appreciate it if you hopped on board." A familiar voice drawled out, bringing my attention back to the ship.

Rook stood in his faded blue robes, a friendly hand on the large man's shoulder.

The man tossed a rope out to me, and I grabbed it. I held on as they reeled me in, feebly kicking and otherwise being nothing more than dead weight. I could hear and see wolves flashing across the scattered remains of the floating harbor, attacking the few gimzers that had survived the flooding of the Below.

Cold and shivering people crowded nearly every space on the ship as Rook and his friend dragged me on board. I stumbled before Rook caught me, showing me to an empty spot on the railing. In the distance, ships were fleeing across the lake in every direction as the Equal flags were being lowered mid-flight.

"Cowards," I spat.

Rook chuckled darkly at that. "It's one thing to fight a bunch of untrained fishermen. It's wholly another to have the courage to stand down against a creath that outweighs you and three of your friends."

I nodded, still too tired to do much else. "Everyone all right?"

Rook raised an eyebrow.

"Everyone you left here, my people," I growled at his unasked question.

He shrugged indifferently. If I could have, I'd have throttled him right then and there.

"Volant, Qaewin, and Insley were picked up by another boat. They're mostly fine." He said after a long moment. "And really, you need to still work on that emotional control. You're an open book, Nil."

I just glared in response.

Shazina appeared from behind Rook. Argo was beside her, dripping wet but possibly even more excited than I'd ever seen him. He was unsuccessfully trying to get the returned creath to play with him. I'd never seen one of the mountain top Night Runners or their companions. They were technically the third and final tribe in Tryst. But seeing Argo next to the sizeable wolfish creature, I realized that we'd saved a puppy cut off from one of these tribes. Maybe a runt, but definitely not your average dog.

Shazina spoke up, seeing the connection I'd made. "In my defense, I'm not from around here either," she said. "And more importantly, Cassiopia seems to be missing."

Of everyone that'd be hard to find, the huge huntress was not who'd I'd expect to be hard to find, or easy to kill.

"Where'd you last see her?" I asked.

Shazina gestured vaguely towards the half-submerged inn. "She'd stayed while it was sinking. Ran out of arrows. Then the waves overtook us. Lost sight after that."

I raised my chin at Argo, the famous dog that was now arguably a famous creath. "Can he find her?"

Shazina seemed caught off guard. "I..," she said, almost embarrassed, "I should have thought of that." She bent down to Argo. "Go find Cassiopia," she said before pointing out towards the sunken inn.

Argo yipped excitedly, ran in a few circles, and then bounded off the ship without the slightest care.

I raised myself up and then slumped against the rail to watch him work. For an animal that hailed from snowcapped mountains, he certainly seemed enthusiastic about swimming in deep water.

It took quite a while for him to cover the whole inn. Another, louder noise and he dove back into the water and paddled his circuitous way to a partially submerged home with only one fallen over wall left on it. He climbed into the shadows and began to bark wildly. Tervlik, still handling the wheel, shouted some orders and sent a small rowboat to the wreckage.

An unconscious form, too large to be anyone but Cassiopia, was pulled from the house's shadows and brought back to the ship.

It took what seemed like half the crew to pull her up and over into the ship. Argo just bounded up the side like some zymph who'd not been told about gravity. He sat protectively next to Cassiopia's still form, some of his exuberance muted in the face of her unresponsiveness.

I hobbled over on unsteady legs. Rook, finally taking pity on me, gave me a plate of fish and a water skin. I devoured it all while moving across the ship. She looked fine for the most part, but there was a nasty bump on her head, and two of her fingers on her left hand were sheared off. It looked like she'd managed to cauterize the stumps, but the pain had made her pass out.

Rook kneeled down next to her and pulled out some small vial of salt. He popped the top off and waved it gently under her nose. With a start, she bolted upright, eyes wide and nostrils flared. She blinked rapidly before raising her left hand to her face.

Tears formed as she took in her mangled hand.

I put a hand on her shoulder. "Hey now, don't worry about that. You got out alive."

She shrugged my hand off and glared. "I'd rather be dead than maimed," she said with cold, angry despair.

In the distance, howls from the Night Runner's creaths rang out and rebounded against the cresting waves as they hunted down the remaining gimzers. Something ancient and innate quaked inside me at the deep, larger-than-life wolf call.

Our ship was brought around in a series of large, pondering circles as we fished additional survivors from the water. A few Equals were fished out and tossed into a makeshift cage at the stern of the ship. They weren't treated unkindly, but neither were they treated with much warmth.

My strength slowly returned, and after a few more skewers of smoked fish, I was walking without too much of a wobble. But, I knew as soon as I fell asleep, my limbs would be taking vengeance on me.

Cassiopia hadn't said anything else after she'd come awake. She was uncharacteristically hunched in on herself and bared her teeth in a snarl anytime anyone else came over. Only Argo was able to go near her. Him, she just ignored.

Volant, Qaewin, and Insley came into view, riding on a long, narrow ship that looked like a canoe built for giants. It, too, had a pair of burly, hairy, and silent Night Runners. Their dark hair and pale skin looked out of place among the rest of the crew.

The two boats made an exchange, which involved several survivors jumping over to the longship and the Nightriders coming over to ours. I warned them away from Cassiopia, but Insley brushed it off, rushing over to the giant woman and dropping down next to her. They argued briefly, but it seemed Insley was made of stronger stuff than I'd guessed, and Cassiopia relented.

While we stood a fair way back, Insley worked the hand over. Grunts of pain and angry muttered curses drifted to us, but Insley ignored them all. She joined us midship, leaving a cleaned and adequately bandaged white hand with Cassiopia, who still seemed like she'd have preferred death over any of this.

There was no celebration. Only a few thousand dead, and multiples upon multiples of that displaced from their homes and loved ones. The only sounds that came with the setting sun were sobs and the oppressive silence of dark thoughts after a day of dark deeds.

Chapter Thirty-Two

A small blessing. Or maybe just a silver lining, so to say, came from the destruction of the city. There were no more gimzers. Whoever had been trying to summon them had been successful and had managed to do it well enough that after Rook and some people far smarter than I worked through the rate of infection they think was possible, there shouldn't have been more than a few hundred gimzers in total. There were just shy of that many drowned gimzers found, with the missing few attributed to the lake creatures or trapped beneath the rubble.

Another blessing seemed to be that many homes had stayed true to their original designs. A small group of older, sturdier ones had floated right up the other air stack. More survivors had chained together the older homes making a raft of sorts. It was woefully too few to make up for the massive amount of losses Brod sustained, but the tied-together homes were a floating beacon of hope for rebuilding the floating harbor. The builder's secrets who'd made the Below had long been lost, and there'd be no reclaiming the lake's floor.

On the other hand, word spread pretty quickly on who'd pulled the lever. Despite the good intentions, Brod's people were pointing a lot of blame in my direction, and there were not many people who were feeling rational on how to deal with it. Not being in Brod seemed like the best idea for us at the moment, so once we'd sorted out all the survivors, Tervlik agreed to take us down the river back towards the rest of Balteris. We took a long, meandering route, one that would bring us both high up through the mountains so the Night Runners could leave, and then down to skirt the edge of the Tryst's plains.

Insley had been quiet. Not Qaewin quiet, the kind when you were reserved but had that kind of inner power and confidence. This was the scared kind of quiet. The kind that didn't bode well for a person's mind.

She'd been too close to the fighting. It was a kind of battle shock, I guessed. When everyone settled down enough, I took her aside with a plate piled high of some of the best food Tervlik could scavenge for me.

She was monosyllabic and had a distant, wide-eyed look about her. I kept her close, had her eat, and told her stories about happier times and good people. She fell asleep in my arms, hair obscuring her face. Hopefully, it was a good start.

We anchored down to fish and get a better idea of what we were going to do after dropping off the small pack of Night Runners. The six men and their wolves had stayed below deck since we launched, occasionally taking turns at rowing but otherwise avoiding all contact with the rest of us. Shazina and Argo, though, had been welcomed to their group without question and had been down below with them.

Rook, Qaewin, Volant, Shazina, and a still subdued Insley sat around a small space in the ship's center. Rook seemed more severe than I'd seen him. Everyone looked tired, worn, and at their wit's end. The softly cloying smell of nearby woods wafted across the river to us. The stolen moon was shining early in the evening sky. It was the part of the day that seemed easiest to be honest and understanding with friends.

"There's some news I've been meaning to share," Rook began. "And I wasn't sure when the best time to do so would be. It's threefold, so hold your questions until the end, if you don't mind. First," he said, with a long sigh, "Kalaran is essentially a fortress now. They've locked all the entrances but the front mountain gate, and that's been reduced to foot traffic and the occasional merchant's wagon. Getting Emerys' Rock is going to be," he paused, "challenging."

Volant began to say something, but Rook shot him a look. In return, Volant, embarrassed, shut his mouth without so much as a sound.

Holding up the second finger, Rook continued. "I believe the rest of my old colleagues, the blue robes, have been roped into the conflict. There's not many, but they are highly skilled. It would appear their name being sullied by that botched job in Erset has given them quite the impetus to throw their lot in with the Equals."

When no one interrupted, Rook nodded as if he expected it. "Third, rumor has it there are stirrings in Wydvis. I noticed your mother and friend have not returned, and they should have done so easily in the time they had. Wydvis has gone silent to outsiders, and the lack of airship support worries me."

"That's... not good," I said.

With a thoughtful nod, Volant seemed to agree. "I'm with Nil. This doesn't seem like a good thing considering the whole civil war bit and the fact that Brod's now sitting at the bottom of a lake."

"And half of Tryst is supposedly burned," Qaewin added with a growl.

Insley shifted, looking at Rook. "Kalaran is my home," she said almost pleadingly. "What's happening to it?"

"Nothing necessarily bad," he replied. "My sources say they've locked down communication to the outside, and are feeding everyone inside a story about crazed Natural's rampaging across the countryside. Unfortunately, I don't think that will last long. It looks like Kalaran will be at the center of this war. Equal sympathizers have been flocking towards Kalaran. In return, those less than fond of Equals have been staking out ground within half a day's march. When news of Brod reaches both group's ears, I believe the only outcome will be violence."

It was unbelievable that we'd come to this point.

Brod was gone. An all-out war on the horizon. Half of Balteris' councils had been destroyed and killed. It seemed Balteris was heading towards a dark age.

Shazina, who'd been silent the entire time, stirred. "I'm tired. I'm tired of not having a home and all the fighting. And everything else. I'm just tired of it. Whatever you all decide to do, I won't be joining. Argo and I are going to leave with the Night Runners and learn their ways."

Qaewin was the first to find something to say. "Are you sure?"

An emphatic nod. "My family is gone and beyond reach. I never wanted any of this. I was just trying to help my people. I want to have a normal life."

I'd almost forgotten just how young she was.

Volant reached over, ruffling her hair. In turn, she smacked his hand away and shot out a jab that would be leaving quite the bruise. Young, but more than capable.

He chuckled while wincing from the strike. "We'll miss you, but that seems like a decent idea."

"Aye," I agreed. "This isn't your fight. Go be a kid and give Argo the life he deserves."

With that, I turned back to Volant. I raised an eyebrow and flicked a quick hand at him. Wydvis?

He shook his head and cleared his throat. "I, for one, would like to try my hand at getting into Kalaran. If there's going to be a civil war, I think the right side should have an edge in that fight." He turned a knowing look my way.

Rook shrugged. "I can't disagree with that. Personally, I'll be heading to Wydvis. I have a trail that needs following."

More than anything, that annoyed me. "Rook, you are one of the most skilled, useful people in Balteris. Why do you keep disappearing when we need you most?" Anger tinged my voice, and it came out harsh and clipped.

Qaewin and Volant both seemed to agree, as they turned expectantly to him. The thought of him leaving us once again seemed to rub Volant the wrong way as well. His mouth had drawn into a line, and his brows furrowed together in a less than friendly manner.

Rook seemed unconcerned. He picked off some invisible speck of dust from his worn robes. "I admire what you all are trying to do. Moreover, I genuinely hope you succeed. But I have my own tasks that need accomplishing. I'm fairly certain that a man I once knew is hiding out in Wydvis and possibly part of the trouble that is brewing there." He gazed sidelong at us. "Besides, you've been mostly fine without me, and there's not much left to teach unless you're ready to become gardeners."

I rubbed at my head, my frustration and lingering overuse of Skill causing a throbbing pain behind my eyes. I wanted to argue with him, but it was Rook. He was probably right, and even if he wasn't, there wasn't much any of us could do to force him to help us.

Qaewin grabbed Volant's hand and nodded. She was in with a Kalaran infiltration.

To my right, Insley still seemed shaken up. But when our eyes met, she gave a small, warm smile.

I thought of Cassiopia down below deck. She was sinking deeper into a dark depression that only she could pull herself out of. She'd be with us, or she wouldn't. She could be as stubborn as Rook, if not more so.

I took inventory of what we had. Volant with the sword master's rapier and more than likely some considerable amount of rope hidden somewhere. My beautiful, black-bladed axes were at the bottom of the lake, and not a single Toron stone was left uncracked. I'd borrowed a knife off of Rook to not feel too naked. Qaewin had her assortment of throwing daggers and the short bow. She wasn't anything like Cassiopia with it but was getting better with time. Insley had her bag of tools, and most importantly, an extensive store of knowledge on how to fix wounds. There was also the zymph Chloe, moody but ferocious, and incredibly stealthy if the environment allowed it.

With a heavy sigh, I wished for one more shot at the storage Supreme Dioden had allowed us to pilfer.

Rook must have read my mind as he tossed a small bundle from his infinite number of pockets in his robes onto my lap. With that, he stood, waved goodnight, and headed downstairs.

I opened the bundle and found it full of coins. As Rook headed down the stairs, I pocketed the coin. "Do you ever feel like he's using us, Volant?"

"That I do, leafer. That I do."

The next day, Shazina and the Night Runners left the ship unannounced and without goodbyes. Argo was the only one who seemed determined to let us know they were going, giving everyone plenty of time to scratch his head before he jumped overboard to follow the rest of his newfound pack.

Despite the whole group of them having avoided us for the entirety of the ride, it still felt emptier after they left. Tervlik's crew was small and busy, and Rook spent most of the ride meditating.

We passed by the edge of Tryst and saw blackened grass stretching in every direction. Qaewin almost left us then, but after she silently shed her tears, new sense of iron resolve seemed to be gained. There was purpose in her that hadn't been there before as she practiced firing arrow after arrow into a makeshift target at the end of the boat. Just when the ash-filled air was almost too unbearable, we hit a curve in the river and began to head back towards the mountains, towards Kalaran. If there was any question about what we had to do, it was no longer there. These people were willing to burn swaths of Qaewin's homeland, killing only gods know how many people and animals in the process. All to keep the Soft Steppers at bay.

It amazed me how foolish the Equals had been. They may have slowed Qaewin's people down some, forcing them to make large detours and flee from what must have been days upon days of billowing smoke and fire. But this would only have enraged the nomadic tribe. There would be no stopping them, not till they were all dead and the Equals no longer walked Balteris.

Finally, we came within spitting distance of the road and disembarked. Tervlik gave solemn, serious goodbyes promising to find us after he helped his people rebuild Brod. Rook waved cheerfully, his nose in a book. Then they were downstream, taking Cassiopia and a promise from Rook to do what he could for her away and heading towards another river crossing that would bring them back to the northwest towards Wydvis.

Before us, the mountains of Kalaran stood, rising above the rolling hills in the distance. Snow-capped peaks disappeared into clouds. Somewhere between Kalaran and us was a small but growing army of people. Unfortunately, we'd have to avoid them as well.

With nearly empty packs, we pushed up onto the road and began walking down the raised, hard-packed path that led to the gates of Kalaran.

A place I'd once have thought of as home, but had somehow become the stronghold for an enemy that wanted us dead.

The End of Book Two

Acknowledgments

A big thanks to those who have been asking me to get this next book out. Your patience and encouragement has been key to making this happen.

A special thanks to Nicki, who went through the very rough second draft and helped with edits throughout the whole document. If you liked the book, she's owed a drink or two for helping it be readable.

About the Author

Andrew Monroe is an avid book monger, tabletop gaming aficionado, fitness enthusiast, obsessive coffee drinker, and can most usually be found thinking about food in its various forms but mostly about what his next dessert will be. There's not much to be said about his writing beyond the fact that he won the third grade Most Persuasive Essay contest in which he wished to convince his teacher to give the class an additional fifteen minutes of recess. When not writing or pursuing one of the above hobbies, he spends most of his time in Amarillo, TX attempting to convince friends and family he's become a somewhat well-adjusted adult who can (mostly) fend for himself.

facebook.com/AndrewMonroeBooks
x.com/Andrew_ific
instagram.com/andrewamonroe

www.ingramcontent.com/pod-product-compliance
Lightning Source LLC
LaVergne TN
LVHW100511110826
845146LV00002B/597